MW00834128

Sovereignty

Sovereignty

Seventeenth-Century England
and the Making of the Modern
Political Imaginary

FEISAL G. MOHAMED

OXFORD
UNIVERSITY PRESS

OXFORD
UNIVERSITY PRESS

Great Clarendon Street, Oxford, OX2 6DP,
United Kingdom

Oxford University Press is a department of the University of Oxford.
It furthers the University's objective of excellence in research, scholarship,
and education by publishing worldwide. Oxford is a registered trade mark of
Oxford University Press in the UK and in certain other countries

Published in the United States of America by Oxford University Press
198 Madison Avenue, New York, NY 10016, United States of America

British Library Cataloguing in Publication Data
Data available

Library of Congress Control Number: 2019946755

ISBN 978–0–19–885213–1

DOI: 10.1093/oso/9780198852131.001.0001

Whom hatred frights,

Let him not dreame on sov'raignty

—Jonson, *Sejanus*, 2.174–5

Acknowledgments

Portions of this book were presented at the Canada Milton Seminar, the Northeast Milton Seminar, the Southeast Milton Seminar, the annual meeting of the Renaissance Society of America, and the annual meeting of the Society for Renaissance Studies, as well as at lectures and seminars in the English departments of Columbia University, the CUNY Graduate Center, Johns Hopkins University, the University of British Columbia-Okanagan, the University of Calgary, the University of Toronto, and Yale University. The first expression of the argument was the 2012 Distinguished Humanities Lecture of the Illinois Program for Research in the Humanities at the University of Illinois. I am grateful to the many faculty and graduate students in these venues who generously hosted me and who have helped refine these pages in various ways. Nicholas von Maltzahn and Ryan Netzley were enormously helpful in offering advice on the Marvell chapter. The anonymous readers for Oxford University Press offered model reports: generous, erudite, and challenging.

Just before embarking on this project, and with the generous support of a Mellon Foundation New Directions Fellowship, I was able to complete an LLM. I am deeply grateful to the Mellon Foundation, as well as to the faculty mentors at Illinois Law who showed great patience with an interloping English professor.

Portions of chapter 3 first appeared as "Milton's Tacitist Sovereignty," in *Milton's Modernities*, eds. Feisal G. Mohamed and Patrick Fadely (Evanston: Northwestern UP, 2017), 241–57; and "Milton, Sir Henry Vane, and the Brief but Significant Life of Godly Republicanism," in the special issue "'Relation Stands': Essays on *Paradise Regained*," edited by John Rogers, *Huntington Library Quarterly* 76 (2013): 83–104. Portions of chapter 1 and the epilogue first appeared as "The Political Theology of Betrayal: Hobbes' Uzzah, and Schmitt's Hobbes," in a special issue on political theology edited by Jason Kerr and Ben LaBreche, *Journal of Early Modern Cultural Studies* 18.2 (2018): 11–33. I am grateful to Northwestern University Press and University of Pennsylvania Press for allowing this material to appear in these pages.

Special mention must go to the graduate students who have been valued interlocutors over the course of writing this book. In our conversations, my dissertation advisees have been patient with various discarded versions of its core ideas: Patrick McGrath, Patrick Fadely, Chihping Ma, and Stephen Spencer. And the students in my Spring 2018 seminar at The Graduate Center, "Sovereignty," engaged many of the texts foundational to this study with energy and insight: Param Ajmera, Noel Capozzalo, Caleb Shaoning Fridell, Aaron Hammes, Nathan Nikolic, Hanna Novak, Lateefa Torrence, and Quixote Radio Vassilakis. Will Arguelles deserves particular notice both for his participation in that seminar and for his assistance in preparing the notes and bibliography. Sukie Kim was of great assistance in preparing the index. Thank you all.

At OUP, Eleanor Collins stood by this project as it took final form, for which I am most thankful. Aimee Wright and Sinduja Abirami steered it through production with efficiency and care.

This is the first book I have written since becoming a father, first to Chloe in 2012 and then to Kate in 2014. They and my wife, Sally, are a daily joy, for which my gratitude is boundless and endless.

Contents

Introduction

From the sixteenth and especially the seventeenth century onward, or at the time of the Wars of Religion, the theory of sovereignty . . . became a weapon that was in circulation . . . both to restrict and to strengthen royal power. You find it in the hands of Catholic monarchists and Protestant antimonarchists; . . . you also find it in the hands of Catholics who advocate regicide or a change of dynasty. You find this theory of sovereignty being brought into play by aristocrats and *parlamentaires*, by the representatives of royal power and by the last feudalists. It was, in a word, the great instrument of the political and theoretical struggles that took place around systems of power in the sixteenth and seventeenth centuries.

—Michel Foucault, *Society Must be Defended*

Foucault is quite accurate in describing the centrality of sovereignty to early modern conflicts over authority, be they within states, amongst states, or between churches and states.[1] He is also typical amongst theorists in pointing to this period as a point of origin for modern ideas and formations of sovereignty. For all that we think of Foucault as a taxonomer of regimes of knowledge and power accompanying the expansion of the state in the nineteenth century, here we find him locating the emergence of the master concept of political modernity in an earlier moment. Whether highlighting Huguenot arguments on the limits of royal authority, or the Treaty of Westphalia, or the thought of Jean Bodin, or Hugo Grotius, or Thomas Hobbes, theorists consistently refer to the sixteenth and seventeenth centuries as the crucible in which modern sovereignty was forged.[2]

---

[1] Epigraph is from Foucault (1997) 34–5.

[2] Such a perception flattens the Middle Ages considerably, but we will bracket that concern. Harold Laski persuasively argued long ago that far from uncritically accepting the dominion of lords and kings "the medieval world, in fact, has a genuine conception of popular sovereignty"; see Laski (1921) 8.

Sovereignty: Seventeenth-Century England and the Making of the Modern Political Imaginary.
Feisal G. Mohamed, Oxford University Press (2020). © Feisal G. Mohamed.
DOI: 10.1093/oso/9780198852131.001.0001

This book contributes to that theoretical narrative, focusing on seventeenth-century England as a case study in characteristically modern ideas on sovereignty. At the same time it aims to complicate that narrative, suggesting a revised view of early modernity's contributions to later thought, one that decenters the emergence of a parliamentary supremacy underwritten by vague notions of popular sovereignty. Of the utility of "popular sovereignty" as a theoretical category I am deeply skeptical. The phrase names the favored window-dressing of various forms of political settlement, absolutist, parliamentarian, and anarchist; it offers little insight on the location of functional authority in a concrete political situation.[3] A case in point is Parliament's January 4, 1649 resolutions on settling the government: "the Commons of *England*, in Parliament assembled, do *Declare*, That the People are, under God, the Original of all just Power: And do also *Declare*, that the Commons of *England*, in Parliament assembled, being chosen by, and representing the People, have the Supreme Power in this Nation."[4] In one reading, this is a great moment in the history of popular sovereignty as a political concept: affirmed by a body actively sweeping away institutions deemed unresponsive to the will of the people, namely the king and the House of Lords. In a more compelling reading, popular sovereignty is here dissolved as soon as it appears, swallowed at birth by a victorious war party claiming supreme power in the realm. We will focus not on whether a certain arrangement of sovereign power claims inspiration from the will of the "people," but on perceptions of the actual power directing the state.

As a work of literary criticism and intellectual history, this book seeks to move away from the limited explanatory potential of some of the categories *en vogue* in current scholarship: "republicanism" and "political theology." The former, which for the past twenty years has dominated critical discussion of political culture from the late Elizabethan period to the Restoration, has taught us a great deal, but can often feel now like a diffuse term naming various strains of neo-Roman thought with little connection to a republican political program. Political theology, more recently coming to prominence, is also too diffuse to be of great critical value, and has been used to describe any kind of interaction between politics and religion. That the two are

---

[3] This is not to deny that "popular sovereignty" has become the default language of modern political sovereignty, but only to highlight that it is only a language, and a highly malleable one at that. For recent work on the emergence of the idea of popular sovereignty in early modernity, see Bourke and Skinner (2016), Lee (2016), and Tuck (2015).

[4] *Journal of the House of Commons*, Volume 6: 1648–1651 (London, 1802), p. 111 (4 Jan 1648/49); available at british-history.ac.uk.

intertwined in the sixteenth and seventeenth centuries should come as no surprise to anyone. Sovereignty is the first-order question of politics lurking beneath both of these critical conversations.[5] And reading the period through the question of sovereignty allows for deeper engagement of the traffic between legal history, political philosophy, and literature.

Why was sovereignty so often debated in early modernity? In no small measure because of the period's seismic shifts in authority, arising from the splintering of Western Christendom with the advent of the Reformation, and from the social consequences of an emerging age of capital. The impacts of these transformations cannot be overstated.[6] Chaucer might have satirized church officials and practices, and implied that a good parson was a creature not of this world, but this is a far cry from the commonplace belief in early modern England that the pope is in fact Antichrist—not a mistaken pope, nor a corrupt one, but *Antichrist*. Incorporation of cities, of professions, and of mercantile ventures, as well as the rise of such voluntary associations as clubs and societies, created a much more pluralist legal and social environment than had been previously experienced.[7] The transformations of the age fundamentally alter perceptions, and experiences, of authority, making its sources more multiform, abstract, and tenuous in a way that feels typically modern. Instead of a single visible church, an invisible one that may or may not be aligned with worldly powers, religious and secular, and a gaggle of sectarians and schismatics claiming to follow divine light. Instead of a social order centered on lord and king, complex and multiplying corporate associations governing civic, professional, and commercial life. In this light, the period's absolutist political theory, which sought in various ways to urge the unique and insuperable authority of the monarch, looks like a frantic reaction to a society already spiraling away from a unified sense of final authority. It would be some time before the expansion of the modern state allowed such control to be reasserted by creating dependencies in such spheres as health and education, and by

---

[5] Kalmo and Skinner (2010) similarly describe sovereignty as the "master concept of legal and political philosophy" (24).

[6] In many ways, this has been the concern across all of my books, which have previously explored ecclesiastical authority in the face of Reformation skepticism on Pseudo-Dionysius' angelology; and the absence of a unified ethics and politics in modernity, early and late. See Mohamed (2008), Mohamed (2011), and Mohamed and Fadely (2017).

[7] On legal pluralism in early modern England, the work of Laski is foundational; see his reading of the seventeenth century in Laski (1997) ch. 1. His insights are recently confirmed by Archer (2002); Clark (2000), esp. ch. 2; Stern, "Bundles of Hyphens," in Benton and Ross (2013) 21–47; Turner (2016); Withington (2010). For recent social history, see Hindle (2004).

monopolizing violence through police forces, standing armies, and incarceration.

The primary concern of this book will not be the place of legal claims of sovereignty in international relations: the legacy of Westphalia affording states legal personhood, which has made international law paradoxically diminish the independence of each while in the same stroke firmly institutionalizing sovereignty.[8] Our focus is on the way that politically engaged thinkers and writers imagine the legitimate political authority directing the state. Bodin's succinct and influential definition comes close to this sense of the term: "Soveraigntie is the most high, absolute, and perpetuall power over the citizens and subjects in a Commonweale . . . that is to say, The greatest power to command."[9] It is at the same time more than supreme power: it is the political situation where *potestas* and *auctoritas* are perceived to come into alignment. Here we will be concerned with seventeenth-century intellectuals in the broad sense of the term: not just a political philosopher like Hobbes, but a key parliamentarian in Lord Saye and Sele, as well as writers of prose romance, the poet and statesman John Milton, and the poet, diplomat, and Member of Parliament Andrew Marvell. This offers a snapshot of the ways in which politically active individuals responded to a period of constitutional strain, allowing us to theorize sovereignty beyond the ambit of political philosophy and to gain a glimpse into the cultural purchase of competing ideas on sovereign power. In energetically engaging with their environment, all of these actors reveal a core idea on the fundamental structure of political authority.

We will find that seventeenth-century England does indeed demand our attention as a major source of modern political thought. It makes especially visible three competing views of legitimacy: 1) unitary sovereignty; 2) divided and balanced sovereignty, which often takes inspiration from the Roman historian Polybius; and 3) the universalist view that sovereign power must be limited by external principles of right order, most evident in the natural law tradition. Each of these divisions, and especially the first two, might be further subdivided into "red" and "black" varieties: "red" thinkers see sovereign power as riding a cresting tide of societal change, as renewing and revitalizing political life; "black" thinkers see societal change as

---

[8] See Kalmo and Skinner (2010) 6. The literature on sovereignty arising in the past decade is large, and we will not seek to address all of its concerns in these pages. See Bartelson (1995); Benton (2010) and Benton and Ross (2013); Bierksteker and Weber (1996); Grimm (2015); Martel (2012); Prokhovnik (2007); and Ward (2003); in more popularizing key is Cocks (2014).

[9] Bodin (1606) 84 (Bk. 1, ch. 8).

inherently disruptive, and urge the exercise of sovereign power to restore and maintain a *status quo ante* of stability and order.[10] Mapping the period's political thought in this way makes proximities and divergences both more visible and more precise: Milton should be classed under "red" unitary sovereignty, Hobbes under "black" unitary sovereignty. This is why both could endorse the rule of the Rump Parliament after the execution of Charles I, but did so on very different grounds. Tensions between these three formations are evident right from the start of early modern thought on sovereignty: they are certainly visible in Bodin, for all that he is often identified in an uncomplicated way with royal absolutism.[11]

The years between the civil wars and Restoration are rife with turncoats shifting allegiance from royalism, to republicanism, to monarchism as occasion demands. But even in jumping from one ship of state to the next, they are remarkably consistent in their views on the nature of sovereignty: once a Polybian, always a Polybian, whether supporting a mixed constitution under the crown or the Commonwealth. This may seem to straightjacket the period's political thought in too-tidy categories, and we will of course complicate them as we proceed. We will see a rare example of a politics reluctant to make a decision on the question of sovereignty in exploring prose romance in the 1650s. And we will see a complex approach to sovereignty in Marvell, who consistently perceives the unitary arrangement as sovereignty's typical form, though he is equally consistent in being horrified by the consequences. More than others in these pages, Marvell is skeptical that *potestas* and *auctoritas* can ever rest easily together. He imagines sovereign power to be typically "black" and unitary, but in his case this does not entail subscribing to a "black" politics.

It is in a reflexive awareness of active competition amongst these forms of sovereignty that the period displays a key characteristic of political modernity, defined in part by the anxiety that the scales could tip at any given moment from a divided and balanced constitution to absolutism, or that reigning powers will trample upon universal principles of justice (whatever those may be). Political settlement, and with it any definition of sovereignty,

---

[10] A source in the background of this distinction between "red" and "black" is Toffanin (1921), oft-cited in applying it to Renaissance Tacitism.

[11] Sovereignty for Bodin is unitary, perpetual, and answerable to none. This distinguishes sharply between sovereign and noble, allowing him to dismiss arguments for shared sovereign power. And Bodin is formulating his theory in response to the popular sovereignty arguments of de Beza and the Huguenots, which would place an external limit on sovereign power. Detailed examination of this sixteenth-century French context is beyond the scope of this book. See Bodin (1606) 85, 91 (misnumbered 73), 95; for a modern edition, see Bodin (1992) 2, 11, 18–19.

is exposed to contingency, destined at some point to collapse. Rome and Israel offer preludes to this condition, but with a key difference: the shifting winds of sovereignty are no longer a subject only for the historian but also become a central concern of the political philosopher—Livy and Suetonius give way to Hobbes and Harrington—which is to say that each kind of sovereignty has an active presence in one's own world. Asserting a particular form of political authority thus necessitates dismissal of the other two, so that sovereignty comes to exist in the modern political imaginary as a set of Borromean rings: each discreet and uninterrupted by the next, though bound so that no single ring can be removed from the others.[12] And each one of these assertions is worried further still by the implacable facticity of the complex and pluriform dynamics of modern power, which provoke the creeping awareness that any attempt to exert political will is futile. To advance a core idea on sovereignty is to be conscious of committing oneself to a necessarily embattled position, one that ultimately can find no ground from which to declare itself history's victor. And yet full participation in modern political life, and modern political culture, demands precisely this self-deluding commitment, this posture of blind optimism in an unfolding tragedy perpetually on the brink of catastrophe. The place of sovereignty in the political imaginary can thus seem like mere representation, but that would be to impose bourgeois ideology on modern politics *tout court*. Certainly bourgeois politics are a major part of the story of political modernity. But it is not my argument that, unmoored from universally recognized loci of intellectual and institutional authority, the political becomes reduced to a circulation of endlessly proliferating and competing signs and images. Rather, we can detect in clashing ideas on sovereignty the central hermeneutics, or ur-narratives, or myths that assign meaning to representations of law, of culture, and of social relations. Sovereignty names the political order emerging most immediately from Order itself.

It may be clear by now that the modern theorist most important to this book is Carl Schmitt. For present purposes, he is doubly important. First, he is the preeminent theorist of sovereignty of the twentieth century and continues to be very frequently cited.[13] He is not as frequently understood.

---

[12] The phrase "political imaginary" holds debts to Taylor (2004). I use it here to evoke the thicket of perceptions and imaginings comprising political consciousness, spanning legal history, political philosophy, cultural texts, economic exchange, and class relations.

[13] For quite different recent books on sovereignty drawing strongly on Schmitt, see Agamben (1998), (2005) and (2015); Brown (2010), esp. ch. 2; Paul W. Kahn (2011); McCormick (1999); and Mouffe (1999). Galli discerns Schmitt's influence among "some of the framers of the Italian

One of the aims of this study is to mobilize a broader range of his thought than tends to appear in early modern literary studies, where engagement of Schmitt centers almost exclusively on his brief polemic *Political Theology*.[14] Second, he is a close, if at times an aggressively misguided, reader of early modern political thought. *Dictatorship*, the book in which Schmitt's mature thought on sovereignty takes shape, opens with an examination of commissarial dictatorship in ancient Rome as presented by Machiavelli, and then proceeds to discuss Bodin, Grotius, Hobbes, the *raison d'état* tradition, and Pufendorf.[15] In fact Schmitt differs from legal theorists of his moment in this respect—one does not find a parallel examination of the sixteenth and seventeenth centuries in Hans Kelsen or Hermann Heller—and it is a large part of Schmitt's point that the nineteenth-century liberal state seeks to mask an earlier moment of decision in which modern constitutional forms took shape, and did so in a hotly contested, often violent, way. In each of this book's four chapters on sovereignty and in the epilogue, we will turn to a key concept in Schmitt's corpus and explore its relationship to the early modern texts under discussion: the mechanization of the state (chapter 1); *nomos*, land-appropriation, and sovereignty (chapter 2); the dynamic obtaining between "the people" and the sovereign (chapter 3); the pluralist state (chapter 4); and the protection–obedience axiom (epilogue). The theoretical excurses at the end of each chapter, and in the epilogue, aim to allow England's seventeenth century to speak to theoretical questions equally significant to later modernity.

Schmitt is also an excellent example of the very tendency that I have described as typical of modern political thought: his strenuous promotion of "black" unitary sovereignty is a conscious attempt to discredit both the divided and balanced, Polybian view that in his mind is the fatal flaw of the Weimar Constitution, and the positivism advanced in neo-Kantian legal theory. The latter of these finds its most important expression in the work of

---

constitution, the French Fifth Republic, and the German *Grundgesetz*, especially regarding the issues of the defense of constitutional legitimacy and the construction of the welfare State as the proper form of democracy"; see Galli (2015) 31.

[14] Much more rarely mentioned are *Concept of the Political* and *Hamlet or Hecuba*. All other work by Schmitt tends to be ignored. See Hammill (2012), Lupton (2005), and the essays in Hammill and Lupton (2012) and Campana (2018). Taking account of a broader range of Schmitt's writings is Kahn (2014), but here he largely serves as a straw man in a celebration of liberal culture and politics.

[15] See Schmitt (2014) ch. 1; for a perceptive reading of Schmitt and Machiavelli, see Galli (2015) ch. 3.

Hans Kelsen, whose positivism would have enormous influence in twentieth-century law, famously, and in a striking contrast to the trajectory of Schmitt's thought, deployed to justify the legal innovations of the trials at Nuremberg. Kelsen plays a leading role in drafting the Austrian Constitution of 1920, consistently making the case that state legitimacy is measured by conformity to legal norms and by the procedures securing that conformity. "The law *qua* system," Kelsen declares, "is a system of legal norms."[16] Coercive sovereign power is emphatically not the source of the law's force, and it is the signal achievement of the modern state to have depoliticized and depersonalized authority in favor of systematic application of legal codes, themselves arising objectively and in a way scrutable to legal reasoning.[17] All of this amounts, as Jeffrey Seitzer and Christopher Thornhill observe, to a "thorough critique of all personalistic or voluntaristic attempts to found a doctrine of political sovereignty" that is "perhaps the most important critical background for Schmitt's work."[18]

At every turn Schmitt is fighting against legal positivism, so it is no surprise that Kelsen is named at several points in *Political Theology*. Such mention is concentrated in the book's eponymous central chapter, where Schmitt opposes "political theology" to neo-Kantian legal thought on methodological grounds.[19] To such methods Schmitt responds with a "sociology of a concept" that deals with perceptions of sovereign power dominant in a particular moment. The key is not the system of law itself, but the way that system is conceptualized alongside a contemporary conceptualization of social order, thus establishing proof of "two spiritual but at the same time substantial identities."[20] In a concrete political situation, rule by norms amounts to rule by jurists: it places ultimate deciding authority in the hands of those claiming expertise in the law.[21] This allows us to clarify a common misconception of Schmitt's political theology: what matters about the political theological moment of early modernity is not that monarchy structurally mirrors divine authority, but that it does so in the "general state

---

[16] Kelsen (1992) 55.

[17] For an excellent exposition of Schmitt's thought and Kelsen's, as well as that of Hermann Heller, see Dyzenhaus (2003).

[18] Seitzer and Thornhill, intr. to Schmitt (2008a) 6.

[19] Kelsen's positivist approach to the law is dismissed, oddly, as both overly natural-scientific and overly belletristic. Natural-scientific in the sense that it expects legal order directly to reflect natural order, and belletristic in that it reduces legal thought to a kind of literary criticism, at its best a learned and sensitive textual interpretation systematically ordering decrees and regulations. Schmitt (2005), *Political Theology*, 40–2, 45.

[20] Ibid., 45.   [21] See Schmitt (2007), *Concept of the Political*, 67.

of consciousness that was characteristic of western Europeans at that time."[22] In a good deal of Schmitt's thought, the realm of culture is important to exploring this "general state of consciousness," and this is the terrain on which we will confront him in this book, which devotes most of its space to exploring key cultural artifacts revealing perceptions of sovereignty.

The aim of *Political Theology* is to elbow aside the Weimar Constitution's balancing of interests and Kelsen's positivism. As emphasized in Carlo Galli's important reading of his work, Schmitt presents modern political forms as incapable of effecting the unity of conflicting peoples and interests, or *complexio oppositorum*, that existed under the umbrella of the medieval church: born in a crisis they are incapable of fully resolving, these forms defer, and distract us from, their inevitable failure, and must rely on violence, actual and threatened, to preserve order.[23] Political community could only be held together in emergency moments with the exercise of the sovereign's power to decide the state of exception. In Schmitt's view, the Weimar framers themselves recognized this in drafting Article 48, the exercise of which he sees as necessary to defeating extremist parties of the left and right.

Preservation of class-based interest is, Schmitt would argue, the core impulse of divided sovereignty, which often justifies itself according to the avoidance of running into tyranny on the one hand and anarchy on the other. Those espousing this argument often express themselves in a legalist or contractualist language: a concentration of power leads inevitably to tyranny, so a harmonious state must strike a bargain of divided and balanced powers that is broadly accepted. But for Schmitt advocates of divided sovereignty wish to secure the interests of a propertied elite, as is evident in the English tradition: "This system contained something especially illuminating for the liberal ideas of the nineteenth century. For it allowed itself to be properly brought into harmony with the principle of the separation of powers and, moreover, provided the opportunity to protect the social power of certain estates and classes against a radical democracy."[24] Schmitt's consistent argument on the Weimar Constitution is that it must be deployed in its entirety: it is both presidential and parliamentary, the president being elected by the whole people and thus carrying their voice in exercising the

---

[22] Ibid.
[23] Schmitt (1996) discusses the medieval *complexio oppositorum*. See Galli (2012) and (2015), as well as Sitze (2012).
[24] Ibid., 318.

power to dissolve Parliament (Article 25) and "to issue measures under the state of exception" (Article 48, 2).[25] The sovereign speaks for the people as organic unity, a voice of the political community standing above class- and interest-based divisions.

It seems an unlikely union, but we shall see how a similar dynamic displays itself in the writings of Milton, long taken to be proto-liberal in his energetic arguments for personal freedoms against the encroachments of church and crown.[26] Those arguments on limiting the state certainly exist, but do so alongside others on the proper wielding of political power. In early and late Milton we find a thoroughly undemocratic logic of popular sovereignty, one that seeks to sweep away institutions and legal apparatuses not answerable to the people's consenting voice. (A consistent rejection of ecclesiastical law and its agents unites the otherwise disparate prose works of the early 1640s: the antiprelatical tracts, the divorce tracts, and *Areopagitica*.) But the "people" fit to exercise political agency remain an imagined elite bearing little resemblance to the nation largely in thrall to stale custom. Thus Milton at crisis points in the Commonwealth period endorses the use of the sword to defend the political rights of the people, though the particular military action in question runs counter to the will of the majority. Sometimes he speaks a language of classical republicanism, sometimes a language of godly republicanism. Consistent for Milton is a view of popular sovereignty emphasizing the sovereign authority of the *maior et sanior pars*. In the critical months following the execution of Charles I, Milton pursues this idea while speaking a Tacitist language of political *prudentia* endorsing unpopular stopgap measures that would, in the long run, advance the cause of a republic of merit. Though Schmitt turned at key moments to Hobbes, he might have turned to Milton in justifying how decisionism in the moment of emergency is necessary to preserving a situation in which the people who are a *bona fide* political unity can exercise their will.

* * *

Each of the first two chapters opens with a core problematic of modern political authority as it presents itself in the legal history of the sixteenth and seventeenth centuries. The first is the nature of obligation in a mechanized

---

[25] Ibid., 316.
[26] For a statement of this "liberal" Milton, see Patterson (1997) ch. 2; Patterson does qualify this designation significantly. More qualified still are Woods (2013) esp. ch. 6, on *Areopagitica*; and Walker (2014) esp. 108–18.

state, where sovereignty is depersonalized and experienced through mediating bureaucracies. We will explore three aspects of legal history making this situation visible: the Court of Wards and Liveries, the rise of corporations, and the legal doctrine of the crown as "corporation sole." That subjects no longer feel their feudal obligations to the sovereign is of deep concern to Hobbes—it is his own version of the Schmittean lament on a lost medieval *complexio oppositorum*—and a major motivation behind his impulse to develop a *nuova scienza* of the state. Developing a natural-scientific language of unitary sovereignty makes Hobbes' seem a quintessentially modern politics, allowing him to present humanistic and natural law approaches to political philosophy as moribund. We will see that his arguments on the nature of the sovereign have much more to do with corporations than they do with Galilean method.

These aspects of Hobbes' thought are read alongside the career of William Fiennes, Lord Saye and Sele, who is equally aware of the constitutional issues surrounding the crown's exercise of its feudal land rights but consistently responds with a commitment to the divided and balanced sovereignty of the traditional constitution. Saye is also of interest in that he is attached to key instantiations of depersonalized sovereign power: the Court of Wards and Liveries and the Providence Island Company, a corporation of merchant adventurers operating under royal charter. In the Providence Island Company we see the circle of individuals who would later become Charles I's chief parliamentary opponents seeking to play a prominent role in power relationships at home and abroad in the era of single rule. Even as Hobbes and Saye have fundamentally different views of the proper arrangement of sovereign power—one advancing "black" unitary sovereignty, and the other "black" divided sovereignty—both are aware that such power is increasingly mediated by bureaucracies and institutions. At the end of the chapter we re-approach a central concern of Leo Strauss' famous critique of Schmitt: the relationship between sovereign power and the mechanization of the state.

Chapter 2 begins with the problematic of the subject seeking to assert political personhood in the face of a hostile sovereign power. On what foundations can one make such an assertion, and how can it carry authority? The legal history we shall consider are Selden's and Coke's arguments before the House of Lords in the wake of the Five Knights' Case, showing how they reveal two different approaches to "liberty of person," the right of the subject against arbitrary arrest at the hands of the sovereign. Despite their different intellectual habits, the opinions of Coke and Selden tend to converge in this instance on a defense of civil law: even as we think of Selden as having a strong intellectual interest in the natural law tradition, that tradition is not the source of legal authority in his arguments. A parallel maneuver takes place in the century's prose romances, which draw on the cosmopolitan heritage of the mode to advance increasingly narrow political insights and arguments. We will chart this development as arising from John Barclay's *Argenis*. Originally published in both Paris and London, and in Latin, and weaving together French and English histories, it clearly seeks to speak across national borders. But its engagements of supra-sovereign cultural norms and traditions lend cover to what is essentially a defense of royal absolutism, especially against the encroachments of overweening nobles. We can follow this trajectory into the 1650s, when Barclay's characteristic marriage of romance and *raison d'état* allows propertied individuals uncomfortable with the Commonwealth to turn to this literary mode as a means of working through the challenges of their political context. Here the aura of traditional order surrounding romance serves a politics where an independent aristocracy increasingly appears to be a counterweight to tyrannous or inept monarchs. The unitary sovereignty of Barclay is transformed into a politics undecided on the question of sovereignty, where the problematic of a noble stripped of political significance remains unresolved. Theorizing this moment with reference to Schmitt and Arendt at the end of the chapter, we can see romance as a site where an aporia in political order is being worked through by those who find themselves in crisis and cling to a sense of independent authority. Though Schmitt's influential definition of *nomos* is attached to the political distinction between friend and enemy, we will see that *nomos* can be a space of custom asserting its legitimacy without reference to sovereign power.

The final two chapters of this book revise our view of the political thought of Milton and Marvell, respectively. Here we see the limits of considering both poets as "republican," which has become an endlessly malleable term. The label certainly fits Milton in many respects, but it can lead us to glide past certain aspects of his thought. As we will see, his early *Maske Presented at Ludlow Castle* defends a controversial branch of royal prerogative, in effect if not in intent. He is quite willing to countenance military evacuation of the English republic's "Supreme Senate," Parliament, endorsing the elimination of the Presbyterian and royalist majority of the Long Parliament in Pride's Purge and, later, the elimination of the Parliament that remained with the advent of Cromwell's Protectorate. And when Milton does offer a model republic, it is pointedly defined against that proposed by James Harrington, one of the most influential republican thinkers of his milieu. A focus on Milton's approach to sovereignty explains these seeming inconsistencies. Milton's engagement of Tacitus and the *raison d'état* writers is especially prominent in the crisis years between Pride's Purge and the advent of the Protectorate, and thus in *The Tenure of Kings and Magistrates*, the *History of Britain* and its digression on the Long Parliament, and *Eikonoklastes*. We will also explore the godly republicanism of Milton's later works, which has no direct precedent in classical or Continental republican thought, and which shares common ground with the younger Sir Henry Vane. Early and late, Milton emphasizes that liberty exists insofar as a fit few are able to exercise political will. The organic and decisionist quality of this sovereignty of the meritorious will be compared to Schmitt's theorization of "the people," in which we will note key distinctions.

The chapter on Marvell finds him not to be an inconsistent republican, but rather an entirely consistent *raison d'état* thinker. If something like a divided constitution appears in Marvell's writings, it is as a practical corrective to be applied to the natural brutality of sovereign power. He is thus not a true Polybian: one never senses a firm commitment to the view that divided and balanced sovereign power yields a harmonious commonwealth. Instead, he is keenly aware that executive power perpetually upsets, or threatens to upset, any constitutional balance enshrined in tradition or statute. For all that he spent the vast majority of his career at the center of England's political life, as tutor attached to the households of Fairfax and Cromwell, as Milton's colleague in the Commonwealth's Office of Foreign Tongues, as diplomat, and as Member of Parliament, it is always with a degree of disengagement that seems to arise from the awareness that politics is, in the final calculus, little more than a bully's game.

This attitude is discernible in his early poetry, such as the Villiers elegy and even *The Picture of Little T.C.*, and in the Cromwell elegy. It matures in the late prose, and especially the *Account of the Growth of Popery* (1677), into the promotion of various legal strategies to contain the potentially destructive energies of the sovereign wielding the power of the sword. Here he advocates measures protecting the subject from royal capriciousness: he promotes *habeas* rights and seeks to end conscription into foreign armies. Even as Marvell largely aligns himself with Anthony Ashley Cooper, first earl of Shaftesbury, at this moment, it is with a different constitutional focus: as is especially visible in their different reactions to *Shirley v. Fagg* (1675), Marvell declines to endorse Shaftesbury's Polybian arguments on the constitutional necessity of a strong and independent House of Lords.

Theorizing these workings allows us to explore a relatively understudied aspect of Schmitt's thought: his approach to the pluralist state, which sees intensity as the key difference between sovereign and other forms of authority. In making that argument, he charges Harold Laski with arguing for pluralism so that the state is weakened and thus more susceptible to the encroachments of international socialism.

As is clear from this chapter summary, a leitmotif of this book is the prevalence of *raison d'état* in early modern thought. This, too, is partly intended as a corrective to the emphasis on republicanism that has animated many studies of the seventeenth century for the past twenty years, an emphasis that has left other kinds of political language largely neglected. In studies of English literature, worldly-wise politics are associated predominantly with Machiavelli, a tendency that overlooks the broad influence of such writers as Francesco Guicciardini and Giovanni Botero, as well as the enormous body of writing devoted to interpretation of Tacitus, including, most famously, Justus Lipsius' *Politicorum*, first appearing on the Continent in 1589, published in London in 1590, and translated into English by William Jones in 1594.[27] The work of Maurizio Viroli and Richard Tuck has made clear that *raison d'état* was very much at the center of sixteenth- and seventeenth-century political discourse, a conclusion that continues to be reinforced by archival discoveries, including Noel Malcolm's recent publication of a *raison d'état* tract translated by Hobbes in the late 1620s and Patricia J. Osmond's discovery of Edmund Bolton's commentary on the first six books of Tacitus' *Annals*.[28] As we might expect, the appetite for treatises on "considerations of State" does not wane as tensions mount in the 1640s, evinced by the appearance in 1642 of the chronicler Sir Richard Baker's translation of Virgilio Malvezzi's *Discourses upon Cornelius Tacitus*, which the printer Richard Whitaker dedicates to Lord Saye and Sele.[29] It has become very clear over the course of preparing this book that arguments on sovereignty in the seventeenth century consistently bear the hallmarks of *raison d'état*: cynical anthropology, calculations of interest, unsentimental views of political authority, extra-legal stratagems to maintain a given political settlement.

---

[27] Lipsius (1590) and (1594).
[28] See Viroli (1992) esp. ch. 6; Tuck (1993) esp. ch. 2; Malcolm, ed. (2010); and Bolton (2017). For an illuminating overview of *raison d'état* in the period, see Burke (1991). Hammill (2012) deals briefly with *raison d'état*; more detail is in Kiséry (2012) chs. 1 and 5 in connection to *Hamlet* and Jonson's *Sejanus*.
[29] Malvezzi (1642) sig. A2.

This book closes with an Epilogue returning to Hobbes and Schmitt, who lurk in the wings of these pages even when not on stage, via a meditation on Uzzah, who is struck dead in 2 Samuel 6 for touching the Ark of the Covenant in an attempt to save it from falling off an oxcart. Hobbes mentions the story in both *Leviathan* and *Behemoth*, each time registering discomfort with Uzzah's death. It serves as a reminder that the subject energetically serving sovereign power may not be rewarded with protection. Quite the opposite. In his book on *Leviathan*, Schmitt faulted Hobbes for not considering this possibility, but clearly he had. For Hobbes and Schmitt, we will see, the point is both theoretical and autobiographical.

1

The Crown as Machine

Hobbes and Lord Saye

> Those that for Princes goods do take some paine
> (Their goods to whom of right all paines we owe)
> Seeke some reward for service good to gaine,
> Which oft their gracious goodnesse doth bestow:
> > I for my travell, begge not a reward,
> > I begge lesse by a sillable, a Ward.
> —Sir John Harington, *To a Great Magistrate, in Re and in Spe*[1]

With the witty compression that we expect from epigram, Harington captures many aspects of wardship as it existed in the sixteenth and seventeenth centuries. By feudal right the crown was chief landlord in the realm, so that a minor heir became a ward of the crown in lands held by knight-service. Henry VIII had done two things with lasting impact on this branch of English law: he dissolved monasteries into lands held by knight-service and created the Court of Wards and Liveries. The former measure increased significantly the number of wardships that came to the crown, and the latter, over time, would assure that it had a mechanism to pursue these claims. For much of the Tudor period, the Court of Wards seems largely to have routinized administration of wardships in a way that did not break with established practices. But in the waning years of Elizabeth's reign and especially under James I and Charles I, the court's activities expanded, with the crown pursuing a greater number of claims and, more significantly, pressuring local feodaries to increase the estimated value of estates.[2] The early Elizabethan Court of Wards generated anomalously large incomes, reaching as much as £29,551 in 1561, though typically the court gathered something in the neighborhood of £13,000. These figures would steadily rise in the early Stuart period: £17,810 in 1607; £25,226 in 1615; £36,731 in 1625;

---

[1] Harington (1618) book 4, number 71 [sig. M3r].
[2] Bell ([1953] 2011) 55–6. Bell provides examples of increases in feodaries' surveys in 56n1.

Sovereignty: Seventeenth-Century England and the Making of the Modern Political Imaginary.
Feisal G. Mohamed, Oxford University Press (2020). © Feisal G. Mohamed.
DOI: 10.1093/oso/9780198852131.001.0001

£49,069 in 1637; £83,085 in 1640.[3] As we might expect, the numbers spike in the period of single rule, when Charles I was in dire need of revenue that did not require parliamentary approval.

Ideally a ward and estate were placed in the care of immediate family. Under objections that the court had not taken sufficient care in this regard, the Master of the court, Sir Robert Cecil, issued instructions in 1610 allowing the ward's family, and close friends named by the deceased landholder, one month's pre-emption in purchasing an available wardship.[4] But family were often unwilling to take on this responsibility or not equipped to pay the requisite fees, and, in a less communitarian spirit, the same instructions of 1610 also give preferential treatment to informers bringing concealed wardships to light; these whistle-blowers often found the court easing the path to purchase of the discovered ward.[5] Thus arises the situation that Harington lampoons, where ambitious souls who once would have taken pains to pursue preferment now take their case to the magistrate. Royal ward replaces royal reward. And, equally significantly, despite the feudal language surrounding knight-service, the path to this royal booty was a court of law, rather than a royal court, with bargain hunters on the prowl for undervalued wardships promising a high return. The "pains" involved are not those of the *cortegiano*—cultivating relationships with the well-placed—but those of the litigant—filing papers, paying fees (above and below board), enduring a lengthy and cumbersome legal process.[6]

The abuses to which the system was prone will be immediately apparent. An investor looking to profit would try to maximize income before a ward came of age, with little regard for long-term effects on the property: soil was farmed to depletion, timber chopped and sold, so that when a male ward turned twenty-one, or a female ward fourteen, and invested the time and resources necessary to sue out his or her livery, the estate had lost much, if not all, of its value. Savvy landholders could protect their children from such eventualities by developing elaborate wills, leases, and conveyances whereby the estate would never revert to a minor heir. These measures appear in the litany of lawyerly tricks that Donne in *Satyre II* associates with the "insolence / Of Coscus" (39–40):

---

[3] See Table A in Bell ([1953] 2011), available at cambridge.org/9780521200288.
[4] Bell ([1953] 2011) 117.   [5] Ibid., 51.
[6] Bradin Cormack similarly observes of the Court of Wards that "the Crown's manipulation of a traditional order meant that a public culture of distributed interest was being transformed into a bureaucratic culture for organizing and managing chiefly one interest"; Cormack ([2007] 2013) 62.

> when he sells or changes land, he'impaires
> His writings, and (unwatch'd) leaves out, *ses heires*,
> As slily as any Commenter goes by
> Hard words, or sense[.][7]

Gregory Kneidel rightly places these lines in the legal context of Elizabeth's final years, and specifically her lawyers' efforts to prevent the execution of leases clearly designed to frustrate the crown's claims.[8] But I would emphasize that the lines are more ambiguous than we have thought: Coscus is not damaging his heirs' prospects, but rather advancing their interests precisely by leaving them out of the voluminous "writings" by which he transfers land. This kind of legal maneuvering assured that a minor heir would not become a ward, allowing a family more efficiently to accumulate wealth, albeit at the monarch's expense. Donne primarily attacks the legal trade, but, as is typical of his satire, the setting of the human errors he lampoons is itself a product of human error.

That both Harington and Donne would expect their immediate audience to be alert to the legal subtleties surrounding wardship suggests that it was a significant presence, and a significant concern, amongst landholders in the period, and became a major prop for monarchs wishing to assert constitutional independence. Extant records certainly bear this out. Although in James' reign net annual income from the court never rose far above £25,000, he refused The Great Contract, a plan put forth by Sir Robert Cecil in Parliament to replace his feudal claims with a set annual payment to the crown of £100,000. James demanded an annual payment of £300,000. An accounting of Prince Charles' income in 1621 lists two sources: "the chardge of Sr Adam Henton" and "the chardge of Sr Richard Smith and the general duchie of Cornwall." The list of disbursements is rather longer.[9] As we have seen, Charles would come in his kingship to lean on this source of income more heavily than his predecessors had done, which would be added to the litany of complaints against him. The Court of Wards appears alongside other branches of the judiciary in *The Grand Remonstrance*:

> The Chancery, Exchequer-Chamber, Court of Wards, and other English
> Courts have been grievous, in exceeding their jurisdiction. The estate of

---

[7] "Satyre II" in Donne (1966), lines 97–100.
[8] Kneidel (2015a) 92–121; reprinted as ch. 2 of Kneidel (2015b).
[9] BL Add MS 33469, f.30v.

many Families weakned, and some ruined by excessive Fines, exacted from them for Compositions of Wardships. All Leases of above a hundred yeares, made to draw on Wardship contrary to Law.[10]

Here a freeborn people has an inalienable right to avail themselves of the lawyerly machinations of Donne's Coscus. That the court had handed down fines or imposed wardship in cases of excessively long leases and other evasions of the crown's claims is, for the authors of the *Remonstrance*, a grievous overstepping of jurisdictional bounds. For at least one member of the Long Parliament it was a personal issue: Sir Henry Cromwell held from the king by knight-service the lands of the Augustinian friary in Hunting-don, portions of which fell to his second son, Robert, who limited use of the lands to his wife for the remainder of her life for a jointure, so that when he died his son Oliver might evade being a ward of the king, which he did.[11]

The Court of Wards was far from immune to the kind of corruption of which the *Remonstrance* complains: the selling of judicial offices endangers the "common Justice of the Kingdom . . . not only by opening a way of employment in places of great Trust, and advantage to Men of weake parts: but also by giving occasion to Bribery, Extortion, Partiality: It seldome hapning that places ill-gotten are well used."[12] An infamous example was Hugh Audley, whose avarice is immortalized in the anonymous tract *The Way to be Rich, According to the Practice of the Great Audley* (1662).[13] In this account Audley began with "two hundred Pound in the year 1605, and dyed worth *four hundred thousand* Pound this instant *November*, 1662."[14] Service to the "Court of Wards" played a significant part in his lucrative career, and with its closing "just before the late War . . . with other Accidents, he lost above an Hundred thousand Pounds. He would say, That his ordinary losses were as the shaving of his Beard, which would grow the faster thereby. The losing of this place, was like the losing of a Member, which was irrecoverable."[15] Audley buys his position for three-thousand pounds, reckoning that it might "be worth some thousands of pounds to him who would go, after his death, instantly to heaven; twice as much to him that would go to purgatory; and nobody knows what to him who would adventure to go to hell."[16]

[10] *Remonstrance* (1641) 10.   [11] Ley (1659) 60; Bell ([1953] 2011) 106–7.
[12] *Remonstrance* (1641) 10.   [13] [G.B.] (1662). See Bell ([1953] 2011) 34–8.
[14] Ibid., title page. Italics in original.   [15] Ibid., 16 [misnumbered 17].
[16] Ibid., 12.

Officers of the court had a habit of acquiring wards themselves—"as often as *Audley* put off his Hat to the master of the Court of Wards and Liveries," quips the author of *The Way to be Rich,* "he gained a young Heir."[17] If this was true for one of the court's attorneys, one could imagine it to be all the more true for administrators. As J. Hurstfield has shown in the case of William Cecil, First Baron Burghley, who was master of the court under Elizabeth I, records show that he acquired three minor wards during his tenure, but he likely held several more: the court has no record of several significant wardships that we know were available during his term, and he likely controlled them. The master could further benefit from court fees: we know that Burghley received £3000 from suitors for wardships, though £906 was entered as the official price for the suits.

The court is eliminated by the Commons in 1646, in an ordinance converting all "Tenures by Knights Service . . . or Soccage *in Capite* of his Majesty" into "Free and Common Soccage."[18] It is the younger Sir Henry Vane who carries the order to the Lords, presumably reflecting his involvement with the measure; we shall return to his uncanny presence in the period's political events in the chapter on Milton, who clearly admired and agreed with Vane on many matters. Under the Protectorate, draft legislation sought to create a system whereby minor heirs were registered and an owner assigned to manage an estate.[19] Even a limited revival of wardship never materialized, which may partly explain why the Restoration effort to resuscitate it quickly ran aground. This was not for want of effort by the brothers Heath, sons of Charles I's Lord Chief Justice Sir Robert Heath, who in 1643 had been appointed auditors of the Court of Wards.[20] The spur of self-concernment prods the Heaths vigorously to petition the committees of the Lords and Commons looking into the court's revival. Robert, the younger compiles and sends to an anonymous MP on 8 May 1661 a catalogue of reasons for restoring the court, though he might have inadvertently persuaded his audience that the court was better left in the dustbin:

---

[17] Ibid., 14.

[18] *Journal of the House of Commons, Volume 4: 1644–46,* 452 [24 February 1645/6]. As opposed to lands held by knight-service or socage *in capite,* the income from land held by common socage is not property of the landlord-king when the land falls to a minor heir. In common socage, a ward may claim income and waste from a guardian. See Milsom (1969) 88–95.

[19] See the draft "Act for the Registring and preserving the Discents of heires and Orphans," BL Add MS 32093, f.395r.

[20] See BL Egerton MS 2978, f. 138–9.

1. That the great men of the land and men of most considerable estates doe hold there land of the King in Capite in Chivalry, or in Soccage in Capite

2. That 100000 le : Anno now offered the King in satisfaccion of the Wardshipps to come is not aproporcionable satisfaccion in lieu thereof

3. That there is above 2 millions of mony due to his Matie for Wardshipps since 1642 . . .

5. That the Greate men & men of most considerable estates in ye Land are subject to those tenures But the abollishing of the Court of Wards will lay the burthen of the paymt of 100000le:Anno as well upon ye poor as the Rich wch will be lookd upon by the generallity of the people as an oppressive Innovacon[21]

Royalist sentiment in the Cavalier Parliament did have its limits. One might see why a landholding Member who wished to shield future heirs from the crown's feudal claims—or who would rather not see Charles II dangle the sword of Damocles in the form of arrears he might pursue when he pleased—would see the Heaths as offering excellent reasons not to restore the court. The healing words of the Speaker of the House upon elimination of the court likely offered little relief to the king:

> Royal sir, your Tenures *in Capite* are not only turned into a Tenure of Socage, . . . but they are likewise turned into a *Tenure in Corde*. What your majesty had before in your Court of Wards, you will be sure to find it hereafter in the Exchequer of your People's Hearts.[22]

A significant constitutional shift takes place whereby the crown's dependence on the goodwill of commoners is more acute. The monarch's remaining sources of revenue would produce immediate backlash if overused: the 1660 bill taking away the Court of Wards and tenures *in capite* replace the crown's revenue with "the Grant of another Imposition, to be taken upon Ale, Beer, and other Liquors."[23] This certainly assured that the crown was far from

---

[21] BL Egerton MS 2979, f.45. Various copies of this list of reasons for reviving the Court of Wards are copied on f. 41–58. See also John and Robert Heath's petition to the subcommittee of the Lords considering the offices of the Court of Wards (f. 26–7); and their petition to the subcommittee of the Commons considering the offices of the Court of Wards (f. 28). John and Robert Heath identified themselves as "auditors of the Court of Wards," with the claim made that Charles I's proclamation under seal to continue the Court at Oxford is still valid (f. 30).

[22] *Parliamentary or Constitutional History* (1763) 23: 86.   [23] Ibid.

impoverished, but the king lost the political benefit of a mechanism whereby he might squeeze landholders at his pleasure. The beneficiaries of this change, we should note, are not the commoners newly burdened with the crown's expenses, but a landholding elite who had successfully shifted that burden away from themselves. We should also note that elimination of the Court of Wards and Liveries is the only constitutional innovation of the Commonwealth period that is retained after 1660. That point is not lost on the eighteenth-century jurist Sir William Blackstone, who takes a dim view of the "crude and abortive schemes" of the Interregnum but declares that "the most promising and sensible" of them were continued in the reign of Charles II, and that the removal of "slavish tenures, the badge of foreign dominion" restored "English liberty, for the first time, since its abolition at the conquest." Along with the Habeas Corpus Act, this retained protection of "the estates of the subject" forms "a second *magna carta*, as beneficial and effectual as that of Running-Mead."[24]

To our consideration of the bureaucracy surrounding feudal rights we can add the emerging legal doctrine of the crown as corporation sole—the "corporation sole" being the English legal paradox of a corporation comprised of a single person. The principle inspires much of Ernst Kantorowicz's work on the king's two bodies, itself inspired by legal historian F.W. Maitland's lively assault on a doctrine flowing from Sir Edward Coke's misapplication, as he sees it, of ecclesiastical law: in *The Case of Sutton's Hospital* (1612), Coke lists as examples of corporations sole "the King, Bishop, Parson, &c." For Maitland the juridic personhood of the crown has no solid legal foundation, and he favors what he describes as the medieval king's single body, where monarchical privileges were attached to a natural person—the point is made with a satisfying allusion to *King Lear*: "The medieval king was every inch a king, but just for this reason he was every inch a man and you did not talk nonsense about him."[25]

What Maitland really wants, one senses, is to make the case for a common law tradition of the permanence of the state, rather than permanence of the crown. In his telling, that legal doctrine exists but cannot speak its name because at the moment when it is taking shape—in the early Stuart period when we begin to see "commonwealth" and "republic" enter the statutes—

---

[24] Blackstone (1791) 438.
[25] Maitland (1911) 246. For a brief analysis of the "corporation sole," see Turner (2016) 11–15.

the civil wars and republican experiments of mid-century arise, lending these terms an anti-monarchical, even treasonous, charge. The insight holds for the print market more generally, as Phil Withington has shown: usage of the terms "commonwealth," "common weal," and "public weal" all drop precipitously after 1660.[26] So even as the monarch's corporation sole is circulated over the course of the eighteenth and nineteenth centuries, as in Blackstone, who lists the crown as an example of corporation sole in his *Commentaries*, it is really in Maitland's terms the permanence of the commonwealth that has legal legitimacy. Or, to present the position in the terms of this book's argument, Maitland uses the tools of legal history to argue that English sovereignty is not only not personal, but not unitary, and to show that the legal doctrine that had been taken as implying such a view of sovereignty instead supports a constitutional balancing of crown, lords, and commons.

But we are still left with one odd implication of the "corporation sole": the implicit sovereignty it grants to the corporation as such. When accounting elsewhere for the independence that English law affords the internal decision-making of a corporation, Blackstone describes the corporation as a "little republic." Certainly the language of the royal patent creating the Providence Island Company, of which Lord Saye, as we will see, was an important member, bears this out. Here we cannot fail to notice that the governor of this "Body Politique," as it styles itself, has powers closely mirroring those of the monarch: to appoint persons and land "for all publique uses Ecclesiastical, and Temporall of what kind soever"; to "fortifie and furnish" the islands "with Ordnance, Powder, Shott, Armor, and all other Weapons, Ammunison [*sic.*], and habilimens [*sic.*] of warre"; and to constitute "Magistrates & Judges Justices, and all manner of Officers" granted full authority to apply law over the king's subjects, as well as foreign mariners and their passengers.[27] As Philip Stern notes, "until the late seventeenth century, it was fairly well established that statute law did not reach beyond the borders of England and Wales, yet there was a sense in which the absolute power of the king to grant charters also ironically limited his powers abroad."[28] Instead of extraterritorial spaces where sovereign

---

[26] Withington (2010) 144–52.
[27] The letter patent creating Providence Island Company is available in the company records: "Book of Entries of ye Governor & Company of Adventurers for ye Plantation of the Island of Providence," National Archives MS CO 124/1, f.2r–10v.
[28] Stern (2013) 28.

power could be exercised without legal restraint, the granting of charters created an increasing number of regions where that power was limited by little republics of planters and adventurers. And they escaped the crown's feudal claims. It had become standard for company charters to indicate conveyance of land with the phrase "as of the Manor of East Greenwich," a formula suggesting that the lands were held from the king, but in the next breath to state that lands were held "in free and common Soccage and not in Capite, nor by Knight's Service."[29] Thus these little republics held land from the crown and evaded its claims in a single stroke.

This is something of a long preamble, but it provides the historical setting for our consideration in this chapter of the depersonalization of sovereignty. By the reign of Charles I, we can see that the crown's ancient privileges come to be focused less on the person of the monarch and are increasingly mediated by relatively autonomous mechanisms, so that their attachment to the king is much more putative. We see sovereignty defined, experienced, and subtly resisted through bureaucracies and legal fictions. The absolutist and personalist brand of royal authority espoused by the early Stuarts comes to look like a desperate attempt to claim a kind of rule that had already been made impossible by the crown's own ambitions, namely its expanding administrative apparatus to pursue property claims at home and its sanctioning of mercantile adventures abroad.

Though one can find other examples of an increasingly associational and pluralist landscape of authority in early modern England, I dwell on these three—the Court of Wards and Liveries, the corporation sole, and the colonial corporation—as especially germane to the lived experience of the crown's authority in the period, and as especially relevant to understanding the thought of the two individuals who are the focus of this chapter, Thomas Hobbes and Lord Saye and Sele. These are two very different political operators, though each engages the question of sovereignty in ways influenced by feudal tenure, mercantilism, and colonial adventure. Hobbes has been credited, not least by himself, with developing a *nuova scienza* of the state, but, as we will see, the terms of his project are often misrepresented. What he seeks most of all is to translate into a modern political language the kind of direct personal authority of the monarch that he associates with feudalism. In order to do that, he relies on a language of contract that had rapidly become more formalized in the sixteenth and seventeenth centuries

---

[29] McPherson (1998) 37–44; Stern (2013) 30.

as a foundation of political relationships. He also summons the language of "interest" that had become broadly current in *raison d'état* literature and defines it in ways that run counter to a Polybian argument for divided sovereignty. Lord Saye, by contrast, is thoroughly committed to the Polybian arrangement, which he sees as enshrined in the traditional constitution of king, lords, and commons. Though they can seem contradictory, his actions throughout 1640s and 50s are in fact highly consistent in cleaving to the view that there is no disposable branch in this arrangement. But even as he invokes the traditional constitution, his career is that of a very modern political operator, one who seeks to rein in the monarch's power through the Court of Wards and through a corporation of merchant adventurers, the spectacularly ambitious and equally hapless Providence Island Company. In these two we see a picture of "black" unitary sovereignty and "black" divided sovereignty: each responds to, and deploys the tools of, modern conditions of politics, and the depersonalization of sovereign power in particular, by seeking to restore a lost *status quo ante*. But the loss is perceived differently. For Hobbes it is the loss of unchallenged royal supremacy; for Lord Saye and Sele it is the loss of a balancing of the estates, and in particular the constitutional independence of the lords.

In applying these insights to a reading of Schmitt, we will look especially at the relationship between the political and the mechanization of the state, a point on which his reading of Hobbes is somewhat fraught. He would appear to enlist Hobbes as an ally of the political defined apart from legality in his 1932 book *The Concept of the Political*; in his 1938 *Leviathan in the State Theory of Thomas Hobbes*, on the other hand, the philosopher of Malmesbury is associated with an anti-political mechanization of the state. Leo Strauss' perceptive critique of *The Concept of the Political* is often described as occasioning this apparent shift in Schmitt's thinking about Hobbes. But we will see that Schmitt had earlier expressed misgivings about Hobbes' natural-scientific turn of mind and the ways in which it anticipated the legal positivism he strenuously resisted.

Hobbes' New Science of the State

Hobbes begins the *Elements of Philosophy* with a swaggering if also sensitive declaration of being the inventor of a discipline: "Natural Philosophy is therefore but young; but Civil Philosophy yet much younger, as being no older (I say it provoked, and that my detractors may know how little they have wrought upon me) than my own book *De cive*."[30] The statement suggests the grounds on which he perceived himself to be making a break with classical authors. Too many thinkers on the subject pass off prevailing political opinion as political philosophy, or simply duplicate Aristotle.[31] The break from Aristotle achieved in natural philosophy, Hobbes here implies, augured the subsequent and similar break made in *De cive*. But even as he claims this "scientific" foundation and beginning, Hobbes lets slip a keen awareness of participating in a dense polemical field: casting his thought as a *nuova scienza* is a means of silencing detractors, a trump in debates centered on classical and Reformation thinkers.[32] James Harrington was unpersuaded, and reclaimed these traditions as equally grounded in natural order. *Leviathan* argued that classical authors simply declared their own commonwealths to be consonant with nature. Harrington replies in good scientific fashion, with a lesson on legitimately drawing conclusions from empirical study: Hobbes' remark is "as if a man should tell famous Harvey that he transcribed his circulation of the blood not out of the principles of nature, but out of the anatomy of this or that body."[33]

If we bracket for a moment these claims of novelty, often taken too seriously by later political theorists, one finds in Hobbes a fairly conservative legal thinker. When he takes up the question of wardship in the *Dialogue Between a Philosopher and a Student, Of the Common Laws of England* (1681), a text that by his own account applies his political theory to English law, it is to claim that feudal rights are necessary to the sovereign's role in defense:

> when Lands were given for service Military, and the Tenant dying left his Son and Heir, the Lord had the custody of both Body and Lands till the heir was twenty one years old; and the reason thereof, that the Heir till that Age of twenty one years, was presum'd to be unable to serve the king in his Wars . . . These services together with other Rights, as Wardships . . . if they

---

[30] Hobbes (1839), *Elements of Philosophy*, vol. 1, ix. On Hobbes and *scientia civilis*, see Skinner (1993).

[31] See Hobbes (1969), *Elements of Law*, 66 [1.13.3]: "those men who have written concerning the faculties, passions, and manners of men, that is to say, of moral philosophy, or of policy, government, and laws, whereof there be infinite volumes, have been so far from removing doubt and controversy in the questions they have handled, that they have very much multiplied the same; nor does any man at this day pretend to know more than hath been delivered two thousand years ago by Aristotle."

[32] For recent discussion of the tension between rhetoric and science in Hobbes, see Evrigenis (2014), esp. Prologue and chs. 3–5.

[33] Harrington (1977) 162.

were holden of the King...could not but amount to a great yearly Revenue. Add to this all that which the King might reasonably have imposed upon Artificers and Tradesmen (for all Men, whom the King protecteth, ought to contribute towards their own protection) and consider then whether the Kings of those times had not means enough, and to spare (if God were not their Enemy) to defend their People against Forreign Enemies, and also to compell them to keep the Peace amongst themselves.[34]

Here lies the solution to the central problems of Charles I's reign, namely that his opponents in Parliament urged him to engage in Continental wars for which they were reluctant to pay, and further deprived him of funds necessary to subdue Scotland and Ireland. If the feudal ground of kingship is kept firmly in sight, then the subject is keenly aware that both body and lands may be summoned against foreign and domestic enemies. With such sources intact, the king can perform these vital offices without any meddling from an upstart Parliament deluded about its right to limit the crown's revenue. The point is quite consistent in Hobbes' thought. As he presents it much earlier in the *Elements of Law* (1640), a Parliament obstructing the king's supply has, in effect, dissolved the commonwealth. Once the sovereign's power of the sword is so denied, "there lieth not upon any of them any civil obligation that may hinder them from using force, in case they think it tend to their defence."[35]

In its language the passage from the *Dialogue* locates such clarity in a lost feudal past, and we might think of Hobbes as striving mightily in his political thought to translate these principles into an equally insuperable modern idiom. Strauss famously, and suggestively, identifies Hobbes' project as "the first peculiarly modern attempt to give a coherent and exhaustive answer to the question of man's right life, which is at the same time the question of the right order of society."[36] But, given the kind of statement on feudal authority quoted above in the *Dialogue*, we might rethink our sense of the impulses leading Hobbes to develop this comprehensive and scientific account of sovereign authority. Hobbes is not making a good-faith methodological improvement upon political philosophy so much as

---

[34] Hobbes (2005), *A Dialogue*, 143.   [35] Hobbes (1969), *Elements of Law*, 114.
[36] Strauss, ([1936] 1963) 1. Strauss and, more recently, Perez Zagorin are rather too eager to take at face value a "*nuova scienza* of man and State" flowing from Hobbes' admiration of Galileo. See Zagorin (2009).

he is engaging in polemics under cover of methodological improvement. As Ioannis Evrigenis notes, Hobbes recognized that "'science' and 'reason' are terms of approbation much in the way that 'rhetoric' is a term of disapprobation," and did not see the method of geometry as transferrable to civil philosophy.[37] Casting his own political philosophy as fundamentally scientific and rational, then, is itself a rhetorical maneuver. If the transition from feudalism to early modernity had led to a misprision of the sovereign–subject relationship, then Hobbes seeks to beat the plough-shares of new logic into swords against fashionable arguments on the nature of political authority—to deploy a hypermodernity that implies the obsolescence of republican and natural law traditions.

At the same time he must confront the transition from landholding to moveable capital, which, as Harrington observed, destabilized any claim to political authority grounded in feudal rights—the demise of the "Gothic balance," in Harrington's view, necessitated constitutional recalibration.[38] The throwaway phrase in the long passage from the *Dialogue* quoted above on taxes reasonably "imposed upon Artificers and Tradesmen" does not sufficiently answer the demands of a political theory adapted to an age of commerce, as Hobbes must have known from the furious response provoked by Charles's impositions on the wool trade. So the emphasis shifts from the political subject as potential soldier to the political subject as war slave—the idea, as Mary Nyquist acutely observes, that consistently underpins his absolutist theory.[39] I would emphasize that Hobbes is not only looking to classical war slavery doctrine, but also finding a way to adapt the feudal rights so visible in wardship to an economy where property and debt were increasingly attached to movable capital. And this new economy was organizing itself through contracts and corporations, which become conceptually central to Hobbes' political philosophy.[40] No longer serving the king as landlord, we must be made to serve by other means: rather than actual tenancy, an internalized and innate possessive impulse that the

---

[37] Evrigenis (2014) 9 and 70.   [38] See Harrington (1977) 164.

[39] See Nyquist (2013) 295: "the contractual character of the subject's submission to the doctrine of war slavery [is bound] to the victor or the despot's power, and to the militarized encounter on which they depend. Presupposing a legitimate, causal connection between the victor's power and a condition of contractual servitude, this encounter becomes... Hobbes's central, ritualized drama, ideologeme or, to use another figure, ruling conceit, by means of which he theorizes sovereignty's origins."

[40] See Turner (2016), esp. 216–17. For the importance of contract to Hobbes' theory of justice, see Foisneau (2004) esp. 108–09, 113; on contract in the period's politics more generally, see Kahn (2004).

sovereign holds in abeyance for the sake of domestic peace. Capital transforms a political economy of military service into one of regulated
acquisition.

The structural resemblance between corporations and the sovereign is
especially visible in the *Elements of Law*, Hobbes' first systematic articulation
of his political thought. Here he distinguishes between corporation and
sovereign in a way that anticipates Schmitt's essay on the pluralist state,
which we will explore in chapter 4: the corporation's partial authority is
made possible by the protection of the sovereign, so that the subject's
obligation of obedience to the sovereign absolutely supersedes any obligation to corporations. But in Hobbes' thought one is simply a smaller, more
limited version of the other:

> as this union into a city or body politic, is instituted with common power
> over all the particular persons, or members thereof, to the common good of
> them all; so also there may be amongst a multitude of those members,
> instituted a subordinate union of certain men, for certain common actions
> to be done by those men . . . and these subordinate bodies politic are
> usually called CORPORATIONS.[41]

Rather than chief landlord in the realm, the sovereign has become, to put it
in modern parlance, Chief of the Chief Executive Officers. One wonders, as
Hobbes must have wondered, if it is a distinction firm enough to support his
absolutist claims on sovereign authority.

That *The Elements of Law* worries in this vein is indicated by a marginal
annotation in Hobbes' hand on a manuscript prepared in 1640 for William
Cavendish. In unpacking the "things that dispose to rebellion," Hobbes seeks
to show, in a way consistent across all of his writings, that Polybian views on
divided sovereignty are simply wrong: "if there were a commonwealth,
wherein the rights of sovereignty were divided, we must confess with Bodin
. . . that they are not rightly to be called commonwealths but the corruption
of commonwealths."[42] The manuscript annotation extends the point significantly, making this one of the longest paragraphs in the chapter, and shows
that, in a way he was still formulating, Hobbes saw himself as likening the
corporation and the sovereign more than his predecessors had done:

---

[41] Hobbes (1969) 104.
[42] Ibid., 172–73. Hobbes here cites "Lib. II chap. I" of Bodin's *De Republica*.

> This errour concerning mixed government hath proceded from the want of understanding of what is meant by this word body Politique, and how it signifieth not the concord, but the union of many men. And though in the Charters of subordinate Corporations a Corporation be declared to be One Person in Law yet the same hath not beene taken notice of in the body of a Commonwealth or City. Nor have any of those innumerable writters [sic] of Politiques observed any such union.[43]

This fascinating emendation must be kept in mind when reading the famous statement in *Leviathan* that a commonwealth is an actual union of men in the person of the sovereign: "This is more than Consent, or Concord; it is a reall Unitie of them all, in one and the same Person."[44] But in the later work, Hobbes suppresses the proximity to the corporation, which is more explicitly offered as a potential menace to political stability: buried amongst the infirmities of a commonwealth is "the great number of Corporations; which are as it were many lesser Common-wealths in the bowels of a greater, like wormes in the entrayles of a naturall man."[45] Here the structural similarity of corporation and commonwealth is briefly acknowledged, but the polemical aim of *Leviathan* is unequivocally to reinforce the obligation of obedience to the sovereign. This leads Hobbes to downplay the way in which his thought on sovereignty has a lot less to do with anti-Aristotelian natural philosophy on human nature than it does with creating a political philosophy responsive to the rising influence of corporations and other contractual associations. Seeing the commonwealth as one corporate association amongst many makes it look a lot less unique, and a lot more alterable by disgruntled subject-investors.

This reaffirms the logic of possessive individualism that C.B. Macpherson associated with Hobbes' thought some time ago.[46] But the advent of a capital economy is not the only thing pushing Hobbes to see interest as the foundation of political life. An emphasis on self-interest has been traced to his close study of Thucydides, and the Athenians' view of "human nature" and its three strongest motives, "honor, fear, and self-interest."[47] He also has

---

[43] Hobbes (1640), Chatsworth MS HS/A/2/B, 251. The addition made in the margin of this manuscript appears in the 1650 edition of the *Elements of Law*, and thence into all modern editions. See Hobbes (1650) 169. On this passage, see also Tuck (2006) 173–5. In discussing the relevance of the corporation to the commonwealth, Aravamudan (2009) argues for the importance of Hobbes' involvement with the Virginia and Somers Island Companies.

[44] Hobbes (2014b) 260.   [45] Ibid., 516 [ch.29].

[46] See Macpherson ([1963] 2011) esp. 70–86.

[47] Thucydides (1919) 1.76. See Evrigenis (2014) 15, Miller (2011) 140–4, and Slomp (1990).

in mind the Tacitist *raison d'état* literature that had become enormously influential in Continental thought. If Noel Malcolm's attribution is reliable, and it has not been challenged, then Hobbes in fact translated a fascinating artifact of this influence in the late 1620s, the satirical advice to Frederick V, Elector Palatine, *Altera secretissima instructio*.[48] In this pro-Habsburg tract, the anonymous author adopts the pose of a friend to the Palatinate offering advice on how to turn his fragile alliances to advantage. Not surprisingly, the chief conclusion of the analysis is that Frederick's cause is lost, that his greatest hope lay in the easy deceit of delivering his children "to be brought up by ye Spaniard, the Emp^r or Bauiere [i.e. the Emperor or the Duke of Bavaria]." Such a move, in the view of this author, would not raise English eyebrows: "the English will never be offended with the so easie selling of Religion."[49] Here the *Altera secretissima* seems to allude to James I's efforts to end the Thirty Years' War by arranging a match between Frederick's elder son and either the daughter of Emperor Ferdinand II or the niece of Maximilian I, Duke of Bavaria, not to mention the king's own pursuit of a Spanish match for Charles.

The text is made persuasive by two chief weapons: the reach and accuracy of its information, which surveys in fine detail the inner workings of power politics from Baghdad to Ireland; and its frequent recourse to plain-speaking, seemingly self-evident aphorisms on the nature of states, in a style reminiscent of Francesco Guicciardini's *Maxims* and its imitators. Thus we find such punchy insights as "at qui pugnat, invitus, spontè fugiet" ("He that fights against his will, will run away of his owne accord"); and "iam etiam odisse incipient; Nam odium tui sine sumptu judicant esse, amicitiam constare impendio" ("now [the Dutch] begin to hate you to boote. For they thinke they may hate you without cost, but your friendship is chargeable"); and finally, in especially Machiavellian language, "leoninae lacerate vulpine succedanea esto" ("when ye Lions skin is worn out, put on the Foxes case").[50] It goes without saying, though the author says it anyway, that the driving force of this analysis is that "causa suprema, causa causarum, RATIO STATUS" ("great cause, the cause of causes, *Reason of State*").[51]

Even if tasked by Cavendish to produce a translation, we can imagine Hobbes reading quite eagerly this supposed insider's view of events on the

---

[48] Malcolm ([2007] 2010); Malcolm's arguments for Hobbes' authorship of this translation appear on 16–29. On "A Discourse upon the Beginning of Tacitus," attributed to Hobbes, see Miller (2011) 138–40.
[49] Malcolm ([2007] 2010) 178.   [50] Ibid., 139, 151, and 173.   [51] Ibid., 145.

Continent, as well as many other *raison d'état* texts that he catalogues, and likely curates, for his master: an extant catalogue of the Hardwick library is in Hobbes' hand, and includes Machiavelli, Lipsius, and Tacitus, as well as Guicciardini, Trajano Boccalini, Giovanni Botero, and René de Lucinge.[52] This body of political thought is likely to have had strong influence on Hobbes' interpretation of interest, which, as Evrigenis aptly describes it, is not related to the pursuit of a *summum bonum* but *bonum sibi*, a constantly changing pursuit of advantage.[53] The recourse to aphorism common in *raison d'état* is, however, at some distance from the method of Hobbes, leaving us with a picture of his political writings as deeply informed by *raison d'état* in content and spirit, and in method informed by the anti-Aristotelian revivification of logic.

Reason of state may have held appeal in offering a distinctly modern language of political action in which all could, and, by Hobbes' time, did participate. Revealing in this respect is Lodovico Zuccolo's 1621 remark that "barbers…and other artisans of the humblest sort, in their shops and meeting-places, make comments and queries on reason of state, and pretend that they know which things are done for reason of state and which are not."[54] Unpacking the connivances of princes, in other words, had become the stuff of common conversation. In the prolegomena to *De juri belli ac pacis*, Grotius declares that his project is necessary because of the ubiquity of *raison d'état*: "Euthydemus's remark in Thucydides is on almost everyone's lips, that for a king or state with sovereign power, nothing which is in their interest is unjust. Much the same are the sayings that when the stakes are high, success is the only justice, or that a state cannot be ruled without injustice."[55] John Morrice, the eighteenth-century English editor of *De jure*, rightly detects here a reference to Tacitus: "*Id in summa fortuna aequius quod validius*" ("With princes might is the only right").[56] Also thinking of both Thucydides and Tacitus, Hobbes recognized that in both its high and low aspects this very modern political culture of divining the venal motives of superiors was a potential threat to authority—one reason why he felt that the nascent news trade ought to be tightly controlled. The low variety of *raison d'état* seems very much to be the target of his remark in *De cive* that "there was never yet any more than vulgar prudence, that had the luck of

---

[52] See Talaska (2013) items 801, 900, 901, 1258–60, 1267–70, 1331, 1368, 1402–5.
[53] Evrigenis (2014) 16, 78, and 102–3.
[54] Qtd. in Malcolm ([2007] 2010) 93. On the broad influence of *raison d'état* in the sixteenth and seventeenth centuries, see Burke (1991); Tuck (1993) ch. 2; and Viroli (1992).
[55] Grotius (2005) 1745.   [56] Ibid., 76n2, citing Tacitus, *Annals*, 15.1.

being acceptable to the giddy people."[57] In his view, it is important not only that the sovereign hold an insuperable power of the sword, but is perceived as holding an insuperable power of the sword.

De cive is pointed in declaring that debates on the limits of sovereign power were a major cause of the English civil wars: "my country, a few years before the civil wars did rage, was boiling hot with questions concerning the rights of dominion and the obedience due from subjects, the true forerunners of an approaching war."[58] Many of the "infirmities" of the commonwealth listed in *Leviathan* amount to the spread of mistaken views, whether such "seditious doctrines" assume that private judgment can determine matters of good and evil, or that one can object to sovereign authority on the basis of religious scruples, or that tyrannicide is legitimate, or that the sovereign is subject to the law, or that the right to property is absolute, or that sovereign power is divided.[59]

The narratives in circulation on the nature of political order, Hobbes makes clear, are central to stability, and *raison d'état* had gained traction in quarters high and low in ways undermining sovereign authority: an "infirmity of a Common-wealth" is "the Liberty of Disputing against absolute Power, by pretenders to Politicall Prudence; which though bred for the most part in the Lees of the people; yet animated by False Doctrines, are perpetually meddling with the Fundamentall Lawes."[60] It is thus a major aim and achievement of Hobbes' political philosophy to take a potentially subversive category, interest, and to make the pursuit of gain inherent to motives of the individual, who then transfers this quality to the sovereign.[61] The memorable *bellum omnium contra omnes* characterizing the state of nature is driven by "equality of hope in the attaining of our Ends."[62] When Hobbes lists the sources of dispute amongst individuals, all are varieties of pursuing and maintaining gain, in terms of goods or reputation: "in the nature of man, we find three principall causes of quarrell. First, Competition; Secondly, Diffidence; Thirdly, Glory." The first "maketh men invade for

---

[57] Hobbes (1991) 90.
[58] Ibid., 103. For a recent overview of the place of the civil wars in Hobbes' thought, see Armitage (2017) 106–20.
[59] See *Leviathan* (2014b) 502–6 [ch. 29].   [60] Ibid.
[61] It is central to Hobbes' thought, of course, that this is not a delegation of power but a transfer of will: "This is more than Consent, or Concord; it is a reall Unitie of them all, in one and the same Person, made by Covenant of every man with every man, in such manner, as if every man should say to every man, *I Authorise and give up my Right of Governing my selfe, to this Man, or to this Assembly of men*" (Hobbes [2014b], *Leviathan*, 260 [ch. 17]).
[62] Hobbes (2014b), *Leviathan*, 190 [ch.13].

Gain," while the second is motivated by a desire to preserve gains, and the last "for trifles, as a word, a smile, a different opinion, and any other signe of undervalue."[63] Once the commonwealth is formed, this pursuit of gain is transferred by contract to the sovereign-actor who uses force against rivals on behalf of the subject-author.[64]

As Elliott Karstadt has recently shown, interest is more prominent in *Leviathan* than in the earlier *Elements of Law* and *De cive*.[65] This prominence arises in no small measure from fuller attention to the informal political culture tending toward obedience. The news writer or barber discussing the political affairs of the day is telling the story of his own interest being pursued when he applies the idiom of *raison d'état* to the sovereign, rather than telling of the ruthless tactics that princes use to maintain power for their own ends. And Hobbes grants space for individuals vigorously to pursue their interests in a way that does not interfere with a prior obligation of obedience arising from an instinct of self-preservation—a natural impulse more foundational than mere interest, which operates in social spheres made possible by the sovereign's assurance of peace.[66] Interest in Hobbes' handling becomes a means by which absolutist authority becomes scrutable and acceptable in a modern society, one where it was no longer the case that relationships of landed property determined social, economic, and political life. The dutiful Hobbesean subject can engage in such narration while celebrating as his own the sovereign's ruthless acquisition of wealth and power, and while being an active player in various forms of social and economic competition.

This is both a new science and a new culture of the state, an edgy modern substitute for the halo of authority that once surrounded feudal kingship (Hobbes' nostalgic view of medieval harmony, not mine). And Hobbes' refiguring of interest has dynamics that forcefully diminish natural law theory and arguments for divided sovereignty. As he claims in *The Elements of Law*, natural law is equivalent to the law of reason that leads each individual to pursue peace, which, in his terms, leads humanity naturally to see the benefit of covenanting to form a commonwealth.[67] Thus rather

<hr/>

[63] Ibid., 192 [ch.13].

[64] See the account of contract and violation of the law of nature in ch.16: "When the Actor doth any thing against the Law of Nature by command of the Author, if he be obliged by former Covenant to obey him, not he, but the Author breaketh the Law of Nature" (Hobbes [2014b], *Leviathan*, 246).

[65] Karstadt (2016) 106.   [66] On this point see ibid., 113.

[67] See Hobbes (1969), *Elements of Law*, 75 [1.15.1]: "all men agree in the will to be directed and governed in the way to that which is the work of reason. There can be no other law of nature

than being a restraint on sovereign power, "natural law" names the impulse driving the individual to transfer his will to an absolute sovereign.

Hobbes is not the first thinker to argue that natural liberty is an alienable property. The point also appears in Grotius, who argues, as Annabel Brett observes, "that an individual can voluntarily alienate the entirety of his liberty, even if this is—in an individual context—a shameful act."[68] For Grotius this is shameful because it is a barbarous, self-imposed slavery, as when Tacitus tells of Germans who "ventured their Liberty upon the Cast of a Die, *He that lost, says Tacitus, voluntarily became a Slave to the winner.*"[69] But the natural lawyers tend to preserve some form of natural liberty held by an individual under political authority, and Grotius makes clear that under normal circumstances an individual may choose simply to leave a sovereign state and so to sever all obligations to it.[70] And the "Generality of Kings," which is to say those who succeed "in the Order established by the Laws" rather than by conquest, do not enjoy absolute power over property: their subjects' natural *dominium* over property is not alienated.[71] Even Bodin retains the natural lawyers' impulse to preserve natural *dominium* in political society, stating that kings are bound by contracts though not bound by law, by which principle the subject retains a right to property.[72] That an aspect of the upright soul remains untouchable by civil authority is particularly significant in terms of Christian liberty, the freedom to follow the dictates of conscience, which must remain beyond the reach of the magistrate.[73] We find this in Saint Thomas, but it persists in a slightly more secular key in Pufendorf, who focuses on the divinely implanted faculties of "Reason" and "Understanding" that must guide human life.[74]

---

than reason, nor no other precepts of Natural Law, than those which declare unto us the ways of peace." Such remarks lead S.A. Lloyd to offer a generous reading of Hobbes' rendition of natural law, arguing that it is not grounded in individual self-preservation but rather in humanity's common good: "The Laws of Nature are precepts discovered by correct reasoning about those of our actions that affect others. But what the specific rules Hobbes discusses as falling under this definition *do* is promote peace. That is, they enable men to avoid or remedy social discord"; see Lloyd (2009) 104.

[68] Brett (2007) 107.   [69] Grotius (2005) 556 [2.5.27].
[70] Ibid., 555 [2.5.24]: "it is to be presumed that Nations leave to every one the Liberty of quitting the State, because from this Privilege they themselves may reap no less an Advantage by the Number of Strangers they receive in their Turn."
[71] Ibid., 1: 280–1 [1.3.11].   [72] Bodin (1606) 93, 106.
[73] On the Jesuit contribution to natural liberty, see Höpfl (2004), 204–9.
[74] See Pufendorf (2003), 73 [1.5.4].

In Hobbes the alienation of natural liberty occurring at the moment of the commonwealth's founding is much more absolute, collapsing Grotius' distinction between conquerors and the generality of kings. Only the sovereign has an absolute right of property, and thus cannot be made to adhere to law or contract. And any space granted to Christian liberty carried a whiff of the kind of radical Protestantism that had bred turmoil at home and on the Continent. Its every trace needed to be eliminated. So when Hobbes reduces natural liberty to mere "absence of externall Impediments," he is not simply taking an extreme position within the natural law tradition.[75] He is invoking the terms of that tradition so that he can completely evacuate them of meaning, so that he can eviscerate natural law's potential threat to a doctrine of absolute unitary sovereignty.[76] He agrees that the sovereign cannot demand that the subject violate natural law, but dramatically reduces the scope of that law so that it includes only physical self-preservation.

Put differently, Hobbes' association of natural liberty with physical movement recalls the tripartite division of law associated with Ulpian: natural law common to *omnia animalia*, the *jus gentium* common to *gentes humanae*, and the civil law of states.[77] In *Leviathan*, natural law and natural liberty are firmly connected to our animal qualities: the one inalienable element of *ius* is a right of self-preservation, which Hobbes casts as an instinctive avoidance of death. Though natural law is associated with the desire for peace, several of Hobbes' interpreters confuse the peace of natural law with that of the *civitas*; it is, more accurately, the kind of absence of immediate threats such as any animal would feel, the peace desired by a rabbit in the woods or a flock of grazing sheep. There does not seem anything uniquely human about

---

[75] Hobbes (2014b), *Leviathan*, 198 [ch. 14].

[76] Lloyd (2001) similarly describes Hobbes as having a "self-effacing natural-law theory" imposing a "duty to treat positive law as authoritative, no matter its substantive merits" (286–87). Zagorin (2009) places Hobbes within the natural law tradition even as he concedes that Hobbes "departed radically from this tradition in his explication of human nature" (32); that "Hobbes broke with this tradition in several major ways that define his subversive character" (47); and departs "from the natural law tradition" in his view of "the legal status of the law of nature" (49) and that his "conception was directly contrary to that of Grotius, Aquinas, and other philosophers of natural law. By absorbing natural law into civil law, he made the law of nature into a pillar of absolutism in the state and affirmed the validity of all civil law in the strongest possible terms" (53–4). On Hobbes, natural law, and natural right, see also Bobbio (1993), Strauss (1953) 166-202, and Tuck (1998).

[77] For Ulpian's tripartite division, see *Digest of Justinian* 1.1.1.3–1.1.1.4, available at thelatinlibrary.com: "Ius naturale est, quod natura omnia Animalia docuit: nam ius istud non humani generis proprium, sed omnium animalium, quae in terra, qaue in mari nascuntur, avium quoque commune est.... Ius gentium est, quo gentes humanae utuntur." See also Tierney (1997) 136, and Crowe (1974), 271–3 *et passim*.

the "reason" employed to determine Hobbes' "Fundamental Law of Nature; which is, *to seek Peace, and follow it.*"[78] With this narrowly circumscribed version of natural law in place, Hobbes then elides the *jus gentium* and civil law in a way that attaches any expression of sociality or political will to a prior loyalty to the sovereign. Any operation of humanity's unique mental and spiritual faculties becomes not a source of rightly determining natural law, such free-floating reason is proper only to human life before the creation of the commonwealth, but rather owes its existence to the protection provided by the sovereign, which creates the space necessary for civilization to flourish.

Likewise, Hobbes shifts interest from its natural home in Polybian arguments on sovereignty. For James Harrington, this is why Machiavelli is "the only politician of later ages," even as he finds that the Florentine "harps much upon a string which he hath not perfectly tuned, and that is the balance or dominion of property."[79] Perhaps the only point on which Hobbes and Harrington agree is that feudal property relationships can no longer be depended upon as the foundation of the commonwealth: if land is divided among the people so "that no one man, or number of men, within the compass of the few or aristocracy, overbalance them, the empire (without the interposition of force) is a commonwealth."[80] In Harrington's terms, a shift had taken place from the "Gothic balance" where the aristocracy were not only chief landholders, but also the chief among them held land directly from the crown: "Earl of the shire or county denoted the king's thane, or tenant by grand serjeantry, or knight's service in chief or *in capite.*"[81] Hobbes' great error, according to Harrington, is to treat the English king as though he is the Turkish Sultan, who holds all property in his realm and can thus exercise absolute authority. That is not the case in England, where a rightly ordered commonwealth must balance the property interests of the few and the many, and create a system of agrarian law whereby these property relationships would become reliably fixed—the redistributive element in Harrington's proposals on agrarian law can tend to be overstated by modern readers.

---

[78] Hobbes (2014b), *Leviathan*, 200 [ch.14]. Another consequence of this very narrow view of natural law is a narrowing of natural *dominium* that often refers to the case of Native Americans. On this point see Nyquist (2013) 279–84; Brett (2007) 37–42, 90–8, 111–14. For the influence of colonial encounters on Spanish thought in natural law, see Pagden (1982) esp. 60–9.
[79] Harrington (1977), 157, 162.   [80] Ibid., 164.   [81] Ibid., 192.

Thus an analysis of interest leads Harrington quite naturally, and in a way that is quite typical, to an argument for divided and balanced sovereignty—Harrington ought to be thought of as advancing a "red" divided sovereignty, a Polybian arrangement advancing reformist republican ideals. Without this foundation in property relationships, the transfer of "interest" to the sovereign as Hobbes uses it is a mere mathematical abstraction offering no firm foundation for political order:

> To erect a monarchy . . . like Leviathan you can hang it (as the country fellow speaks) by geometry (for what else is it to say that every other man must give up his will unto the will of this one man without any other foundation?), it must stand upon old principles, that is upon nobility or an army planted upon a due balance of dominion.[82]

Interestingly, Harrington takes a dimmer view of human nature here than Hobbes does. Even as Hobbes offers will as an insatiable appetite, he argues that individuals can come together and agree to set will aside for the sake of a common peace from which all will benefit. Rather than a single sovereign acknowledged to hold the power of the sword, Harrington, good proto-liberal that he is, offers as necessary to order a standing army's tangible threat of state violence.

By making interest the driver of human will—an anthropological quality that is not scaled to the size of one's possessions—Hobbes is able consistently to argue that the Polybian scheme does not achieve its aim of balancing interests. Rather, as he puts it as early as the *Elements of Law*, it introduces instability by pitting constitutional branches against one another:

> The division therefore of the sovereignty, either worketh no effect, to the taking away of simple subjection, or introduceth war; wherein the private sword hath place again. But the truth is . . . the sovereignty is indivisible; and that seeming mixture of several kinds of government, not mixture of the things themselves, but confusion in our understandings, that cannot find out readily to whom we have subjected ourselves.[83]

Instead of ending the state of perpetual war, a mixed constitution creates it at one step up, at the level of government rather than of individuals. The

---

[82] Ibid., 198–9.   [83] Hobbes (1969), *Elements of Law*, 115.

same point is made in *Leviathan* with greater force: the "confusion" on this point of sovereign power had been the chief cause of England's civil wars.

Harrington thus alerts us to the ways in which Hobbes provides an unlikely prefiguration of the liberal democratic state: he erects a fiction by which all are rendered equal subjects to an artificial sovereign. Faced with the Polybian and natural law challenges to unitary sovereignty, and with an increasingly juristic state and mercantilist economy, the *nuova scienza* of man and state that Hobbes generates mechanizes political obligation in a way that against its own will displaces the sovereign's personalist authority. In Hobbes we thus see dramatized the impossibility of a fully modern theory of sovereignty that does not bear the trace of its own untenability. We will explore the "mechanization of the state" more fully at the end of this chapter via the Schmitt–Strauss debate on Hobbes.

Lord Saye and Sele, the Corporation, and the Mixed Constitution

In a 1657 letter to Wharton, Lord Saye and Sele makes clear his assessment of Hobbes, of conquest theory, and of lawyers:

> for your lawers I looke uppon them as wethercockes which will turne about with the winde for theyr own advantages . . . with them thearfore whear thear is might thear is right, it is dominion if it succeed, but rebellion if it miscarry, a good argument for pyrates uppon the sea, and for theaves uppon the highway, fitter for hobbs & athiests [*sic.*] then good men and christians.[84]

The context of this remark, as we will see, is a critical constitutional moment, and we need not spell hard to divine which conqueror Saye rejects. In the same stroke he places himself at some distance from Tacitean *raison d'état*, a discourse with which he has been associated, suggesting that it yields a politics unfit for "good men and Christians." Though that phrase signals his godly bent, it does not offer much guidance on just what Saye is after in the seventeenth century's various crises of authority. That is a complex question if also an underserved one precisely because he falls outside of

---

[84] Fiennes (1895) 107.

the tensions between crown and commons that tend to occupy our attention—the only book-length discussion of the fate of the lords temporal in the period is C.H. Firth's *House of Lords During the Civil War* (1910). When noticed, he can be presented, as in the view of Richard Tuck, as a Lord arguing for the place of the Lords in the traditional constitution.[85] In this light he looks like something of a dinosaur. He has been alternately presented, notably by Diane Purkiss, as marching in stride with the Puritan camp in Parliament and as carrying Pym's torch after 1643, with the two attacked in the same breath by the author of the 1648 *Mercurius poeticus*:

> At this time Pym, and Say, upon their beds
> Lay plotting mischiefes, and their cursed heads
> Were busied, while they inventing were
> How to invade the *King*, and *Bishops* Chaire.[86]

In this light Saye appears to be on the vanguard of the Puritan Revolution.[87] A closer look suggests that he is both of these and neither, a complex figure who at times defends the rights of the commons and seeks to limit the powers of the crown, and who argues for the place of the Lords out of a consistent commitment to divided and balanced sovereignty that, in his eyes, is at the heart of England's constitutional tradition. But the tools that he would use to advance this traditionalist position are distinctly modern: the colonial company and the Court of Wards.

Saye was a leading figure in a corporation formed at the dawn of Charles I's era of personal rule: the Providence Island Company, patented in December 1630 to engage in commercial activity on the tiny volcanic island now known as Providencia and under Colombian control, 220 km off of the coast of Nicaragua. The list of investors in the company is something of a catalogue of those destined to become the king's parliamentary opponents in the 1640s: in addition to Lord Saye are Robert Greville, Lord Brooke; Edward Montague, Earl of Manchester; John Pym; Sir Nathaniel Rich; and Oliver St. John, to name but a few.[88] The company is founded in the same year as the Massachusetts Bay Colony, and shares many investors with that other adventure in the Americas.

---

[85] Tuck (1993) 75.   [86] *Mercurius poeticus*, 5–13 May (1648) p. 3.
[87] Purkiss (2006) 327.
[88] For a full list of company members, see Kupperman (1993) Appendix I.

But there were also differences. Unlike North America, where land was plentiful though hard to bring to profit, the investors here had a very small island in a tropical climate that they felt could readily produce any commodity they pleased. So they did not allow colonists to hold shares in land and claimed 50 percent of all crop yields. They were also generous with advice, and in ways that colonists may not have found welcome, overestimating the extent to which the soil and climate would favor a broad range of crops. Investors repeatedly urged commodities valuable in the English market, even when colonists had limited success in producing them. Thus tobacco was discouraged owing to competition from Virginia and elsewhere, and such commodities as juniper juice actively, even obsessively, promoted: one searches in vain for a letter to colonists from company secretary William Jessop that does not urge cultivation of the piney elixir.[89] Letters from Nathaniel Rich collected in company records likewise encourage Hugh Wentworth and George Hanmer to "good husbandry and specially to attend the juniper."[90] The market soon made other demands, so the parcel of letters from company headquarters in August 1634 urge Cammock flax with equal zeal.[91] Along the way, investors also pressed planters to cultivate the castor oil plant, rhubarb, cotton, madder, and mechoacan, and grew increasingly frustrated with their inability instantaneously to obtain high yield. In Karen Kupperman's suggestive comparison to Barbados, that colony also went through a decade of struggle until it focused its efforts on developing sugar production, importing Dutch expertise in the early stages of transition.[92] The Providence Island investors were more interested in making

---

[89] Jessop's 1634 letter to Hugh Wentworth is typical: "I have received three hogsheads of tobacco ... I wish I could give you better encouragement concerning the price than the market affords, but we hope tobacco is improvable to a better rate if those great quantities come not in which are much talked of in this City.

I hope by this time you have had further experience of the juniper, and have thus encouraged revival which have not lately seemed to indicate. Of the commodity itself there can be no question if after deduction of the charge it may be able to turn to good account." (BL Add MS 63854B, f.13).

[90] BL Add MS 63854B, f.5. See also f.18 Rich's letter to Thomas Durram of 19 July 1634: "I should be glad to hear that your hope of the juniper is by this time confirmed, and strongly desire you not so much to remember your own advantage and mine as to follow that commodity with all convenient industry. I hope Mr. Parker's engine is brought to good purpose, and able to prepare the juniper in such a manner as it may turn to good account." And again f.20, a letter to Thomas Kemble, "I commend to your special care the planting and preparing of the commodity of juniper juice."

[91] See, for example, Jessop's letter to Captain Ax, BL Add MS 63854B, f.42: "if Cammock flax will but grow I shall heartily persuade and entreat you to return thither, with assurance of all convenient regard and engagement from the Company."

[92] See Kupperman (1993) 110–14.

demands from London than in allowing planters to draw on their experience and expertise, and to import old Caribbean hands familiar with various crops, all of which prevented the enterprise from succeeding. Records show early encouragement of sugar production, which was quickly abandoned when not immediately successful.[93]

Also unlike their North American counterpart, the Providence Island Company was consciously setting up shop in the heart of the Spanish Americas, and one of the aims of this godly band was to annoy the great Catholic power: after a Spanish attack on the island in 1635 they seek and are granted letters of reprisal to engage in privateering, or licensed piracy. Ostensibly the practice allows the company to recover losses from the attack, but Sir John Coke's report to the Privy Council on the issue also suggests that privateering would bolster the profitability of a venture teetering on the brink of collapse.[94] That view promoted by the company's investors may have been exaggerated for rhetorical effect, but other evidence certainly shows them to be eager to see a return on their significant investments. Though fortifying the island became a major priority, with the number of soldiers coming to rival the number of planters, the colony ultimately fell to the Spanish, who attacked in 1640 and overtook the island completely in 1641, the final nail in the coffin of a venture that had never enjoyed success. Retaking the island became one of the pretextual claims of waging war against Spain during Cromwell's Western Design.[95]

Even though it was operating under royal patent, then, we can read the company's activities as a subtle challenge to the crown. This is not the same as open hostility toward Charles I, which is not discernible in the company's records. On the contrary, we find William Jessop reporting to correspondents that "here at home the Ministers meet with many difficulties, but yet we enjoy glorious season. The Lord enables us to walk like children of the light before the night comes wherein no man can work"; by contrast the "people of Germany lie still sweltering in blood."[96] The planters' oath declares

[93] Records of Providence Island Company, National Archives CO 124/1, f. 18r. Leaves are numbered twice in this manuscript, once in a seventeenth-century hand and again using a later ink stamp, the latter usually being one numeral larger than the former. In all references to CO 124, the ink-stamped folio numbers are used.

[94] See Kupperman (1993) 106–7.

[95] See the declaration available in Milton (1931–38) 13: 541–3; though this is included in the Columbia *Works*, Milton's involvement in drafting the declaration is far from certain. For this reference I am indebted to Paul Stevens.

[96] For this positive assessment of Charles I from within the Providence Island Company, even well into the decade of single rule, see William Jessop, letter to Mr. Sherhard, April 9, 1635, BL Add MS 63854B, f.113. See also Jessop's letter to C Camock, August 11, 1634, BL Add MS

allegiance to true religion as practiced in "reformed Churches, and established in the Church of England," that they "abhorre and oppose...the Jurisdiction of the Bishop and Church of Rome, and all Popish authoritie and superstition," and hold "Allegianse to our Soveraigne Lord king Charles."[97] We are not yet at a point in history when these declarations would widely be deemed self-contradictory amongst godly Englishmen. Still, the desire to trouble Spanish interests in the Americas does inherently rival the king's projection of English power abroad. The investors wished to consolidate their influence in London, maintained a strong hold on territory and demanded a great share of their tenants' crops, and sought under their own flag to achieve victories against England's great rival. In all of these respects the company is a structure that mirrors the crown, and allows these very prominent Parliamentarians to assert their political role, and to build important working relationships, in a decade when Parliament was not sitting. To adapt Henry Turner's core insights, we see an especially clear example of the ways in which corporations inherently created a pluralist environment of authority in early modern England, with the Providence Island adventurers occupying a place challenging to Caroline absolutism in the era of single rule.[98] The corporation marks precisely the kind of shifting social and political dynamics that worried Hobbes, as he would have observed in his experience with the Virginia and Somers Island companies.

In addition to this effort to amass wealth with investment in the Americas, Saye exercised considerable influence as master of the Court of Wards and Liveries, the revenues from which, as we have seen, Charles came increasingly to pursue over the 1630s. It was in a climate of resistance to Charles' enthusiastic use of the institution that Lord Saye became master of the court in 1641. His appointment may of itself have been an attempt to stave off parliamentary agitation: as one of the Twelve Peers who urged Charles to summon the Long Parliament, he would have been a popular

---

63854B, f.47: "the state of Germany is still very troublesome . . . At present we do here enjoy our former peace and plenty, every man sitting on his own vine and fig tree." Corporations' interests nonetheless conflicted directly with the king's in several ways, as investors sought to maximize profit by minimizing payments to the crown. See the comparison of the crown's 1622 contract with the Virginia and Somers Island Company alongside proposed revisions in BL Egerton MS 2978, f.10v‾11v. The comparison shows that the company sought to reduce payments to the king from £37,500 per annum to £20,000.

[97] Records of Providence Island Company, National Archives CO 124/1, f. 14r.
[98] See Turner (2016) xiv–xv.

replacement for the controversial Lord Cottington, who had been accused of taking bribes and, in the account of Clarendon, rendered "the rich families of noblemen and gentlemen exceedingly incensed" and eager "to take the first opportunity to ravish that jewel out of the royal diadem."[99] When Charles moved his court to Oxford, he commanded Saye and other court officials to follow. Rather than obeying, Saye put the question to the Lords, who predictably advised him to continue the court's work at Westminster. An incensed Charles issued a royal proclamation bewailing his lost income, and threatening all officials who refused to recognize the Oxford court:

> We would severely punish all those Escheators, Feodaries, and other Ministers of Our said Court, who should in their respective places neglect their duties to Our disservice. And whereas, notwithstanding Our severall Proclamations, the late Viscount *Say* and *Seale*, late Master of Our said Court of *Wards and Liveries*, who is now Outlawed, and attaynted of High Treason, did not only neglect to attend Our said Court at Our said City of *Oxford*, contrary to Our severall Commands and directions, and contrary to the duty of his Place but hath also withheld, and kept, and doth still withhold and keep from Us, Our Seale of Our Said Court.[100]

Thus arose the twin Courts of Wards and Liveries, one at Westminster and the other at Oxford, the former operating under the seal it always held and the latter under the new seal described in this proclamation and to "remain in the custody of Our Right Trusty, and Right Wellbeloved Councellor *Francis* Lord *Cottington*."[101] As Bell describes it, the Westminster court seems to have had the greater success, likely because it was the devil known to the local feodaries, though it may not have helped matters that Charles selected as master of his new court the widely disliked Cottington.

Unlike the Westminster court, Oxford had to create bureaucratic networks afresh, and the result, so far as can be discerned from its limited records, was a severely compromised ability to secure revenue for the crown: in its lifespan of nearly three years, it collected £26,066 and noted payments in arrears of £82,454.[102] In the single court term of 1642–43, by contrast, the Westminster court secured £17,369 in income from wards' lands and £13,461 from the sale of wardships. The likeliest explanation for the discrepancy is a bureaucratic affinity for established procedure. The feodaries

---

[99] Bell ([1953] 2011) 148.   [100] Stuart (1643) 1–2; italics in original.
[101] Ibid., 2.   [102] Bell ([1953] 2011), 153.

passed their information along to Westminster as they had always done, regardless of the king's directives. It is striking that a majority of the officers of a court inextricably tied to the crown's feudal prerogatives would operate in the teeth of Charles' objections, some we may presume for reasons political, others, perhaps even the majority, for reasons inertial.

Colonial companies and the Court of Wards are important spheres of activity for Saye before and during the 1640s, an eventful decade in English history, to say the least, that was the zenith of his political career. If we follow J.S.A. Adamson's conclusions on the authorship and date of the *Vindiciae Veritatis* (1654), then we have in this tract a record of Saye's constitutional thought in the latter half of the decade: he most likely wrote the bulk of the treatise immediately after the Newcastle negotiations with Charles I in 1646, with additions after attempts again to treat with the king in 1648, and further, relatively minor, passages added during the 1649-53 rule of the Rump Parliament.[103] In the seventeenth century only Anthony à Wood attributed the tract to Saye alone; Thomason assigned it to Saye's second son, Nathaniel Fiennes, and an annotation on the Bodleian copy is ambiguous. Because even the more conservative view has Saye co-authoring the tract, we can safely turn to it as reflecting his views on constitutional matters.[104]

As we might expect, the *Vindicae* argues above all for limiting the powers of the king within the traditional mixed constitution. In this respect it is entirely consistent with Saye's Polybian bent, if also rhetorically inflected by Parliament's cause against Charles I. As Adamson describes it, the crown occupies a "third and distinctly inferior place" in the mixed constitution that the tract advances, being an executive branch in the narrow sense: the king is to implement the legislative will of the commons and lords.[105] Important to limiting the king's power is the elimination of the lords spiritual, whose dependence on the favor of the crown tilts the House of Lords in the monarch's favor. In developing these ideas, Saye depends on a kind of language of disembodied royal authority that we have been tracking in this chapter. He reads the constitutional notion of the King-in-Parliament as only an abstract legal fiction. The two Houses of Parliament are the "*Supream Power*," the "*King in supposition of Law being ever present in his Authoritie, and not to be separated from that great Council of the*

---

[103] Adamson (1987) 51.
[104] Pearl (1968) assumes co-authorship of the *Vinidicae Veritatis*.
[105] Adamson (1987) 54.

Kingdom."[106] But when the king was physically present in the House of Lords during the impeachment of Strafford, Saye declared on his departure that the proceedings should be begun anew because the Lords "was not a House while the King was there."[107] The priority of a House of Lords independent from the king's influence explains Saye's opposition to the lords spiritual and his stipulation in the *Vinidicae* that any lord appointed by the king must receive the approval of both Houses. This, in addition to more limited powers for the king and expansion of Parliament's ability to act independently on matters of national concern, amply justifies Adamson's remark that this mixed constitution was not a mixture of equals.[108]

The *Vindiciae* gives us a sense, then, not only of what Saye thought about the English constitution in the 1640s, but also of potential continuities with his activity in the 1630s. His involvement in such ventures as the Providence Island Company allowed him to forge working relationships with those who would become the king's most formidable opponents in Parliament—that these relationships were forged in the smithy of failure did not seem to diminish the confidence of future success that is the most reliable trait of the godly. The experience also allowed for a decade's worth of encountering the king's share of sovereignty as a dividuall moveable, an abstract commodity that could be transferred in part to a colonial governor answerable to investors pursuing their own interests. Corporate charters and contracts become a piece of the king's political body subject to manipulation, leaving in its wake a more legalistic and depersonalized experience of the king's share of sovereign power. What's more, in the seventeenth century these charters place limits on the monarch's unfettered, extraterritorial sovereignty, as a 1689 letter of the East India Company makes clear: "In all other places & Plantacons his Majesty's Charter gives the Law and his power is despoticall, if he has not bounded it by some Charter of his own to the first Planters or Adventurers."[109] That experience is only more pronounced after Saye's tenure in the Court of Ward and Liveries, which operates in the name of the king's feudal rights but through institutions and practices that are increasingly independent—as became undeniably clear in the period of the two courts, Westminster and Oxford.

With this background in view, we can return to the moment with which we began this discussion of Saye's career: the creation of the "other House"

---

[106] Fiennes (1654), "Epistle to the Reader," sig. *.*v.   [107] Qtd. in Adamson (1987) 55.
[108] See Ibid., 62–3.
[109] London to St. Helena, 5 April 1689, IOR/E/3/92, f.17; see Stern (2013) 28–9.

in the Humble Petition and Advice of 1657. Despite having balked at the regicide, we can see why Saye may have seemed a natural choice: he had worked in the Providence Island Company alongside many who would form the Puritan camp of Parliament; he was imprisoned after the dissolution of the Short Parliament with Brooke, Pym, and John Hampden; and he had collaborated with Pym and Oliver St. John in the Petition of the Twelve Peers. Unlike many of the other peers involved in that effort, he remained loyal to Parliament throughout the civil wars—Charles had sought to win many of them over with honors and perquisites, making William Seymour, for example, a privy councilor and governor to the Prince of Wales; the king may have hoped that appointing Saye to the Court of Wards might also make him an ally. Those among the Twelve Peers with the most radical sympathies—Robert Greville, Lord Brooke, and Robert Devereux, Third Earl of Essex—are dead by 1649, so could not be invited to join the other House in 1657.

When the Humble Petition and Advice is issued, there are exactly four living members of the Twelve Peers who had sided with Parliament during the war: Saye and Sele; Edward Montagu, Second Earl of Manchester; Robert Rich, Second Earl of Warwick; and Philip, Baron Wharton.[110] Manchester was one of the six members impeached by Charles in 1642, but still opposed the trial of the king and refused the Commonwealth's Engagement. Warwick served as one of Parliament's naval commanders during the civil wars. Of the group he is perhaps most sympathetic to the Commonwealth: in the June 1657 inauguration of the Lord Protector, he bore the sword of state and draped Cromwell in a robe of purple velvet. Cromwell courted all four of these peers to join the other House. And all four of them refused.

Saye's letter to Lord Wharton, dated 29 December 1657, is the best surviving explication of this rebuff. Here he makes a plea for the old constitution of king, lords, and commons, claiming that such a "mixture of the 3 lawfull governments" prevents each from slipping into extremity: it prevents monarchy from turning into tyranny, aristocracy into oligarchy, and democracy into anarchy.[111] For Saye, the problem of the other House is that it has no constitutional independence: it is initially nominated by the Lord Protector, though in replacing members who die or are removed, the House must consent. That consent of the House is eliminated in the June 1657

---

[110] Wharton makes the twelve peers a baker's dozen: his signature is not on the original petition but on subsequent copies.

[111] Fiennes (1895) 106.

Additional Petition and Advice, which modifies the fifth article of the Humble Petition so that replacements in the other House are made only by the Lord Protector's appointment.

Saye is more than a little justified, then, in seeing the other House as "chosen att the pleasure of him that hath taken power into his hands to doe what he will," and as offering only a patina of adherence to the traditional constitution as it in fact completes the "overthrowing" of the "House of Peeres."[112] Participation in this house would forfeit the traditional privileges of the lords temporal. Lest we think that this is only a conservative argument, we should notice that Saye's own career shows that he takes seriously the role of the peers in limiting the ambitions of the crown. And he is not conservative in every aspect of his constitutional thought: the *Vindicae* advocates elimination of the lords spiritual. When Lord Saye was among the ten peers reclaiming his seat in the Lords in April 1660, he did so with the intention of limiting the powers of the crown as Parliament readied itself to reintroduce monarchy: if Charles II was to be invited to take up his father's throne, it would be on the terms presented at Newcastle in 1646. The mood of the time would not admit such efforts, and Saye ultimately abandoned them.

Over the course of his career, Saye is thus remarkably consistent in his commitment to a mixed constitution. But the tendency we have been charting is that one not only adheres to a particular view of sovereignty, but does so in a way conscious of, and ultimately arguing against, competing alternatives. We can certainly see in his career an emphatic rejection of the unitary sovereignty of Charles I and Cromwell. As for natural law tradition, Saye responds in good Puritan fashion: by casting the order of grace at a distant remove from the order of nature, and thus eschewing application of universals to the political realm. One senses his hope that the reforms he proposes, especially his congregationalism in church affairs, would allow godly energies to percolate into public life, but an obscure Providence occupies the space of supra-legal principle in a way that deprives natural law of its force. In this way we should be reluctant to align him with the godly republicanism of Milton and the Vane circle that we will explore in chapter 3. He will make a tantalizingly brief appearance in our discussion of romance in chapter 2, suggesting that in the Commonwealth period the mode is much more than a refuge for defeated royalists.

---

[112] Ibid., 107.

Schmitt and Hobbes Revisited

We have seen thus far tangible examples of the early modern "mechaniza-tion" of sovereignty in the Court of Wards and the corporation, as well as offered two case studies, Hobbes and Lord Saye, showing how these examples impact the period's political imaginary. With all of this in mind we might approach Leo Strauss' critique of Schmitt, centered as it is on the extent to which the mechanization of the state informs the political thought of Hobbes. The exchange between Strauss and Schmitt on the subject of Hobbes continues to be a source of debate and interest, as furnishing key insights on these two twentieth-century critics of liberalism.[113] Our particu-lar focus will be Schmitt's reading of Hobbes' response to the depersonalized authority that we have charted as a phenomenon to which he is consciously reacting.

In Schmitt's *Political Theology*, Hobbes is praised for emphasizing the "decisionist" and "personalistic" aspects of sovereignty. Though he is essen-tially a "natural-scientific" and "juristic" thinker, Hobbes postulates "an ultimate concrete deciding instance" who "heightened his state, the Leviathan, into an immense person and thus point-blank straight into mythology."[114] This Schmitt opposes to the tendency of Enlightenment thinkers increasingly to cast sovereignty as a function of the law, to conceive of the sovereign as legislator rather than "creator and legislator." Ideas of popular sovereignty derived from Rousseau made sovereign power a "quantitative determination with regard to its subject" the virtue of which is measured against its conformity to a popular will presumed to be virtuous.[115] But in the legalistic state that will is reduced to a particu-larized set of interests overlapping in some matters and diverging in others—here Schmitt critiques Rawlsean overlapping consensus *avant la lettre*. In the politics for which Schmitt is striving, narrow interest is set aside for the "organic unity" and "national consciousness" of the *Volk* finding expression in sovereign decision. Hobbes, Schmitt argues in *Politicial Theology*, is the last European thinker to offer such a possibility. After him the "decisionistic and personalistic element in the concept of sovereignty was . . . lost."[116]

---

[113] On Strauss and Schmitt, see Meier (1995), Scheuerman (1999) ch. 9, Kahn (2011) ch. 1, Behnegar (2014), and Moyn (2016).
[114] Schmitt (2005), *Political Theology*, 47.   [115] Ibid., 48.   [116] Ibid.

It is frequently claimed that Strauss critiqued this reading in ways that prompted Schmitt to shift emphasis in his later work on Hobbes.[117] In Strauss' arguments, Hobbes anticipates liberal political theory much more than Schmitt allows. For Strauss, as we have noted above, Hobbes occupies a central role in a different origin myth of modern political theory: Hobbes "was the first who felt the necessity of seeking, and succeeded in finding, a *nuova scienza* of man and State," one founded in the methodology of Galileo.[118] The argument receives its full expression in his 1936 book *The Political Philosophy of Hobbes*, but some of its major claims had earlier appeared in notes on *Concept of the Political* that he sent to Schmitt in 1932. Schmitt's critiques of liberalism flounder, Strauss argues, because they fail to take into account Hobbes' role in establishing core liberal ideas.[119] With his emphasis on an inalienable right of self-preservation, Hobbes limits the power of the state and thus, as Strauss puts it, "sets the path to the whole system of human rights in the sense of liberalism." Despite this limit the state in Hobbes is also essential to the existence of civilization, which Hobbes holds up as an ideal and opposite to the *bellum omnium contra omnes* of the state of nature. "By this very fact," Strauss remarks, "he is the founder of liberalism."[120]

It sounds very much like Schmitt is incorporating Strauss' insights when his 1938 book on *Leviathan* describes Hobbes' "concept of the state" as "an essential factor in the four-hundred-year-long process of mechanization, a process that, with the aid of technical developments, brought about the general 'neutralization' and especially the transformation of the state into a technically neutral instrument."[121] This is done by transferring the "Cartesian conception of man as a mechanism with a soul onto the 'huge man,' the state, made by him into a machine animated by a sovereign-representative person."[122] Schmitt explicitly states that Strauss is "correct" in identifying the central aim of Hobbes' political philosophy as a "restoration of the original unity" of spiritual and secular power, and concludes in this book that the myth of the leviathan fails to effect such a unity.[123] But well before these remarks, Schmitt is ambivalent about the philosopher of

---

[117] The connection between Strauss and Schmitt has been the subject of considerable debate. See Balakrishnan (2000) 215; Kahn (2014) 31–3; McCormick (1994) and (2016); and especially Meier (1995).

[118] Strauss ([1936] 1963), 1. See also Strauss (2011) 29.

[119] See Strauss, "Notes on Carl Schmitt," in Schmitt (2007) 114–15.

[120] Strauss, "Notes on Carl Schmitt" in Schmitt (2007) 107.

[121] Schmitt (2008b), *The Leviathan*, 42.   [122] Ibid., 32.   [123] Ibid., 10–11.

Malmesbury.[124] He clearly wishes to distance himself from Hobbes in *Dictatorship* (1921). Schmitt underscores in that book a sharp distinction between commissarial dictatorship and sovereign dictatorship. In the former, a dictator can be entrusted with broad powers at a moment of emergency when a political constitution is under threat. Those powers, importantly, do not include legislative authority, and, even more importantly, they are limited to a specific political situation, which, once resolved, brings the dictator's powers to an end. The commissarial dictator is empowered to defend a constitution, but has no constituting power, or *pouvoir constituant*. Sovereign dictatorship, by contrast, exists when a constitution has been suspended and an individual, or body of individuals, claims to hold the *pouvoir constituant*, either directly or on behalf of the people.

The polemical aim of the work is to advance Schmitt's interpretation of Article 48 of the Weimar Constitution, which grants emergency powers to the president of the Reich. Indeed, he appends to *Dictatorship* an extended commentary on this article of the constitution.[125] In the face of objections that emergency powers would amount to an abrogation of the constitution, Schmitt wishes to argue that such powers are within the terms of the constitution itself—it is the argument he makes most consistently in the Weimar years, receiving extended treatment in *Constitutional Theory* (1928).[126] For this reason, in *Dictatorship* he distances his arguments from those of Hobbes. Here Hobbes holds debts to a sixteenth- and seventeenth-century absolutist tradition of sovereign authority based on divine right, which "did not find its legitimation in any consensus of the people."[127] For Hobbes "sovereignty emerges from a constitutive act of absolute power, made through the people," but once the state is formed "private conscience" no longer exists. This places Hobbes at odds with a natural law thinker like Grotius, for whom there is a law prior to the state. Where Grotian natural law "takes its start from interest in certain understandings of justice, and therefore a certain *content* of the decision," for Hobbes "the interest only

---

[124] Galli sees this ambivalence toward Hobbes as reflecting Schmitt's ambivalence toward the state: "Schmitt's fundamental disposition toward the State is ambivalence, as demonstrated by his tormented relationship with Hobbes, whom he sees as the emblem of modern statuality" (Galli [2015] 1).

[125] See Schmitt (2014), *Dictatorship*, 180–226.

[126] Dyzenhaus (2003) persuasively argues that Schmitt wishes to show in *Dictatorship* that Article 48 extends to the president the role of commissarial dictator, but is vague enough also posit in him "at least a residuum" of the power of sovereign dictator (75). On Schmitt and the Weimar Republic, see Caldwell (1997), and Kennedy (2004).

[127] Schmitt (2014), *Dictatorship*, 2.

consists in the fact that a *decision* as such has been made at all."[128] Already in *Dictatorship*, then, Hobbes is being associated with a decisionism that does not take the concrete political situation into account, a sort of decisionism reduced to pure procedure, that anticipates Schmitt's objections to legal positivism. Even without the intervention of Strauss, we already detect that Hobbes is being associated with the march toward replacing legitimacy with pure legality, to adapt Schmitt's 1932 title.[129]

That point on positivism is more visible in the 1928 book *Constitutional Theory*, the work with strongest claim to being Schmitt's *magnum opus*. Here Schmitt argues that a pure legal positivism is a form of nihilism that has no recourse to values beyond proceduralism and rule of law. Rather than core constitutional values that the state is erected to protect, the persistence of legislative bodies and procedures is taken to be the primary end of a given constitutional settlement.[130] Kelsen's positivism, Schmitt claims, thus offers an ultimately baseless normativity:

> The political *being* or *becoming* of the state unity and order is transformed into that which merely functions, the opposition of being and the normative is constantly mixed up with that of substantial *being* and legal *functioning*. . . . With Kelsen . . . only *positive* norms are valid, in other words, those which are *actually* valid. Norms are not valid because they *should* properly be valid. They are valid, rather, without regard to qualities like reasonableness, justice, etc., only, therefore, because they are *positive* norms. The imperative abruptly ends here, and the normative element breaks down. In its place appears the tautology of a raw factualness: something is valid when it is valid and because it is valid. That is "positivism."[131]

Bourgeois rule of law was a "logically consistent normative order" in the "seventeenth and eighteenth centuries," when the "bourgeoisie mustered the strength to establish an effective system, in particular the individualistic law of reason and of nature, and formed norms valid in themselves out of concepts such as private property and personal freedom." Those last two

---

[128]   Ibid., 17–18.
[129]   Moyn (2016) argues that Meier (1995) overstates the impact of Strauss' criticisms, and points, following Scheuerman (1999), to the influence of Hans Morgenthau.
[130]   On this point see Scheuerman (1999) 65.
[131]   Schmitt (2008a), *Constitutional Theory*, 64.

qualities could contain a "genuine *command* without regard to the actual existing, that is, positive-legal reality."[132]

The point places us in Hobbes' moment, but sounds much more like a defense of Locke, who elsewhere in *Constitutional Theory* is described as providing "the classic Rechtsstaat [legal state] formulations and speaks of previously established positive laws (antecedent, standing, positive laws), while all ex post facto laws are contrary to law." Hobbes, by contrast, is associated with the absolutist principle, drawn from *Leviathan*, that "auctoritas, non veritas facit legem."[133] Schmitt also quotes this passage in *Dictatorship* and in *Political Theology*, though each time with slightly different inflection.[134] It is a very short step from Schmitt's reading of Hobbes in *Dictatorship* and *Constitutional Theory* to his 1938 association of Hobbes with the advent of a "technically neutral" machine that "realizes 'right' and 'truth' only in itself" and "guarantees me the security of my physical existence; in return it demands unconditional obedience to the laws by which it functions."[135] The later book makes most explicit Schmitt's association of Hobbes with a concept of the state that was thoroughly "a product of men," the "first product of the age of technology, the first modern mechanism in a grand style."[136]

With these readings in view, we can re-approach the praise of Hobbes offered in *Political Theology* (1922). We should first notice that the praise is more narrowly circumscribed than it first appears. Hobbes is described as primarily "natural-scientific" in his turn of mind, and thus, as was visible in *Dictatorship*, distanced from a political theory concerned with substantive core concerns, such as the advancement of justice—Kelsen's positivism is likewise described as scientific in its orientation, though also associated with literary criticism in its attempt to solve legal aporiae and impasses with an infinite regression of readings of legal texts. But despite this core impulse, Hobbes nonetheless generates the political myth of the Leviathan. And the reason he does so is as a "postulate" by which he might explain the idea of sovereignty predominant in his moment:

> The seventeenth and eighteenth centuries were dominated by this idea of the sole sovereign, which is one of the reasons why, in addition to the decisionist cast of his thinking, Hobbes remained personalistic and

---

[132] Ibid.   [133] Ibid., 182.
[134] See Schmitt (2014), *Dictatorship*, 16, and (2005), *Political Theology*, 52.
[135] Schmitt (2008b), *The Leviathan*, 45.   [136] Ibid., 34.

postulated an ultimate concrete deciding instance, and why he also heightened his state, the Leviathan, into an immense person and thus point-blank straight into mythology. This he did despite his nominalism and natural-scientific approach and his reduction of the individual to the atom. For him this was no anthropomorphism—from which he was truly free—but a methodical and systematic postulate of his juristic thinking.[137]

The strength of Hobbes is not that he effects a translation of theological concepts into political ones, but that he is alert to the theological charge of sovereignty in his moment and does not shy away from naming it, even as doing so conflicts with many of his intellectual aims and habits. Hobbes recognized the limitations of a natural-scientific approach to the question of sovereignty, in addition to recognizing that there must be an "ultimate concrete deciding instance." We tend see the importance of the latter to Schmitt, without fully seeing the significance of the former.

But in the account we have given in this chapter, we should be reluctant to claim either Hobbes' natural-scientific language or his departures therefrom as offered entirely in good faith. Rather, both are rhetorical postures deployed against competing arguments. If we accept this view, it shifts significantly the role that Schmitt and Strauss have assigned to Hobbes in the story of modern political philosophy. What we find is that the worries driving Hobbes' political theory are not unlike those driving Schmitt's political theory: that increasingly depersonalized notions of political authority had taken root in ways that threatened political stability. Just as Hobbes sees the proliferation of forms of authority not centered on the sovereign as a major cause of political upheaval, so Schmitt sees the liberal state as untenable because it could not duplicate the Catholic Church's *complexio oppositorum* (complex of opposites).[138] The ways in which Hobbes himself recognizes, and sees himself as responding to, a modern age of depersonalized and pluralist authority, the ways in which Hobbes himself is attuned to a concrete political situation—as much if not more than he is to developments in natural philosophy—are not fully recognized in Schmitt's writings. Rather than a response to an age of corporations and contracts, Schmitt presents Hobbes' myth of the leviathan as a response to a Christian rupture between religious and worldly authority reopened by the Reformation, reflecting his own concern with the loss of unity provided by the medieval

---

[137] Schmitt (2005), *Political Theology*, 47.   [138] See Schmitt (1996) 7.

church. The "failure" of Hobbes' political myth is the inevitable failure of a modern political idea seeking universal acknowledgment as the proper focus of the spiritual and secular lives of its subjects. Under the surface of the *Leviathan* book is an acknowledgment that Schmitt sees himself as implicated in the same inevitable failure. Galli perceptively describes "the true outcome of Schmitt's thought" to be "a paradoxical renewal of the political efficacy of the State that he obtained through the full acceptance of its instability."[139] The same could be said of Hobbes' thought.

In this story, Lord Saye and Sele is precisely the kind of person Hobbes would see as particularly dangerous: a new man with a sense of ancient privilege. In every one of the multiple facets of his career, Saye leads an influential political life in the teeth of the demands of the sovereign, whether nurturing Puritan connections, or joining the Providence Island Company, or pressing Charles to summon the Long Parliament, or refusing to move the Court of Wards to Oxford, or defying Cromwell's invitation to join the upper house. Through Saye we gain a glimpse into precisely the qualities of this political moment that Hobbes most feared: the absence of a sense of obligation to the king even amongst the aristocracy, fueled by institutions conceiving of themselves as operating independently of the sovereign's protection, whether the separatist prayer meeting, or the corporation, or the courts, or Parliament. Hobbes with Schmitt worried that political life was being increasingly characterized by the thickening of relationships within such associations and a thinning sense of obligation to the political community as a whole and to the sovereign power at its head.

This awareness shared by Hobbes and Schmitt lends an air of desperation to each man's strident claims for decisionist unitary sovereignty, not to mention a reactionary posture marking each as "black" in orientation. We will return to that theme in the Epilogue of this book, where we will see Hobbes and Schmitt confront a collision between their theoretical projects and the actual workings of sovereign power.

---

[139] Galli (2015) 2.

2

Provincializing Romance

One fascinating episode of Charles I's early battles with Parliament is the Lords' 1628 Conference on the Liberties of the Subject, which featured two of the most important legal minds of the century, Sir Edward Coke and John Selden. Both were summoned to represent the Commons' alarm over the broad discretionary power of arrest claimed by the crown during the Five Knights' Case, a claim to which the Lords had acquiesced.[1] Especially in the Elizabethan phase of his career, Coke is rightly associated with promoting the interests of the crown. But in the 1620s his thinking reveals its full complexity, locating sovereignty in the King-in-Parliament, rather than in the person of the monarch, and placing *lex* firmly above *rex*. This is the Coke who joined the outcry against the king's protection of the Arminian Richard Montague, and who collaborated on drafting the Petition of Right.[2] With the "corporation sole," as we saw in chapter 1, Coke summoned a legal fiction supporting the crown's claims to perpetual property ownership: these were held by the monarch as undying corporate entity, rather than by an individual monarch with a limited natural life. But as lawmaker the king was at the acme of his power when operating with parliamentary consent, and his power over existing law was exercised through the judges he appointed. Unlike Hobbes, Coke argues that the subject, too, had a right of inheritance, which could be extended to include other liberties enshrined in law. This is not a Polybian position where sovereignty is divided. Rather it shows that defenses of unitary sovereignty could admit differences of degree and did not necessarily amount to an apology for authoritarian rule.

Coke displays this turn of mind in his contribution to the Conference before the Lords. The speech as recorded in manuscript ends with a slightly garbled quotation of Cicero. The original, a passage in *Pro Caecina*, makes clear the necessity of law to the enjoyment of one's inheritance:

---

[1] See Zaller (2007) 649–52. The Five Knights' Case is sometimes styled Darnel's Case.
[2] See White (1979) esp. chs. 5 and 7.

Sovereignty: Seventeenth-Century England and the Making of the Modern Political Imaginary.
Feisal G. Mohamed, Oxford University Press (2020). © Feisal G. Mohamed.
DOI: 10.1093/oso/9780198852131.001.0001

Mihi credite, maior hereditas unicuique nostrum venit in iisdem bonis a iure et a legibus, quam ab iis a quibus illa ipsa bona relicta sunt. Nam ut perveniat ad me fundus testamento alicuius fieri potest; ut retineam quod meum factum sit sine iure civili non potest

("Believe me, the property which any one of us enjoys is to a greater degree the legacy of our law and constitution than those who actually bequeathed it to him. For anyone can secure by his will that an estate comes into my possession; but no one can secure that I keep what has become mine without the assistance of the law.")[3]

The particular "inheritance" that Coke has in mind is a man's "libertie of his person, for all others are accessorie unto it."[4] The legal basis for this liberty resides in *habeas* rights. The law provides a "diversitie of remedies" against imprisonment, including imprisonment by order of the king or privy council, given in "the statute of Magna Charta, ca: 26." Furthermore, the "statute 42.Ed.3.cap:10" ordered "that all statutes made against Magna Charta are voyde."[5] In a well-worn rhetorical move amongst parliamentarians, Coke casts this brake on the king's authority as dignifying English kingship, for "it should be no honour to ye King, to be a King of Slaves."[6]

Selden joins Coke in defending liberty of person, and also emphasizes that it is already law. He offers even more substantive arguments to that effect: it is supported by "7 severall acts of Parliament"; the "writte of Habeas Corpus"; and, the prong of his argument to which he devotes the vast majority of his attention, a clear line of precedents for, and dubious precedents against, the liberty in question.[7] As with Coke, a major conclusion of his argument is that "Letters from the councell or from ye King cannot alter the Law in any case," even when the king's letter carries the Great Seal.[8] We sense here that Selden is speaking not only as Member of Parliament, but as an attorney deeply annoyed by his failed defense of Edmund Hampden in

---

[3] Cicero (1927) p. 170. The passage appears as follows in BL Stowe MS 333, f.82r: "Cicero. Maior hereditas venit unicuque nam a legibus quam a parsutibus[?]."

[4] BL Stowe MS 333, f.82r. See also *A conference* (1642) and Johnson et al. (1977) entries for April 3, 7, 16, and 17.

[5] BL Stowe MS 333, f.81r. [6] Ibid.

[7] Ibid., f.66r, 67r. Selden declares there to be twelve precedents proving "that persons so committed are to be delivered upon bayle" (f.69r). In addition to the many precedents directly cited, Selden refers to a book of cases collected by a "learned ... cheefe justice of the comon pleas ... I mean the Lord cheefe Justice Andirsonne" (f.78v), i.e. Sir Edmund Anderson. A much briefer list from Selden appears in *Commons Debates, Volume III: 21 April–27 May 1628* (1977) 16.

[8] Ibid., f.74v.

the Five Knights' case. We also catch faint glimpses of a legal mind different from Coke's, one more given to legal reasoning that ought to apply in all legal systems. It is not just that this particular right has a remedy, but that any right must have a remedy: "In all cases (my Lords) wher any righte or libertie belongs to the subject by any positive law... if there were not also a remedie by law for the enjoying or regaining of this righte or liberty which was violated or taken from him, the positive lawe is most vaine, and to no purpose."[9] Denying liberty of person is contrary to "all usages of law" and subverts "the cheefest liberty and right belonging to every freeman of the Kingdome."[10] The language of inheritance that is a central theme of Coke's argument is significantly absent from Selden's.

Still, in reading the two speeches, and in considering their collaboration on the Petition of Right more generally, convergences between Coke and Selden are much more visible than differences. We are reminded of their common interest in Sir John Fortescue's *De laudibus legum Angliae*. Coke refers repeatedly, and admiringly, to this "Man of excellent Learning and Authority" throughout the *Reports*, marshaling him to support the larger historical point that "the ancient and excellent *Laws of England* are the Birth-right and the most ancient and best inheritance that the Subjects of this realm have, for by them he injoyeth not only his Inheritance and Goods in peace and quietness, but his Life and his most dear Country in safety."[11] Selden's comments on Fortescue signal other intellectual sympathies, but in their most famous passage arrive at similar ends:

all laws in general are originally equally antient. All were grounded upon nature, and no nation was, that out of it took not their grounds; and nature being the same in all, the beginning of all laws must be the same. As soon as *Italy* was peopled, this beginning of laws was there, and upon it were grounded the *Roman* laws,... yet remained always that they were at first, saving that additions and interpretations, in succeeding ages increased, and somewhat altered them, by making a *determinatio juris naturalis*, which is nothing but the civil law of any nation. For although the law of nature be truly said immutable, yet it is as true, that it is limitable, and limited law of nature is the law now used in every state.... This rationally considered,

---

[9] Ibid., f.66v. See also Zaller (2007) 667.   [10] Ibid., f.78r.
[11] Coke (1697) *Reports*, Part 3 sig. a4r; and *Reports*, Part 5 sig. A3r; for other references to Fortescue, see *Reports*, Part 6 sig. A2r ("*Fortescue*... who (besides his profound knowledge in the Law being also an excellent Antiquary[)]"); and *Reports*, Part 8 sig. A4v.

might end that obvious question of those, which would say something against the laws of *England* if they could. 'Tis their trivial demand, *When and how began your common laws?* Questionless it is fittest answered by affirming, when and in like kind as the laws of all other states, that is, *When there was first a state in that land, which the common law now governs:* Then were natural laws limited for the conveniency of civil society here, and those limitations have been from thence, increased, altered, interpreted, and brought to what now they are.[12]

The passage makes clear Selden's approach to natural law, which shares the comparative spirit of his considerations of religion: the impulse to follow the law of nature, like the impulse to worship, had been planted in the heart of humankind, but became limited and modified as societies evolved. Once an individual or group of individuals makes a determination from natural law, the result is an artifact of civil law, which is normative in subsequent determinations. Rome is significantly diminished in this narrative as the source of a *jus commune* more closely reflecting the law of nature than various forms of civil law do. Meditations on natural law might exercise the scholar, but they have little impact on deciding live legal issues, which are matters of civil law alone. As Richard Tuck observes of this passage, "this was in fact already the Burkean theory of English law, and its influence ... can be traced directly to Matthew Hale, Selden's friend and executor, and thence to Blackstone and the mainstream of eighteenth-century English legal thinking."[13]

From their different intellectual and political backgrounds, Coke and Selden are able to find a consensus that centers on laws that have accrued in the realm, and to cast the king as straying from them. As Robert Zaller puts it, they pit a *lex terrae* against the *lex coronae* that Charles claimed to be insuperable.[14] Or, nearer to our concerns, they are advancing an argument on the source of the law's authority, claiming that it does not emanate from the person of the king but rather resides in a given conjunction of land settlement and custom. This brings to mind Schmitt's theorization of *nomos* as a land-appropriation that is the foundation of political order, though with an important difference: Coke and Selden are striving for a sense of *nomos*

---

[12] Selden (1726) col. 1891–2. On this work, see Toomer (2009) 174–85. On English law and *jus commune* generally, see Helmholz and Piergiovanni (2009).

[13] Tuck (1998) 84. Cromartie (2006) similarly observes of this passage that Selden's remarks "could be made the basis of almost positivist attitudes" (199).

[14] Zaller (2007) 655.

limiting the prerogative of the sovereign in a way at odds with Schmitt's formulation. Both are grappling with the problematic of limiting the sovereign's power over the physical liberty of the subject. And while their arguments may prefigure later developments placing *lex* above *rex*, the effects of Charles I's arrest of the five knights are worked out through political negotiation between king and Parliament. In claiming the authority of a nexus of person, land, and national tradition that can check sovereign power, Coke and Selden cannot expect to be supported by the robust institutions of the modern state—they are, in fact, quite at odds with the chief justices of the realm. They can draw on precedent, and statute, and the conduct of civilized nations with free citizens, but they and their allies in the Commons are, to no small extent, floating in the breeze.

Slippage between land and custom on the one hand and sovereignty on the other will be significant to the romance literature that is the focus of this chapter. And also the consciously tenuous claim of traditional authority—of class and of culture—that is no longer recognized by the sovereign holding the power of the sword. The core *mentalité* of romance is economically expressed by Northrop Frye: it is the literary form nearest to "the wish-fulfillment dream," and thus the one where a "ruling social or intellectual class tends to project its ideals." These qualities produce an "extraordinarily persistent nostalgia," marked by the "search for some kind of imaginative golden age in time or space."[15] In this respect romance resembles a translation into literature of the utopian impulse visible in natural law: measuring worldly authority against cosmic order, finding a common language of right rule reaching well beyond individual principalities, defining by contrast the perversions of order beyond the pale of this broad social and cultural code. Romance explores these themes in a more conformist, middlebrow key than do the natural lawyers. But it shares the ambition of embodying a set of standards common to the civilized world, even when speaking in the vernacular.

In many ways that ambition is dashed on the flinty rocks of the Reformation and the social upheavals of modernity. From the very advent of Protestantism, romance summons its cultural resources to cast confessional enemies as agents of Satan responsible for dividing Western Christendom. Martin Luther is satirized in *Orlando Furioso* through Rodomonte, the "monarch of Algiers" likened in a memorable epic simile to a snake rearing

---

[15] Frye (2000) 186.

"Itself in glistening pride, its triple tongue / Vibrating."[16] Babel becomes the direct antecedent for the fracturing of the church: "Proud as was Nimrod Rodomonte is. / No climb for him could ever be too steep."[17] As in so many other respects, Spenser follows Ariosto's lead and adapts these new values of romance to a Foxean emphasis on the papal antichrist. Redcrosse is pulled into a history anticipating, in the standard view of sixteenth-century English Protestantism, the collapse of Antichrist's thousand-year reign over the church. In the portions of the *Faerie Queene* that Spenser did not write, Arthur was to engage in a crusade, but this bit of hostility toward Islam seems merely literary, a nod to the conventions of romance with little relevance to the epic's immediate concerns. Spenser knows that a romance must at some point find creative and entertaining ways to kill off a few thousand Muslims, but he procrastinates on this task and it becomes a conspicuous absence in the unfinished work he leaves behind. The real fantasy affirming right rule in the *Faerie Queene* is not a successful crusade against the Muslims, but a successful conquest of Christian enemies.

In the period that is our focus, then, the implicit claim of romance to express the values of Western Christendom is already a distant memory. As with Selden's approach to natural law, cultural and political commonality is consigned to an irrecoverable past, and more local concerns animate the mode. But even as a decayed piece of cultural memory, romance still has an aura of carrying the civilized world's core values, a status that could serve polemical ends: a work could offer itself as cosmopolitan and universal when in fact it consciously served a much narrower cultural agenda. Though romance had always been embedded in particular national stories, whether the Matter of Britain or the Matter of France, the seventeenth-century turn on which we will focus is an increasingly provincial expression of the mode. A sense of political and religious values extending well beyond the sovereign is placed in service of an elite whose power is in crisis. And the idealized landscape of romance incongruously becomes a staging ground for the disenchanting gaze of *raison d'état*. The effect in the mid-seventeenth century is to create a space where nobility and gentry skeptical of the Commonwealth can lend cultural heft to a *nomos* newly unmoored from state power, and meditate on the political form that might enable their return to prominence. Instead of a common cultural language of Western

---

[16] Ariosto (1975) 17.11. On romance and the racialization of Christendom, see Britton (2014); on prose romance and formation of masculinity, see Stanivukovic (2016).

[17] Ibid., 14.119.

Christendom, romance serves as a common cultural language of a propertied class seeking to consolidate group identity and interest in a time of political uncertainty.

We will trace the roots of this development to John Barclay's *Argenis*, a work of early Stuart apology seeking to advance a stridently monarchist view of political authority, and one that effects an unlikely marriage between romance and *raison d'état*. We will then turn to various forms of romance appearing in the 1650s, England's constitutional tumults and innovations make this a literary space for working out the challenges of a dramatically altered social and political environment. To label these later works as "royalist romance" indebted to Barclay, as has often been done, is to miss their very different approach to political authority. Put simply, where Barclay's emphatic unitary sovereignty views a powerful nobility as a threat, the romance of the 1650s is much more open-ended in its political views. And it is much more inclined to see a powerful nobility as a stabilizing bulwark against an autocratic monarch and unruly commoners.

Under the Commonwealth, romance's ambience of social tradition and stability thinly disguises the anxieties of royalists thinking through their political fate. The upheavals of the mid-seventeenth century place these authors' turn to romance at odds with their actual environment, but also opens up this literary mode in unprecedented ways. Its meditations on the traffic between ideal and real worlds become much more genuinely speculative. In the pages of this book, mid-century romance is a unique case of politically engaged writing purposefully holding the question of sovereignty in suspense while seeking political unity founded in a traditional nexus of land distribution and authority. That is an exceedingly rare, perhaps even unique, cultural occurrence. We will contemplate it in the final section of this chapter by re-evaluating Schmitt's concept of *nomos*, with its roots in Pindar and Aristotle, in light of Hannah Arendt's definition of the same concept and its relevance to her theorization of the *vita activa*.

Barclay's *Argenis*: Modern Monarchy in Ancient Costume

That Barclay first publishes the *Argenis* in Latin signals the work's aspiration to speak to a broad European audience, and advertises the author's own cosmopolitan background and experience: Barclay is born and educated in Lorraine, and served on a diplomatic mission for James I in 1609. The enthusiastic epigraph by Grotius appearing below the frontispiece portrait of Barclay in the 1622 Paris edition proclaims these qualities: "*Gente Cale-donius Gallus natalibus hic est / Romam Romano qui docet ore loqui* ['Scottish by race, French by birth, this is the man / Who taught Rome to speak in the Roman language']."[18] And many of the work's political statements were readily visible at the time as remarks on England's place in a larger European landscape. The key of characters included in most early editions, beginning with the 1627 Elzevier edition, makes clear the work's Continental setting: it identifies King Meleander as Henry III of France, Poliarchus as Henry IV of Navarre, and Radirobanes, his rival for the hand of Argenis, as Philip II of Spain.[19]

But not all of the action is meant to comment on the past and on Continental affairs. Nicopompus, clearly a stand-in for Barclay himself, offers a lengthy account in book 2 of his decision to write a romance. Though loyal to Meleander, he is also frustrated that the king's actions have contributed to instability in the realm. Rather than turning to open criticism at a time of political unrest, which would display the "swelling pride of an unseasonable censurer," and likely lead "to the Gallowes," Nicopompus turns to the gentle instruction of a "delicate fiction": "Perhaps [readers] will bee ashamed to play any longer that part upon the Stage of the World, which they shall perceive in my Fable to have beene duely set out for them. And lest they should complaine that they are traduced, there shall be no mans picture to be plainely found there."[20] This explicitly places the political commentary of the text in Barlcay's present, and suggests that romance writing is an outlet for the frustrations he had felt in his service to James. During the Oath of Allegiance controversy, Barclay had continued the family trade of Catholic apology for royal absolutism: he edits a new edition of his father William's *De potestate Papae* in 1609 and responds to Bellarmine's attack on this work with his *Pietas*, published in Paris in 1612.[21] In preparing the Latin edition of the *Premonition*, James sought Barclay's assistance—the manuscript has a note in the king's hand, "remember to speake with barclaye"—and his 1609–10 embassy was to deliver that work to the Emperor of Germany, the King of Hungary, and the Dukes of Bavaria,

---

[18] Barclay (2004) 2. Barclay also referred to as a "French poet" in Carleton (1609). There is relatively little critical work on Barclay's *Argenis* and its influence on romance of the 1650s. See Kahn (2002) 625–61; Salzman (1985) ch. 11; Smith (1994) 233–49; Bush (1952) 54–5; and Fleming (1966) 228–36.

[19] Ibid., 45–8. A key of characters is first provided in the 1627 Elzevier edition, numbered 12 in the list of editions that Riley and Pritchard Huber provide as Appendix 2. The key is incorporated into Roger Le Grys' 1628 English translation; see Barclay (1628) 485–9.

[20] Barclay (2004) 130–1.   [21] See Barclaii (1612).

Lorraine, and Savoy. By Isaac Casaubon's account, the king had come to value the "eruditissimo et amicissimo Barclaio" as an interlocutor in scholarly discussion. Though he is referred to by Dudley Carleton as a "French poet," and though by the time *Argenis* appears he had, ironically, retired in Rome on a pension from the Vatican, Barclay's most active service in the cause of royal absolutism was to King James.[22]

That his political remarks can point toward either side of the Channel is visible in the intermittent attacks on the Hiperephanii, a stridently predestinarian and iconoclastic religious sect attractive to "as many as loved the license of sedition" and led by "Usinulca," an anagram for Caluinus.[23] Immediately after his victory in the civil war, Meleander rejects the congratulations of commissioners sent by the Hyperephanii because they have placed their religious identity above their identity as subjects: "Why doe they not send to me in the name of the Provinces or Cities, but in that of a faction? which, let them know, are alwayes hateful to Princes." Here we sense Barclay observing that the sect as a form of social organization is inherently threatening to stable kingship. Given that this comes from the mouth of Meleander, we think of it first as a remark on the Huguenots, but its applicability to English Puritans is plain enough.

The first translation of the *Argenis* into English is, famously, a false start: Ben Jonson undertakes the labor at James' request only to see the manuscript burn in his 1623 library fire. His poetic account of the fire laments the loss of "three Books not afraid / To speake the Fate of the *Sycilian* Maid / For our owne Ladies," even as it takes aim at romance as being worthy of Vulcan's flames, which makes one wonder how eager Jonson really was to translate Barclay.[24] The 1625 effort of Kingsmill Long proves to be wildly popular well into the eighteenth century. By the beginning of the nineteenth century Coleridge could lament that it was "*unknown* to general readers" despite having been admired "by great men of all ages"—that last remark is hard to square with a work less than two centuries old, though Barclay's romance had been widely admired for at least an age and a half. While less popular and less stylistically accomplished, Roger Le Grys'1628 translation

---

[22] Carleton (April 27, 1609). See Introduction to Barclay (2004) 5–10; Westcott (1911), lxii–lxiv.

[23] Barclay (2004) 269. When civil war erupts, the Hyperephanii are too internally fractious uniformly to side with either King Meleander or Lycogenes, as is emphasized in the Le Grys translation: "with no general resolution of the whole Sect, did rebell, but as the private humours of every one carried them; some served on the Kings part, others on that of Lycogenes" (Barclay [1628] 152; cf. Barclay [2004] 373).

[24] Jonson (1640) sig. B3r.

is notable in claiming for the *Argenis* an identity as a semi-official publication of the Caroline court. The translation is commissioned by Charles I, as announced both on the title page and in Le Grys' dedicatory epistle to the king. It thus takes its place alongside the several printings of Sidney's *Arcadia* in the late 1620s, and the appearance of Francis Quarles' *Argalus and Parthenia* (1628), in attempts by Charles and his supporters to associate the king with chivalric virtue.[25]

Whatever cosmopolitan intentions it hoped to signal in its first publication, and whatever historical references it made to late sixteenth-century affairs on the Continent, the work could also speak to the priorities of an English audience in the throes of the religious and constitutional controversies of Charles I's reign. This is true in both political and literary terms. Politically, an English audience would be alert to the text's intermittent defenses of court favorites, a major point of controversy in the early Stuart period.[26] The point is repeatedly made that kings are uniquely equipped to hand-pick individuals on the basis of merit alone, and indeed that showering perquisites on such individuals is a sound public investment. The multitude will always resent those favored by the king "because that lofty place is not open to the multitude."[27] "Imagine . . . that the most excellent in war, learning, and all manual arts . . . were met together under one prince, like many stars in heaven," Arsidas declares in a lengthy instruction of the African king Archombrotus, "how would the whole world esteem such a court?"[28] Archombrotus' doubts are cleared, but one wonders how many English readers would be so easily persuaded.

In literary terms, the debts to Sidney's *Arcadia* are limited, but an English audience would likely be attuned to strong resonances with Shakespeare. When Argenis is distraught by a report of the death of Poliarchus and attempts to kill herself, her maid Selenissa reminds her of the story of Pyramus and Thisbe: "Have you not heard the error of Pyramus, so famed in writing only that we might learn how dangerous it is to decide upon the first apprehension?"[29] The episode recalls the intimate scenes between heroine and worldly-wise maid in *Romeo and Juliet* and *Othello*. The Pyramus and Thisbe reference is reminiscent of *A Midsummer Night's Dream*, a play further evoked by a hapless band of rustics who mistake the

---

[25] See Patterson (1984) 168, 171, 180, 183.
[26] On animosity toward court favorites as a site of constitutional tension, see Perry (2006). Ch. 3, on defenses of the political value of favorites, is especially relevant to Barclay's *Argenis*.
[27] Barclay (2004) 135.   [28] Ibid., 177.   [29] Ibid., 149, 151.

African king Archombrotus for Poliarchus.[30] In another trope familiar from drama, language marks these peasants' social status: Archombrotus "though he understood Greek, yet in their rustic speech perceived nothing but that they would have him to prison," a double gesture marking the foreignness of the African king and the distance from the metropolis of the "peasants."[31] Shakespearean intertexts could also be introduced by Barclay's translators. In a long diatribe against a would-be court astrologer, the Le Grys translation has Nicopompus ask Meleander why he should not "fall foule upon this Juggler that usurpes a more large authoritie over thee, then the Starres themselves, which he prates and lyes of, can challenge?"[32] The Latin "*veteratorum*" is more accurately rendered "old impostor" in the Long translation. But "Juggler" ingeniously recalls the usurper Macbeth's too-late remarks on the witches' prognostications: "be these juggling fiends no more believed, / That palter with us in a double sense."[33]

With these topical references, paratexts, and literary allusions, English readers encountering the *Argenis* after it is twice translated in the late 1620s would receive a clear message on the dignity of kingship that is in several ways recognizable as intended for their especial benefit. Dignity, but also fragility. Meleander, the king of Sicily, temporarily mismanages his realm, losing territories to the popular rebel Lycogenes, with whom he then must negotiate a humiliating peace. Here the king's acquiescence to the counsel of his self-interested nobles hollows his authority.[34] The choice to follow such advice, Meleander reveals to his daughter Argenis, is made out of paternal care: "You, daughter, were the only cause that I desired rather to hold my crown upon any conditions than to disinherit you by a violent defence of my own majesty."[35] Here the Le Grys translation is less literal and speaks more

---

[30]   The mistake is amusing to King Meleander not only as a confusion of identity, but also as an absurd misreading of sartorial convention: "when in jest they began to speak of the peasants' violence, Meleander conjectured that besides the countenance and youth of Archombrotus, his foreign habit had also caused their mistake, and the ignorant people thought because Poliarchus was a stranger, that he always used a foreign habit" (193).

[31]   Ibid., 185.

[32]   Barclay (1628) 143. The Riley and Pritchard Huber edition, based on the Long translation, has the same passage as follows: "Why should I not rebuke this old impostor, Sir, who would by this means assume to himself more power over you than these very stars have, which he so falsely magnifies?" (357).

[33]   Shakespeare (2008) 5.10.19–20.

[34]   See Barclay (2004) 157: "most dangerous are those who are in my bosom and dive into my counsels, observing me more truly like a captive than a king . . . They urged how necessary it was to make a league; that a strong part of the people favoured Lycogenes . . . And they were so bold as even to excuse Lycogenes."

[35]   Ibid.

directly to English constitutional concerns: for "obstinata defensione maies-tas" it has "obstinate defence of my Prerogative Royal."[36] Meleander's bargain is consistently figured negatively, as is especially apparent in his willingness to allow Poliarchus to be outlawed for killing three of Lycogones' agents in self-defense—a chaotic reversal in the values of this romance, whereby villainous servants of a traitor are valued above a virtuous royal affianced to the princess. Even Argenis is moved to question her father's wisdom, though quickly corrects herself for such disloyalty, and is later enthused by his preparations to renew the war against Lycogones.

In reclaiming his kingship, Meleander must display even more cunning than the cunning rebel. Even as book 2 builds great anticipation of a battle between his armies and those of Lycogones, it ends with Meleander per-suading a good many enemy troops to lay down their arms. Once Meleander has a visible military advantage, he offers pardon to enemy defectors, of which pardon many Lords and rank-and-file soldiers in Lycogones' camp avail themselves.[37] He thus creates disturbance and division in the enemy camp, a tactic that, Botero remarks, had been expertly used by "the pre-tended queen of England," Elizabeth I, in her handling of Continental monarchs and of Mary Stuart.[38] It is an opening gambit that all-but assures Lycogones' later loss in battle. The mild, virtuous king of book 1 who fritters away his power seems by the start of book 2 to have taken a crash course at the Machiavelli School of Government, for which he rises significantly in the text's esteem. The ideal king, we are explicitly told, must command fear: "a good document for mortal men that whatsoever high or excellent virtue be in a king, yet unless he have the fame of fortitude ['nisi fortitudinis opinio accedat'], he shall be condemned, and that no princes are more faithfully beloved of their people than such as have deserved to be feared ['nec fidelius ullos principes amari a populis quam qui timeri meruerint']."[39] The principle is straight from Machiavelli and Francesco Guicciardini. And we are made especially to see the susceptibility of senators and magistrates to Lycogones' anti-monarchist views.

---

[36] Barclay (1628) 32.
[37] For these episodes, see Barclay (2004) 263–5 (Lycogones feasting magistrates), 281–7 (Lycogones' plot regarding the bracelet), 343–7 (deception inducing confession of Lycogones' associates), 397–401 (Meleander's offer of pardon on the eve of war).
[38] Botero (2017) 115 [Bk. 6, ch. 8].
[39] Barclay (2004) 350–1. See also 447–9, on swelling ambitions of nobility when king is not feared.

Constitutional concerns are thus, and for romance rather oddly, at the center of the work's narrative tensions. This is why in his dedicatory poem Owen Felltham praises the *Argenis* for its "Worth, and State Philosophy," praise later underscored by Nahum Tate: "The Philosophy and Politics deliver'd in the Romance of Barclay have render'd it worthy the perusal of greatest Statesmen."[40] An extended dialogue late in the first book openly displays these qualities. Here the philosophically inclined Anaximander makes a full-throated case for the civic virtue cultivated in republics:

> how many more would fit themselves to serve the commonwealth, would exercise their wits, practice the wars or peaceful eloquence, and lastly, seek the good opinion of their fellow citizens, when they knew by their votes that there were rewards to be had for virtue and the chief dignities of the commonwealth were awarded by merit, than when the disposal of these things is confined to the pride of one house and scarce ever conferred by merit or by the judgement of common fame upon honest and industrious men?[41]

Before his speech begins we are told that Anaximander is a nephew of the rebel Lycogenes, so that this "show of his own Philosophy" looks a lot like ambition and irrational hostility to kingship.[42] And lest we have lingering questions on the justice of Anaximander's cause, Barclay has Mount Aetna erupt on him and his troops as they are laying siege to a town loyal to Meleander.[43] The firebrand republican dies from his burns after being captured. Such resting finds the soles of unblessed feet, as Milton tells us of Satan, drawing with Barclay on Virgil's association of Aetna with Jove striking down the Giant Enceladus.[44]

In a way not untypical of the period's republicanism, Anaximander speaks of liberty as the birthright of all, but fudges on whether his imagined republic is fully democratic or ruled by an aristocracy. (We will see a similar ambiguity regarding liberty of "the people" in Milton's political thought.) On this point he is pressed by Nicopompus, the stand-in for Barclay who is described as "a man brought up in learning from his childhood, but scorning to dwell altogether in his books, he left his tutors when but a young man so

---

[40] Felltham, "Authori," qtd. in Barclay (2004) 79; Tate qtd. in Riley and Pritchard Huber's introduction to Barclay (2004) 14.

[41] Barclay (2004) 205.   [42] Ibid., 203.

[43] Ibid., 407. For Anaximander dying from his wounds, see 439.

[44] See Milton (2007) 1.230–7; and Virgil (1916), *Aeneid* 3. 578–82.

that in the courts of kings and princes, as in a true and free school, he might lay the foundation of a public life."[45] Anaximander "played fast and loose," he claims, "in confounding democracy and aristocracy, which are far different from each other; for to ensnare us with a show of liberty you mention the people's power, and to show us its utility, you speak of the wisdom of senators." If "the people govern," they will "bestow offices upon men ignorant and unworthy." If "you insist upon an aristocracy," then "multiplying the number of masters increases the baseness of the bondage. For instead of one sovereign, you make as many as a full senate consists of men."[46]

To justify his own designs on the crown, Lycogones declares his preference for an elected monarchy. He agrees that "under one man the commonwealth is best governed," but bemoans that hereditary monarchy can place the crown on the head of either "an infant or a fool." Better to let the people choose the individual most worthy of kingship, which might encourage "those who are born of royal blood" to "devote themselves to the noble arts, being certain that they cannot succeed their ancestors in their sceptres unless they imitate them in those virtues for which they were chosen kings."[47] We already know Lycogenes to have rebelled against his king, and not without the acclaim of the nobility and the people. For sympathy he turns to the churchman Dunalbius, who, he imagines, would agree given that his proposal resembles the selection of "high priests"—Le Grys again adapts the phrase to an English context, rendering it "chusing of Prelates."[48] That we have already been told of his "excellent endowments of the mind" makes it unsurprising when Dunalbius does not agree at all.[49] Succession promotes peace by disarming "the ambition of great men who would make combustions and assault the king's person in hope of the crown." Lycogenes should of course grasp that point well enough. Further, Dunalbius claims that hereditary monarchs "labour for the good of their kingdom, as being the patrimony of their own children," whereas an elected king would wish to shore up his power by buying and otherwise influencing "those in whose power the election is," or at least of using his office to enrich his family so that "all men may take notice that one of that house had once reigned."[50] All of this in addition to the "bribing or open force" that would attend the election itself.[51]

---

[45] Barclay (2004) 205–7.   [46] Ibid., 207.   [47] Ibid., 209–11.
[48] Ibid., 211; cf. Barclay (1628) 63.   [49] Ibid., 203.   [50] Ibid., 213.
[51] Ibid., 215.

Even as this defense of hereditary kingship appears in a romance setting of loyal knight-service, we cannot mistake its distinctly modern tang. Kings are defended, but good laws are defended more. It is important to our view of Meleander that when he discovers the plot to poison Poliarchus, the plotters are placed on trial, despite the desire of the mob to have them immediately stoned.[52] In a similar key Nicopompus tells us that obedience is necessary to any political settlement; given "the wickedness of men...that form of government comes nearest to nature that forbids men to wander from the rules of virtue or of nature herself. So that the matter is not how many or how few are governors, but under what government the people live best ['*in utro regimine sanctius cives agant*']." Le Grys with more justice translates "*cives*" as "the Subject."[53] This speaks a language of natural law, but deploys a very limited portion of it, to an extent that its core sentiments are quite at odds with that tradition. The pattern of law may be nature, but a nature that imposes necessary limits on an innately vicious human race. No mention is made of humanity's innate sociability, or of the capacity of right reason to descry the law of nature. As in Hobbes, the chief effect is to render moot an appeal to nature as justification for liberty. The subject who here walks upright has been straightjacketed by a law that bars corrupt action, which is much more an apology for the limits on liberty imposed by civil law than it is an argument moving from natural law to natural liberty. Monarchy is more likely to yield effective law, in Nicopompus' argument, because the factionalism pervasive in other political settlements will foster corruption as groups vie for power. The political settlements favored by Amaximander and Lycogones thus give more space to the ill inclinations of men. With this very dim anthropology in place, Barclay through Nicopompus makes clear this text's promotion of a "black" unitary sovereignty attached to a hereditary monarch, and dismisses competing alternatives.

These values become more clear still after Meleander has put down Lycogones' rebellion and contemplates the future stability of his realm. Here Cleobulus, whom Meleander praises for his "*prudentia*," offers lengthy advice that amounts to an evisceration of the political power of the nobility so that the crown might be secure.[54] It does not make sense, he argues, for the island of Sicily to have so many "strongholds, castles, and garrisons," and to appoint "rulers of provinces so absolute that they shall hold their places

---

[52] Ibid., 344–7.   [53] Ibid., 207; cf. Barclay (1628) 61.

[54] Barclay (2004) 468. Long translates *prudentia* as "wisdom" (469), where Le Grys translates it as "prudence" (in Barclay [1628] 205).

during their life."[55] Each of these governors then commands an *imperium in imperio*, with his fortress and militia holding his subjects in awe and all towns becoming "slaves to the captains of the garrison."[56] The only outposts worth maintaining are those necessary to defense of the island as a whole, and Syracuse in particular; the rest of the island's forts ought to be razed. Further, rather than selecting governors from the "greatest nobility" and installing them for life, Meleander should appoint those "neither poor nor proud of too much wealth" for "some few years."[57] Such appointees would likely see themselves, and would be seen by those below them, as only administrators within an order where all real power was held by the sovereign, rather than as potential rivals to the authority of the crown. Cleobolus is clear that the existing system is a vestige of a bygone era when "Sicily was not all under one king, or else every province had a prince who acknowledged subjection only by some small tribute or little homage."[58] Now a fully-fledged island kingdom, Sicily had outgrown this arrangement. The advice hews closely to the principles of Botero, who argues against permanent offices and praises England's Henry II for causing "all the private castles that had been permitted by King Stephen to be razed to the ground."[59] Meleander is sympathetic to this analysis and responds only with practical objections: that he cannot repay the loyalty of those lords who had come to his assistance during the civil war by razing their forts and eliminating their power. Cleobolus avers that the process of phasing them out must be a gradual one, that as each lord dies he ought to be replaced by the kind of term-limited bureaucrat he has described.[60] Lest we think that Barclay is writing only with France in mind, Cleobolus refers to the example of the country on the "opposite shore," with its "proud company of castles and forts" and whose "nobility were so great in faction and strength that they would make their kings afraid."[61]

---

[55] Barclay (2004) 469.   [56] Ibid.   [57] Ibid., 473.
[58] Ibid., 471.
[59] Botero (1956) 87 and Botero (2017) 88. Botero (1956) is based on the 1598 Venice edition, the last that Botero oversaw. The passage on Henry II razing private castles does not appear in Botero (2017), which is based on the first edition, appearing in 1589. See also Botero (1990) 122, and Botero (1601) 30, which notes that "in England the nobility possesse few castels."
[60] Barclay (2004) 473–4.
[61] Ibid., 475. Commentary on the English constitution is more direct still when Poliarchus and Hyanisbe, the Queen of Mauritania, discuss taxation. Riley and Pritchard Huber rightly note that Poliarchus uses the term "free monarchy" as James does in his *True Law of Free Monarchies*, to mean one where the king has no constitutional constraint on levying taxes; see ibid., 733n2.

All of this amounts to a strong argument for the sovereign power of the crown, but not to an idealized view of kings. The *Argenis* is conspicuously unmagical, and expends little energy investing its royal characters with the celestial aura that we expect in romance.[62] Cleobulus argues that setting up a king is a bargain accepted by the subject where some of the liberty enjoyed under a republic is sacrificed for the sake of stability:

> Heretofore the people had recourse to their princes for the appeasing of these troubles lest ambition should knock together and break the nobility, lest factions should divide a friendly country and they should fear from their countrymen that which enemies use to threaten. Therefore they bestowed that honour, sword, and throne upon the king. But if they are yet troubled in the kingdom with the calamities of the commonwealth, what will it avail them to have given up their right or enthralled themselves to any man? Therefore either restore them to their liberty or settle their domestic peace for which they have left their liberty.[63]

By this contractarian reasoning, subjects must see that loyalty to the king remains in their interest, and a king cannot reasonably expect anything more from them.

True to this dispassionate account of the foundation of royal authority, kings can receive rather rough handling in this romance. Meleander, as we have seen, is not always a model of strength and wisdom. More subtly, even the work's ideal king, Poliarchus, is forced to endure several indignities— and narratively gratuitous indignities at that, as though Barclay is inviting us to delight in royal humiliation. In an odd security measure, he disguises himself as a young woman and gains entrance to the private quarters of Argenis. His cover is blown when he fends off a late-night attack by Lycogenes' thugs, a reversal of the gender dynamics of Britomart's self-defense in Castle Joyeous. While Poliarchus loses his sanctuary, he wins Argenis' affections. This is one of several disguises, including a set of false beards that were used by a famous thief to avoid detection, and which had worked only so long before the thief was caught and crucified. Poliarchus is uneasy with this provenance, but accepts the gift. While wearing the disguise, an encounter with Argenis is arranged as she presides over rites in the

---

[62] Patterson (1984) associates unmagical romance with the influence of Heliodorus; see 163 and 180.

[63] Barclay (2004) 451.

temple of Athena. Dwelling too long at the feet of his lover, he is beaten with a stick by a noble "thinking the fellow in rustic simplicity had lain still at her feet."[64] We learn that this particular noble is in fact a friend of Poliarchus, striking a skeptical note on royalty's grandeur: a simple costume change and a prince is utterly unrecognizable, even to his intimates. And disguise cuts both ways: during the battle against Lycogenes, the visiting African royal Archombrotus volunteers to enter battle disguised as Meleander. Not only does this fool Meleander's own army, but they marvel that the old man can still fight with such vigor.[65]

The natural body of the king is held cheap. Replaceable, imitable, easily concealed, it holds few qualities strictly essential to wielding sovereign power. Again we are reminded of Shakespeare's affinity for disguised and substitute kings, whether in *Henry V*, or *Measure for Measure*, or *Hamlet*, though Barclay has even less of the countervailing enchantment of kingship that we associate with the procession of Banquo in *Macbeth*. Even as the *Argenis* consistently defends hereditary kingship as a political settlement, royalty is utterly demystified. *Raison d'état* has very much left its mark on the courtly values this romance espouses, suggesting that interest analysis purporting to have insider information on political conflict had become the stuff of courtly conversation—we have seen hints of this in chapter 1, in discussing Hobbes' translation of the *Altera secretissima instructio* for Cavendish. With its pessimistic anthropology, Barclay's *Argenis* makes a case for absolute monarchy as the worst sort of government except for all the rest.

In supporting the publication of *Argenis*, Charles I may have been promoting a more pragmatic and worldly royalism than we have thought. He may also have been promoting a more pragmatic and worldly royalism than he had thought. Barclay opens a passage by which romance comes to contemplate the practical dynamics of various constitutional settlements: through his efforts, the human counterpart to post-apocalyptic purity that Frye terms an "analogy of innocence" is disrupted in ways later put to other political use.[66] Which is precisely what happens with the revival of romance in the 1650s, often also referred to as "royalist" in a way that does not capture the complexities of its self-positioning. The absence of the supernatural and the debts to drama are key features of Davenant's *Gondibert*. Having looked at the *Argenis*, the combination of romance and political philosophy in Harrington's *Oceana* looks far less unique. In genre it places

---

[64] Ibid., 231. [65] Ibid., 419–21. [66] Frye (2000) 151.

itself in the company of Barclay's very popular work, implying, as Jonathan Scott and J.C. Davis have argued, that its political ideas should not be deemed so alien to royalist readers and advancing its mission of "healing and settling" the realm.[67]

Barclay's strongest influence is on the prose romances of the 1640s and 1650s, which follow the *Argenis* much more closely than they do Sidney's *Arcadia*. As is visible from their full titles, these works, like Barclay's, marry romance narrative with pragmatic political commentary: *Cloria and Narcissus, A Delightfull and New Romance, Imbellished with divers Politicall Notions, and Singular Remarks of Modern Transactions* (1653); *Theophania: Or Severall Modern Histories Represented by Way of Romance: And Politickly Discoursed Upon* (1655); and *Panthalia: Or the Royal Romance, A Discourse Stored with Infinite Variety in Relation to State Government* (1659).[68] Equally clearly, these later romances were much more receptive to the kind of political settlement that Barclay strenuously opposed: one where the nobility has a significant share of sovereign power and exercises salutary limits on royal absolutism.

That is visible right from the earliest of them, *Theophania*, likely written in 1645 though not published until 1655. Like Cowley's *Civil Wars*, it is an unfinished royalist work optimistically embarked upon when the king's supporters felt that their victory was inevitable, and later published as a work of defeat. Even so, it is a great deal less absolutist than Barclay's *Argenis*: much space is given to the history of Cenodoxius, a stand-in for the third Earl of Essex, who criticizes Charles for rebuffing his attempts to negotiate a settlement that would have prevented the outbreak of war. *Theophania* undercuts an association of Charles with unitary sovereignty by stating that in fact Henrietta Maria is his "associate in sovereignty," and that she populates the court with fops and sycophants while sidelining civic-minded nobles.[69] This is the explicit claim of Alucinus' complaint to Cenodoxius in book 6:

---

[67] See Scott (2011) 191–2 and Davis (2014) 66–7.

[68] Cf. the full titles of English translations of the influential romances of Madeleine de Scudéry: *Ibrahim, or, The Illustrious Bassa an Excellent New Romance, the Whole Work in Four Parts* (1652); and *Clelia, An Excellent New Romance Dedicated to Mademoiselle de Long-ueville* (1656). Both are printed for Humphrey Moseley.

[69] *Theophania* (1999) 256. Pigeon justly notes that the attribution to "Sir W. Sales," sometimes "Sir William Sales," rests on slender evidence provided in an 1852 entry in *Notes and Queries*: the book collector James Crossley states that his copy has "Sir W. Sales" inscribed on the title page under "By An English Person of Quality" (see *Theophania* (1999) 12).

How often whilst the buffon Crotus, the chief poet, and the chiefest of poltroons Valerius, the strong gaming wit Andemus, the playwright Dante, the railleur Arterius, the intriguer Grollio, with the rest of that cabal and their chief patron, the luxurious Vitellio, have been admitted to the privacy of councillors, have the chiefest of the nobility, upon urgent affairs, like so many lackeys attended in the antechamber for an audience? And no sooner dismissed, but every one of you passed under the censure of those flattering critics?[70]

The printed key appearing in some copies identifies Andemus as Sir John Suckling and Vitellio as Sir Henry Jermyn, and in her recent edition Pigeon plausibly conjectures that Valerius refers to Richard Lovelace, Dante to Sir William Davenant, and Grollio to Edmund Waller.[71] For all of his flaws of ambition and pride, Cynodoxius/Essex is justifiably piqued that such men find royal favor, as even the young prince Alexandro, a stand-in for Charles II, grudgingly concedes after hearing his lengthy tale: "I must confess that if [Cynodoxius] had avowed his cause, I should not have been so much offended with his actions, nor altogether so averse from a reconciliation: for great men that are sensible of their own dishonor are the fittest ministers for princes, and being cherished, the chief supporters of the Crown."[72] It is no minor fantasy to place these words in the mouth of a young Charles II.

In a stark contrast to the *Argenis*, favoritism is presented as a major political ill, and Synesius—a stand-in for Robert Sidney (1595–1677) and the chief moral authority in the text—intriguingly remarks that robust constitutionalism would assure that only those contributing to the health of the commonwealth are rewarded and promoted.[73] As Pigeon notes, it is revealing that the romance seeks to praise Sidney above all others, a "royalist" who did not fight in Charles I's cause.[74] In a way that will become typical, skepticism on the absolutism Barclay endorses arcs toward claiming

---

[70] Ibid., 260.

[71] Ibid., 316n61. Pigeon provides the printed key, and the manuscript key in the Michigan copy, as an Appendix.

[72] Ibid., 278.

[73] See *Theophania* (1999) 280–1: "All other nations in the world, when they first established their empire, aiming at continuance, prescribed to themselves certain fundamental laws, as well concerning the succession as the government . . . And considering their own true proper interest, in relation to other people, proposed a certain end, and ordained politic maxims, by which those that are entrusted with the management of affairs must direct their counsels for the advancement of their interest, so that whosoever is ambitious to participate [in] the honors of the commonwealth frames his studies and actions wholly according to those principles."

[74] *Theophania* (1999) 58–9.

the importance of the nobility to a realm that had been torn asunder by a negligent king and fickle commoners. Though often styled "moderate royalism," that label does not capture a core emphasis on the place of an independent nobility in a stable constitutional arrangement, an emphasis deeply skeptical of depositing unitary sovereignty in the monarch.[75]

The 1650s: Romance without a King

We will focus on prose romance of the 1650s, but it is worthwhile momentarily to consider it alongside verse romance. These two expressions of the mode certainly have a strong family resemblance, even if prose dresses in homelier weeds than its Italianate cousin. Once we take this broad view, we realize that there was quite an output of romance in the 1650s, including the efforts of Abraham Cowley and Sir William Davenant, of Richard Brathwaite and Roger Boyle, of George Mackenzie and James Harrington.[76] To these we might add translations of French romance, though the quality of these efforts is derided by Dorothy Osborne in a letter to Sir William Temple: "I have no patience . . . for these translations of romances. I met with *Polexander* and *L'illustre Bassa* both so disguised that I, who am their old acquaintance, hardly know them."[77] That Osborne considers these works old acquaintances offers a glimpse into their popularity amongst royalist gentry and nobility, both men and women.

In the same letter, Osborne declares she had heard rumor that Lord Saye and Sele and Edmund Waller had both composed romances. Neither has been found, a hint that there may be several lost romances of this period, but we might consider the possibility of Saye's project alongside Thomas Fairfax's manuscript translation of the romance "Barlaam and Josaphat" as complicating the extent to which we consider the mode to be the demesne of the defeated party: Puritans skeptical of the regicide, and, later,

---

[75] Pigeon likewise emphasizes the importance of a "stronger nobility" to the author of *Theophania*; see *Theophania* (1999) 53.

[76] I have in mind Roger Boyle's *Parthenissa* (1651, four-part in 1655, 'six volumes compleat' in 1676); Brathwaite's *Panthalia* (1659); Cowley's *Davideis*, appearing in his *Poems* (1656); Davenant's *Gondibert* (1651); Mackenzie's *Aretina* (1660); and Harrington's *Oceana* (1656).

[77] Osborn (1888) 161. Henry Cogan's translation of de Scudéry's *Ibrahim, or the Illustrious Bassa* appeared in 1652; William Browne's translation of Gomberville's *History of Polexander* in 1647. To these we can add John Davies' and George Havers' translation of de Scudéry's *Clelia*, which appeared in 1655.

republicans skeptical of the Protectorate, also turned to romance.[78] A spectrum emerges in the Commonwealth period, with a right wing expressing nostalgia for the old order and a left pointing toward a new settlement. Not all of this material can be called "royalist romance." Boyle's *Parthenissa*, with its absurdly mannered courtliness, is on the farthest reaches of the right wing, but still has some internal qualities pointing leftward: it claims to follow Polybius more closely than any other Roman author and tells the story of the Second Punic War, both qualities that we would otherwise associate with republican culture. Harrington's *Oceana* shores up the left wing of this spectrum by delivering republicanism in a mode that held appeal across political divisions. We might think of Davenant's *Gondibert* as resting somewhere in the middle: it advertises itself as offering a path forward for a national literature that will reconcile readers to the new regime, a quality praised by Hobbes in his response to the preface, though also seeks to incorporate traditional tastes and standards.

With Barclay we saw cracks appearing in the gilded surface of romance, revealing the ugly realities of politics. In the 1650s appears a deep chasm in the mode, so that the aristocratic-cum-Christian values of chivalric romance are consciously at odds with those of prevailing authority, namely the Commonwealth. When noticed, romance of this decade is often deemed a literature of exile, a fantasy of shelter from a world turned upside down, anxiously awaiting a restoration of monarchy. While that tendency exists, we can also see romance becoming a vehicle for working through political anxieties, both for those who would adapt to the new regime and for those who would reject it. It is an odd phenomenon, we should note, for prose romance especially, a breezy object of delight now bearing, after Barclay's example, the thick knuckles of *raison d'état*. After charting these dynamics in Sir Percy Herbert's *Cloria and Narcissus* (1653–54), we will seek to theorize their political engagements with reference to Schmitt's unconventional interpretation of the term *nomos*, which seeks to uncover the anchoring of law in a particular landed settlement.

Cloria and Narcissus, first published anonymously in 1653, is explicitly royalist in allegiance, if also signaling the ways in which royalist political sentiment had changed by this juncture: its primary sympathies lay with an aristocracy betrayed by a politically inept king and discarded by upstart commoners. Now known to have been written by Sir Percy Herbert, a Catholic

---

[78] On Fairfax's manuscript works, see Major (2014) 173–4.

supporter of the king who had been despoiled of his properties in 1651, the affinities of the romance are clear, but this does not preclude the sprawling text from providing complex and subtle commentary on the decade preceding the civil wars, taking into account, as Barclay does, England's place in European affairs. An early moment points to political principles to which Charles should have adhered, in the form of advice from the mouth of King Euarchus' trusted counselor, Polinex. Despite a desire for war amongst the people and corrupt members of court, Polinex counsels peace for the simple reason that the king cannot afford to raise and maintain an army:

> your treasure, notwithstanding it be sufficient to maintaine the expence of your peaceable Government; yet, it will be found no way able to undergoe the charge of a powerfull Army.... Therefore my opinion is, that until you can provide a store out of your owne revenew, without depending altogether upon the uncertainty of your Subjects bounty, no warlike undertaking can prove glorious or beneficiall, but of the contrary danger-ous and unprofitable[.][79]

King Euarchus is "extreamely pleased" with the advice of pursuing peace. This creates tensions within his own court, as the self-seeking Dimogoras rouses opposition to Polinex and to the king's "cold newtrality."[80] As Paul Salzman notes, the early pages of this romance comment on the Thirty Years' War,[81] and we find here Euarchus serving as a stand-in for Charles I, who, in the face of parliamentary objection in the 1620s, was reluctant to engage in a defense of the Protestant cause on the Continent. Much as we admire the wisdom of Polinex, we are also made aware that wisdom is not always politically advantageous: when the "Senate," through the plotting of Dimogoras, wishes to strike at the "root" of the king's authority, Polinex is tried and condemned.[82] King Euarchus detests the judgment, but ultimately executes it in order to avoid political unrest: "though long he disputed with his *Flamins* about it, who all perswaded him to the compliance, rather then hazzard his own person, and the Kingdoms ruine."[83] We recall that in the opening pages of the romance, Euarchus was aware that Dimogoras was murmuring at court about the course of peace that Polinex had advised. He responded by calling a hunt "to remedy (the sweetest way he could) these growing inconveniences."[84]

---

[79] [Herbert] (1653) 21–2.   [80] Ibid., 46.   [81] Salzman (2001) 224.
[82] [Herbert] (1653) 129.   [83] Ibid., 131.   [84] Ibid., 24.

Such measures may reflect a nature too sweet effectively to deal with the politic spirits of his own court. That Euarchus' political naiveté leads to a crisis of authority is just one way in which Herbert may be offering very faint praise of Charles I. The flash of sound judgment apparent in his reluctance to enter the fray on the Continent in the 1620s is thoroughly overshadowed by defeats in the bishops' wars and civil wars. Through Euarchus, Herbert is critical of both James I and Charles I, and offers detailed accounts of key royalist losses to parliamentary forces. Further, the romance is no simple political allegory: political ideas that have direct bearing on the English context are not attached only to the house of Euarchus, creating an ongoing meditation on corruptions of political stability leaving neither king, nor Lords, nor Commons unslapped.

Sympathies quite different from Barclay's are most visible in the handling of royal favorites. Where the *Argenis* makes the case that hereditary monarchs are best equipped to seek out and reward exemplary individuals on the basis of merit alone, and that they serve the public good in doing so, *Cloria and Narcissus* is much more ambivalent about favorites and the monarchs who promote them. This is especially visible in the "politicke braine" of Philostros, who serves his own ambitions by manipulating the unruly passions of Prince Orestes, brother of King Orsames.[85] With the prince desiring a politically disadvantageous match, Philostros orchestrates his imprisonment and carefully transforms his initial rage into slow submission to the king's will: "*Philostros* plaid with him like a huge Fish intangled with an angle . . . letting him by degrees worke himself out of breath, that at last he might deale with him according to his pleasure."[86] Orestes' unruly nature makes him especially susceptible to Philostros' machinations. Disappointed that he can no longer pursue Alciana, the prince takes comfort in the company of her cousin Phalarius, in language that leaves little doubt about the sexual comforts the relationship provides: "With this taking the Boy by the white hand, he led him into his owne Lodgings, enforming every one that he was a neere Kinsman to the Princesse *Alciana*, his passion not being able to hide what his discretion should have concealed." Just in case we miss the broad hint, Herbert drives the point home: "In conclusion he made the

---

[85] Ibid., 83.
[86] Ibid., 85. He later manipulates the prince into lighting upon a new love interest, Philostros' own niece who is firmly under his influence, and draws Orestes into an argument on her honor before the king, adding to the prince's disgrace at court. Thus "poor *Orestes*" was "unawares surprised by the wise favourite" (102).

daintie *Ganymed* not only his daily play-fellow, but his night companion."[87] With his hot passions and unruly appetites, Prince Orestes is marked as having an utter lack of prudence.

His brother the king also declines in the text's estimation for treating Philostros' power as a synecdoche of his own, feeling that "as long as his Favourite is safe and powerfull, himself with security may freely enjoy his own pleasures." And so Philostros is granted "a new guard," a sign of growing power and growing unpopularity: "to defend his person from such dangers as his over-great interest, and absolute bold execution, threaten; especially, since not onely the States of the Kingdome are highly offended against his pride, but the common people became exceedingly burdened by his taxations."[88] Once he has "established his own power," he moves to suppress "the greatnesse of all the Nobility of *Syria*, who during the Kings infancy had alwaies demanded conditions for themselves by force of Armes; and having now no more opposition in his own Countrey, resolved to contend with the mightinesse of the *Ægyptian* Monarchy."[89] The political lessons are somewhat ambiguous. A corrupt, unpopular, and power-hungry favorite defangs the nobility and thus removes potential resistance to the will of the king. But that resistance is not necessarily positive, waiting eagerly for an ebb in the king's power so that it can advance its interests with the threat of civil strife. With such resistance cleared, the king is secure enough at home to project power abroad. Nonetheless, a comparison to Barclay's Cleobulus is revealing: Herbert is much more willing to show the corrupt motives behind an effort to secure the crown's power at the expense of the nobility. With Botero, Herbert seems to present a strong nobility as necessary to political stability despite their challenges to monarchical authority: though their "authority and power" is "suspect to the sovereign," nobles are "as the bones and firmness of the states which, deprived of them, would be as it were bodies composed of flesh and pulp."[90]

Taking all of this together, the effect may be neither encomium to nor attack on the Stuarts, nor uncomplicated praise of royalist nobility, but rather an attempt to translate recent experience into political wisdom. Barclay's pairing of romance and *raison d'état* is redoubled in response to the constitutional crises following the removal of Charles I, now with less emphasis on the practical benefits of unitary sovereignty in the hands of a hereditary monarch. Herbert would later finish his work and publish it as

---

[87] Ibid., 92.   [88] Ibid., 118.   [89] Ibid., 125.   [90] Botero (2017) 85.

the five-part *Princess Cloria* in 1661, a move that then projects anticipation of a return to Stuart rule onto its previously released parts. If we bracket that later release from consideration and take the earlier parts at face value, we find the politics of *Cloria and Narcissus* to be quite complex. In such works, as Nigel Smith observes, we find an exiled parliamentary nobility working through questions on the foundations and limits of royal authority, though romance of this moment "had no answers within itself for the predicament in which many of its readers found themselves."[91]

Davenant's position in the preface to *Gondibert* is that poetry has an important role to play in cultivating obedience to authority:

> Poets (who with wise diligence study the People, and have in all ages, by an insensible influence govern'd their manners) may justly smile when they perceive that *Divines, Leaders of Armies, States-men* and *Judges*, think *Religion,* the *Sword,* or…*Policy,* or *Law*…can give, without the help of the *Muses,* a long and quiet satisfaction in government.[92]

His real ambition, of course, is to introduce theatre in the Commonwealth, something, in his account, at which English poets had excelled amongst the moderns. He thus strategically deploys romance in a larger poetic project seeking to cultivate—and, equally importantly, to be seen by the powerful as cultivating—quiescence in its readers. But saying this must also leave us wondering if legitimation runs in the other direction, for Davenant's and all of the romance projects of its moment, which is to say that given the altered political environment even verse romance can no longer stand on its own feet—despite its high-Renaissance pedigree, verse romance, too, finds itself in search of a politics to embellish. Rather than offering a diverting means of inculcating proper aristocratic conduct as it had always done, romance is now marshaled as a medium of the more weighty and complex meditations of an age saturated with political philosophy. It simultaneously loses its status as a mode of wonder and delight.

Nomos without Sovereignty

"Poor Schmitt," writes Hannah Arendt in the margin of her copy of Schmitt's Nomos *of the Earth*, "the Nazis said Blood and Soil—he

---

[91] Smith (1994) 239.   [92] Davenant (1650) 83.

understood Soil—the Nazis meant *Blood*."[93] Wonderfully scornful of the jurist's dirty bargain with the National Socialists, the remark equally signals Arendt's recognition of the central place of land in Schmitt's thought. His definition of *nomos* has received a good deal of attention in recent years, especially as it contributes to his analysis of America's role in international relations.[94] Even so, it is widely recognized that the Greek etymology central to his definition is highly dubious—this does not of itself diminish its utility as a theoretical category, but in the instant case we will see other thinkers drawing more fruitfully than Schmitt does on the range of meanings available in the original Greek. It is Schmitt's central concern to distinguish between *nomos* as a spatial enclosure marking the border between friend and enemy, and Ciceronian *lex* as a depoliticized, rational order of law that does not necessarily refer to a particular space.[95] To his mind, Cicero's misleading translation of *nomos* as *lex* sets the path to "the further development of the law-state and... the present crisis of legality."[96] Through our consideration of romance, and through Hannah Arendt's consideration of the distinction between Greek *nomos* and Roman *lex*, we will see an alternative to Schmitt's theorization of *nomos*.

Though *nomos* is typically translated as "law," Schmitt returns to Greek sources to associate the term with property settlement. This is partly achieved by setting Plato against Aristotle. For Plato, "*nomos* signified a *schedon*—a mere rule—and Plato's *nomoi* already contain something of the utopian plan-character of modern laws."[97] Schmitt has the *Laws* ["*NOMOI*"] and also the *Statesman* in mind: "law ['νόμος'] could never, by determining exactly what is noblest and most just for one and all, enjoin upon them that which is best." Here *nomos* is limited by the diversity of human thought and action, which prevents "any science whatsoever to promulgate any simple rule for everything and for all time."[98] We can imagine Schmitt approving of this critique of legality divorced from the concrete situation of a people pursuing its way of life, but Plato's use of

---

[93] Arendt's note on p. 211 of Schmitt's *Der Nomos der Erde*: "Arme Schmitt: die Nazis sagten Blut u. Boden—er verstand Boden—die Nazis meinten Blut." Image available at bard.edu/library/archive/arendt/marginalia.htm. For deciphering Arendt's hand, and translations from German, I am indebted to Jurkevics (2017).

[94] See especially Benhabib (2012), Hooker (2009) ch. 2, Koskenniemi (2004), Legg (2011), Mouffe (2005), Odysseos and Petito (2007), and Scheuerman (2006).

[95] See Adam Sitze's introduction to Galli (2010) lxviii, and Galli (2000) 1598 and 1610.

[96] Schmitt (2006), Nomos *of the Earth*, 342.

[97] Schmitt (2006), Nomos *of the Earth*, 67.

[98] Plato (1925), *Statesman*, 134–5 [294B].

the term *nomos* does not perform all of the work he wishes it to do. He emphasizes instead a distinction he finds in Aristotle between "the concrete order as a whole, the *politea*, and the many individual *nomoi*," with the "rule of the *nomos*" being "synonymous with the rule of medium-sized, well-distributed landed property." When Aristotle says that "*nomos* as such should govern," Schmitt argues, he is not defending modern rule of law *avant la lettre* but arguing against rule by the very wealthy and rule by the masses.[99]

Schmitt's argument is hard to square with the *Politics*, where *nomos* can designate law in a way detached from property: Book 1 declares that "law is a principle of justice ['ὁ γὰρ νόμος δίκαιόν τι']."[100] He does speak more suggestively, however, in attaching his claims to Pindar, in no small measure because the fragment in question is profoundly unclear in its use of *nomos*. Cited by Plato in the *Gorgias* and by Herodotus, the poem does suggest some traffic between law, custom, and property in its use of the term:

> *Nomos*, the king of all,
> of mortals and immortals,
> guides them as it justifies the utmost violence
> with a sovereign hand. I bring as witness
> the deeds of Heracles,
> for he drove Geryon's cattle
> to the Cyclopean portal of Eurystheus
> without punishment or payment[101]

It is "rightly said in Pindar's poem," Herodotus tells us, "that use and wont is lord of all."[102] As Schmitt reads the passage "the theft of cattle, an act of Heracles, the mythical founder of order" is the means "whereby, despite the violence of the act, he created law."[103] And thus *nomos* manifests the connection between the "first concrete and constitutive distribution, i.e. land-appropriation" and legal order: "all subsequent regulations of a written or unwritten kind derive their power from the inner measure of an original, constitutive act of spatial ordering. This original act is *nomos*."[104] The antistrophe implies that Geryon has a good death, that with Heracles he is

---

[99] Schmitt (2006), Nomos *of the Earth*, 68.
[100] Aristotle (1932), *Politics*, 24–5 [1255a]; see also 264–7 [1287a–b].
[101] Pindar (1997), fragment 169a, lines 1–8.
[102] Herodotus (1921) 51 [3.38].   [103] Schmitt (2006), Nomos *of the Earth*, 73.
[104] Ibid., 74, 78.

acting consistently with *nomos* in a way that must produce the death of one them: "it is better to die when possessions / are being seized than to be a coward."[105] With this implication, we can see *nomos* not only as tied to an order arising from land distribution, but as a political unit in Schmitt's sense of the term, as defining a nexus of land and custom that adopts a posture of war toward outsiders.

Schmitt must have been aware that his Greek etymology was highly selective, and that he was ignoring associations of *nomos* with nomadism in order to advance his claims.[106] That association is developed by Deleuze and Guattari, who argue that *nomos* names a particular form of distribution defined against that of a settled community:

> the nomadic trajectory... *distributes peoples (or animals) in an open space, one that is indefinite and noncommunicating.* The *nomos* came to designate the law, but that was originally because it was a distribution... one without division into shares, in a space without borders or enclosure. The *nomos* is the consistency of a fuzzy aggregate: it is in this sense that it stands in opposition to the law or the *polis*, as the backcountry, a mountainside, or the vague expanse around a city ("either nomos or polis").[107]

For Deleuze and Guattari, *nomos* thus designates the opposite of the marking of an enclosure that then becomes the source of legal authority. Its root in νέμω (*némō*, "I distribute"), and the fact that Aristotle contrasts it against the *polis*, point to a distribution standing apart from the city, a distribution that does not lose its sense of fluidity and that is attached to a space that is not parceled into properties.

We should be conscious of this alternate sense of *nomos* that Schmitt seeks to bury, and be alert to the ways in which it raises questions on the formula provided by Wendy Brown in her compelling analysis of sovereignty and enclosure: "There is first the enclosure and then the sovereign.... Schmitt's etymology of *nomos* may be contested... but his appreciation of enclosure as a prerequisite of political order and law is difficult to set aside."[108] This insight might be expressed slightly differently. Sovereign power seeks to contain the various dynamics of *nomos*: of settlement and

---

[105] Pindar (1997), fragment 169a, lines 16–17.
[106] On this point, see Meierhenrich and Simons (2016) 54–5.
[107] Deleuze and Guattari (1987) 420; italics in original. In making these claims, Delueze and Guattari draw on Laroche (1949).
[108] Brown (2010) 45.

distribution, of law and custom, of violent appropriation and free use. Even as sovereign power presents itself as the inevitable next step of *nomos* in Schmitt's sense of the term, his suppression of its contradictory meanings teaches us that this is an ideological maneuver. At the same time, in brushing against the grain of this maneuver Deleuze and Guattari engage in their own ideological distancing of *nomos* and law, in a way that also forecloses certain implications of the term.

A more nuanced approach to *nomos* would allow us to keep several of its senses in play. Here we might turn to Arendt, who contrasts Greek *nomos* and Roman *lex*. The latter conceives of itself as an agreement between men, and so has a contractual basis and becomes the foundation of law conceived as the product of mutual agreement amongst politically interested elements of society. For the Romans, then, "legislative activity, and with it the laws themselves, belong to the realm of politics."[109] For the Greeks, by contrast,

> the legislator's activity was so radically disconnected from the truly political activities and affairs of the citizens within the polis that the lawgiver did not even have to be a citizen of the city but could be engaged from outside to perform his task, much like a sculptor or architect commissioned to supply what the city required.[110]

Nomos names the just bounds to be placed on human action, and it is by respecting these bounds that a person is deemed within a *nomos*. These moderating bounds are necessary not because humanity is inherently immoderate or corrupt, but as a means of organizing and directing human action in a way advancing the aims of a particular group. *Nomos* thus encloses the "web of ties and relationships" constituted by human action.[111]

It is this sense of enclosure that drives Arendt's reading of the term. And here she seems to be consciously adjusting Schmitt. Schmitt's account of enclosure in the spatial sense as bracketing the domain of war is marked with several emphasis lines in Arendt's copy of Nomos *of the Earth*.[112] But

---

[109] Arendt, *Promise of Politics*, 179.   [110] Ibid.

[111] Ibid., 186. "To the Greek mind, this lack of moderation did not lie in the immoderateness of the man who acts, or in his hubris, but in the fact that the relationships arising through action are and must be of the sort that keep extending without limits."

[112] See Arendt's copy of Schmitt, *Der Nomos der Erde*, 44; images available at bard.edu/library/archive/arendt/marginalia.htm. Several pages in the chapter "On the Meaning of the Word *Nomos*" have annotations; Jurkevics (2017) remarks that "the most sustained subject of the marginalia is Schmitt's inability or unwillingness to comment about right and wrong" (350), a charge of ignoring the question of justice reminiscent of Strauss' critique of Schmitt.

she comes to a radically different view of spatiality, one that accords with her thought on plurality and the possibility of action. Even as Arendt retains a spatial emphasis, it is without the equation so automatic for Schmitt that an enclosure necessarily divides friend from enemy. "The Greek word for law, *nomos*," *The Human Condition* states in a footnote, "derives from *nemein*, which means to distribute, to possess (what has been distributed), and to dwell."[113] A reader of seventeenth-century English literature will be reminded immediately of the closing lines of Jonson's *To Penshurst*: "they that will proportion thee / With other edifices, when they see / Those proud, ambitious heaps, and nothing else, / May say, their lords have built, but thy lord dwells."[114] It is the nature of Penshurst, as Jonson figures it, to have walls that serve no defensive purpose: they certainly are not a social barrier, as the Pembroke estate is a space of grateful gifts from tenant to lord, and endless bounty from lord to tenant. To "dwell" here is to inhabit a sphere of customary relationships animating a defined space. As Hans Lindahl has put it in his recent elaboration on Arendt, "a phenomenology of *nomos* suggests that ... two meanings are internally connected: *abiding*, in the twofold sense of abiding by the law and abiding in a place, is one of the spatial modes of appearance of legal validity. When abiding, an individual is emplaced, located where she or he ought to be." The opposite of abiding is trespassing, "in the double sense of becoming misplaced and crossing the law."[115]

The account of *nomos* that Arendt provides is thus closely tied to her theorization of action. Unlike labor, which satisfies life's necessities, and work, which engages in fabrication, action cannot be performed in isolation: "to be isolated," Arendt declares, "is to be deprived of the capacity to act."[116] Arendt describes action as a new beginning producing reactions that themselves may have the character of action. It is thus not a pebble tossed in the water creating ripples of displacement in its medium; it is instead the initiation of a chain of events producing unanticipated consequences beyond its control. It is illumining to note that Arendt began her project as a critique of Marx, whom she accuses of seeing political action as flowing from labor and work.[117] Action is the aspect of the human condition for which a view of the subject as *animal laborans* and *homo faber* cannot account, and it is vital to the lived experience of political relationships. But

---

[113] Arendt (1998), *The Human Condition*, 63n62.
[114] Jonson (1947), *To Penshurst*, 100–3.   [115] Lindahl (2006) 887.
[116] Arendt (1998), *The Human Condition*, 188.
[117] See Canovan introduction to Arendt (1998) xi. For a lucid account of labor and action in the context of Arendt's views on human rights, see Gündoğdu (2015).

in order for action to be politically productive and cohesive, rather than anarchic and disruptive, it must tighten a web of relations and advance the aims of a group.

Narrative in this theorization hovers between fabrication and action. If "the light by which to judge the finished product is provided by the image or model perceived beforehand by the craftsman's eye," then we are in the realm of fabrication.[118] If that light appears only at the end "frequently when all the participants are dead," then that narrative is a record of action. In articulating the distinction, Arendt insists on using "historian" and "story-teller" interchangeably: "action reveals itself fully only to the storyteller... What the storyteller narrates must necessarily be hidden from the actor himself, at least as long as he is in the act or caught in its consequences, because to him the meaningfulness of his act is not in the story that follows."[119] If the storyteller—or historian, or political philosopher—substitutes "making for acting," then the result is a "degradation of politics into a means to obtain an allegedly 'higher' end—...in the Middle Ages the salvation of souls, in the modern age the productivity and progress of society" (229). That remark will recall *Oceana*, which, as J.C. Davis argues, is framed "to bring the reader to participate imaginatively in the steps required to rebuild the commonwealth on a stable basis."[120] But this desire for stability is antithetical to the *vita activa*: it is an attempt to put a brake on action by circulating already known forms and stories associated with cohesion and stability. Harrington is a *de jure* thinker in every respect: his use of romance chimes well with a political philosophy that has substituted making for acting, subordinating politics to the "higher ends" of balanced interests and legal order. In their use of romance, Davenant and Cowley are further removed still from action: then and now, readers encounter them as converted royalists—*Davideis*, we'll recall, appears in Cowley's 1656 *Poems*, with its preface famously declaring obedience to Cromwell. Their literary efforts under the new regime thus take on the survivalist quality of labor, signaling a view of humanity as *animal laborans* whose efforts are centered on the continuation of life.

The story we have been telling about prose romance of the 1650s is a bit different. On first blush, we see a literary mode firmly in the realm of fabrication: we expect romance to cleave closely to its own conventions, foregrounding the writer as craftsman ingeniously recombining them in a

---

[118] Ibid., 192.   [119] Ibid., 192.   [120] Davis (2014) 74.

way that does not fail to deliver its own kind of surprise and delight. With its foregrounding of history and political philosophy, Barclay's *Argenis* alters this narrative dynamic. We might see his mid-century imitators as engaging in political action: not practicing a non-thinking nostalgia that is a kind of collective isolation, but opening up a received form in a way that is genuinely uncertain about political future even as it solidifies the social bonds of the audience it addresses. Barclay shows a tendency to introduce the historical and political so that it can then be easily explained away. The established conventionality of romance narrative thus imposes similar bounds on the threat of action: the defeat of republicans and other enemies of absolute monarchy are a foregone conclusion. But the introduction of history and political philosophy amongst romance writers who follow his example is significantly more open-ended, responding as it does to the political action of the trial and execution of Charles I—the first trial and execution of a head of state—and to the widespread transfers of landed property taking place over the 1640s, from the confiscation and sale of land held by the bishops, to the paying of army arrears with lands held by the Crown, to the confiscation of the estates of leading royalists.[121]

We might think of royalism in the 1650s as happily unburdened of an actual king to support. In this condition its political thought could roam more freely, and the royalist romances of the 1650s suggest that, in ways we have not fully appreciated, it had fully internalized the unsentimental politics of *raison d'état*, itself a product of constitutional crises on the Continent. One senses a growing royalist view that kings could unsettle the traditional constitution as much as they preserve it. In this way there is an important cleavage between 1650s royalist romance and a progenitor like *Argenis*. As a romance first published in Latin by a poet with a reputation for cosmopolitanism, *Argenis* tries to take an ambassador's-eye view of political tumults, and to speak from a cultural position spanning Western Christendom. I say "tries to" because, as we have seen, its forays into practical political philosophy attach romance to particular historical tensions that it seeks to resolve with apologetics for royal absolutism easily recognizable as marching in stride with those of James I.

The complex dynamics at play in the term *nomos* are also at play in the mid-century's turn to romance. The provincializing of romance begun by Barclay is perfected by romance writers speaking in the vernacular and in

---

[121] See Aylmer (1963) 142, 161.

the aftermath of bewildering alterations in government and of widespread seizure of royalist property. When noted, such a trajectory is described as a prehistory of the emergence of the novel. That tendency is under the surface of Victoria Kahn's recent work on romance, which, like this chapter, focuses on the crisis in loyalty to the crown visible in *Cloria and Narcisus, Theophania*, and *Parthenissa*. In Kahn's argument, the development of the mode in the seventeenth century evinces a heightened anxiety on genre that leads to a rising sense of fabrication as an independent realm of political engagement, one resting on affective modes of political community and with the formation of an "aesthetic interest" as the "basis of political settlement."[122] Thus romance takes its place in her larger, triumphalist story of the rise of bourgeois liberal culture.[123] But I wish to resist that narrative and to place these works in their immediate milieu, to see them as consciously opposed to bourgeois politics in their patrician sensibilities, though arising from patricians uncertain about how to project power in an altered social and political environment. The received traditions of romance create their own space where abiding within a customary settlement—in land and law—remains possible. And this is an Arendtian *nomos* rather than a Schmittean one: romance becomes a textual act consolidating a web of association amongst its readers and writers that will then produce further action allowing a politically marginalized elite to reassert its place in a new order. This is neither a commitment to a particular arrangement of sovereign power nor a posture of ongoing war.

It is notable that amongst the relatively few publications of Anthony Williamson in the 1650s are *Cloria and Narcissus* and two tracts by John Moore, "Minister of the Church at *Knaptoft* in *Leicester-shire*,"[124] on the evils of land enclosure, a hint of the complex set of concerns animating a disempowered and disillusioned nobility, ranging from changes in land use that had altered traditional social order (for which they were themselves often responsible), to the elimination of their constitutional role, to resentment of the Stuarts' failure to hold the realm together.[125] For these nobles,

---

[122] Kahn (2002) 628. There are many similarities between Kahn's analysis and that offered in this chapter. Perhaps the largest difference is that Barclay's introduction of *raison d'état* receives scant mention in Kahn's analysis, which sees romance as becoming increasingly opposed to interest, which she identifies primarily with Hobbes. But *raison d'état* is much more visible than this argument allows, and can be used to apply critical pressure on absolutist theory of all stripes.

[123] This celebration of the "liberal idea of culture" (115) is the aim of Victoria Kahn (2014). See my review of this book, Mohamed (2015b).

[124] Moore (1656) t.p. (italics in original); see also Moore (1653).

[125] See Moore (1653) and Moore (1656), both printed for Anthony Williamson.

the kind of unitary sovereignty espoused by Barclay had been co-opted by the new regime: if authority arises from the power of the sword, then, as Hobbes famously argues, it can be transferred by conquest. One senses that some form of Polybian division of sovereign power feels congenial for writers like Herbert, but the details of that division have not been worked out. Political crisis has freed political judgment to entertain various possibilities, and the marriage of romance and *raison d'état* effected by Barclay provides a forum in which to do so.

That this exercise of judgment yields a more worldly-wise royalism might make more legible some of the paradoxes of the Restoration settlement: a forceful purging of commonwealthmen that in the same stroke sought to limit the traditional prerogatives of the crown. A case in point is the elimination of the Court of Wards and Liveries by the Tenures Abolition Act of 1660.[126] An invention of Henry VIII, as we saw in chapter 1, the court had been used by the early Stuarts strongly to flex the feudal property rights of the crown in a way generating large revenues without parliamentary oversight.[127] The impulse of the parliamentary aristocracy at the Restoration is to put a brake on political action from above and from below. But after 1660 these are the political maneuvers of an interest group vying for influence within a familiar constitutional arrangement: the brief moment of uncertainty, of a *nomos* without sovereignty, has closed.

It is fitting that Herbert completes *Cloria* after the Restoration, when the storyteller can safely contain the wild events of mid-century in the realm of fabrication: "it cannot be denied," he declares in the 1661 epistle to the reader, "but the Ground-work for a *Romance* was excellent; and the rather since by no other way almost, could the multiplicity of strange Actions of the Times be exprest, that exceeded all belief, and went beyond every example in the doing."[128] Though we tend to see seventeenth-century romance as anticipating the rise of the novel, we might view the case as more complicated if we think of its aristocratic *mentalité* as not merely residual: it is the cultural product of a class undergoing its own significant transformations over the course of the seventeenth century. A precise reading of romance in the period must be attuned to the political ferment taking place within the English gentry and nobility.

---

[126]   Tenures Abolition Act, 1660 c. 24 (12 Cha. 2), available at legislation.gov.uk.

[127]   As noted in chapter 1, the court's activities expand in the early Stuart period, with the crown pursuing a greater number of claims and pressuring local feodaries to increase estimates. See Bell (2011) 55–6. Bell provides examples of increases in feodaries' surveys in 56n1.

[128]   [Sir Percy Herbert] (1661) A1v.

3

Milton's Unitary Sovereignty

Milton was certainly capable of admiring politically prominent men with Puritan leanings. Lord Saye and Sele, who, as we have seen in chapter 1, was at the very center of the Puritan faction in the Long Parliament, does not appear to have been one of them. The two men come into direct contact over the course of Milton's most extended Chancery litigation, which arose from his 1638 loan of 150 pounds to Sir John Cope. Milton believed Saye to be one of the trustees of Cope's estate. In response to a subpoena sent at Milton's request, Saye writes a long, and somewhat haughty, letter in January 1656 denying all connection to Sir John Cope and all knowledge of his debts. We do not have a record of Milton's reply, but we can safely assume that the encounter is not likely to have filled either man with great affection for the other. Whether it created personal resentments that then became political ones is open to speculation.[1]

The exchange fairly closely antecedes Lord Saye's efforts to scuttle the "other House" in late 1657, and might lead us to look with fresh eyes at Milton's publications of 1658: his May edition of the *Cabinet-Council*, attributed to Raleigh, and his reissue of the first *Defense*. If Milton's 1658 publications do respond to the peers' rejection of the other House, they do so by offering a two-pronged attack on the idea of mixed government that Saye articulates. First with the *Cabinet-Council*, which makes the case for unitary sovereignty and cites Aristotle, Thucydides, and Tacitus in presenting the role of councils as advisory.[2] Insisting on mixed government, such sources suggest, is the constitutional innovation, and the other House of the Humble Petition is not so inconsistent with the views of a previous generation. Reissuing the first *Defence*, which had also argued for unitary, rather than divided, sovereignty may register both sympathy with and resistance to the Humble Petition and Additional Petition. The *Defence* argues for the ancient privilege of Parliament to appoint Councils of State, which had been done by the Rump and which the Instrument of Government had sought to

---

[1] See French (1939) 124, 126, and 132–3.
[2] Raleigh (1658) Wing R156, chs. 2 and 14.

Sovereignty: Seventeenth-Century England and the Making of the Modern Political Imaginary.
Feisal G. Mohamed, Oxford University Press (2020). © Feisal G. Mohamed.
DOI: 10.1093/oso/9780198852131.001.0001

implement. The Humble Petition and Additional Petition, by contrast, gave the Protector much more power over the other House.

We hear hints, then, that Milton's own views are not in stride with the ideas on mixed government recorded in the Commonplace Book, whether arising from Polybius or from Machiavelli. Those hints are confirmed in his practical proposals for an English republic, as found in *The Readie and Easie Way to Establish a Free Commonwealth*, which largely seek government by a small body of men loyal to the republican cause, a perpetual Rump Parliament. We will see how those proposals directly respond to the divided sovereignty espoused by Harringon. Though *The Readie and Easie Way* is often deemed, not inaccurately, an expedient addressing the Commonwealth's immediate needs, it is also a tract not inconsistent with the unitary popular sovereignty that is typical of Milton's thought. *Eikonoklastes* declares that because Parliament is the highest court in the realm, it must also hold the power of the sword:

> As for sole power of the *Militia*, which [Charles I] claimes as a Right no less undoubted then the Crown, it hath been oft anough told him, that he hath no more authority over the Sword then over the Law; over the Law he hath none, either to establish or to abrogate, to interpret, or to execute, but onely by his Courts and in his Courts, whereof the Parlament is highest, no more therefore hath he power of the *Militia* which is the sword, either to use or to dispose; but with consent of Parlament; give him but that, and as good give him in a lump all our Laws and Liberties. (*OM* 6: 342)[3]

Here Milton agrees with Hobbes to the extent that the sovereign power of decision cannot be separated from the power of the sword. But of course the two put that central premise to very different uses. For Hobbes, dividing sovereign power creates a climate of competition amongst constitutional branches, and so threatens stability. For Milton that competition creates conditions whereby force will always abrogate law and deprive the people of liberty. Rather than "entrusted Servants of the Common-wealth," kings grow "to esteem themselves Maisters" (*OM* 6: 360–1).

---

[3] When possible, citations refer to the ongoing Oxford Milton, Milton (2008–), indicated in parentheses by the abbreviation *OM*. At this writing, volumes 2, 3, 6, and 8 are available. Prose works not yet available in the Oxford Milton are cited from the Yale edition, Milton (1953–82), indicated in parentheses by *YP*. References to *Paradise Lost* are to the Lewalski edition, Milton (2007), and indicated in parentheses by the abbreviation *PL*.

This is the kind of hostility toward royal prerogative, and defense of Parliament using the language of popular sovereignty, that we expect from Milton. Things become rather less straightforward when we scrutinize his use of the term "the people," which is to say the class of individuals whose liberty must be protected and whose political will is sovereign. In his recent full-length study of Milton's use of the term, Paul Hammond concludes that Milton uses the term positively when describing the *pars potior et sanior* leading England to its divinely appointed greatness, and negatively when describing the *plebs*, the internal slaves styled "pork" in *Tetrachordon*. True enough, but this is only part of the picture. It did not escape contemporary notice that Milton's notions of popular sovereignty rest on the authority of only a fraction of the people. In his *Observations Concerning the Original of Government*, a sustained critique of Hobbes, Milton, and Grotius, Sir Robert Filmer takes Milton to task for the slenderness of his definition of "the people." Aristotle, notes Filmer, is ambiguous on the qualifications of a free citizen if also clear that democracy is "a Corrupted sort of Government" because it extends political agency to those who are born servants.[4] So Milton is not alone, nor is he on unsteady ground, in restricting "the people" to "*pars potior & sanior*" or "the better part and the sounder part."[5] Milton's argument runs aground, according to Filmer, when the liberty of the better and sounder part becomes indistinguishable from the liberty of the Army to abrogate the law, which is equivalent to saying that "the Souldiers are the People."[6] If Filmer mounted this objection to Milton's first *Defense*, one could imagine it becoming louder after Milton's defense of Cromwell's expulsion of Parliament. The *Second Defense* underscores the destructive alliance between tyrants and the "mob" in terms that make clear in the language of the time that the majority are natural slaves: "the common people, maddened by priestly machinations, sunk to a barbarism fouler than that which stains the Indians, themselves the most stupid of mortals" (4: 551).

The case becomes more complicated still if we take seriously Milton's early acceptance of the constitutional primacy of the crown. Coming to mind is *Of Reformation*, with its memorable "Tale": "the Body summon'd all the Members to meet in the Guild for the common good . . . the head by right takes the first seat, and next to it a huge and monstrous Wen little lesse than the head it selfe."[7] The lesson is clear, that the Wen is a "heap of hard,

---

[4] Filmer (1652) 13. On this tract see Cuttica (2014), 35–51.
[5] Filmer (1652) 17.   [6] Ibid., 18.   [7] Milton (1953–82) 1: 583.

and loathsome, uncleannes, and ... to the head a foul disfigurment and burden," and that it is "sound Policy" to "cut away from the publick body the noysom, and diseased tumor of Prelacie."[8] Milton is of course turning tables on the oft-repeated dictum attributed to James I, "no bishop, no king," by claiming that in fact the bishops weaken and obstruct monarchical authority. He is also making a constitutional statement, where England's government is superior to that praised by "the wise *Polybius*": rather than a Roman balancing of estates, it is "equally ballanc'd as it were by the hand and scale of Justice ... where under a free, and untutor'd *Monarch*, the noblest, worthiest and most prudent men, with full approbation, and suffrage of the People have in their power the supreame, and finall determination of highest Affaires." The King-in-Parliament is here presented as bearing full sovereign power, though later in the tract Milton suggests that the king is supreme in this arrangement if also limited by the law.[9]

Such early statements are often considered to pre-date Milton's political awakening as a firebrand republican deeply hostile to the Stuarts. But it is one argument of this book that despite shifts in political allegiance thinkers are remarkably consistent in their view of the legitimate structure of sovereignty, and we will see a young Milton accepting a "red" unitary sovereignty located in the king. The text we will consider is the Ludlow *Maske*, which will be placed in the legal context of the Council in the Marches of Wales, of which Milton's patron, John Egerton, first Earl of Bridgewater, was president. As an irregular court propped up by royal prerogative, the Council was resented especially in the English counties under its jurisdiction as impeding the subject's right of access to courts of common law. From the moment that Egerton was appointed president, he worried that the legal status of the court was on unsteady ground. Milton's masque responds by celebrating his household as a seat of virtue and justice in a hostile wilderness, which implicitly defends what many perceived to be an overextension of royal prerogative.

This reading of *A Maske* participates in the re-evaluation of the young Milton that has taken place especially since the appearance of Gordon Campbell and Thomas Corns' landmark biography.[10] Rather than being a

---

[8] Ibid., 584, 598.

[9] Ibid., 606: "The K. may still retain the same Supremacy in the Assemblies, as in the *Parliament*, here he can do nothing against the common Law, and there neither alone, nor with consent against the Scriptures."

[10] Campbell and Corns (2008) esp. chs. 5–7. On early confessional allegiance, see also McDowell (2011) and Jones (2013), esp. Jeffrey Alan Miller's chapter on Milton and conformable puritanism. A launching point for such questions is Lewalski (1998), though it is committed to Milton's reformist and resistance energies.

discrete phase in Milton's career, however, we will see an early acceptance of monarchical authority as part of a career-long affinity for unitary sovereignty, which is defended in various incarnations: an early masque that is a product of patronage defends a controversial branch of royal prerogative, then a more politically engaged Milton locates unitary sovereignty in Parliament, and finally, when his immediate political hopes are dashed, he crafts a late politics looking forward to an enlightened unitary sovereignty whose time had not come. If Milton promotes in the wake of the regicide a government reflecting the will of "the people," the Restoration Milton must concede that "the people" have not yet fully emerged as a political entity, and thus he speaks a language of godly republicanism where the immediate aim is to create conditions conducive to their arrival in God's time. In this respect his late political thought, as we shall see, closely resembles that of the younger Sir Henry Vane. And we shall also see that despite many changes in his thinking, he consistently imagines final authority on matters legislative, judicial, and military to be held by a single body.

In the final pages of this chapter, we will turn to Schmitt in parsing Milton's ideas on popular sovereignty. I have suggested elsewhere that in *The Tenure of Kings and Magistrates*, Milton sounds very much like he is advancing a friend–enemy distinction as central to political constitution: "if an Englishman forgetting all Laws, human, civil and religious, offend against life and liberty, to him offended and to the Law in his behalf, though born in the same womb, he is no better then a Turk, a Sarasin, a Heathen" (*OM* 6: 163).[11] "The political enemy," Schmitt remarks, "is the other, the stranger . . . he is, in a specially intense way, existentially something different and alien."[12] This is not an abstract remark, but an effort to "raise the intensity of a unity or separation," to draw a distinction between actual subjects, between the sovereign people and the enemies in their midst—if disapproval of the regicide were the litmus test, those enemies comprised the majority of the realm. At key moments, Milton seeks to thicken the meaning accruing to "the people" in a way reminiscent of Schmitt's remarks on the subject:

> Representation is not a normative event, a process, a procedure. It is, rather, something *existential.* . . . Something dead, something inferior or

---

[11] For brief discussion of this passage in light of the friend–enemy distinction, see Mohamed (2015a) 68–70.

[12] Schmitt (2007), *Concept of the Political*, 27.

valueless, something lowly cannot be represented. It lacks the enhanced type of being that is capable of an *existence*, of rising into the public being. Words like size, height, majesty, fame, dignity, and honor seek to express this peculiarity of enhanced being that is capable of representation . . . . The idea of representation rests on a people existing as a political unity, as having a type of being that is higher, further enhanced, and more intense in comparison to the natural existence of some human group living together.[13]

For all that he is a self-proclaimed champion of liberty and parliamentary supremacy, Milton's thought has never rested easily with later liberalism, and we can see why when we consider this brief passage from Schmitt, who is most useful as a trenchant critic of the liberal state. Parliament in Milton's writings is the sovereign representative of a freeborn people, a dignified category if also one with stringent qualifications. Not stringent qualifications of rank or estate, which separates Milton from classical republicanism, but of civic virtue and Protestant spiritual fitness. The optimism of Milton's politics is aligned with the location of power in the hands of those most fit to wield it.

For Milton, as for Schmitt, the sovereign power wielded by those worthy of representation must be unitary. The proximity to aspects of Schmitt's thought teaches us that Milton's sovereignty is modern, popular unitary sovereignty. This explains why he finds elective monarchy inoffensive, and oligarchy positively inviting. When he turns decisively against the Stuarts, it is because theirs was a kind of anti-sovereignty: an exercise of power motivated by pure self-interest rather than a desire to advance the good and implement the will of an enlightened political community, which always for Milton marks the difference between a tyrant and a king. The principle of unitary sovereignty suggests an intellectual foundation for Milton's willingness to work on behalf of Cromwell's Protectorate, and explains the grounds of his disagreements with Harrington's Polybian republicanism.

As we explore Milton's thought we will account for the influence of Tacitus in two ways: as a key source of the principle of unitary sovereignty, and also as a Roman historian clearly on Milton's mind in the crisis years between the execution of Charles I and the advent of the Protectorate. The latter influence tends to be neglected as we have aligned Milton with more

---

[13] Schmitt (2008a), *Constitutional Theory*, 243. On this aspect of Schmitt's thought, see Dyzenhaus (2003) 51–8.

explicitly republican thinkers like Cicero and Sallust, though that would suggest a reductive view of Tacitus as a proto-Kissingerian exponent of *realpolitik*, a view that has been recently refined.[14] Quietly but discernibly, Tacitus does articulate ideas on liberty, and his enormous influence throughout the sixteenth and seventeenth centuries demands recognition in our reading of the valences of Roman thought.

The Ludlow *Maske* as Defense of Royal Prerogative

On every conceivable level, Milton's *Maske Presented at Ludlow Castle* is a complex negotiation of center and periphery: its 1634 title page foregrounds the role of the court musician Henry Lawes, on whose coat-tails the young Milton is not unreluctant to ride; it is a form of entertainment strongly associated with the Stuart court, thus meant to add luster to the Welsh border country and to glorify the Bridgewater household. In a way that has gone unremarked, the text reproduces in these respects the legal ambiguities of Egerton's appointment. He was president of the Council in the Marches of Wales, and as such held a judicial role. But that role was an unsettled one, and had been perceived in several quarters as an extra-legal imposition of the crown's sovereign power, with other courts guarding against its encroachments upon their jurisdiction.[15] Certainly the ecclesiastical courts did not appreciate its settling of legacies. And litigants could justly claim that matters of property ought to be settled in Chancery or, where bills of discovery were at issue, as they often were, at courts of common law.

These issues come to the fore in the case of *Vaughan v. Vaughan*, which stretched from the death of Sir Robert Vaughan in 1624 to the late 1630s and beyond, involving several courts, including Chancery, King's Bench, and Star Chamber. In dispute were the estates at Llwydiarth, which in February 1622 Sir Robert had conveyed to his brother Edward as an act of spite toward his wife, Catherine Herbert, and, indirectly, their son, Herbert

---

[14] For a recent reevaluation of Tacitus, see Joseph (2012). On debts to Virgil and Lucan in diction, narrative structure, and imagery, see Kapust (2011). Sailor (2008) points to Tacitus' pervasive concern with cultivating a position of political and intellectual independence under the principate, and with "the tenuous place of speech in the principate" (113). The classic study is Syme (1958).

[15] The Council did have statutory basis in An Acte for Certain Ordinaunces in the Kinges Majesties Domynion and Principalitie of Wales (34 & 35 Hen.VIII c.26), but also used as basis for its activity instructions from the crown, which instructions James I and Charles I clearly saw as a firm foundation for the court's jurisdiction.

Vaughan. Catherine turned to her father Sir William Herbert, after 1629 the first Baron Powis, who took up the legal cause. The Council in the Marches found in Sir William's favor, despite Edward's claim that his brother had bequeathed the estate to him by entail. It was both a battle of families, hostilities between the Vaughans and Herberts were longstanding, and a battle of lawyers, with Sir Robert Vaughan and his three brothers all trained at Inner Temple, and Sir William Herbert having served on James I's Council in the Marches (which may in part explain his favorable ruling before that body). Bridgewater watched the progress of the case with great anxiety, fearing that his perpetually cash-strapped Council was on the brink of losing a major source of fees.[16] In a letter of November 1637, he worried that Vaughan's efforts would all but end the Council's ability to settle legacies. This adds to concerns over challenges to the Council's assessment of fines in criminal causes, and to the ecclesiastical courts' taking "greatest exception" to hearing of cases of "Bona notabilia," or the disposition of property beyond a deceased person's home parish. All of this, Bridgewater worries, bodes of deprivations that will make it impossible to maintain Ludlow Castle: the outcome of the Vaughan case would "either adde muche luster to the Courte or very much dampn & blemishe it ... [if] the fines be lessened, I scarcely knowe howe the house will subsist, though with disgrace and blemish, which I shoulde be loathe to see."[17] In the same letter, he refers to the longstanding hostility of the English counties within the Council's territory: "if [the] foure Countyes have not beene yett of power to doe more harme unto it then to grinne & shewe their teethe I shoulde be very sory to finde it nowe so bitten & crushed that it shoulde not be hable to

---

[16] See Huntington mssEL 7520, a motion for prohibition claiming that if Canterbury had settled a case pertaining to a will, then it ought also to decide a legacy arising from that will; and mssEL 7523, a draft letter from Bridgewater to John Bridgeman of 24 November 1637, reporting a conversation with the king in which Charles requests that proceedings in the Council be stayed until the jurisdictional dispute with the ecclesiastical courts is resolved: "he wolde not have any further proceeding to be had there [in the Council], in the case of the Legacye between Vaughan & Vaughan, until suche time as he had hearde the differences between the Prerogative Courte & that his Counsell upon the Article concerning Legacyes."

[17] Huntington Library, mssEL 7521. See also 9 July 1636 letter from John Bridgeman to Bridgewater, mssEL 7508: "if those things be taken from this councell, there wille shure be decay of the fines that they will not support the charge of the house ... or the Counsell broke up unlesse some other cause be taken for supplye." Details of the dispute over Llwydiarth drawn from Bowen (2007b), esp. 1264–65, and from *Dictionary of Welsh Biography* (1959), esp. articles "Vaughan family of Llwydiarth," "Vaughan, Edward," and "Powis, earls of (Herbert)." See also Roger Holland's account in Huntington mssEL 7518 of Vaughan's pressure to have the matter heard before a common law court.

breathe or move within the limits of its Jurisdicon & Instruccons."[18] The counties in question are Gloucestershire, Herefordshire, Shropshire, and Worcestershire.

Adding to Egerton's headaches on the status of his Council was its association with the Council in the North, led by the not-yet notorious Thomas Wentworth, later Earl of Strafford. Egerton recognized that his fate was shackled to that of his counterpart in Yorkshire, who enjoyed little popularity. In a letter of 1633, he complains to Strafford that a litigant in Star Chamber had "cast out words of disrespect" toward the Council in the North, and makes clear his fear that he might "receive prejudice by being ... wounded through [Wentworth's] sides."[19] Resentment of the two councils did not abate, and objectors seized the opportunity to eliminate them with the advent of the Long Parliament in 1640, led by MPs from the four English counties under the jurisdiction of the Council in the Marches. Parliament considered the fate of the two Councils alongside that of Star Chamber. All of these, the argument ran, denied freeborn Englishmen the right of access to common law courts. And the two Councils in particular rankled as the kind of obtrusive exercise of royal prerogative to which Charles was prone.

But the fate of the Councils in the Long Parliament is a later development. The moment with which we are concerned is that of the performance of Milton's masque, roughly two years after Egerton is appointed president of the Council in the Marches.[20] Even at this earlier juncture, Egerton was cognizant of the precarious position of his Council. Mixed in with papers from the first year of his tenure as president are detailed demonstrations of the Council's jurisdiction over the four English counties.[21] A 1632 letter from Charles suggests that the king was not insensitive to Egerton's plight, and that he was willing to press for the jurisdiction of the Council:

---

[18] Ibid.   [19] Qtd in Bowen (2007b) 1263n18.
[20] Egerton is appointed 26 June 1631; the masque is first performed 29 September 1633 (see "Egerton, John, first earl of Bridgewater," *ODNB*).
[21] For documents on jurisdiction over English counties, see mssEL 7462–5; 7469 (in which is underlined "for the quiet and good government of the Inhabitants of the English bordering counties, as well as those of Wales"); mssEL 7472, which gathers arguments against the Council's jurisdiction over the English counties, including that "the pointe of prerogative is noe way in question in this cause, for the aucthority of that counsel is not grounded upon any pretense of prerogative , but by force of statute made 34o:H:8" (f.2r) and "yt wilbe obiected that the fynes arisinge out of those foure counties are a great meanes of supporte to that counsel. A worse argument cannot be made against that counsel than that their support must prove out of the punishments of the people" (f.2v); and mssEL 7473–4.

Whereas the Intent of Our Establishing a President and Council in the Principality of Wales, and the Marches thereof, hath ever been for the more speedy Administration of Justice, and ease of Our good People, in those remote Parts.... Wee are nevertheles given to understand That the proceedings before Our said Council, grow much perplexed, and Our Subjects disappointed, of the just fruites of their suites there more then in the happy Reigns of Queen Elizabeth and our Father of blessed Memory hath been accustomed, and then stood with the quiet, and good government of those parts[.] All which proceeds, from the too frequent granting of Prohibicions forth of Our Courts of Common-Law in Westm[inster] much more then in former times, have either been permitted or Practized ... We have thought it very necessary hereby to Admonish you, to be very carefull, that you do not in any thing Transgress from Our Instruccions, But in all Causes wch shall come before you keep yourselves punctually there unto ... cause our Decrees to be fully & speedily performed, by all such ways, and meanes, as is used in our Court of Chancery, Notwithstanding any Prohibicon to be granted to the contrary, to stay such your Proceedings Warranted by Our Said Instruccons.[22]

We should note the social harm that Charles is seeking to prevent: if justice could only be obtained at Westminster, then Welsh poor would have no forum in which to seek remedy from the oppressions of wealthy landowners. This had been a longstanding concern of the crown, and one of the motivations for sustaining the Council over the protestations of grandees from the four English counties.

Despite his reference to their "happy" reigns, Charles must have known that the Council had been consistently resisted under Elizabeth and James. The former acceded to the demands of incorporated cities like Bristol and Cheshire to be exempted from the jurisdiction of the Council—another example, to be added to those we saw in chapter 1, of the period's ongoing negotiations between corporate and sovereign authority. Over his reign James grew increasingly annoyed with prohibitions from King's Bench that limited the Council's activity and amounted, in his mind, to an assault on the principle that law is *voluntas regis*. Charles is grinding an old axe in pressing

---

[22] BL Egerton MS 2882, f. 179r. The letter is dated "the 24th of July in the Seaventh year of Our Reign." See also Huntington mssEL 7480, scattered notes, presumably by Bridgewater, on prohibitions: "any time before sentence a prohibition may be Granted / it does but Affirme: the old common law."

the Council to be more active. As his father did, he sees the jurisdiction granted by his instructions as superseding prohibitions placed on the Council by common law courts. This is precisely the position that later irked the Long Parliament, and we can see that longstanding jurisdictional wranglings are becoming swept into a mounting constitutional crisis.[23]

And what might we learn from the "Instruccons" to which Charles refers? They are almost entirely a word-for-word restatement of the ones that James I had given to Egerton's predecessor. But some significant changes appear in paragraph 8, which addresses the president and Council's role in general law and order. Both versions include the prosecution of "Forgeries, Extorcons, Briberies, Evacons" of "beginge or unlawfull gateringe of Money," of manipulation or destruction of "Bills, pleadinge, orders," and of "unlawfull assemblies." Just after mention of unlawful assemblies, the directions from Charles add spreading "roumrous falshoode" and "hunting in farmse... Parkes and warrens not mendinge hyge wayes and bridges... takeinge in or keepinge of Inmates, keepinge of disordered Alehouses." In both instances, the council is charged with prosecuting these faults in a long list of local officials—bailiffs, sheriffs, clerks, and the like—as well as "other persons whatsoever."[24]

The additions in the instructions from Charles shift the emphasis significantly. Where the Jacobean Council seems in this paragraph to be tasked primarily with preventing corruption in financial transactions and amongst local officials, the Caroline Council is being tasked with broader social oversight. The provisions seem anxious about the unruliness of the lower sort, and the tendency of the better sort in the Marches to renege on their civilizing obligations. Gentry are suspected of tending toward neglect of public accommodations like highways and bridges, of menacing cottagers, and of turning a blind eye to riot. To put it in jurisdictional terms, the Jacobean directions made the Council likely to step on the terrain of the quarters and assizes; to this the Caroline directions added significantly the prospect of stepping on the terrain of the ecclesiastical courts. More

---

[23] In the Huntington collection of Egerton's papers from the 1630s is a summary of a 1608 debate at Serjeants' Inn on Parliament's intent in establishing the Council in the Marches (mss EL7502). Williams (1961) argues that what started as a battle over fees early in the seventeenth century, with an expanded class of lawyers interested in extending the reach of King's Bench and the Common Pleas, became by the end of James' reign a battle between "common law and royal power" (14).

[24] BL Egerton MS 2882, f.164v–165r. The corresponding passage in James I's instructions is on f. 30r–30v.

than his predecessors, Egerton was being asked to preserve general decorum and decency.

This complicates the picture of Bridgewater as energetic legal reformer that Leah Marcus offered as a significant background to the Ludlow masque.[25] If he was taking a more active role in such matters as sexual violence, as suggested by his scrutiny of the case of Marjorie Evans, it was part of a larger effort to uphold morality and stanch social harm, as well as to expand the activity of his Council. And we must see this as a flexion of royal prerogative that is perceived, especially by those who would become the Independent gentry opposed to Charles, as an assault on the right to seek remedy before common law courts.[26] This is frontier justice, where rule of law is most directly an imposition of sovereign power, made particularly fraught by the fact that the English counties in Egerton's jurisdiction didn't wish to be lumped in with Wales.

We must keep the embattled position of the Council in the Marches in mind as we approach Milton's masque, especially as it is a work deeply concerned with the location of virtue fit to administer justice. Whatever Milton's intentions, the effect of his masque was to add luster to the household of the president of the Council, and to lend cultural support to his controversial legal role. But we are also concerned here with Milton's emerging politics, and so must wonder how much we might reasonably expect him to know about Egerton's worries. As a budding poet commissioned by Lawes to produce this masque, and one likely writing far from Ludlow in Hammersmith, Milton is not likely to know intimately the jurisdictional battles portentously hanging like a dark cloud over Ludlow Castle.[27] He is likely to have known the mood of the time, to know that the Council in the Marches was a prerogative court long viewed with skepticism and hostility, and to have some sense of the priorities of the King and of the ways in which he might appeal to Egerton's sensibilities. So it does seem significant that Comus is, to put it simply, keeping a "disordered Alehouse." And that drunkenness in the masque is the gateway

---

[25] Marcus (1983) 294–5.

[26] See Huntington mssEL 7492, which lists "the misheefes and inconveniences that the Kynges Maties subjects have and doe endure by the goverment of the Councell in the Marches of Wales." Listed second is "They doe ordinarilie restrayne the subjects from aserting theire lawfull suits at the common lawe and from all courts in Westminster."

[27] There is no evidence that Milton made the trip to Ludlow, and he is not likely to have done so. See Campbell and Corns (2008) 79.

to a "sensual stie."[28] We learn that Comus is the son of Bacchus and Circe, which explains the association with drink and shape-shifting. It is the thirsty country labourer who seems most susceptible to his enticements:

> offringe to everie weary traveller
> his orient liquor in a Christall glasse
> to quench the drouth of Phebus, wch as they taste
> (for most doe tast through fond intemperate thirst)
> soone as the potion workes their humane Countenance
> th'expresse resemblance of the Gods, is chang'd
> into some brutish forme
>
> (BridgeMS 84–90)

"Orient liquor" adds an exotic touch to this corrupting influence in the wild wood, reaffirming its status as a zone of barbarity. Also working subtly here is a blaming of the thirsty for their thirst, which they foolishly allow to become intemperate, leaving them vulnerable to temptation, another mark of the social and cultural distance the text generates between the Egerton children and Comus' brutish rout.

The Lady's first response to this unruly crew is to identify them with low social standing:

> This waye the noise was, if my eare be true
> my best guyde now, methought it was the sound
> of riott and ill-manag'd merriment
> such as the iocund flute or gamesome pipe
> stirrs vp amonge the [rude] loose vnlettered hindes
> when for their teeminge flocks and granges full
> in wanton daunce they praise the bounteous Pan
> and thanke the Gods amisse
>
> (BridgeMS 190–7)

"Ill-manag'd" stands out for present purposes. From her very first lines, the Lady is making clear that the merriment of these "loose vnlettered hindes" needs to be well managed. Equally significant, Comus identifies her holiness

---

[28] Milton, *Maske* (2009), 77. References to Milton's *Maske* are to the Bridgewater Manuscript, the extant version closest to the performance text, available in Milton (2009) and indicated in parentheses by the abbreviation BridgeMS.

as foreign to his parts: "Haile forreigne wonder / whome certaine these rough
shades did never breede" (BridgeMS 252–3). In his disguise as shepherd, he
similarly describes the two brothers as not of his uncouth world:

> Two such J sawe, what tyme the labour'd oxe
> in his loose traces from the furrowe came
> and the swink't-hedger at his supper sate ...
> J tooke it for a faerie vision
> of some gaye creatures of the Element
> that in the cooleness of the raynebow live
> and playe i'the plighted clouds; J was awe-strooke
> and as J past J worship't
>
> (BridgeMS 278–89)

The "barbarous dissonance" of the revelers is diametrically opposed to the
tuneful singing of the Lady, reinforcing our sense of the Egerton household as a
moral mainstay at the edges of a wilderness populated by those with no human
countenance. The brothers famously cannot release their sister, but they can
lay waste to the alehouse, rushing in with swords drawn to break Comus'
"glasse, / and shed the lussious liquor on the ground" (Bridge MS 632–3).

The masque develops in the strongest possible terms an opposition
between the menacing wood and Ludlow Castle, emphasizing deep divisions
of civilization, of class, of religious virtue. Images of productive country life,
and orderly jollity, are in the guardian spirit's telling centered on Egerton
himself:

> your fathers residence,
> where this night are met in state
> many a freind to gratulate
> his wisht presence, and beside
> all the swaynes that neere abide
> with Jiggs, and rurall daunce resorte
> wee shall catch them at this sporte,
> and our suddaine Cominge there
> will double all their mirth, and cheere
>
> (Bridge MS 868–76)

Given everything we have seen, we should read this as a carefully qualified
version of the conventional portrait of a country house, with bounty and

social harmony radiating from the master of the estate. Our attention is drawn to Egerton's official capacity: the "friends" gathered at Ludlow Castle are "in state," several of them presumably being members of the Council in the Marches. And together they observe wholesome country celebration, a final scene of rightly regulated merriment amongst the lower sort.

Masques are a technology of augmented reality: we see through them the world that the elite think they are creating. And in this case we see Ludlow as a beacon of civilization on a wild and potentially dangerous frontier. Milton's is often called a "reformed" masque. It might be, though not quite in the way we have thought. We should be skeptical of the extent to which it is a performance straining against the values of the Caroline court. I am unconvinced that any masque dedicated to Charles' appointee and advertising its association with Henry Lawes ought to be read that way. The Ludlow *Maske* critiques Comus' courtly revelry by creating a dramatic space in which one can indulge in its pleasures, a maneuver firmly within the conventions of the antimasque. Its first printing in 1637 makes an association with controversial aspects of royal prerogative only more pronounced: by that point, Egerton's headaches were increased significantly by the ship money writs of 1634–36, which required him to press local gentry who wished neither to pay nor to collect.[29] Milton does not appear to have had much of a hand in that printing; he also did not attempt to disown the masque, and of course includes it in his 1645 *Poems.* But this is not to say that no reformist impulse is visible in *A Maske.* On the contrary. Here domestic Protestant virtue is located in the Egerton family in a way that has legal ramifications, in a way that underwrites the role Bridgewater was expected to play in securing order, which is to say stanching riot and lawlessness in remote parts. These qualities become in our imagination much more naturally centered on the Egerton household, a beacon of right order in the wilderness, than on a sense of rule of law in which Westminster or Canterbury hold cultural or legally normative sway. Egerton and his children seem specially equipped to translate virtue in its pure, divine form into enlightened action in their inhospitable physical environment.[30]

This is, as in the traditional view of *A Maske,* usurping the role of the church, but in light of what we have said here it is the legal and social

---

[29] See Bowen (2007a) 154–84 and 201–6, which draws on figures from Gordon (1910).
[30] On this performance as an occasion of state, and as showing the Egerton children to be preparing to "assume the obligations of the ruling class," see Campbell and Corns (2008) 79, 82. Of their conclusion that it is an "Arminian masque" I am more skeptical (83).

function of the church—rather than its claims in the realm of theology or its efforts toward religious uniformity. Fines arising from cases of sexual immorality had become an indispensable source of revenue for the Council, adding to the ecclesiastical courts' annoyance.[31] It is worth noting that as the Council is taking shape during the reign of Henry VIII, the presidents are all bishops, forestalling this potential rivalry. Headed by a member of Charles I's privy council who is not a clergyman, Egerton's Council is an extension of the crown's power coming at the expense of the church. And Milton is lending cultural support to this controversial branch of royal prerogative, one that would come to be seen as trampling upon the legal rights of English subjects. He is offering a reformed masque to the extent that he may already be contemplating removal of the Wen from the commonwealth's body, with the king still very much as its head. This is not yet the Milton of *The Tenure of Kings and Magistrates*, nor of *Eikonoklastes*, with its sneering reference to Charles' prerogatives as the "Toys and Gewgaws of his Crown" (*OCM* 6: 358). Though he is far from his revolutionary awakening, his fundamental position on the structure of political authority has revealed itself: sovereignty is not divided and dispersed, meant to spread power and preserve order, but unitary and reformist, meant energetically to sweep away moribund institutions and to guide subjects on the path of virtue. He would grow much more hostile to the view that the law is *voluntas regis*, and especially *voluntas Caroli*, but there remains in his later thought a unitary will from which the law rightly emanates. Stuart monarchy would soon become in Milton's mind an obstacle to the emergence of such a will, but the basic structure of sovereignty remains the same: legitimate authority is that of an enlightened, civic-minded minority whose political liberty might lift the polity as a whole.

Tacitus on Liberty

Before moving to Milton's more mature political thought, it is worthwhile to pause for a moment on the early modern influence of Tacitus, influence that tends to be overlooked given scholarly focus on neo-Roman republicanism in Milton and his contemporaries. Taking this into account changes significantly our picture of Milton's republican thought, making it look less like an

---

[31] See Williams (1961) 16–17. For further background, see also Williams (1958).

outgrowth of high-minded humanism and more consistent with pragmatic and unsentimental early modern *raison d'état*. Tacitus is central to that body of early modern political thought, and inspires a small army of editors, translators, and commentators who turn to him as the Roman historian exposing high-flown republican principles to the harsh glare of reality.[32] By his lights, the harmoniously balanced republican constitution praised by Polybius is a nice idea that Rome never achieved. Thus arises a host of commentaries amongst the generation of Continental thinkers who them-selves had seen republican experiments buckle under pressures internal and external.

Tacitus is often, then, the Roman to whom the period turns to show why republicanism does not stand a chance against power politics. He might not be entirely eager to claim this legacy, and there are other lessons to be gleaned from his writings. Rather than a historian of either republic or empire, he is the historian who makes us aware that political life is always a mixed bag. Republics must always fear being rent asunder by competing factions, and principalities must always fear the reign of a despot. How do we choose between them? For Tacitus a positive political settlement is one allowing for the liberty of a civic-minded senatorial class.[33] That can happen in a republic, provided it is not overrun by the *plebs*, or it can happen in an empire, provided that it is led by a Trajan rather than a Nero or Domitian.

We can locate these ideas in his most mature work, *The Annals*, and especially in Book 1, which describes the transition from the reign of Augustus to that of Tiberius. Here we find Tacitus lamenting the decline of the senate, not only because of Augustus' deft consolidation of power, but also because senators had allowed themselves to be converted into a tribe of sycophants. Augustus was able to "unite in his own person the functions of the senate, the magistracy, and the legislature" because many nobles "found a cheerful acceptance of slavery the smoothest road to wealth and office" and because the provinces had grown to distrust "administration by the Senate and People" due to the "feuds of the magnates and the greed of the officials."[34] All of this destroys "the old, unspoilt Roman character": "Equal-ity was an outworn creed, and all eyes looked to the mandate of the sovereign."[35] Augustus thus ripened conditions for his successor's tyranny,

---

[32] See Tuck (1993), esp. chs. 2 and 3; Gajda (2009) 253–68; and Burke (1991) 479–98. Burke counts 100 commentaries between 1580 and 1700 and sixty-seven editions between 1600 and 1649 (see 484–85).

[33] See Oakley (2009) 185.   [34] Tacitus (1931–37), *The Annals,* 1.2.

[35] Ibid., 1.4.

and praise of Roman liberty appears only momentarily in book 1 as Tiberius sits in the senate and seeks to vote on a case of treason:

> breaking through his taciturnity, [Tiberius] exclaimed that, in this case, he too would vote, openly and under oath,—the object being to impose a similar obligation on the rest. There remained even yet some traces of dying liberty. Accordingly Gnaeus Piso enquired: "In what order will you register your opinion, Caesar? If first, I shall have something to follow: if last of all, I fear I may inadvertently find myself on the other side." The words went home; and with a meekness that showed how profoundly he rued his unwary outburst, he voted for the acquittal of the defendant on the counts of treason.[36]

The victory for liberty is twofold: the treason laws that Tacitus consistently associates with tyranny are not applied, and for a fleeting moment the senate defends its independence. Still, in the next breath Tacitus concedes that Tiberius' influence on justice is sometimes positive. When the emperor sits in the "common courts" (*praetorem curuli*), he often assures that cases are decided fairly, even going so far as to dip into his own coffers to assist hard-luck litigants. Even these instances of justice, however, are harmful to liberty: "while equity gained, liberty suffered" (*dum veritati consulitur, libertas corrumpebatur*).[37]

How so? Because all aspects of law and public life had coalesced around the emperor. In a final illustration of this destructive tendency, Book 1 closes by noting that Tiberius manipulated the election of consuls in a way that rendered the office meaningless, "destined to issue in a servitude all the more detestable the more it was disguised under a semblance of liberty."[38] Those espousing unitary sovereignty in this book of the *Annals* tend to be supporters of Tiberius, and are clearly offering a debased form of the principle. In advising Livia and Tiberius, Sallustius Crispus declares it "a condition of sovereignty that the account balanced only if rendered to a single auditor" (*eam condicionem esse imperandi, ut non aliter ratio constet quam si uni reddatur*).[39] In attempting to assuage Tiberius after misspeaking in the senate, Asinius Gallus similarly declares that "the body politic was a single organism needing to be governed by a single intelligence"

---

[36] Ibid., 1.74.   [37] On this statement see Oakley (2009) 187.
[38] Tacitus (1931–37), *The Annals*, 1.81.   [39] Ibid., 1.6.

(*unum esse rei publicae corpus atque unius animo regendum*). This as an example of the senate "descending to the most abject supplications."[40]

Through a fascinating portrait of Galba, the *Histories* offer a different path to dashed liberty. For a brief moment, it looks as though the senate might resume its central political role: Galba is not named emperor in Rome itself, which looks to the senate like a symbol of their possession of the capital, and he chooses in Piso a successor outside of his own household and one known for public spirit, lamenting in the same breath that Rome is not ready to return to a republican settlement. All seemed well pleased with the appointment of Piso but were not all. Galba is disastrously rigid in his principles, bungling the transition with his scruples about handing out gifts to the soldiery, a decision about which Tacitus makes his feelings clear: "There is no question that their loyalty could have been won by the slightest generosity on the part of this stingy old man" (*Constat potuisse conciliari animos quantualcumque parci senis liberalitate*). Common soldiers are then all-too receptive to the enticements of Otho, who encourages resentment of Galba's "avarice" (*avaritia*) and easily gains the loyalties of the rank and file with promised largesse.[41] The form of his rebellion augurs a world turned upside down: Otho is supported chiefly by the common soldiers, rather than centurions, who "seized arms without regard to military custom or rank" and subjected Galba to a ruthless murder: "They thrust aside the rabble, trampled down senators; terrifying men by their arms, they burst into the forum at full gallop."[42] With "the soldiers' will . . . supreme," a fearful senate reduced itself to sycophancy yet again, tripping over itself to vote Otho "the tribunitian power, the title Augustus, and all the honours granted the other emperors."[43]

The lessons that such moments provide *raison d'état* thinkers are clear enough: Galba's high ideals are detached from reality, leading to political disaster because they blind him to the measures necessary to stable transition. He imagines that the army is motivated by public spirit, when in fact it differs little from the mob in having more stomach than head. That kind of

---

[40]   Ibid., 1.12.

[41]   Tacitus (1925–31), *Histories*, 1.18. Early in Book I we learn that "there was the saying of Galba's to the effect that he was wont to select, not buy, his soldiers—an honourable utterance in the interests of the state, but dangerous to himself" (Tacitus [1925–31] 1.5). Later Galba names Piso as his successor before the praetorian camp without "flattery of the soldiers, nor . . . mention of a gift" (1.18).

[42]   Ibid., 1.38, 40.   [43]   Ibid., 1.46-7.

wisdom from Tacitus we might associate with Guicciardini.[44] But Tacitus is also telling a story of how liberty makes its way in the world. Its natural repository is clearly the senate, but a senate that feels itself unthreatened by emperor, or army, or plebs. Here we might be reminded of Sallust's emphasis on free institutions, but with a much keener awareness of the senate's record of abandoning its principles at the slightest touch. The promise of Trajan's reign, then, is that it will take measures necessary to preserve order without seeking to concentrate power in the hands of the emperor and his inner circle. This is the kind of cool analysis we expect from Tacitus, here placed in the service of identifying properly Roman political authority.

Milton's Sovereign Parliament

The prospect of liberty under a precarious political settlement is central to Milton's concerns at the tail end of the 1640s. It is as his disenchantment with the Long Parliament grows that we begin especially to see his position on sovereignty emerge. But even as early as the antiprelatical tracts, he tends not to speak much about the traditional constitution of kings, lords, and commons. *Of Reformation* perhaps comes closest in the image we have seen in this chapter of the bishops as a "Wen" on the neck of the body politic, but the image inaugurates a theme that ties together the tracts of 1640–45, and which is one implication of the Ludlow *Maske*: a sustained assault on ecclesiastical law, whether arguing for the removal of its administrators, the bishops, or against its jurisdiction over marriage and the press. The very existence of this body of law seems inherently in Milton's mind to be an encroachment upon parliamentary sovereignty. Such sympathies indicate why he pivots quite naturally in *Areopagitica* to speaking of Parliament as a Senate, and is comfortable addressing its Erastian members. And when Parliament proves not to be an assembly of the wise, Milton has little philosophical problem with altering the body itself—rather than balancing it against other branches of the constitution—so that it is better able to shepherd the liberty of "the people."

---

[44] Of "the people," Guicciardini (1970) 76 [series C, 144] offers a less than charitable evaluation in the *Ricordi*: "To speak of the people is really to speak of a mad animal gorged with a thousand and one errors and confusions, devoid of taste, of pleasure, of stability."

Here the first four books and the Digression to the *History of Britain* are particularly relevant, for we notice a marked shift from the earlier polemical prose in that Milton must take up the question of placing judicious constraints on Parliament, something he does not do in the antiprelatical tracts, or divorce tracts, or in *Areopagitica*. If we take Milton's claim in the *Second Defense* at face value, and it has not yet been disproven, then the first four books of the *History of Britain* were composed in the month between the publication of the *Tenure* and his appointment as Secretary of Foreign Tongues by the Council of State (*YP* 4: 627). On this and other evidence, Nicholas von Maltzahn has argued that the Digression was written in the wake of the execution of Charles I, expressing frustration with the Long Parliament's actions in the years between the end of the first civil war and Pride's Purge. By Milton's telling, the house had more than its share of plebeian, self-interested members squandering revenue and levying new taxes: as he puts it, those "who had bin calld from shops & warehouses without other merit to sit in supreme councel & committies, as their breeding was, fell to hucster the common-wealth" (*YP* 5: 445). The "offices, gifts, and preferments bestow'd and shar'd among themselves" (ibid.) had not only shown a lack of public spirit but also further corrupted the capacity for civic virtue of a people already unaccustomed to liberty:

> Thus they who but of late were extolld as great deliverers, and had a people wholy at thir devotion, by so discharging thir trust as wee see, did not onely weak'n and unfitt themselves to be dispencers of what libertie they pretented [*sic*], but unfitted also the people, now growne worse & more disordinate, to receave or to digest any libertie at all. (*YP* 5: 449)

In a way akin to his earlier prose works, which lean heavily on the distinction between the liberty loved by good men and license craved by the corrupt, Milton here asserts that liberty "hath a sharp and double edge fitt onelie to be handl'd by just and vertuous men, to bad and dissolute it become a mischief unwieldie in thir own hands" (ibid.). But we ought to notice that Milton abandons the liberty–license distinction and suggests that liberty itself can be abused: he is no longer simply agitating for the sweeping away of institutions like Stuart monarchy, which gives space to license without cultivating liberty, but arguing that a legitimate body pursuing liberty must be chary of extending it to the wrong people. Skilled government thus entails granting "good me[n] . . . the freedom which they merit and the bad the curb which they need" (ibid.).

This is a significant change in Milton's rhetoric, to be sure. For the first time he is arguing that parliamentary rule may not in fact create a climate conducive to liberty. And in saying why Britain is not ready to be a republic, Milton twice refers to a key Tacitist political virtue:

> For Britain (to speake a truth not oft spok'n) as it is a land fruitful enough of men stout and couragious in warr, so is it naturallie not over fertil of men able to govern justlie & *prudently* in peace; trusting onelie on thir Mother-witt, as most doo, & consider not that civilitie, *prudence*, love of the public more then of money or vaine honour are to this soile in a manner outlandish.   (5: 451, emphasis mine)

Thanks in part to the great emphasis Justus Lipsius places on it,[45] there is no political virtue more often associated with Tacitus than *prudentia*, which we find displayed especially in the life of Agricola, the British subject of which drew Milton's attention at this moment: it is a text that he cites in the *History* and the first *Defense* (*YP* 5: *passim*, 4: 479). Agricola's great triumph is to have served the empire well if also not overly conspicuously under the rule of Domitian, who, in the way of tyrants, was jealous of glory—Milton would later mark this tyrannical inverse of civic-minded *prudentia* when Satan prevents all reply in the Parliament of Hell:

> Prudent, least from his resolution rais'd
> Others among the chief might offer now
> (Certain to be refus'd) what erst they fear'd;
> And so refus'd might in opinion stand
> His Rivals
>
> (*PL* 2.468–71)

Satan's is the prudence of a Machiavellian prince guarding against future threats to his power, not to be confused with the public virtue that Agricola displays, one that eschews acclaim in favor of quiet and diligent public service.[46] Or, Satan's is the prudence of false reason of state, governed by the kind of "necessitie" that is "the Tyrants plea" (*PL* 4.393–4). After his

---

[45]   See Burke (1991) 485.

[46]   See, for example, Machiavelli (1971) 39 [ch.3]: "In these instances [of seizing new provinces], the Romans did what all wise [sometimes translated as prudent] rulers must: cope not only with present troubles but also with ones likely to arise in future, and assiduously forestall them."

conquest of the island of Anglesey, Agricola does not affix "laurels to his despatches; yet his very deprecation of glory increased his glory."[47] He further assures that conquest is not followed by the kind of plunder and corruption that yields unrest, picking by hand those conducting public business on the basis of ability and virtue, rather than "personal likings, or private recommendation, or entreaty."[48] Tacitus praises these qualities in Agricola not simply because they allow for stable rule, but also because they brush against the grain of the corruption and tyranny of the age of Domitian insofar as one man is able to do without resorting to rash, and therefore fruitless, acts of defiance.[49]

Such is the kind of *prudentia* that Milton might see as necessary in a nascent Commonwealth that needed to balance liberty and constraint, to reap the benefits of a tenuous military victory while gaining the trust, or at least the quietude, of a skeptical and factious populace. While *prudentia* also had strong associations with Cicero, by Milton's time it had very much become associated with Tacitist reason of state.[50] And Milton's internalization of the lessons of Tacitus might run deeper still. Like Tacitus he defines liberty as the liberty of a senatorial class equipped to advance the public good, and it is this group of individuals who are the source of true authority. Sound political order does not allow their liberty to be threatened from below by the huckstering *plebs*, nor from above by an overreaching *princeps*. Milton could support Pride's Purge or the advent of the Protectorate on grounds practical and intellectual: by authority of "the people" he never meant the will of the populace as a whole or a balancing of estates traditionally represented in a full sitting of Parliament, but the will of the enlightened few advancing the cause of national virtue. Theirs is the only politically significant liberty, and it must be defended by force if necessary.

These ideas on political order are discernible as Milton becomes the official mouthpiece of the new regime, and must cast the Rump's actions as flowing naturally from English constitutional tradition. By the time his first official publication appears, *The Observations upon the Articles of Peace* (May, 1649), the Long Parliament had done away with the Lords Spiritual, and the Rump had not only tried Charles but then proceeded to do away

---

[47] Tacitus (1970), *Agricola*, par. 18.   [48] Ibid., par. 19.
[49] On these qualities in *Agricola*, see Kapust (2011) 135–7.
[50] "Botero and [Pedro de] Ribadeneira," Harro Höpfl observes, "tended to equate reason of state with prudence." See Höpfl (2004) 165.

with the office of king and the House of Lords.[51] Milton has to find a language by which this can seem legitimate, and to redeem the Commonwealth from the charge of military dictatorship, or, worse still, innovation. And the language he hits upon is an early expression of the principle of popular sovereignty—though, as in much of the Anglo-American tradition, popular sovereignty is not equivalent to democracy.[52] The "People" are in *Eikonoklastes* the "iron flaile . . . that drove the Bishops out of thir Baronies . . . threw down the High Commission and Star-chamber [and] gave us a Triennial Parliament" (*OM* 6: 306). As the representatives of this freeborn people, it is Parliament that has "both the life and death of Lawes in thir Lawgiving power: And the Law of England is at best but the reason of Parlament" (*OM* 6: 340). Because of its legislative and judiciary power, Parliament must also wield the power of the Sword.

Though in the same passage Milton refers to property rights, it is only to argue that something more fundamental is at stake: "not to have in our selves, though vanting to be freeborn, the power of our own freedom, and the public safety, is a degree lower then not to have the property of our own goods" (*OM* 6: 342). In this statement added to the second edition, Milton is manifestly not engaging in Coke's common law language of liberty, where all rights flow from rights of property, nor is he engaging in what C. B. Macpherson would call a political theory of possessive individualism.[53] Political freedom is here divorced from and made prior to the liberty of holding property. In fact a right to property without political liberty is likened in *Eikonoklastes* to the condition of minorities living in the Sultan's territories: "for the injoyment of those fruits, which our industry and labours have made our own upon our own, what Privilege is that, above what the *Turks, Jewes,* and *Mores,* enjoy under the Turkish Monarchy?" (*OM* 6: 408). This is directly opposed to a "Christian libertie" that does not "depend upon the doubtful consent of any earthly Monarch" (*OM* 6: 363–4).

With these values in place, sovereignty need not be divided according to estates, and so, to speak the language of Harringtonean republicanism, Milton has no concern with a balancing of the few, the one, and the many. *Eikonoklastes* leaves the impression that the king in Parliament holds no

---

[51] For texts of the Act Abolishing the Office of King and the Act Abolishing the House of Lords, see Gardiner (1906) 384–8.

[52] When "the People" has plebeian connotations, it is used derisively in *Eikonoklastes*: "Such Prayers as these may happily catch the People, as was intended: but how they please God, is to be much doubted" (*YP* 3: 601).

[53] Macpherson ([1963] 2011).

more constitutional authority than does any other sitting member. The lords are similarly denied independent constitutional value. Even as he recognizes that some were instrumental in pressuring Charles to summon the Long Parliament (*OM* 6: 287), and even as he draws on the Magna Carta as an important constitutional text, Milton does not afford the upper house the sort of special consideration that one encounters in political thinkers of the Polybian variety. And he is emphatic that the crown should not be able to create lords, just as it should not be able to appoint bishops (*OM* 6: 368). This would limit and frustrate the operation of the people's political will and concentrate power in the hands of the monarch, who can deploy it according to private whim.

Charles I, then, is damnable for an abnegation of sovereignty in his manipulation of national institutions for the sake of private interest. In *Eikonoklastes* this becomes an excellent means of turning tables on the king's expressions of private conscience in the *Eikon Basilike*: "for certainly a privat conscience sorts not with a public Calling; but declares that Person rather meant by nature for a privat fortune" (*OM* 6: 295). As in *The Tenure of Kings and Magistrates*, Milton emphasizes that kings are public servants entrusted by the people "to govern them as Freemen by Laws of thir own framing" (*OM* 6: 360). In a free and happy nation, those laws flow naturally from the virtues held by the people themselves, and Milton has little patience for Charles' language of paternal suffering:

> He would work the people to a perswasion, that *if he be miserable they cannot be happy.* What should hinder them? Were they all born Twins of *Hippocrates* with him and his fortune, one birth one burial? It were a Nation miserable indeed, not worth the name of a Nation, but a race of Idiots, whose happiness and welfare depended upon one Man. The happiness of a Nation consists in true Religion, Piety, Justice, Prudence, Temperance, Fortitude, and the contempt of Avarice and Ambition. They in whomsoever these vertues dwell eminently, need not Kings to make them happy, but are the architects of thir own happiness; and whether to themselves or others are not less then Kings.   (*OM* 6: 391–2)

We cannot fail to notice that "race of Idiots" introduces the language of wardship, a condition of dependency on a superior diametrically opposed to a race of citizens who are architects of their own happiness. Here the Stoic virtue of magnanimity is adapted to Reformation values, in a way that Milton will later explore, if also fly above, in *Paradise Regain'd*. Milton's point is that Charles' desire to impose his will in the teeth of parliamentary objection indicates his utter lack of sovereign legitimacy.

The *Defenses* cleave to this position of parliamentary sovereignty. In response to Salmasius' attack on the novelty of the Supreme Council and its president, Milton emphasizes that its powers remain subordinate to those of the body that created it: "the Council you dream of is not supreme, but rather appointed for a specified time by the authority of Parliament and composed of forty men from its ranks . . . It has always been the practice for the Parliament, which is our Senate, to appoint a few of its members when it seemed necessary" (*YP* 4: 317). Just as the king is a mere Member of Parliament, so the Council of State is in this argument little more than a parliamentary committee. One wonders how much they would appreciate such a defense.

As we have been charting throughout this book, we see Milton's argument on unitary sovereignty confront natural law arguments in the exchange with Salmasius. Or, more precisely, both Milton and Salmasius invoke an external limit on arbitrary rule only to dissolve it with differing versions of unitary sovereignty: for Milton, that limit is popular sovereignty, which then shades into oligarchy; for Salmasius, it is natural law, which is then used to justify royal absolutism. Salmasius invokes natural law to claim that nature has ordered the relationships between ruler and ruled to the benefit of all societies, the reasonableness of which law is "infused into the minds of all men" (qtd. 4: 425n7). The Aristotelian provenance of this view is certainly not lost on Milton. Though he at times endorsed Aristotle's view of "natural-born slaves," his riposte to Salmasius describes the condition of freeborn men in a way rather unlike Aristotle and consistent with the language of political compact that he had used in *The Tenure*:

> Since a king has no right to do wrong, the rights of the people remain supreme; and so the right by which men first combined their judgment and strength before kings were created, and by which they placed one or more in charge of the rest to preserve the safety, peace, and freedom of all, is the same right by which they can check or depose either those same persons who for their courage or judgment were put in command, or any others if through sloth, folly, wickedness or treachery they misgovern the state: For nature has always looked, as she now does, not to the dominion of one man or a few, but to the safety of all, whatever may become of the dominion of the one or the few. (4: 425)

This rapidly shifts ground from natural law. Salmasius claims that it is the office of reason to see the benefit of the law of nature, which favors the security offered by existing powers; Milton counters with a view of human reason as equipped in and of itself to weigh the liberty and security that a given political arrangement provides. In the space of a few sentences he has leapt from "book III of Aristotle's *Politics*," and the Averroist tradition that it inspires, to a language of popular sovereignty.

Milton makes short work of Salmasius' sneer that the elimination of the House of Lords was a piece of "Anabaptist doctrine," declaring that it is rather "democracy, a much more ancient thing" (4: 632–3). But in the next breath we find Milton defending rule by an enlightened minority: "Those whose power lies in wisdom, experience, industry, and virtue will, in my opinion, however small their number, be a majority and prove more powerful in balloting everywhere than any mere number, however great" (4: 636). This is not slippery rhetoric or inconsistency, but a discernible set of ideas, democratic to the extent that rank does not determine political status but imposing qualifications of civic virtue on admission to the *demos*.[54] As the text proceeds, his exhortations to Cromwell look rather like those of Tacitus to Trajan: to exercise power in a way that placates noisy factions and the army, and to allow a political elite the liberty to guide the commonwealth on the path to national glory.

Creating a Poetry of Godly Republicanism

In exploring Milton's late, godly republicanism as a further instance of his affinity for unitary sovereignty, we will first examine the tumultuous years between the death of Oliver Cromwell and the Restoration, when a profusion of last-ditch efforts to save the Good Old Cause, including Milton's own, make especially visible the fault lines of Interregnum republican thought. Looming large at this moment is James Harrington, who revived *Oceana* (1656) in a 1658 edition and sought further to advance his ideas through the Rota Club and in an avalanche of tracts clinging to *de jure* republican principles: settle a republican constitution, his argument ran, and

---

[54] Hammond (2014) 176 similarly notes that in the Latin defenses "*virtus*" distinguishes "a *populus* from a *vulgus*," See also his treatment of *The Tenure* as typical of defenses of the regicide in trying, with noticeable strain, to claim this unpopular action as a victory of "the people," esp. pp. 118–25.

a Parliament positively stuffed with royalist members still could not reintroduce monarchy.[55] Even the printer of the first edition of *Oceana*, John Streater, was skeptical, and his own proposals at this juncture reflect the prevailing sentiment that royalists had to be kept away from the polls, and out of Parliament, if the republic was to survive the crisis: he endorsed the Army's resettling of the Rump in his *Continuation of this Session of Parliament, Justified* (1659), though that Parliament was not destined long to continue.[56] Milton clearly agreed with that view: *The Readie and Easie Way to Establish a Free Commonwealth* (1660) was in title and in content opposed to Harrington's *Wayes and Meanes Whereby an Equal and Lasting Commonwealth May be Suddenly Introduced and Perfectly Founded* (1660). In the first edition of his tract, Milton essentially proposed ossification of the ruling Rump Parliament, and tepidly modified the second edition to give more space to election even as he voiced objections and declared rotation to have "too much affinitie with the wheel of fortune" (*OM* 6: 497). Milton's departures from Harrington and his followers are much more pronounced than his agreements with them, and they have both practical and theoretical dimensions. Practically, he is much more aware of England's constitutional crises being decided by intervention of the army, rather than by legislators. And theoretically, Milton's recipe for stability is fundamentally at odds with the Polybian division of sovereignty that Harrington inherits from Machiavellian republicanism: as he had done in the early years of the Commonwealth, Milton argues for a single body that holds final legislative, judicial, and military authority.

---

[55] Harrington's productivity between 1658 and 1660 is remarkable: a new edition of *Oceana* (London, 1658; Wing H810); *The Stumbling-Block of Disobedience* (London, 1658; Wing H822); *Half a Sheet Against Mr. Baxter* (London, 1658; Wing H813A); *Brief Directions Shewing How a Fit and Perfect Model of Popular Government may be Made, Found, or Understood* (London, 1659; Wing H807); *The Art of Law-Giving in III Books* (London, 1659; Wing H806); *Valerius and Publicola* (London, 1659; Wing H824); *Pour Enclouer le Canon* (London, 1659; Wing H819); *A Discourse upon this Saying* (London, 1659; Wing H813); *Aphorisms Political* (London 1659; Wing H804); *A Parallel of the Spirit of the People* (London, 1659; Wing H817); *Politicaster, or a Comical Discourse, in Answer unto Mr. Wren's Book, Intituled, Monarchy Asserted* (London, 1659; Wing H818A); *The Use and Manner of the Ballot* (London, 1660; Wing H823); *Political Discourses Tending to the Introduction of a Free and Equal Commonwealth* (London, 1660; Wing H818); *The Rota: or, A Model of a Free-State* (London, 1660; Wing H821); *A Letter unto Mr. Stubbs in Answer to his Oceana Weighed* (London, 1660; Wing H814A); and *The Wayes and Meanes Whereby an Equal and Lasting Commonwealth may be Suddenly Introduced and Perfectly Founded* (London, 1660; Wing H825). The finest modern edition of Harrington's writings remains Harrington (1977).

[56] Streater (1659), Thomason dates this tract May 16, ten days after the Rump Parliament is recalled.

Read alongside his 1659 tracts on the deinstitutionalization of the church, *A Treatise of Civil Power in Ecclesiastical Causes* and *Considerations Touching the Likeliest Means to Remove Hirelings*, his model of government can also be seen as participating in the language of godly republicanism. In the palazzo of republican thought, godly republicanism has an admittedly small gallery—small and to Whig, Marxian and revisionist tour guides alike, one best overlooked as the only distinctly English contribution to the republican tradition.[57] Nonetheless, the Interregnum's latter years yield a set of discernible principles with no direct provenance in classical or Continental thought. These arise in part as a reaction of the Protestant left to the Protectorate's imperfect dismantling of priestcraft, which took aim at ceremonialism but left the national church largely intact by refusing to dispense with tithes. Godly republicanism forcefully urges liberty of conscience for sectarians and demands that the church no longer be enervated by the organs of the state, seeking to end tithes, central organization, and a university-trained ministry. It values republican government as that most likely to practice noninterference in religion—which is why it can sometimes align itself temporarily with non-republicans promising to secure liberty of conscience—in the hope, and here is its distinctive mark, that noninterference will allow the Saints to rise to a position of unchallenged political sovereignty in God's time.

We find these ideas expressed most programmatically in the writings of the younger Sir Henry Vane (1613–62), that remarkable mix of administrative exactitude and radical spiritualism uncannily present in every major event of the period on both sides of the Atlantic. He became governor of Massachusetts less than a year after his arrival in October 1635, in which post he secured the purchase of Rhode Island with the assistance of Roger Williams. His sympathy with Massachusetts antinomians would lead him to confrontation with John Winthrop, a confrontation that Vane would lose and that would prompt a return to England in 1637. He sat for Hull in the first year of the Long Parliament and was no idle member: he furnished key evidence against the Earl of Strafford, which was procured by rummaging through his father's bureau; with Cromwell and Sir Arthur Hesilrige he

---

[57] There are several outstanding accounts of seventeenth-century English republicanism, intellectual and literary. See especially Norbrook (1999); Pocock (1975); Rahe (2008); Skinner (1998); van Gelderen and Skinner (2002) vols. 1–2; and Worden (2007). Giving some space to godly republicanism is Scott (2004) esp. 151–69, and Nelson (2011) 23–56. Also treating overlaps between republicanism, nationhood, and religion are Achinstein (2003), Guibbory (2010), Trubowitz (2012), Sauer (2014), and Hackenbracht (2019).

initiated the bill for "root and branch" elimination of episcopacy; and he led negotiation of the Solemn League and Covenant. After removing himself from Parliament during Pride's Purge and the trial and execution of Charles I, he resumed his seat in February 1649 to become treasurer of the navy, a post in which he oversaw supply of Cromwell's Irish and Scottish campaigns, as well defeat of the royalist fleet and of the Dutch. Vane, with Algernon Sidney sitting next to him, is supposed to have come into direct confrontation with Cromwell in the 1653 expulsion of Parliament that forced him into retirement—to Cromwell and his musketeers, according to Ludlow, Vane cried defiantly if also idealistically "This is not honest, yea, it is against morality and common honesty." His disagreement with Cromwell would lead to forced retirement, and brief imprisonment, during the Lord Protector's reign. But after Cromwell's death his star would rapidly rise, sitting in Richard's Parliament and playing a large part in the restored Rump. His cooperation with Lambert's Council of State, through which he introduced measures to secure liberty of conscience, was deemed an unforgivable betrayal when the Rump returned to power. And the Restoration led to his execution in 1662, much more for his political efficacy and unrepentant anti-Stuart sentiments than for the regicide, in which he did not take part.[58]

Vane's writings of the latter 1650s provide the spiritualist justification and political implications of his consistent efforts to advance liberty of conscience. *The Retired Mans Meditations* (1655) describe liberty of conscience as a necessity in an age where the Saints had not yet fully revealed themselves. In such a time the magistrate must be confined to the government of externals only, allowing the elect to follow their divinely appointed path and to begin in God's time the millennial reign in which they will exercise "Judicial power" in matters civil and spiritual. The jurisdiction of that power spans both heaven and earth, and its final authority to exercise divine will Vane identifies with "the power of the KEYS."[59] Though, as we shall see, he does not appoint the time of this reign with the confidence of a Fifth Monarchist, he does make clear that he believes the defeat of Antichrist to be imminent, a belief to which he attributes his defiance of worldly authority. These ideas undergird the republican model of government that he offers in *A Healing Question* (1656, 1660) and *A Needfull Corrective* (1660); the latter,

---

[58] On the 1653 confrontation between Cromwell and Vane, see Hosmer (1889) 409; for biography of Vane, see especially Rowe (1970). Parnham (1997) explores Vane's theology.
[59] Vane (1655) 410.

written in the form of an epistle to Harrington, opposes the principle of rotation in settling for life a senate willing to preserve liberty of conscience.[60] In its single, appointed body exercising sovereign power, Milton's *Readie and Easie Way* resembles no republican model more closely than it does Vane's, and Milton's *Civil Power* and *Hirelings* share views on the church very close to those of Vane and his confidant Henry Stubbe. Stubbe would also advance Vane's model republic in *Malice Rebuked* (1659), where he defends Sir Henry against the attacks of Richard Baxter, and justifies a permanent senate in his *Essay in Defence of the Good Old Cause* (1659). *Civil Power* prompted a letter from another member of Vane's circle, Moses Wall, who hoped that Milton had returned to his "former Light" after a period of Cromwellian darkness (*YP* 7: 510).[61] Whatever rift had developed during the Protectorate, Milton is clearly keeping company with the Vane circle in the critical years of 1659–60, and the ideas he promotes at this moment remain pervasive in his major poems. The proximities between Milton and Vane are readily apparent, as we will see, if we read *Paradise Regain'd* alongside Vane's unpublished works, which include a lengthy commentary on the Book of Job.

Lending primacy to liberty of conscience bars the magistrate from interfering in religious matters, clearing human obstructions to the radiant beams of divine light. In this it distinguishes itself from other kinds of republican thought, which tend to endorse some measure of religious conformity or to see the rule of the virtuous as encompassing determination of acceptable modes of worship. Representation does not matter in the liberal democratic sense of having every individual serve in some fashion as author of the law that he or she must obey. Rather, effective representation empowers those fit to exercise sovereign power, with the fitness of the polity measured by its ability to be so led. If in Milton's earlier Tacitism the installation of a civic-minded elite capable of filling this role seems like a possibility of the near future, it is less so in his later godly republicanism.

---

[60] Vane (1656) [reissue London, 1660] and Vane (1660). The latter tract is most likely Vane's, but a note in a seventeenth-century hand on the title page of the Bodleian copy leaves some doubt: "This was writt by Sr. Henry Vane or (at least) by his advice, and approbation"; see Worden (2007) 363n22, and Woolrych (1957) 154n112.

[61] Stubbe (1659d) and (1659a). The title page of the Thomason copy of Stubbe (1659b) is marked "A dangerous fellow; Sr Henry Vanes Advisor"; see Woolrych (1957) 155. On the proximity of Milton and Stubbe in 1659–60, pointing especially to views on the church in Stubbe (1659c), see Hawkes (2004) 76–7. On the Vane-Moses Wall connection, see Parker (2003) 2: 1069n89, which states that Vane sends Wall to meet Lord Lovelace, the king's representative in 1643–4; and von Maltzahn (2008b) 65–6.

The late Milton remains committed to unitary popular sovereignty, but, ironically, in a way both more religious and more secular than is visible in his early Commonwealth writings: more religious in that preparing the way for the rule of the Saints becomes central to his thought, and more secular in that the consequence of this core principle is an expectation that for the foreseeable future civil authority must limit itself to externals. In its more flamboyant moments, Milton's prose of the 1640s fashions an image of the Long Parliament as leading a reformation of religious and political life. By 1659 Milton has lowered his expectations of MPs, even those with estab-lished allegiance to the Good Old Cause.

A powerful symbol of this deferred ideal polity is Milton's turn to Job in *Paradise Regain'd*, which is interesting not only in and of itself, but also in suggesting a Dissenting counter-narrative to the currency of David amongst defenders of the restored monarchy and its conformist church. In sermons and poems celebrating the Restoration, as Stella Revard shows, Charles II is frequently described as a David who had suffered persecution before begin-ning his divinely appointed reign, a comparison "J.W." makes with particu-lar force in a published 1660 sermon: "as *David* in his Kingdom, Christ in his Kingdome, so King CHARLES in his Kingdome *is a stone, a tried stone.*"[62] Dryden not surprisingly takes up the comparison, likening Charles to David in "Astraea Redux" and again in "A Panegyric on His Coronation."[63] But David could be reclaimed by Dissenters pointing to his Job-like endurance of trial. Upon his ejection from the national church in 1662, the former Smectymnuan Edmund Calamy delivered a farewell sermon on 2 Samuel 24.14: "I am in a great strait: let us fall now into the hand of the Lord; for his mercies are great: and let me not fall into the hand of man." In his handling David is a believer preferring divine to human law, a point Calamy emphasizes with citations of the Book of Job. When that sermon is published in 1663 alongside those of other ejected ministers, Calamy is far from the only one turning to that book to explain the plight of the godly party; Job also appears in the sermons of William Bates, Thomas Brooks, Daniel Bull, Thomas Case, George Evank, John Gaspine, Thomas Horton, Thomas Jacombe, Philip Lamb, Thomas Lye, Matthew Mead, Lazarus Seaman, George Thorne, Ralph Venning, and Thomas Watson.[64]

---

[62] W[hite] (1660) 9.   [63] See Revard (2010) 219–20 and 224.
[64] Calamy et al. (1663) sigs. B1r, B4r, D2r [unpaginated until p. 649]. Other references to Job in this collection are in the sermons of William Bates (sig. Q4r-v), Thomas Brooks (sigs. Ll3r-v, Ll4v), Daniel Bull (sig. Bbb4r), Thomas Case (sig. F3r), George Evank (sigs. Uuu1r, Uuu2v-Uuu3r, Xxx2v), John Gaspine (sig. Sss2r), Thomas Horton (sigs. Oo4v, Pp2v), Thomas Jacombe

In *Paradise Regain'd* it is Satan who is obsessed with reading the messianic progress of history through the lens of David's earthly kingship. Jesus is equally preoccupied with Job, whose single resistance to temptation neither depends on nor culminates in a publicly ordered religious settlement. The debate is between the sovereignty of a monarch whose authority spans both religious and civil government, and the self-rule of the enlightened, who wait upon God's will.

Milton's literary choices in developing this image of earthly authority are clarified by comparison to Giles Fletcher and Francis Quarles. Milton was clearly familiar with the work of Du Bartas and Giles Fletcher. Equally clearly, he departs from these predecessors, and assertively rejects the Spenserian allegory and romance that Fletcher embraces. Milton likewise sets himself against the work of Francis Quarles, a poet whose very different literary and politico-religious sensibilities are revealed in his handling of the Hebrew Bible figures central to Milton's 1671 volume, Job and Samson. Put simply, Quarles' reading of Job through the lens of Stoicism and reading of Samson through romance convention both rhyme well with his defenses of the king and national church at the outbreak of the civil wars.

Milton's relationship to Quarles is not so much literary rivalry as it is literary antipathy. The young Milton is likely to have been conscious of the reputation of his predecessor at Christ's College, Cambridge.[65] And the two shared a printer in Humphrey Moseley, who issued a number of releases of Quarles' *Argalus and Parthenia* and *Enchiridion* over the 1650s while Milton's 1645 volume of poems laid fallow.[66] Perhaps one indication of

(sig. O4v), Philip Lamb (sigs. Hhh1v, Hhh2v, Iii2v, Iii4v, Kkk1v, Kkk3v, Lll3r), Thomas Lye (sigs. Z1r, Tt4r, Tt4v, Uu4v, Xx2r), Matthew Mead (sig. Cc2r), Lazarus Seaman (sig. Ff4v), George Thorne (sigs. Mmmm4r; p. 653, 655 [misnumbered 650]), Ralph Venning (sigs. Hh2r-v), and Thomas Watson (sigs. V2r, X2r).

[65] Early in his career he may have been as receptive as he ever would be to Quarles' work: *Areopagitica* in particular might have in mind some of Quarles' language in a way that has been undetected. The apology to Quarles (1642) describes his muse as "unbreath'd, unlikely to attain / An easie honour" and in the first meditation he describes how God "daily sends the Doctors of his Spouse, / (With such like oyl as from the Widows Cruse / Did issue forth)" (4,5). Did Milton borrow these turns of phrase in reproving a "fugitive and cloister'd virtue, unexercis'd & unbreath'd," and in worrying that the "cruse of truth must run no more oyle" (*YP* 2: 515, 541)?

[66] The number of bibliographical entries for Quarles' works reflects wide and sustained interest, with Humphrey Moseley acquiring *Argalus and Parthenia* and *Enchiridion* in the 1650s and passing the profitable venture on to his posterity after his death in 1661—the "A. Moseley" of the 1664 printings of Quarles is his widow, Anne (see Wilcher [2004]). After seven entries published by John Marriott from 1629–47, Moseley issues *Argalus and Parthenia* in 1654 (Wing Q41), thrice in 1656 (Wing Q41A, Q42, and Q42A), and again in 1659 (Q43); A. Moseley publishes the work in 1664 (Q43A), and there are three additional entries for the work in

Milton's disdain for the emblematist is the uncharacteristically disparaging entry in his nephew and pupil Edward Phillips' catalogue of poets ancient and modern, the *Theatrum Poetarum* (1675):

> *Francis Quarles*, the darling of our Plebeian Judgments, that is such as have ingenuity enough to delight in Poetry, but are not sufficiently instructed to make a right choice and distinction . . . his Feast of Worms, or History of *Jonas*, and other Divine Poems have been ever, and still, are in wonderful Veneration among the Vulgar, and no less his *Argalus* and *Parthenia*.[67]

We would expect Milton strongly to distinguish himself from Quarles in his handling of Job and Samson in the 1671 volume. The meditations of Quarles' *Job Militant* often refer to Stoic principles. To a pious statement on vitiated human nature—"*No Flesh and Blood / Deserves the stile of Absolutely Good*"—he adds a marginal reference to Horace's ode 2.16: "nihil est ex omni parte beatum" ("Nothing is happy altogether").[68] Horace reappears in Quarles' eighth meditation, in a marginal note on accepting the life appointed by God.[69] The point is reinforced with reference to Epictetus' *Encheiridion*.[70] Job's speech on his grief in chapter 9 of the biblical book is interpreted by Quarles as the pangs of conscience, on which subject he turns to Juvenal: "occultum quatiente animo tortore flagellum" ("the mind is a torturer wielding an invisible lash").[71] In the same meditation a single marginal note cites Horace alongside Luke 16.22, both as a gloss on the

---

Milton's lifetime. After three entries for *Enchyridion* from 1641–49 (STC 2053, Wing Q86, Q87, and Q117A [printed with *Solomons Recantation*]), Humphrey Moseley prints the work in 1654 (Wing Q89), and twice in 1658 (Wing Q90 and Q90A); A. Moseley prints the work in 1664 (Wing Q91) and 1667 (Wing Q92); and there is an additional entry in Milton's lifetime (Q93).

[67] Phillips (1675), *The Modern Poets*, p. 45. Cf. the more charitable handling of a poet esteemed among the "Vulgar" in Phillips' entry on George Wither (56–7).

[68] Quarles (1624) sig. F1v. English translations of *Odes* from Horace (1988).

[69] The ode here cited points to the inevitable end of our turbulent lives: "omnium / versatur urna serius ocius / sors exitura et nos in aeternum / exsilium impositur cumbae" ("The lot of every one of us is tossing about in the urn, destined sooner, later, to come forth and place us in Charon's skiff for everlasting exile") (Horace [1988], *Odes*, 2.3.25–8).

[70] The marginal note to Epictetus refers to a non-existent chapter 77; it is likely paragraph 7 that is intended. See Epictetus (1928) 488–91: "Just as on a voyage, when your ship has anchored, if you should go on shore to get fresh water, you may pick up a small shellfish or little bulb on the way, but you have to keep your attention fixed on the ship, and turn about frequently for fear lest the captain should call . . . So it is also in life: If there be given to you, instead of a little bulb and a small shell-fish, a wife and child, there will be no objection to that; only, if the Captain calls, give up all these things and run to the ship, without even turning around to look back."

[71] Quarles (1624) sig. H1v; Juvenal (2004), Satire 13, 195.

statement that *"The secret disposition / Of sacred Providence is lockt and seal'd / From mans Conceit"* (italics in original).[72] In addition to further references to Horace, Quarles also cites Martial and Seneca.[73]

The effect of these references is to turn Job into a model Stoic who learns not to place too much emphasis on worldly tribulations and rewards. The joys of the world are fleeting and suffering is inevitable, so the judicious soul will remain indifferent to things of this world and focus on the realm of eternals. When Quarles' *Historie of Samson* has been compared to *Samson Agonistes*, it is to note that Milton is more sophisticated in his handling of Dalila: Quarles presents a "naively-drawn portrait," observes Merritt Hughes, while Milton is a more complex poet who offers a more complex character.[74] True enough, but the tables turn if we consider representations of the woman of Timnath (Judges 14). Here it is Quarles who offers the more dynamic interpretation of the biblical story, providing a Samson who loves truly and must confront his skeptical parents, of a Manoa and wife who approve the marriage with mixed parental joy and anxiety, and of a woman of Timnath torn between real love of Samson and self-preservation in the face of Philistine threats.[75] If, as Judges 14.4 tells us, this marriage is "of the Lord," Quarles interprets that statement in the spirit of Renaissance Neo-platonism, where romantic love leads us upward on the *scala* toward divine love: *"Love is a noble passion of the heart / ... Fill'd with celestiall fier"* (italics in original).[76]

The collapse of this marriage is thus a story of the human frailty that too often leads us away from such heavenly ascent, and God remains a majestic, largely absent, figure in Quarles' divine economy. In thus presenting the story, the literary structure of this interpretation of Samson is that of romance, where, to paraphrase Spenser, it is fierce wars and faithful loves that moralize the song. And romance is typically a mode surrounding an existing order of power with the mystique of heavenly virtue—Northrop Frye sees this clearly in his comments on the mythical structure of romance, where love of the king and the courtly love mistress "is an educating and informing power which brings one into unity with the spiritual and divine worlds."[77]

---

[72] Quarles (1624) sig. H1v; Quarles quotes Horace, *Odes*, 3.29.29–30—"prudens futuri temporis exitum/calignosa nocte premit deus" ("With wise purpose does the god bury in the shades of night the future's outcome").

[73] See Quarles (1624) sig. L1r, L3v, M2v (Horace), sig. H4v-I1r (Martial and Seneca).

[74] Hughes (1957) 534; see Dobranski (2009), 14, 313 n. ad. 960–96.

[75] Quarles, (1631) 38–9, 39–40, and 62–3.   [76] Ibid., 40.

[77] Frye (2000) 153.

These approaches to the Job and Samson stories are consistent with Quarles' defenses of the king and the national church during the civil wars. They are also consistent with the tendency we have associated in chapter 2 with Barclay's *Argenis*: Quarles appropriates the universalizing language of Neoplatonism, and the broad cultural roots of romance, in an apology for royal absolutism. The exordium to the first of his defenses of Charles I, *The Loyall Convert* (1643), feigns internal division between the claims of Parliament and the king, until Quarles is resolved neither by reason nor policy, but by scripture, the *"Great Oracle,"* which he opens in his confusion, happening upon Proverbs 20.2: *"The feare of a King is as the roaring of a Lyon, and who so provoketh him to Anger, sinneth against his own soule"* (italics in original).[78] As he sets out the standard biblical passages supporting the divine right of kings—Romans 13.1 makes its inevitable appearance, *"Let every soule be subject to the higher Powers, for there is no Power but of God"*[79]—he also points to Shadrach, Meshach, and Abednego as models of righteous resistance:

> The King, a known *Pagan*, commands a grosse *Idolatry*; Did these men conspire? Or (being Rulers of the Province of *Babel*) did they invite the Jews into a *Rebellion*? . . . . No, being called by their *Prince*, they came, and being commanded to give *actuall* obedience to his *unlawfull* Commands, observe the *modesty* of their first answer, *We are not carefull to answer thee in this matter* [Dan 3.16], and being urged, mark their pious *resolution* in the second, *Be it knowne, O King, we will not serve thy Gods, nor worship the golden image thou has set up* [Dan 3.18].[80] (italics in original)

Though conscience can justly lead one to reject the false worship demanded by Nebuchadnezzar, that rejection is a private matter and such non-obedience must not extend to fomenting resistance to monarchical authority. Scripture is deployed here to justify obedience to a monarch, even when he tramples upon right religion. Godliness most certainly does not offer a staging point for justified resistance to a king, nor for the inauguration of a new, and more enlightened, politics.

In *Paradise Regain'd* the *kenosis* by which the Son is emptied of his divinity in becoming Jesus plays a vital role in the literary unity of the work: it creates an internal drama of being refilled by divinity in a way

---

[78] Quarles (1643) 3.   [79] Ibid., 4.   [80] Ibid., 5.

that condenses the human story into the span of Jesus' life.[81] The incompleteness of the "thoughts following thoughts" and contingency of the journey into the desert create a space for revealed truth to appear. And, in a way unlike Quarles' majestic divinity, appear it does. The life of Jesus in Milton's brief epic emphasizes moments of divine presence: the virgin birth of which Mary gives him an account, the baptism reported repeatedly, and the final triumph over Satan and over the Temple.

We are also aware that such events are, to use Michael's phrase in *Paradise Lost*, "not but by the Sprit understood" (12.514). Satan, of course, witnesses the baptism and remains unable or unwilling to read it aright. Even such believing souls as Mary, Andrew, and Simon can hearken toward divine truth and be slightly baffled in their attempts to ascertain the ways of the Word made flesh, showing that its full significance is revealed in God's time and according to the light planted within. Milton's handling of Samson's marriage to the Woman of Timnath thus interprets Judges 14.4 in a way quite unlike Quarles: that the marriage is "of the Lord" is taken to be a sign of the "intimate impulse" of divine illumination. Many of the concerns that Quarles develops in presenting Samson's first marriage arise upon the entry of Dalila, who in *Samson Agonistes* claims the divided loyalties of nation and marriage. The burden of that internal conflict is more attenuated than it is for Quarles' woman of Timnath. Dalila's life is not threatened in Milton's version, leaving her open to the charge that she follows her compatriots' demands for the sake of money and fame. Her constant equivocation renders her sincerity dubious at best, so that we learn just how base and hollow human motivation can be. Reinforcing the point are Samson's hollow human motivations in this episode, ranging from simplistic deduction on the legality of marrying Dalila to the violent hostility of an emasculated and betrayed lover. Read alongside the later exchange with Harapha, we see in the dramatic poem a dismissal of the "long and tedious havoc" of romance love and war (*PL* 9.30). Rather than being coopted for royalist ends, romance conventions are actively criticized, even lampooned. In his version of the Samson story, Milton's general discomfort with romance in favor of celebrating "Patience and Heroic Martyrdom" takes direct aim at Fletcher and Quarles (*PL* 9.32).

Irruptions of divine will clear the havoc of human confusion, and these forcefully punctuate the 1671 volume, first with Jesus standing on the temple

---

[81] On *kenosis*, see Lewalski (1966), esp. 148–56.

top and next with the return of Samson's strength. Where Quarles uses biblical paraphrase as impetus to tentative mystical flight toward a majestic God, Milton's volume is structured around the upright soul's attunement to moments of divine presence in the natural world. Jesus is the perfect king because he is the perfect subject to the Father, filling himself with divinity and inviting others to do the same. Samson is redeemed insofar as he recovers his ability to hear God call. In this landscape, Andrew, Simon, and Mary also play an important role: they are keenly aware of their imperfect understanding and humbly follow Jesus to learn more. Manoa and the Danite chorus are less virtuous in their imperfect knowledge: they jump to hasty conclusions and use Samson's memory as a means of promoting shallow nationalist sentiment.

If politics is the human art of bringing society into alignment with the good, then we are learning through these examples just what this entails: patience, waiting upon divine will, humble receptiveness to the leadership of the enlightened. Despite the distracting cataclysm of Samson's divinely inspired slaughter of the Philistines, we are seeing a vision of political change much more patient than a younger Milton had imagined in the heady 1640s. And we are also seeing that *Paradise Regain'd* and *Samson Agonistes* offer an alternative to the religious and political order imagined in romance, a mode strongly critiqued in *Paradise Lost*, which had been associated with monarchical absolutism or, as we saw in chapter 2, with the values of a politically displaced aristocracy. In the late poems the political itself, in all of its received iterations, is a site of rupture and violence, of deep disorder thinly veiled by corrupt and tenuous forms of human authority. The inherent tragicity of modern politics is resolvable only by divine intervention, of which Samson's triumph offers a foretaste.

Vane, Job, and the Rule of the Saints

These messages of Milton's 1671 volume are underscored when read alongside the younger Sir Henry Vane's commentaries on Job. The commentaries appear in a manuscript book prepared by his daughter Margaret that also contains his final sermon before being sent to the Tower, various other biblical commentaries, and a letter to Henry Cary.[82] The last of these jars

---

[82]   Vane (1677) Forster MS 606 (48.D.41).

with our image of Cary as a hardliner against the regicides, and suggests that he may have inherited some of the intellectual and religious inquisitiveness of his father, Lucius Cary. Vane's final sermon is on Jeremiah 45.2–5 and emphasizes Baruch's confusion as to why God allows oppression of his faithful servants. Identifying himself with Baruch, he laments the faithful witness that has been given to a rebellious people while also declaring that the Saints are exposed to the world as just punishment for their sins.[83]

A commentary on Romans 6.3–7 that is dated "1658" emphasizes how the profane are justly damned for choosing evil when offered enlightenment, perhaps reflecting Vane's resentment of the Cromwellian rule that had forced him into retirement and brief arrest, and anticipating his return to prominence in the final throes of the English republic.[84] Though undated, the commentaries on Job, like the final sermon, focus on the suffering of the faithful, strongly suggesting that they were composed between the Restoration and his execution in 1662. Vane is concerned especially with how God's faithful servant can be visited with great affliction, a point, he says, on which Job "stumbles."[85] The chapters discussed at greatest length are those where Job's friend Elihu defends God's punishment of the righteous (Job 35–6); such affliction has the double benefit of seasoning the just for their return to the Creator and of ripening the wicked for Judgment. And Vane refers explicitly to the wicked of his own nation who will be judged. The day "wherin we live," he claims, offers temptation to judge the chosen and side with the wicked, but even "if the whole world give a wrong Judgment of God & the whole stream run yt way," the righteous "yet chuse affliction rather then sin."[86] We must recall that God "sits in heaven & laughs at ye day yt is coming upon ye wicked in wch they will be overtaken in a moment." As is typical of his religious writings, Vane describes Christ as the Mediator from the beginning of time, so that it is not anachronistic to say that Elihu shows the benefit of being a holy man whose sins are folded in Christ.[87]

Perhaps most suggestive in their anticipation of *Paradise Regain'd* are the claims Vane makes on the inward turn of the chosen as they wander in the wilderness. In Milton's brief epic God the Father turns to Gabriel and tells us that he means to "exercise" the Son "in the Wilderness" (1.155–6). Vane similarly tells us that the afflictions suffered by the righteous are intended for their spiritual benefit: "if they be not exercised in a life of faith their best professions will turn into a life of vanity therfore God chastens them as sons

---

[83] Ibid., 4, 7–8.   [84] Ibid., 57.   [85] Ibid., 118.
[86] Ibid., 186; see also, 135, 142.   [87] Ibid., 159, 130–1.

not as bastards." Commenting immediately thereafter on Job 35.13—"Surely God wil not hear vanity, neither will the almighty regard it"—Vane tells us that it "teaches gods people what their duty is in ys day, tis to be looking more inward, entering into a more secret fellowship with God, till his indignation be overpast."[88] The righteous man may suffer afflictions of sense, but "injoys feasting between god, & his own soul"; that feast is figured as a "refreshing" song "in the dark night," making the suffering of the world "light" when compared to the weight of sin.[89] In *Paradise Regain'd* we find Jesus pursuing his "holy Meditations" into the wilderness (1.195). A rare bardic interjection—"ill wast thou shrouded then, / O patient Son of God" (4.419–20)—emphasizes the stormy night that Jesus endures in the fourth book, only to have its afflictions quickly evaporate in lovely lines on the tuneful birds of morning who "After a night of storm so ruinous, / Clear'd up their choicest notes in bush and spray / To gratulate the sweet return of morn" (4.436–8).

As in Calamy's farewell sermon, David appears in Vane's commentaries not in his kingship, but as a "righteous man" to whom "the lord gives a reward even in his affliction," quite like the "Shepherd lad" to whom Milton's Jesus refers (2.439). "The Lord deprives us of the life & comfort of sense," Vane continues, "& gives us a better Good the keen eye of faith."[90] For Vane's Elihu consolation does not arise from "the wisdom of the Creature," but rather depends on "Gods wisdome"; only divine consolation can quiet the "fretting thoughts" that "lye close in a good man."[91] It is through the wisdom that "christ ministers to his people" that we become "wiser then the beasts of ye feild [*sic*], wiser then our enemies nay wiser then the angells & in Gods light we are made to see light," as seen in the Manna of Deuteronomy 8, which "trained" the fathers up in God's wisdom.[92] "[H]e who receives / Light from above," Milton's Jesus "sagely" tells us, "No other doctrine needs" (4.285–90), a reliance on God that he also figures with reference to Deuteronomy 8.[93]

Through Vane's commentaries we may also clarify the ways in which the theodicy of *Paradise Regain'd* is in harmony with that of *Samson Agonistes*. All of these works, Vane's and Milton's, focus on worldly trial as exercise leading to fuller spiritual awakening. "It sho[ul]d exceedingly stir up the excersise of our faith whenever we are brought to straights & tryalls," Vane

---

[88] Ibid., 150–1.   [89] Ibid., 120, 128.   [90] Ibid., 120.
[91] Ibid., 153, 125.   [92] Ibid., 140.
[93] Vane cites Deut 8.16; Jesus paraphrases Deut 8.3.

tells us, "then let our spirituall sense be awakned." "There is a weak side" Vane declares in his final sermon, "in the best of gods Saints, wch will be sure to shew it self in the day of tryall."[94] Even "the choicest saints of god ... cañot forbear making provision for the flesh & if the lord would suffer it they would never give over gratifying their fleshly lusts."[95] We see beyond such fleshly concern only with "heavenly eye salve," rather than through a human "judiciall blindness" that Vane likens to the Church of Laodicea, which "did not know the very light she had was blindness." God's wisdom is "above the reach of our naturall understandings ... therfore will the Lord pour out ys annointing on us; without it 'tis no wonder if we judg God, his wayes, & people since we want ys wisdome wch is from above."[96] The trials of the suffering saint should thus be borne with "chearfullness," "the hatred & malice of men for righteousness sake ... for the Lord will return & will have mercy for Zion"; the Lord tries the faithful by exposing them to worldly powers "then he comes forth & avenges their wrong."[97] Where the Saints had come to rely on their outward strength rather than inner light, Vane's final sermon states that now God "sweeps all those confidences off the stage."[98] These are precisely the lessons of Milton's brief tragedy, which shows us one of God's chosen falling prey to fleshly lusts, straying from his divinely appointed path, resisting the limited reasoning of his agonists, and finally following heavenly light.[99]

Through this manuscript we might add to our understanding of the proximity of Milton's and Vane's ideas. They agreed, of course, on the Root and Branch elimination of episcopacy in the early 1640s. Milton's nineteenth-century biographer Masson hazarded that Vane was the acquaintance mentioned in Cyriack Skinner's biography as approaching Milton with the offer of becoming the republic's Secretary of Foreign

---

[94] Ibid., 170, 4.   [95] Ibid., 13.   [96] Ibid., 157, 155.
[97] Ibid., 149, 248.   [98] Ibid., 5.
[99] As Milton does in *Samson Agonistes*, Vane makes us keenly aware that God's return will be a time of judgment: God may "suffer" the trampling of His people "for a while but he has a time to right them & yt nation yt wrongs them God will judg"; by granting prosperity to the wicked, the Lord "expose[s] ym & lay[s] ym open to a day of slaughter"; the righteous must not forget in their moment of trial that God shall "crush [the wicked] to powder & hide them in the dust" (ibid., 166 [misnumbered 165], 163, 230). In a way that might remind us of Manoa or the Danite Chorus in *Samson Agonistes*, Job's three friends can sometimes play a part in a hero's self-discovery, though they do not directly enjoy the benefit of God's favor: "these 3 men understood not Jobs case, but condemned him of hypocrisy, ignorant they were of the end the lord had in Jobs sufferings & of the true christian Gospell frame of spirit yt God had to bring forth in him" (245). We see this especially in Milton's introduction of Samson's father, Manoa, serving as a relic of the old law whose logic is surmounted by the inner refreshing and faith in things not seen that will ultimately mark Samson as a hero of faith under a "Gospel frame of spirit."

Tongues; though that speculation has fallen out of favor, we do know that Vane was among the twenty-one members present in the Council meeting where Milton's appointment was approved.[100] Their mutual involvement in foreign relations would have put them in close contact in the republic's first years.[101] Milton's sonnet was likely composed as a response to Vane's sagacity in handling naval confrontation with the Dutch in 1652 and to Vane's anonymous pamphlet in the same year, *Zeal Examined*, which urged greater liberty of conscience than more conservative Independents like Ireton and Cromwell were willing to allow—Thomason's date for the pamphlet is June 15, and Sikes claims that the sonnet was sent to Vane on July 3. This may explain why Milton's sonnet to Vane praises his knowledge of "spirituall powre & civill, what each meanes" (10) where the sonnet to Cromwell is more hortative: "Helpe us to save free Conscience from the paw / Of hireling wolves whose Gospell is their maw" (13–14).[102] Though Milton served in the Cromwellian regime to which Vane objected, Sir Henry would return to public life in the Parliament of Richard Cromwell, a moment at which Milton mounts a return of his own to vernacular controversy and does so, as we have seen, with ideas very close to those of Vane and Henry Stubbe. There is every evidence to suggest that Milton with Algernon Sidney lamented the execution of Vane as the loss of England's "greatest ornament."[103]

The late proximity to Vane shows how Milton's unitary popular sovereignty had adapted itself to an anticipation of the rule of the Saints.[104] At the

---

[100] See Parker (2003) 1: 354, and 2: 980n107 on the copy of *Defensio* sent to Vane by the printer William Dugard.

[101] Vane was treasurer of the navy and one of the new republic's most skilled diplomats. See Mayers (2015) and Rowe (1970) 134.

[102] *Zeal Examined* is published anonymously by Calvert, see [Vane] (1652). On the Vane sonnet and naval battle with Holland, see Dzelzainis (2009), 550. The very plausible suggestion that Milton's sonnet is a response to *Zeal Examined* is advanced by Mayers (2015). See also Parker (2003) 1: 413–14, 417, 2: 1015n3; Campbell and Corns (2008) 246, 280 describe the Vane and Cromwell sonnets as "twin" sonnets, noting their similar syntax.

[103] "The Character of Sir Henry Vane by Algernon Sidney," available as Appendix F of Rowe (1970) 282. Milton's emphasis on acting in God's time differs from the political machinations with England and France by which Sidney hoped to restore the republic. See Greaves (1990) ch. 1.

[104] Perhaps one indication of Vane's continued reputation is the especial ire reserved for him in William Baron's attack on those regicides praised by Ludlow. Baron places a comparably long attack on Vane last in his catalogue of regicides, and brands him a fanatic expressing "whatever came uppermost in his *freakish* head, [so] that the common Appellation men gave him was, *Sir Humerous Vanity*." During his retirement under Cromwell, the temperamental and self-interested Vane "Tyranniz'd over his Tenants and Neighbours, obliging the former to take new *Leases*." All this to quash Ludlow's suggestion that Vane's successful management of the navy was a mark of the kind of even-tempered and public-spirited individual who rose to the fore under the Commonwealth. See Baron (1700) 95, 100.

same time we must recognize that both Milton and Vane were reluctant to declare when that reign might occur: it is the error of Satan in *Paradise Regain'd* to assume that a lack of "date prefixt" in "the Starry Rubric" makes Messiah's terrestrial reign uncertain: "eternal sure, as without end, / Without beginning" (4.391–3). Whatever storms Satan and his late-Stuart servants are able to produce, their fleeting discomforts are easily brushed aside as "false portents" that make no less inevitable the monarchy "that shall to pieces dash / All Monarchies" (4.491, 149–50).

Schmitt, Milton, and the "People"

Addressing our own moment, when a politics of the "people" has been appropriated by reactionaries of varying kind, Alain Badiou frames the questions that might relend the term a progressive charge: "Can't the 'people' be a reality that underlies the progressive virtue of the adjective 'popular'? Isn't a 'popular assembly' a kind of representation of the 'people' in a different sense than the closed, state-controlled one masked by adjectives of nationality and the 'democratic' legalization of sovereignty?"[105] Schmitt's sense of himself as a theorist of popular sovereignty offers an excellent case study in the perils of a unitary sovereignty founded on the insuperable will of an exclusivist "people." But we should be reluctant to seal him up safely as a Nazi artifact. His thought in fact highlights an under-appreciated aspect of the modern political imaginary: the persistence *within* notions of popular government of the idea of right rule by a fit people. One of the key insights of Paul W. Kahn's work on political theology is that liberal political theory avoids the question of sovereignty and so can treat state violence only as a deviation from a rightly constituted liberal democracy, a tendency especially apparent in American political thought of the Cold War era: "Rawls and his followers never took seriously the violence of the state . . . It is as if the violence of the United States is simply an accidental characteristic of an essentially liberal political order: a posture forced upon the liberal state by threats from abroad."[106] If that view was tenable in the face of a Soviet nuclear threat, it has become much less so during the war on terror, where the asymmetry between foreign threat and US state violence is rather more pronounced. Kahn has thus emphasized the ways in which

---

[105] Badiou (2016) 25.   [106] Kahn (2011) 7.

the US constitutional tradition has demanded love and sacrifice even as it espouses a language of Enlightenment republicanism. Here again, recourse to the "people" underwrites the state's extra-legal violence and abrogation of liberal procedures, and so seems a political category that is only destructive. This, Badiou's worry runs, is a conclusion eminently convenient for the modern liberal state, which aims to replace, indeed considers it a virtue to replace, a "people" capable of political will with a "population" to be perennially managed.

As Wendy Brown observes, Foucault offers insights on the emergence of the "population" as the object of state activity, of the ways in which power lays claim to *homo economicus* or *homo juridicus*. But Foucault, Bown continues, tends to ignore *homo politicus*:

> there is an absent figure in Foucault's own formulation of modernity, when he offers us the picture of *homo economicus* and *homo juridicus* as the two sides of governance and the human being in modernity. Foucault just says you've got on the one hand the subject of interest, *homo economicus,* and on the other hand *homo juridicus,* the derivative from sovereignty, the creature who is limiting sovereignty. But for Foucault there's no *homo politicus,* there's no subject of the demos... [I]sn't it striking for a French thinker that there's no democratic subject, no subject oriented, as part of the demos, toward the question of sovereignty by or for the people?[107]

Appearing in Aristotle as the *zoon politikon,* the term *homo politicus* describes a sociability fundamental to human identity that seeks a public life grounded in virtue and justice. Though Brown is certainly onto something in this observation, if we were to summon Foucault to respond to the charge of neglecting *homo politicus,* he might say that the history of the modern state is one of creating subjectivities that marginalize or silence the truly democratic subject: rather than justice, we have the liberal administrative state or a neoliberal governmentality that defines all forms of social action in market terms. On this reading, it is exactly right that *homo politicus* is absent in a taxonomy of modern apparatuses of power.

The absence of *homo politicus* in the liberal state is one of Schmitt's driving concerns, and we can productively think of his project as seeking to recover the subject of the *demos*: his focus on sovereignty reflects a

---

[107] Celikates and Jansen (2012) 70.

broader desire to revive a politics where collective identity finds expression in sovereign decision. In *Political Theology*, Hobbes is the last European thinker to retain the "decisionistic and personalistic element in the concept of sovereignty."[108] As we have seen in chapter 1, Schmitt's readings of Hobbes are more ambivalent than would appear from this assertion, and he consistently worries that the "natural-scientific" approach to politics with which he associates Hobbes is an early precursor of legal positivism, the dominant theoretical movement of his moment against which he consistently strains. In his late work especially, Schmitt claims that Hobbes paves the way for a full conversion to the mechanistic state: the "personalistic" element of sovereignty is "drawn into this mechanization and becomes absorbed by it."[109] It is precisely this mechanization that occludes and neuters the political, founded, in its modern instantiations, in the unity of a people adopting a posture of war against enemies threatening their way of life. And when the political is so occluded, the state is vulnerable to the opposite of popular sovereignty: the advancement of interest groups seizing state power in a way that promotes their particular concerns. This, in Schmitt's terms, is the fatal flaw of the liberal state, which replaces a "politically united people" with "on the one hand, a culturally interested public, and, on the other, partially an industrial concern and its employers, partially a mass of consumers."[110]

The organic unity of free citizens animates Milton's politics, which can endorse exercise of the power of the sword to establish the normal situation of rule by the *pars potior et sanior*. So there seems as much common ground between Milton and Schmitt as there is between Hobbes and Schmitt. Making that common ground visible suggests an alternate narrative of Milton's place in intellectual history, not as bending toward Enlightenment liberalism, not as looking back to classical republicanism, but as resisting both absolute monarchy and the expansion of democracy in a way not untypical in modern political thought. In Milton, as in Schmitt, we see a politics of crisis making especially keen the desire to have sovereign power reflect the will of the people as a political unity.

Noting this common ground raises the question: are the differences between Milton and Schmitt only historical, or are they also theoretical?

---

[108] Schmitt (2005), *Political Theology*, 48. On the complexities of this assertion, see chapter 1 and epilogue.
[109] Schmitt (2008b), *Leviathan in the State Theory*, 98.
[110] Schmitt (2007), *Concept of the Political*, 72. See also Wall (2012) 78–86.

Context rightly conditions a great deal of our response to texts and thinkers—it is why Schmitt's anti-Semitism is a good deal more horrifying than Martin Luther's. If Schmitt and Milton share an affinity for unitary popular sovereignty founded on a worthy "people," then context may be the chief difference between them. Each seeks to mobilize political will against prevailing institutions deemed destructive precisely because they are indifferent or deleterious to such mobilization. For Milton this is rule by the bishops and king, tyrannous in their indulgence of license. For Schmitt it is the factionalism of parliamentary democracy and the liberal logic underpinning it, which seeks to silence or defer the political so that powerful interests can maintain control over public life; this is to be countered by awakening the people's sense of unity in a shared way of life. The similarity of ideas is hiding in plain sight, occluded by distracting dissimilarities of context. Milton was an agent of England's seventeenth-century republic, which often, if not always with great precision, has been seen as inaugurating the modern relationship between crown and Parliament, or, more distantly, as anticipating the Enlightenment republican experiments of America and France. Schmitt was an agent of a Nazi regime that has become to the modern imaginary what Satan was to the medieval imaginary: the source and measure of all evils befalling humanity. Our views of these contexts are poles apart.

If the differences of context are stark, the differences of ideas are more subtle, and largely center on each thinker's relationship to modernity's upheavals, social, institutional, legal, and intellectual. In the terms we have been developing in this book, Milton adopts a "red" unitary popular sovereignty where Schmitt adopts a "black" one. These are fundamentally opposite postures on the relationship between sovereign power and society, with one seeing rightly exercised sovereign power as advancing the progressive energies of the polity it governs, and the other seeing it as imposing order upon potential chaos. But even as the "red" variety names a certain imagining of the role of the sovereign, it is not at all "progressive" in any grand sense of that term: so naming a politics makes no claim for the enlightenment or desirability of any of its substantive claims. Milton interprets the seismic event of Reformation, with its splintering of Western Christendom, as an opportunity to embrace a politics giving fullest possible expression to vigorous spiritual and intellectual seeking. He offers a high humanist version of the Puritan impulse to reform top to bottom, to leave no aspect of public or private life governed by stale custom potentially stifling to the pursuit of calling. This is why he virulently opposed Roman Catholicism and the canon law, the bishops and established church, the Stuarts and their courtiers. His is a virtue-based politics assuming that virtue takes many, and sometimes conflicting, forms. He also took an unpardonably narrow view of politically valuable virtue, so that he deemed the vast majority of individuals to have little to offer—most obviously women, non-Protestants, and non-Europeans. We thus may place Milton firmly within views of liberty in the European West premised on, and indeed animated by, exclusion undertaken in the name of progress—the views driving Lisa Lowe's reading of the liberal tradition as furnishing logics of imperial governance more reliably than principles of equality.[111] Or, in the language of Miltonic Tacitism, prudent advancement of the cause of liberty depends upon placing restrictions on the majority, who are incapable of using it to good effect.

Schmitt, by contrast, sees the Reformation as throwing a wrench in the *complexio oppositorum* by which the medieval Roman Catholic Church synthesized rational and vital, formal and concrete in a way that no other imperium has ever achieved.[112] Modern politics is a story of loss and inevitable failure, where various settlements emerging from violent conflict can never repair the divisions that brought about their existence.[113] Schmitt thus tends to see the diversity and polyphony of modern society as a perennial threat to political stability. This is why his political thought seems always to be yearning for a lost past of powerful, traditional institutional forms that to his mind promise a sense of unity, whether monarchy or papacy. We have lost the unity by representation of absolutism, whereby "*L'État c'est moi* means I alone represent the political unity of the nation," and so must rely on a unity of "identity," which exists "by virtue of a strong and conscious similarity, as a result of firm natural boundaries, or due to some other reason."[114] While I have emphasized in this chapter that Schmitt is a theorist of popular sovereignty, an aspect of his thought that can tend to be neglected, we must also recognize that he comes to be so as a grudging concession to the conditions of modern politics: any modern theory of sovereignty, Schmitt laments, simply must be a theory of popular sovereignty by virtue of the predominance of this concept in the modern political imaginary. This is an even more reactionary relationship to modernity than

---

[111] Lowe (2015), esp. ch. 4.
[112] See Schmitt (1996), *Roman Catholicism and Political Form*, 8.
[113] See Sitze (2012) 50.
[114] See Schmitt (2008a), *Constitutional Theory*, 239. Georges Didi-Huberman similarly notes Schmitt's "nostalgia for monarchic power"; see Didi-Huberman (2016) 67.

that of Hobbes, an intellectual guide by whom Schmitt ultimately feels betrayed—a point to which we shall return in the epilogue of this book.

To put it differently. A person so inclined could engage in a bad-faith reading of Miltonic politics by which it would advance a vision of the "people" not at odds with present-day progressivism: it is a sovereignty of powerless bearers of truth in the mode of to come. And it demands that magistrates anticipate and enable the disappearance of the state at the moment when the true people appears, to govern in a manner conscious that the state is a temporary institution preparing the way for the arrival of Truth. To mistake this passing nature of sovereign power is to do the work of Antichrist. In this way, Milton's late parliamentarianism is not that of Enlightenment republicanism, which, as Schmitt remarks, aims to assemble the minds fittest to govern by reason alone; nor is it that of the present-day liberal state, which, as Badiou remarks, summons the "people" only to perpetuate the state's existence. Instead Milton might be forced to advance what Badiou calls "a politics that would put an end to politics," becoming a champion of the "people" who have "a positive sense only with regard to the possible nonexistence of the state," and implying "the disappearance of the state itself, from the moment that political decisions are in the hands of a new people assembled on a square, assembled *right here*."[115] This is deferred to a point in the future: it is a gathering of real existents, but they are invisible to us and will assemble we know not when or where.

---

[115] Badiou (2013) 109 and (2016) 31, 27.

4
Marvell's Dread of the Sword

Cease quoting laws to us who have arms girt about us!
                                        —Pompey, in Plutarch's *Lives*

If these the times, then this must be the man.
                                        —*The First Anniversary*

The carefully qualified praise of Cromwell in the above line from the *First Anniversary* reveals a good deal about Marvell's views on political power.[1] Perhaps we are on the eve of the Apocalypse, in which case Providence guides the contraction of time visible in the Protectorate's hyperactive first year. But Marvell also makes clear that God's calendar is beyond the ken of "mortal eyes" (142), strongly implying that any eschatological justification for Cromwell's sweeping actions could be entirely baseless. Thus the *First Anniversary* sustains some of the ambivalence of Marvell's first Cromwell poem, the *Horatian Ode*, which lays bare the violence of a climacteric shift in political authority—be it the inauguration of the English Commonwealth or of the ur-republic Rome, both erected on the cornerstone of a severed head—so that celebration of the achievements of power politics are always also celebrations of bloodshed. In the line above, Plutarch's Pompey, much more than his counterpart in Lucan, reveals a quality never far from our attention in Marvell's portraits of Cromwell: even a modest and dutiful general will impose his will in the teeth of the law. Marvell registers these sentiments even as he crafts an epideictic poetics reflecting the values of the Commonwealth and Protectorate.

This is political theology, Marvell style: if modern political concepts are secularized theological ones, then for Marvell they do not carry with them the absolute value of the sacred but rather are never free of the profane. He is keenly aware that a single sovereign power decides on the state of exception, and that even when such decisions are necessary they carry an undercurrent

---

[1] Epigraphs are from Plutarch (1917), 137 [par. 10] and Marvell (2007), *First Anniversary*, line 144. Parenthetical references to Marvell's poetry are to this edition.

Sovereignty: Seventeenth-Century England and the Making of the Modern Political Imaginary.
Feisal G. Mohamed, Oxford University Press (2020). © Feisal G. Mohamed.
DOI: 10.1093/oso/9780198852131.001.0001

of brutality for its own sake. In what could be a reading of the *Horatian Ode*, Tacitus has the jurist Gaius Cassius declare that "All great examples carry with them something of injustice—injustice compensated, as against individual suffering, by the advantage of the community."[2] A poet coming of age with the advent of the Long Parliament might readily see a Polybian dividing and balancing of sovereignty as a delusion, a refusal to acknowledge the zero-sum game playing itself out between constitutional branches vying for supreme authority. As Warren Chernaik suggestively observes, Marvell tends to accept the core principles of conquest theory, or *de facto* political authority, stated by Marchamont Nedham at the height of the Engagement Controversy: "the *Power of the Sword* ever hath been the Foundation of the Titles to Government" and "the People never presumed to spurne at those Powers, but (for publique Peace and quiet) paid a patient Submission to them."[3] But Marvell also tends over his career to favor a legalist expansion of the political tent, an impulse that one certainly does not detect in the reference to Horace closing Nedham's chapter on *de facto* authority: "Nescio an Anticyram ratio illi destinet omnem" ("wisdom, I rather think, would assign them all to Anticyra").[4] For all that his allegiance to the Protectorate is real, we do not find Marvell fantasizing about shipping recalcitrant subjects off to an island famous for its abundance of hellebore. Consent to conquest is only one piece of a larger puzzle for him: he emphasizes not mere submission to the power of the sword, but a patient advancement of the rights of the subject slowly limiting and renegotiating the scope of sovereign decisionism.

Put differently, this chapter will argue that the royalist James Scudamore's famous gibe, that Marvell was "a notable English Italo-Machavillian," says a great deal more than it knows.[5] Marvell had internalized many of the lessons of reason of state literature that Annabel Brett aptly describes as "both anti-Machiavellian and profoundly Machiavellian at the same time," and he gives that literature English inflection and application.[6] Francesco Guicciardini had argued that every state is founded in violence and, true to this origin,

---

[2] Tacitus (1931–37), *Annals*, 14.44: "Habet aliquid ex iniquo omne magnum exemplum, quod contra singulos utilitate publica rependitur."
[3] Nedham (1650) 16. See Chernaik (1999) 199.
[4] Nedham (1650) 17. Translation is from Horace (2005), *Satires*, 2.3.83.
[5] Qtd. in Smith (2010) 133, and in Kelliher (2008). Kelliher cites BL Add. MS 15858, f. 135.
[6] Brett (2019) 432. Brett convincingly sees *raison d'état* at work in Marvell's *Horatian Ode*, and suggests that if Marvell spent time in Madrid in 1646-7, he might there have "become familiar not only with Tacitist reason of state in substance but with … poetic understanding of its particular *acutezza*" (434).

does not follow the dictates of conscience.[7] The ruler solidifying his power creates a large web of personal obligations centered on himself, generating a political climate favorable to the pursuit of interest rather than republican magnanimity.[8] Interest is emphasized further still in the writings of Giovanni Botero, where it becomes the prime category of political analysis: "Let it be taken for a settled matter," he declares, "that in the deliberations of princes interest overcomes every other consideration."[9] Even as Guicciardini could praise Florentine republicanism, he recognized that the Medici empire that he served both created and was responsive to a set of political realities utterly opposed to the nurturing of civic virtue. Greasing the wheels of commerce seemed in his world to be the impetus of politics, for all that he retained the republican ideal of cooperating citizens as a political aspiration.

Taking all of this together, we start to come to a complete picture of the reason of state tradition that Marvell inherits. Though an emphasis on competing interests often leads to an embrace of a Polybian dividing and balancing of powers, we will see that Marvell's view of sovereignty is unitary and holds strong debts to Renaissance Tacitism. We said the same thing of Milton, but the differences between the two are stark. For Marvell it seems a simple if also repellent fact that political order is centered on a single person deploying, or threatening to deploy, the force of arms. If Milton had somewhat more idiosyncratically found in Tacitus a source for prudently working toward a republic of merit with sovereignty residing in a supreme senate, Marvell is closer to the mainstream of the period's Tacitism in taking a thoroughly unidealistic view of political order as such.[10] Even if dividing and balancing sovereign power were favorable, and one searches in vain to find a place where Marvell argues that it is, it did not seem to him to be a viable possibility in his time and place. In his Restoration prose he could sometimes speak the language of liberty, but did so in a limited, strategic way, and largely to promote a pro-Parliament faction at the expense of the court party. Such guarding against single rule chimes with Tacitus' perennial worry over the concentration of power in the hands of the emperor, often effected through the machinations of self-interested senators vying for

---

[7] See Viroli (1992) 194, 198.   [8] Ibid., 184, 185.

[9] Botero (2017) 41 [II.6]. See also Malcolm (2007) 94. On Marvell's affinity for the interest theory prevalent in international relations after the Treaty of Westphalia, see von Maltzahn (2008a), esp. 52–5.

[10] The distinction is reminiscent of that between "red" and "black" Renaissance Tacitism, following Toffanin (1921). See the Introduction to this book, as well as Malcolm (2007) 96, and Burke (1991) 484.

preferment. These concerns are especially close to the surface in the *Account of the Growth of Popery*, the most detailed of Marvell's political statements.

But we shall see that the mentality at the core of the *Account* is visible across many of Marvell's writings, early and late, and that the political life he imagines is one of attenuating the exercise of sovereign power, and, in the case of the bishops or Roman Catholics, opposing factions that tend to endorse authoritarian government as a host favorable to their parasitism. By the same standard Marvell opposed those seeking to advance themselves by eviscerating existing sovereign authority in the months following the death of Oliver Cromwell. In both situations powerful groups were willing to overrun state institutions in an aggressive program of self-advancement, rather than to promote the interests of subjects within limits imposed by established order. We have seen throughout this book how thinkers and writers of the seventeenth century are aware that modern sovereignty is increasingly mediated by state institutions. This space where sovereignty is buffered is the mature Marvell's chief sphere of action. The task of the active political subject is to take a measure of the sovereign's propensity for destructive action better to forestall it, lest, in the words of the *Account*, he become the "ill Woodman that knows not the size of the Beast by the proportion of his Excrement."[11]

We might expect this kind of patient, incrementalist approach to liberties from someone who had spent his career in cordoned off rooms where the wheels of government churn at their most glacial pace: those of diplomacy and of the parliamentary committee. Here especially a person skeptical of politics as an intellectual pursuit might feel justified. What idealism Marvell had would be easily crushed in the mill of his daily work in government, with its routines aimed at deferring action and its ample opportunity to observe with quiet scorn the doings of mediocre and venal parliament-men. These are places where political life resembles a meeting of the associate vice provost's subcommittee on revisions to section four of the campus strategic plan.

It is also no accident that such an outlook comes into its full flowering during the Restoration, a period of legal reforms in spite of the excesses of the Stuart court, or, as the eighteenth-century jurist Charles James Fox famously put it, "the era of good laws and bad government."[12] Here it is

---

[11] Marvell (2003) 2: 376. All parenthetical references to Marvell's prose works are to this edition; references to the letters are to Marvell (1967) vol. 2.

[12] Fox (1888) 22.

worthwhile to recall Sir William Blackstone's famous assessment of this moment in English legal history: "the constitution of England had arrived at its full vigor, and the true balance between liberty and prerogative was happily established by *law* in the reign of king Charles the second." Even though "some invidious, nay dangerous branches" of royal prerogative remained, "the people had as large a portion of real liberty, as is consistent with a state of society; and sufficient power, residing in their own hands, to assert and preserve that liberty, if invaded by the royal prerogative." Blackstone goes further still and pinpoints this "*theoretical perfection* of our public law" as taking place in 1679, "after the *habeas corpus* act was passed, and that for licensing the press had expired: though the years which immediately followed were times of great *practical* oppression."[13]

If these the times, then Marvell was the man. If his political *mentalité* is informed by Renaissance Tacitism, his is also a more familiarly modern, legalistic response to the dangers of royal absolutism: good laws passed by the people's representatives in Parliament were the best defense against the expansion of sovereign power. Even so he seems always conscious that such an approach must avoid achieving only a theoretical perfection of public law while practical oppressions grow in weight and number. This explains his uncharacteristically public effort to disgrace the court and church alliance in the mid-1670s, when their growing power seemed to be reaching a tipping point and when an effective opposition was gathering under the banner of the Country party.

As we move now to more specific readings of some of Marvell's works, it will be with this overview in mind. At first glance Marvell looks very much like one of the period's turncoat-poets, joining the likes of Abraham Cowley, Sir William Davenant, John Dryden, Edmund Waller, and George Wither. Just a poet being a poet, navigating an uncertain world, projecting the political views that patrons and potential patrons wished to see, committed only to the continued march of his own verse feet. A chameleon, as in the title of Nigel Smith's recent, magisterial biography. I suggest that this is both true and untrue. Of course there are changes in allegiance discernible in Marvell's writings. But there is also a core approach to politics that proves to be remarkably consistent. In making the case for that core approach, we will look at works from all three major phases of his career, each of which coincides with a moment of political crisis: the early verse, where the

---

[13] Blackstone (1791) 439–40; italics in original. See Cross (1917) 530–2, and Willman (1983) 39–70.

influence of the Cavalier poets is most visible; the Cromwell poems, with an emphasis on the elegy, the one most often overlooked; and the late prose, where Marvell aligns himself with Shaftesbury, albeit with important differences. We will find that the kind of ambivalence toward the power of the sword often associated with the *Horatian Ode* and *Upon Appleton House* is quite typical, and that his anxieties on this power animate a good deal of his rhetoric on the English constitution rightly conceived.

Some of the resonances between Marvell's thought and Schmitt's will be clear. Of central concern to both is that strong factions with narrow, self-serving interests will disrupt, or take over, sovereign authority. But in his late thought Marvell emphasizes that arbitrary rule can be forestalled by advancing the rights of the subject. Schmitt eschews such an emphasis in his trenchant critiques of the liberal state. In the closing section of this chapter, we will focus on an important aspect of Schmitt's writings: the status of pluralism in his thought on sovereignty. It has been suggestively noted that Marvell is both a product and a career-long supporter of a system of civic patronage. Acknowledging *de facto* unitary sovereignty is only one part of his politics, in which order is a dynamic, ongoing negotiation between force and consensus, between the imposition of power holding the nation together and the various spaces of individual and associational liberty limiting the scope of that power. In the pages of this book, he is a unique case study in that his view of sovereignty as such does not point in the same direction as his politics: sovereign power is an unruly, if also necessary, beast that only sometimes, and never fully or entirely willingly, exerts itself in ways aligning with the interests of citizens. In these ways, Marvell may be aligned with Schmitt's arguments on the special intensity of political association within the pluralist state, arguments not fully appreciated by those who associate his work with sovereign decisionism alone.

Rewriting the Cavaliers

Marvell's 1648 commendatory poem on Richard Lovelace's *Lucasta* begins with two simple premises that will inflect his verse for the next half-decade: "Our times are much degenerate" and "Our wits have drawn th'infection of our times" (1, 4). This goes well beyond Herrick's "The Bad Season Makes the Poet Sad," with its nostalgic longing for a return to a "golden Age" of the 1620s and 30s, when the peaceful reign of Charles I and Henrietta Maria seemed especially "smooth and unperplext" by comparison to the

Continent, mired as it was in the Thirty Years' War.[14] Herrick's is also a fantasy of return to the height of his career, in a way that we would not expect of a young poet just starting to make his way in the world. Marvell's poem on *Lucasta* offers a grim view of the very different social world in which a poet must move in the late 1640s—by infected "wits" he seems primarily to refer to writers, rather than his or others' mental faculties. London is no longer a place for polite literary exchange, but a gritty and competitive city where reputation is a weapon used to destroy others:

> These virtues now are banished out of town,
> Our civil wars have lost the civic crown.
> He highest builds, who with most art destroys,
> And against others' fame his own employs.
>
> (11–14)

However much this participates in a rosy fiction of the Tribe of Ben, we can readily imagine Marvell mourning the loss of a world where a self-effacing poet could earn recognition amongst a group of discerning peers. News and polemics had made writing a more rough-and-tumble, intensely public pursuit. Relevant for our purposes is Marvell's perception of this poetic condition as a political one: civic virtue is lost in a world where civil war is a condition of public life extending well beyond the battlefield.[15]

Even as the cluster of poems on Villiers, Lovelace, and Hastings are rightly described as Marvell's most Cavalier verse, it must be with the recognition that they also seem darkly aware of celebrating lost worlds, social, political, and poetic. The Villiers elegy begins with Marvell reading of his subject's death in what is often taken as a news pamphlet.[16] To take it this way may impose a later meaning of the word "news" (2), which is not used as a shorthand for newsbooks until the eighteenth century; in this case "news" could refer to any account of recent events.[17] Marvell may be fresh

---

[14] Herrick (1968), "The Bad Season Makes the Poet Sad," lines 7 and 9.

[15] On the "collapse of the classical ideals" in this poem, see Patterson (2000) 15. McDowell explores Marvell's connections to the Stanley circle, though the slender manuscript evidence of circulated poetry suggests that this was a much more limited forum than we associate with Jonson and the Tribe of Ben; see McDowell (2008) esp. 13–31 and cf. Hirst and Zwicker (2012) ch. 2, Loxley (2019), and von Maltzahn (2019) 43–4.

[16] McDowell (2008) finds parallels to the 29 June 1648 edition of the royalist newsbook *The Parliament Kite*; see McDowell (2008) 166–7.

[17] See *OED* "News" *sb.* 5, citing Swift's *Complete Collection of Genteel and Ingenious Conversation* (1738) as the first example of this usage; cf. *OED* "News" *sb.* 2 ("tidings; the report

from reading the anonymous broadside *Elegie on the Untimely Death of the Incomparably Valiant and Noble, Francis, Lord Villiers*, which Thomason dates July 11, a short four days after Villiers' death on July 7. He seems in some ways to be responding to this bit of poetasting, assuring that Villiers receives a finer tribute. The anonymous elegy makes the inevitable reference to the Trojan war, casting Villiers as Memnon:

> So in his height of youthfull Pride
> 'Fore Troy the beauteous Memnon dy'd.
> Nor with such teares bewail'd was he,
> Though wept for by a Deitie.[18]

As Hesiod tells us, Tithonus and Eos had two sons, Memnon and Emathion, who might parallel the Villiers brothers.[19] Though king of Ethiopia at the outbreak of the Trojan war, Memnon returns to take up arms on behalf his uncle, Priam. The allusion places some distance between the Villiers family and the royal household: though he is a loyalist, Memnon is not one of Priam's sons. The distinction is quite pronounced because Memnon, like Hector, falls at the hands of Achilles; to compare Villiers to Memnon is explicitly to eschew a comparison to Hector.

Also invoked in the anonymous *Elegie* is the moving scene in Ovid's *Metamorphoses* where Aurora weeps over the death of her son Memnon and pleads with Jove that he receive some form of recognition. Jove obliges by bringing the ashes from Memnon's funeral pyre to life in the form of two factions of birds that then fall to war against one another.[20] The *Elegie* alludes to this moment in having Villiers declare from the grave that his "glad ashes . . . shall rise" when each reader of the poem has crowned his

---

or account of recent events or occurrences," first usage 1423) and 3 ("a piece or item of news," first usage 1574).

[18] *Elegie* (1648).   [19] Hesiod (2007), *Theogony*, 984–5.
[20] See Ovid (1916), *Metamorphoses*, 13.600–16: "Jove nodded his consent, when Memnon's lofty pyre, wrapped in high-leaping flames, crumbled to earth, and the day was darkened by the thick black smoke . . . Dark ashes whirled aloft and there, packed and condensed, they seemed to take on form, drew heat, and vitality from the fire . . . At first,'twas like a bird; but soon, a real bird, it flew about on whirling pinions. And along with it were countless sisters winging their noisy flight; and all were sprung from the same source. Thrice round the pyre they flew and thrice their united clamour rose into the air. At the fourth flight the flock divided and in two warring bands the fierce contestants fought together, plying beak and hooked talons in their rage, wearying wing and breast in the struggle. At last these shapes kin to the buried ashes fell down as funeral offerings and remembered that they were sprung from that brave hero."

sword with "a Death like that [he] found." It is a call not only to avenge the
death of Villiers, but to meet cruelty with multiplied cruelty. Even if the
poem voices muted ambivalence about the cult of Villiers in its Memnon
allusion, this final plea is delivered with unfaltering earnestness.

Marvell's elegy takes up similar allusions and themes. He enthusiastic-
ally forms the association that the anonymous elegizer makes a display of
avoiding: he likens Villiers to Hector, bracketing the poem with references
to Virgil's *Aeneid*. The parallel allows him to put a heroic spin on the
ruthless disfigurement of Villiers that would become a sensation in royalist accounts of his death. It also allows for fuller praise of the first Duke of
Buckingham, Francis' father, who becomes a Priam figure by implication
and who is directly celebrated in Marvell's elegy in a way entirely absent in
the anonymous *Elegie*. If the latter does not wish to elide the royalist cause
with a defense of Buckingham, Marvell more exuberantly praises a household to which he had personal attachment.

But on other fronts his praise is more skeptical. The opening lines of the
anonymous *Elegie* celebrate Villiers' beauty alongside his virtue without
hesitation: "in him, Courage, Beauty, Blood, / All that is Great, and Sweet,
and Good" have "their Grave." Marvell similarly casts Villiers as an ideal
chivalric hero, allowing him to paint the final, and fatal, dalliance with
Mary Kirk in a flattering light. But there is a defensive tone to his
celebration of male beauty, one implicitly recognizing that it does not
sort well with the republican masculinism gaining traction as a cultural
value:

> 'Tis truth that beauty does most men dispraise:
> Prudence and valor their esteem do raise.
> But he that hath already these in store,
> Cannot be poorer sure for having more.
> And his unimitable handsomeness
> Made him indeed be more than man, not less.
>
> (41–6)

Marvell allows the clumsiness of "unimitable handsomeness," and its rhyme
with "less," to steal away a good deal of the force of this passage. More
significantly, these lines show awareness that the terms of praise and dis-
praise had shifted: Villiers has to be praised as an exception to the neo-
Roman rule that pleasure and beauty do not rest well with virtue, properly

located in military valour and political prudence.[21] The ideal Cavalier hero in whom beauty and virtue are gracefully intertwined can no longer be celebrated in the straightforward catalogue of the anonymous *Elegie*. With its mention of "prudence," the Villiers elegy touches on the reason of state literature that Marvell ironizes in the Hastings elegy composed the following year, which refers to "maxim[s] of ... state" and "some prince, that, for state-jealousy, / Secures his nearest and most loved ally" (23, 27–8).

It is not surprising that Marvell's Villiers elegy runs out of steam once it has closed the circle on the comparison to Hector, and imagines Villiers stolen away, like Adonis, to "gardens of sweet myrtle" where Venus "kisses him in the immortal shade" (113–14). These gently sibilant and assonant lines bring the poem's literary energy to an elegantly quiet rest. But Marvell goes on for another two verse paragraphs, in an ugly and uninspired celebration of Villiers' slaughter of parliamentary forces and with a call to arms:

> Yet died he not revengeless: much he did
> Ere he could suffer. A whole pyramid
> Of vulgar bodies he erected high:
> Scorning without a sepulchre to die.
> . . . . .
> And we hereafter to his honour will
> Not write so many, but so many kill.
> Till the whole Army by just vengeance come
> To be at once his trophy and his tomb.
>
> (115–18, 125–8)

The effect of this closing maneuver is to collapse any moral distinction between royalist and parliamentary forces, a duplication of the desire for retribution closing the anonymous *Elegie* that in this poem conspicuously falls flat. There is nothing high-minded in this fantasy of building a monument to Villiers out of heaped corpses, so that the opening verse paragraph, where Marvell wishes that Fame would deliver news of the death of "heavy Cromwell" or "long-deceivèd Fairfax" (14, 16) is not a longing for a return to right order so much as it is another expression of the brutal impulses so prominent in the poem's closing lines.

---

[21] Referring to Marvell's engagements of Carew, McDowell similarly finds in the poem an interrogation of Cavalier values; see McDowell (2008) 172–9.

Even as he makes these statements, Marvell fascinatingly places himself in a Cavalier camp whose conventions of genteel conduct put a thin veneer of respectability on the barbarism of war—a veneer that enduring hostilities had stripped away. Where the anonymous *Elegie* introduced the voice of Villiers' ghost, here the poet-speaker himself delivers the final call to arms with a significant "we": "we...will / Not write so many, but so many kill." Marvell also exerts his presence in his personal recollections of Villiers:

> Lovely and admirable he was,
> Yet was his sword or armour all his glass.
> Nor in his mistress' eyes that joy he took,
> As in his enemy's himself to look.
> I know how well he did, with what delight
> Those serious imitations of fight.
> Still in the trials of strong exercise
> His was the first, and his the second prize.
>
> (51–8)

"Strong exercise" here seems to span sex, and battle, and fencing, all treated as equivalent expressions of physical vigor. Ostensibly "I know how well he did" places Marvell with Villiers in the fencing hall, but in context one cannot escape the sexual undercurrent of this remark—either homoerotic or that of a blokey insider. Whatever its nature, the intimacy described plays up obligations of honour and affection put to grim use in a world where sword and armor are no longer guided by noble conduct. Very much a Trojan in this poem where Hector has fallen and virtue fallen with him, Marvell is also an agent in the desperate, ignominious, self-preserving violence that must ensue.

This kind of rewriting of Cavalier poetry, with a strong sense of its obsolescence, is given most economical expression in *The Picture of Little T.C. in a Prospect of Flowers*, Marvell's wonderfully weird poem to the young Theophila Cornewall.[22] From the outset it calls to mind Cavalier imagery of idyllic country life. The first image of T.C. is that of a Flora-like "nymph" who with Edenic innocence names "The wilder flowers" (2, 5). Though giving a lover a "green gown" was a common image of Cavalier "cleanly

---

[22] I am grateful to Edward Holberton for suggesting *The Picture of Little T.C.* as a poem worth exploring in this chapter.

wantonness," T.C. is not on her back submitting to a male figure but alone and on her stomach, gazing on the flowers she commands.[23]

The second stanza makes clear that this is not simple innocence, but a subtle reworking of the relationships fundamental to Cavalier verse: those of natural fecundity, sexual delight, and harmonious social order under the patronage of a benevolent nobility. Order remains mysterious in the poem. All we can know are the visible workings of power:

> [T.C.] only with the roses plays;
> And them does tell
> What colour best becomes them, and what smell.
> Who can foretell for what high cause
> This darling of the gods was born!
> Yet this is she whose chaster laws,
> The wanton Love shall one day fear,
> And, under her command severe,
> See his bow broke and ensigns torn.
> Happy, who can
> Appease this virtuous enemy of man!
>
> (6–16)

The relationship between T.C. and nature becomes a closed loop, inscrutable and impenetrable. The "tell" and "smell" rhyme (7–8) emphasizing T.C.'s command over even the fragrance of the flowers is emphasized further still by the internal rhyme with "foretell" (9). Scent often presages the arrival of a human or divine lover, as in the Song of Solomon: "Who is this that cometh out of the wilderness like pillars of smoke, perfumed with myrrh and frankincense, with all powders of the merchant?" (4.6). In this instance smell does not foretell, but serves only as a sign of T.C.'s rule, whether she is assigning a fragrance to a rose or demanding that tulips have one (28). Here Marvell is taking an image from Edward Benlowe's poem to Theophila Cornewall, *Theophila* (1652), in a strikingly different direction. For Benlowe, Theophila is herself a bud breathing in her own developing perfume, her emerging beauty a sign of grace radiating through her: "Breathe in thy dainty

---

[23] The most famous example of the "green gown" appears in Herrick's *Corinna's Going a-Maying*: "Many a green-gown has been given; / Many a kisse, both odde and even" (Herrick [1968] lines 51–2).

Bud, sweet *Rose*; 'Tis *Time* / Makes Thee to ripened Virtues clime, / When as the Sun of Grace shall spread *Thee* to thy Prime."[24] Marvell transforms Benlowe's image by making Theophila's early command of the roses' fragrance a sign of emerging power that must be chary of affronting the gods.

Similarly, in the conventions of Cavalier verse Love's arrows unsettle all human affairs.[25] That disorder is not a sign of love's higher harmony; here Eros himself is defeated by a virtue paradoxically associated with Satan through the epithet "enemy of man."[26] Marvell's "nymph" surpasses Pan in power and denies love this role in nature. In both of these respects she is defined in ways that brush against the grain of pastoral, and Marvell does not miss the opportunity to imply that this opposition to classical gods typically likened to Christ makes her a Satan figure. We are left only to "Appease" this despot in waiting, whose power is to be admired from a safe distance: the "glancing wheels" of her "conq'ring eyes" will one day "drive / In triumph over hearts that strive" while Marvell is "laid, / Where [he] may see [her] glories from some shade" (18–24).

Yet the gods do still have their say. Even as T.C. is a "darling of the gods" (10), the poem closes with a warning on the wrath of Flora:

> Gather the flowers, but spare the buds;
> Lest Flora angry at thy crime,
> To kill her infants in their prime,
> Do quickly make th'example yours;
> And, ere we see,
> Nip in the blossom all our hopes and thee.
>
> (35–40)

---

[24] Benlowe (1652), Canto 3, stanza 23; italics in original. On similarities to Marvell's poem, see Smith's headnote in Marvell (2007) p. 113.

[25] See, for example, Shirley (1646), *Cupid's Call*, appearing first in his *Poems*:

> Ho! Cupid calls; come, lovers, come,
> Bring his wanton harvest home...
> Let hinds whose soul is corn and hay
> Expect their crop another day.
>
> (1–6)

[26] This subtly dark association of T.C. with Satan gains significance as an assault on pastoral conventions if we recall that Pan was, according to Conti, thought by the ancients to have lost a wrestling match with Eros. In Conti's reading, this shows that "Love quickens the substance of nature into life, and shapes it into all the different forms that define created beings." Conti (2006) 375, 378.

Herrick's famous lyric "To the Virgins, to make much of Time" is significantly recast. The message is not an invitation to pleasure before beauty fades and the opportunity passes—Herrick's "Gather ye Rose-buds while ye may"—but to "spare the buds" so that the exercise of power does not frustrate nature's rebirth. Loss of beauty is here associated with loss of the power to "charm" and "reform" nature, rather than with loss of the ability to attract the opposite sex and to indulge in sensual delight.

The explicit reference to Flora in the poem's closing lines hearkens back to the image of T.C. in the first stanza, which has been associated with Ovid's Flora in the *Fasti*.[27] But the message of the poem is that T.C. is emphatically not Flora; she is a human counterpart aping the goddess in some respects. If T.C. is a kind of human Flora, then she may be a "darling of the gods" more directly: the Italian mythographer Cartari describes Roman rites to Flora as a polite version of celebrating the courtesan Larentia, who, in Plutarch's influential account, spends a night with Hercules.[28] As a reward, Hercules advises her to shower affection upon the first man she meets the next morning. That man turns out, according to Plutarch, to be the wealthy old bachelor Tarrutius, who marries Larentia and leaves his fortune to her.[29] With no heir of her own, Larentia bequeaths this large inheritance to the people of Rome, and is thus celebrated in civic rites. Tertullian and Augustine take up this story and make it widely known to Christian readers—for Augustine it represents the perversity of Roman civil theology, which is willing to give credence to fables and bestow divine status on just about anyone.[30] Marvell, like Ovid, may have in mind the common association of Flora with Larentia.

Is this story under the surface of his play on the name Theophila, "lover of God"? If, as we think, it was composed late in 1652, around the time of the Larentalia, the December festivals to Larentia mentioned by Ovid in the *Fasti* (3.55), then the association would be stronger, but it was most likely composed in the fall, before Marvell's return to London at the tail end of the year.[31] In some ways the allusion would be consistent with the emphases of

[27] See Ovid (1931), *Fasti*, 5.200–14.

[28] Cartari (2012) 184–5. On the association, and confusion, of Flora and Acca Larentia, see also Felix (2008) 375 [ch. 25]; and Ovid (2015) 19 [commentary on 3.55].

[29] Plutarch (1975) 135 [Question 35, "Why do they so honour Larentia, who was a common prostitute?"].

[30] Augustine, *The City of God* [*De civitate Dei*], 6.7. See also Tertullian (2008), ch. 25, which describes Larentia as "the most infamous of prostitutes."

[31] See von Maltzahn (2005) 37.

the poem. Like the implication of a "green gown," it strongly suggests a sexual source of T.C.'s power even as she resists romantic love. Larentia's celebration in civic rites is non-dynastic; like T.C.'s it does not reproduce itself through heirs.

Most importantly, the poem is profoundly anti-Cavalier in its starkly asocial portrait of worldly authority. The kind of human coupling that is an extension of natural fecundity is here replaced by a laying bare of romantic love as a power relationship, one of victor and vanquished. There is no self-perpetuating political and social order here mirroring a self-perpetuating natural order. What we have instead is one darling of the gods ruling absolutely over men until she oversteps her bounds and is punished with death. We should be reluctant to read this witty engagement of Cavalier conventions as a political allegory, but also should not fail to notice that we are witnessing not just a young poet's rivalry with his seniors and contemporaries, but a very different vision of the relationships defining human power. In this brief poem Marvell distances himself from the harmony promised both by a traditional sociopolitical settlement of crown, lords, and commons, and by Benlowes' Neoplatonic language of a higher law working mysteriously through human affairs. An ordering assertion of force is the way of the world. And as with the Villiers elegy, the violence of this imposition of force gives the lie to claims of enlightened, peaceable political settlement founded on harmonious and natural differentials of authority.

Cromwell's Bourgeois Dynasty

By his own account, 1657 is the year in which Marvell becomes active in public service, joining the office of John Thurloe as a secretary of foreign tongues. That account is written in 1673, and under fire of polemical attack from Parker, when Marvell has incentive to massage the evidence: clearly he had attached himself to key commonwealthmen well before this date, serving as tutor in the household of Fairfax in 1649 and as governor of Cromwell's protégé William Dutton from 1653 to 1657. And he certainly seemed to be seeking further preferment in the Protectorate by writing a commendatory poem on the first anniversary of Cromwell's reign. That he was not paid a government salary until 1657 seems primarily attributable to factors well beyond his control: Milton had recommended him to Bradshaw in 1653, likely with his knowledge if not at his request, though he was passed over in favor of Philip Meadows.[32] On the evidence it is difficult to think of him as a conscientious objector to the Commonwealth before 1657, or to take him entirely at his word when in the second part of the *Rehearsal Transpros'd* he describes it as an "usurped and irregular Government, to which all men were then exposed" (1: 288).

Even as we keep all of this in mind, there are reasons to think that Marvell would have found the government under Cromwell to be more congenial after 1657. Perhaps because we now know it to be a very short-lived constitution, we tend to overlook the Humble Petition and Advice passed in the summer of that year—a major advance toward regularity, and a second attempt at an English constitution after the failure of the Instrument of Government, which Marvell praises in the *First Anniversary*. The clear aims of the Humble Petition are firmly to establish elected, triennial parliaments; to pull inclinable nobles into an upper house and to expand the powers of Parliament; and to assert greater parliamentary authority over the military, an aspiration that in the unstable years following the death of Cromwell would sow the conflict and mistrust with leading army officers on which the hopes of the English republic were dashed. As in the Instrument of Government, "the standing forces of the Commonwealth shall be disposed of by the Chief Magistrate, by the consent of both Houses of Parliament" when Parliament is sitting. The document also recognizes that paid soldiers would be loyal ones, setting aside a million pounds per year for the Protector to administer an army and navy.[33]

It is often noted that Marvell's poem on the death of the Lord Protector has a markedly different tone than his two previous Cromwell poems. No longer celebrating a prolific career of military conquest, Marvell's gaze turns to the private Cromwell and his domestic affections. The effect is to emphasize the legitimacy of Richard's succession, not only by thickening the culture surrounding the house of Cromwell but also by associating the son with the finer impulses of the father. Of course the second Cromwell's reign was over by the time Marvell's elegy would have appeared in print, and it was replaced in the *Three Poems* (1659) by Waller's effort—though one should note that Thomas Sprat's elegy, which also ends by praising Richard, did appear in this publication. More to the point, Marvell is casting

---

[32] On patronage relationships in the years following the regicide, see von Maltzahn (2019) 48–53 and Hughes (2019) 64–77.

[33] The Instrument of Government and The Humble Petition and Advice, in Gardiner (1906) 406 [*Instrument* art. 4] and 453 [*Humble Petition* arts. 7–8].

Richard's rule as flowing naturally from the arts of peace nursed by Oliver in his final years. In this sense, he continues in the spirit of the *First Anniversary* to praise the *government* under the Lord Protector as much as he praises the Cromwells themselves.

That Richard ultimately could not wield his father's constitutional authority is lampooned in the tract *Fourty-four Queries to the life of Queen Dick*, which wonders "whether R.C. might not get favour amongst the Ladies, though he hath lost himself amongst the People, if he had but his Fathers *Long Instrument*?"[34] This distills concerns over Cromwellian government later expressed in Bulstrode Whitelocke's *Memorials of English Affairs*, first appearing in print in 1682. In a piece of hindsight masquerading as foresight, Whitelocke offers an account of a November 1652 conversation in which Cromwell expressed a desire to assume the title of king, citing the difficulty of quieting army factions, the ineffectiveness of Parliament, and the concern that English statutes passed without the signature of a king might be open to legal challenge. With no small irony, Whitelocke places in Cromwell's mouth precisely the arguments that the Lord Protector dismissed when being urged to take up the crown in 1657. Completing this turning of the tables, Whitelocke reserves for himself the role of arguing against Cromwell's kingship, claiming that taking up the crown would not give Cromwell any more control over the army or Parliament, since the general had already brought both to heel. Whitelocke further argues that assuming the title of king would reduce the political question before the English people to a choice between the house of Stuart and the house of Cromwell:

> one of the main points of Controversie betwixt us and our Adversaries, is whether the Government of this Nation shall be established in Monarchy, or in a Free State or Common-wealth .... Now if your Excellency shall take upon you the Title of King, this State of your Cause will be thereby wholly determined, and Monarchy established in your Person; and the question will be no more whether our Government shall be by a Monarch, or by a Free-State, but whether Cromwell or Stuart shall be our King and Monarch.... Thus the State of our Controversie being totally changed, all those who were for a Common-wealth (and they are a very great and

---

[34] *Fourty Four Queries* (1659) 4. Thomason dates his copy June 15, placing it shortly after Richard Cromwell's resignation on May 25.

considerable Party) having their hopes therein frustrate will desert you, your hands will be weaked, your Interest streightned, and your Cause in apparent danger to be ruined.[35]

Despite these objections, it was Whitelocke in his role as committee chair who later presented the Humble Petition and Advice to Cromwell, urging the Lord Protector to accept the crown. And that at the same moment when a plot was discovered "by the vigilancy of *Thurlo*, of an intended Insurrection by Major-General *Harrison*, and many of the *fifth Monarchy-Men*."[36]

Such is the climate in which Marvell enters Thurloe's service. The elegy for Cromwell that he would write roughly a year later sets the terms of Richard's legitimacy in important ways. To put it in Whitelocke's language, it is precisely his aim to prevent the controversy from becoming a simple choice between a king Cromwell and a king Stuart, and to show instead that the house of Cromwell embodies Commonwealth values in ways that the house of Stuart never could. This to retain in the Protectoral tent at least some of those adherents to the Good Old Cause whom Whitelocke imagined might abandon the regime, allies who were especially necessary as the Army increasingly became a menacing source of resistance, and who were already uneasy with the royal trappings of Oliver's final years. Richard's slim chance of success rested on a potential alliance of the officers willing to support him, a pro-Parliament faction seeing the new Protector as a lesser evil than a return to the Stuarts, and a monarchist middle party who might be satisfied that the Humble Petition sufficiently resembled the traditional constitution. Even in making an effort to speak to this potential alliance, Marvell may have suspected that the settlement would not hold. Writing to George Downing on the first sitting of Richard's Parliament, he offers a roll call of members, many of them leading republicans, intent on using every parliamentary trick at their disposal to press for parliamentary supremacy: "Sr Arthur Haslerig, Sir Henry Vane, Mr Weaver, Mr Scott, Mr St Nicholas, Mr Reinolds, Sr Anthony Ashly Cooper, Major Packer, Mr Henry Neville, the lord Lambert, and many more" whose "Doctrine hath moved most upon their Maxime that all pow'r is in the people That it is reverted into this house by the death of his Highnesse."[37] One notes that as soon as its name is spoken, popular sovereignty becomes a justification for the sovereignty of

---

[35] Whitelocke (1682) 525.   [36] Ibid., 646.   [37] Marvell (1967) 2: 294.

Parliament, a repetition of the January 1649 resolutions that we saw in the opening pages of this book.

To Marvell's eye such "doctrine" looked like self-promotion masquerading as principle, revealed in its willingness to jettison the "petition and advice" in favor of declaring a single person's powers, or such limited powers as they were willing to concede, as arising "by adoption and donation of this House" (ibid.). The remark recalls the impulse in the *First Anniversary* to emphasize, more than the facts allowed, the constitutional order secured by the Instrument of Government: "Such was that wondrous order and consent, / When Cromwell tuned the ruling Instrument" (67–8). Marvell there makes Cromwell an architect of a new state, the greater Amphion than is Charles I in Waller's poem on the renovation of St. Paul's.[38] (In the event, both comparisons to Amphion would prove dubious: the Instrument of Government was never approved by Parliament, and the renovated St. Paul's was crumbling by the mid-1650s.) Though the Cromwell elegy does not explicitly name the Humble Petition, it is no less invested in preserving the settlement that document provided. The result is a poem on the death of Cromwell that is not only less militaristic than the *Horatian Ode* and *First Anniversary*, but less Augustan and less Providentialist. Its world, strikingly, is that of the novel, where domestic virtues are celebrated and then find public expression in socially constructive ways. Marvell finds a poetic key in which to celebrate a dynastic bourgeois constitutional monarchy.

This was, and remains, an unknown category in the European tradition and true to form Marvell rises to the challenge of creating a suitable brand of epideictic verse. This is the true shared project of the three Cromwell poems: each is responsive to the immediate need for a new kind of public poetry of praise that remains legible within received literary traditions. Marvell adroitly adapts across these poems not the subject of portraiture but the frame, developing economies of praise suited to a rapidly shifting political environment.[39] In this he stands discernibly apart from those poets who do take part in the *Three Poems Upon the Death of . . . Oliver Lord Protector* (1659), John Dryden, Thomas Sprat, and Edmund Waller. Dryden cannot

---

[38] On reference to the Instrument of Government in the *First Anniversary*, see Chernaik (1999) 205; Raymond (2011) 144–6; and Holberton (2008) 108–17. On Marvell's repurposing of the Amphion allusion in Waller's *Upon His Majesty's Repairing of Paul's*, see Norbrook (1999) 344–5.

[39] These are "experiments in praise," as Annabel Patterson terms them; see Patterson (2000) ch. 2. Holberton (2008) similarly finds in Marvell's elegy a "sophisticated formal syntax that questions how the conventions of public praise and grief . . . can offer consolation and guidance appropriate to Oliver's case" (182).

escape a royalist language, placing Cromwell within a tradition of English kingship even as he seeks to distinguish him: "But to our *Crown* he did fresh *Jewells* bring, / Nor was his Vertue poyson'd soon as born / With the too early thoughts of being King."[40] None of these poets strays far from what one might expect to be praised in a Cromwell elegy: mounting a glorious military career, bringing order to a realm divided, proving himself more than kingly in refusing the crown. When Sprat concludes, as Marvell does, by praising Richard, it feels very much like an afterthought; the move has no organic connection to the poem as a whole, with the son being simply praised as "not only heire unto [Oliver's] Throne, but minde."[41]

Marvell recognized that a poem praising the government under Richard Cromwell must not celebrate military achievement in quite the same way as did the *Horatian Ode* and *First Anniversary*. Richard's base of support was certainly not in the Army, as events shortly following his installation as Lord Protector made clear. The poem begins by sharply dividing Providential design from the popular desire to see Cromwell die a general's death. With Marvell's characteristic play on mirroring and perception, the six-line verse paragraph with which the poem opens offers an image of Providence as reflecting only upon itself:

> Now in itself (the glass where all appears)
> Had seen the period of his golden years:
> And thenceforth only did attend to trace
> What death might least so fair a life deface.
>
> (3–6)

The effect of the account of human affairs in the following verse paragraph, also six lines, is to present them as occurring quite apart from, and blind to, this self-contained realm of heavenly direction. The values of "[t]he people" are clearly debased: "what most they fear esteem, / Death when more horrid, so more noble deem" (7–8). Like a theater audience, they "blame the last act.../ Unless the prince whom they applaud be slain" (9–10). The tepid providentialism of the *First Anniversary* that we saw at the beginning of this chapter here grows cool. Now it is not only the sectarians' strident readings of Providence that are impugned, but all those who would see military action as central to political life in the Commonwealth—the kind of energy that

---

[40] Dryden (1659) 3.   [41] Sprat, in Dryden et al. (1659) 29.

Lambert embodied. In this poem, Marvell veers away from the view that "The same arts that did gain / A pow'r must it maintain" (*Horatian Ode* 119–20). Nature had made Cromwell "all for peace," his "mighty arms" exercised in the elegy not in dispatching Irish but in flourishing his baby daughter, Elizabeth (15, 32). Instead of being clad in armor, his "steely breast" here is a mirror reflecting Elizabeth's suffering in her final illness, being clouded by "the damp of her last gasps" and ultimately broken by her departure (73–8).

Human misperception is cleared by the intimacy of this domestic bond. Each reads the other's heart too well, as father and daughter cannot hide the anguish arising from Elizabeth's illness:

> She, lest he grieve, hides what she can her pains,
> And he to lessen her's his sorrow feigns:
> Yet both perceived, yet both concealed their skills,
> And so diminishing increased their ills[.]
>
> (61–4)

The encounter makes public Cromwell's private mildness, of which "the people" are unaware. The poet-speaker's famous declaration "I saw him dead" not only places him in the room with Cromwell's corpse, but draws on personal recollection of the "piercing sweetness" of his glance and his "majestic" deportment (247, 250–1). It is a strategy that we have already seen Marvell employ in the Villiers elegy: casting himself in a supporting role as he composes a political martyrology. If the effect in the earlier poem is a self-implication in the declining righteousness of the Cavalier cause, here it is quite the opposite: his intimacy of access to Cromwell marks him as a discerning reader of precisely those peaceable qualities being associated with father and son. In a world where subjects are increasingly aware that they encounter sovereign power through mediating agents and institutions, Marvell is advertising himself and his poetry as filling this role.

Naturally an elegy on Cromwell has to say something about his military career, and this one does so without allowing it to be the hallmark of his political success at home. The poem deftly shifts the scenery of Cromwell's military triumphs, from British ones of the late 1640s to foreign ones of the late 1650s. In the verse paragraph most directly addressing Cromwell's career in arms, Marvell moves from victories over the Scots at Preston (1648) and Irish at Clonmell (1650), to that over the Spaniards at Fenwick (1658) where with "the sea between, yet hence his prayer prevailed"

(187–90). The kind of instability requiring military intervention within the British archipelago is implicitly a thing of the past; recent victories are on foreign soil. Mention of these military successes is immediately preceded by celebration of England's increased international standing under Cromwell, "Who once more joined us to the continent; / Who planted England on the Flandric shore, / And stretched our frontier to the Indian ore" (172–4). Dryden's elegy takes a similar approach, presenting Cromwell as having won peace at home from which "forraign-Conquests flow."[42]

In the *First Anniversary*, the disorder threatened by the sectarians' Hammish ingratitude, and fear over the loss of Cromwell after his coach accident, is used to solidify support for the Protectorate. In the elegy the home front is presented as already won, despite the attempted uprising in April 1657 by Thomas Venner and the Fifth Monarchists that Thurloe had uncovered, and despite the Cavalier plot of April 1658 prompting Cromwell in his final months to establish a High Court of Justice "for the tryal of Conspirators now in Prison."[43] The narrative of the Commonwealth offered in the poem is in this respect like that in the Humble Petition and Advice, where Cromwell has already restored the realm to "peace and tranquility" and can now turn to "settling and securing ... liberties," where there is "an opportunity of coming to a settlement upon just and legal foundations."[44]

Equally significantly, language typically styling Cromwell a godly general is repurposed to create an image of a godly *pater patriae* wielding a spiritual sword on behalf of left-leaning Protestants. His armor is "that inward mail" of conscience, referring to a favorite sectarian text, Ephesians 6. Marvell likewise invokes the army only to extend Cromwell's care beyond their ranks, in a passage yoking together his paternal regard both for Eliza and for the saints:

> If so indulgent to his own, how dear
> To him the children of the highest were?
> For her he once did Nature's tribute pay:
> For these his life adventured ev'ry day.
>
> (211–14)

The phrase "children of the highest," as Smith notes, is strongly tied to the Army, but Marvell strives to expand its scope of reference. The dangers

---

[42] Dryden (1659) 7.   [43] Whitelocke (1682) 674.
[44] Humble Petition and Advice, in Gardiner (1906) 448 [preamble].

encountered "ev'ry day" include those on the battlefield and in office, so that a case is being made for Cromwell's self-endangerment in campaigns military and political. Army stalwarts would certainly see themselves in these lines, but others could, too. And the fatherly dimension of his character anticipates a catalogue mixing neo-Roman and bourgeois virtues: "Valour, Religion, Friendship, Prudence died / At once with him, and all that's good beside" (227–8). In his simple goodness Cromwell does not resemble Dryden's substitute king so much as he does Fielding's Parson Adams in purple velvet and ermine. The "milder beams" and largely "private" life of Richard are thus entirely consistent with the kind of virtue that the poem has praised in his father, and with the picture Marvell paints, counterfactually, of an England ready for a ruler fitted to "calm peace" (321).

As with the *Horatian Ode*, there is an element of fantasy in the political imaginary of the Cromwell elegy. The earlier ode celebrates a republican order where a general's victories are laid at the feet of a senate wisely pursuing the public good, even as it registers anxieties on just where the new Commonwealth's frenetic militarism will tend and whether its most active general can be contained. The elegy presents England as ripe for the reign of a monarch innocent of the arts of war, one who embodies the pacific virtues of his father. Its effort to thrust armed civil strife into the national past also registers anxiety on the precariousness of the political settlement under Richard. One senses that the elegy is not entirely convinced of its own statements that order will hold without the exercise, or at least the credible threat, of force. The kind of strong sovereign presence of which Marvell is consistently ambivalent is a conspicuous absence in the elegy, replaced by a reign of private decency turned outward to kindly reign. Such a center, in Marvell's politics, cannot hold. The terms by which he celebrates Richard's reign thus suggest the ways in which he must have recognized that it was doomed to fail.

Constitutionality in the Moment of the *Account*

Shaftesbury begins his speech on *Shirley v. Fagg* (1675), a case that had brought the two Houses of Parliament into very heated dispute, with a less than understated claim on its significance: "Our All is at stake."[45] On the

---

[45] Cooper and Villiers (1675) 1.

surface the case seems an innocuous enough appeal of a decision in Chancery, where Dr. Thomas Shirley had lost his case against Sir John Fagg. An estate that had been held by Shirley's family before the civil wars was acquired by Fagg during the Interregnum, and Shirley sought to reclaim it. When he was unsuccessful in his Chancery suit, he appealed to the Lords; under normal circumstances this might have been uncontroversial. But Fagg was MP for Steyning, and the Lords were simultaneously taking up equity petitions involving other MPs—*Crispe v. Dalmahoy* and *Sloughton v. Onslow*—which looked like an aggressive attack on privilege in the eyes of the Commons. The lower house dispatched a message to the Lords warning them not to hear the case, and attempted to serve Shirley with a warrant for breach of parliamentary privilege. This quickly devolved into a battle of arrests. Declaring that he wished to settle the matter without further disturbing the House, Fagg filed a response with the Lords against the order of the Commons; for this his fellow MPs had him sent to the Tower.[46] The Commons also ordered the arrest of the attorneys involved in the Crispe case, and of Crispe himself. Dalmahoy escaped arrest because his case before the Lords was dropped.[47] The Lords' Usher of the Black Rod was then commanded to liberate the *Crispe* attorneys and arrest the Sergeant of the House who had imprisoned them, but he was unsuccessful in the attempt.

Shaftesbury's speech in response to this conflagration is printed twice, once as half of *Two Speeches* alongside a November 1675 address to the Lords by George Villiers, Second Duke of Buckingham, and again in 1679, we think, as *Notes taken in Short-hand of a Speech in the House of Lords*.[48] Both publications are surreptitious, with the former being printed, or claiming to have been printed, in Amsterdam, and the latter indicating no author or printer. Clearly publishing tracts by Shaftesbury and Buckingham recommending the dissolution of the long-sitting Cavalier Parliament could earn a printer some powerful enemies. For Shaftesbury, all is at stake because conceding the point of privilege in *Shirley v. Fagg* to the Commons would be equivalent to nullifying the constitutional independence of the Lords. We can thus hear echoes of the arguments we have seen in this book from William Fiennes, Lord Saye and Sele in his defenses of the constitutional independence of the upper house. Shaftesbury urges his colleagues in the Lords to move immediately to hearing the case, rather than appointing a day to debate whether to hear the case, and presents the appellate role of the

---

[46] See Grey (1763) 113.   [47] Ibid., 219–20, 229.
[48] [Cooper] (1679?), Cooper and Villiers (1675).

Lords as fundamental to its constitutional purpose: "My *Lords*, to these give me leave in the first place to say, that this Matter is no less then Your whole *Judicature*, and Your *Judicature* is the life and soul of the Dignity of the *Peerage of England*, you will quickly grow burdensome, if you grow useless."[49] How prescient that remark now seems.

What's more, the judicial function of the Lords prevents "future *Princes*" from handing out appointments to the realm's law courts as perquisites, an eventuality that would give the crown excessive power and lead it to encroach upon that great English bugbear, liberty of property.[50] Fundamental to English law are that "*the King is King*," that "*the poor man Enjoys his Cottage*," and that "*the Lords House, and the Judicature and Rights belonging to it, are an Essential part of the Government.*"[51] Shaftesbury explicitly dismisses all "reason of State" arguments that would urge the Lords to drop the dispute over *Shirley v. Fagg* in favor of cooperating with the Commons on more pressing issues.[52] Threatening the legal order of the traditional constitution is the prospect of a future with "a King governing by an Army, without his Parliament" and on the basis of divine right kingship, a pernicious notion that Shaftesbury attributes to "Arch-Bishop *Laud*."[53] In many minds, as Shaftesbury well knew, that "future" was not so very distant.

And one of those minds was Marvell's, as the full title of his 1677 tract makes clear: *An Account of the Growth of Popery and Arbitrary Government in England*. Even as he is largely in agreement with Shaftesbury, we can detect important differences in emphasis. Though he acknowledges the controversy surrounding *Shirley v. Fagg* in both *Mr. Smirke* and the *Account*, it is with considerably less alarm than we see in Shaftesbury. In the former tract it is used only to make an allusive gibe against Turner.[54] The *Account* consistently praises Shaftesbury and Buckingham in glowing terms, especially for their opposition to the Oath—they surpass the drafters of the Magna Carta in that they pressed their cause "under all the disadvantages imaginable"—immediately before mentioning the "great Controversy betwixt the two Houses" over the Shirley case (2: 285–6). Here Marvell

---

[49] Cooper and Villiers (1675) 4.   [50] Ibid., 3.   [51] Ibid., 10.

[52] Ibid., 6–7.   [53] Ibid., 10.

[54] Turner, having achieved the secret ambition of all aspiring prelates by arrogating to himself the position of "the whole Representative," suffers an internal dispute between houses before he can pass an order for the public burning of Croft's *Naked Truth*: "what security can he have himself, but that there may rise such a Contest between the Lords and Commons within him, that, before they can agree about this Judicial Proceeding against the Book, it may be thought fit to Prorogue him" (2: 48). For a recent overview of the context of the *Account*, see Goldie (2019).

asserts that the Lords have an "undoubted Right" to take cognizance of the case, being "the Supream Court of Judicature in the Nation," but that some members of the Commons claimed a violation of privilege for political reasons: "the Commons, whether in good earnest, which I can hardly believe; or rather some crafty Parliament men among them...took hold of, and blew the Coales to such a degree, that there was no quenching them" (2: 286). This point of "their own Priviledge" and "ancient Jurisdiction" brought together the two main factions in the Lords, those for and against extension of the Test Act to exclude Catholics from the upper house, making the Commons and Lords so irreconcilable that prorogation became inevitable (ibid.).

"Ancient," as Marvell well knew, was stretching the Lords' historical claim to appellate jurisdiction over the courts of Chancery. As a member of the Commons' committee on privileges, his news letters to the Mayor of Hull carefully report the facts of the "unhappy misunderstanding betwixt the two Houses," and also the "long and late sitting" in which he must have heard rehearsed at length the Commons' arguments against the jurisdiction claimed by the upper house.[55] In the parliamentary debates on the subject, Henry Powle voiced the common recognition that such jurisdiction was "of no antiquity," that the first example of it "was in the case of Magdalen College in Oxford, 18 James," and that precedents of the Lords "taking Appeals" are concentrated "in the Long Parliament, in irregular times."[56] Sir Matthew Hale, praised in the Account for his "Wisdom and Probity of the Law" (2: 291), had authoritatively made the same legal argument in a widely circulated manuscript that would be published in the late eighteenth century as The Jurisdiction of the Lords' House.[57] By "irregular" Powle likely refers to the various reforms of the courts that the Long Parliament had

---

[55] Marvell (1967) 2: 150–1.

[56] Debates (1763) 3: 142. Sir Heneage Finch, who served as Lord Keeper from 1673 until 1682 and became Earl of Nottingham in 1681, has little patience with the Lords' claim of appellate jurisdiction over Chancery courts. In 1673–75 he prepared his Prolegomena of Chancery and Equity; see Finch (1965) 185: "'Tis more natural and legal the appeal should be to the King in person, whose conscience is ill administered. So it was done in Sir Moyle Finch's case, and so it ought to be done in cases before Constable & Marshal. But Lord Coke says the first decree in Chancery was 17 R.2, and that as appears was examined in Parliament. By the Journal of the House of Commons, 18 James, divers bills read for vacating several decrees in Chancery. So it was conceived fit for the legislative power, and not proper for the judicial power of the lords as now is used"; Nottingham here cites Coke, 4 Institutes 83. This passage from Nottingham cited in Hale (1796) clii note n. See also materials collected on judicature in Parliament in BL Stowe MS 1042.

[57] Though first printed in 1796, Hale's tract arises from the controversies surrounding the Lords' appellate jurisdiction in equity causes arising shortly before his death in 1676.

undertaken, from abolition of the privy council's judicial function, to abolition of Star Chamber and the high commission, to the impeachment of judges.[58] The issue had come up, as Marvell notes in his letters, in *Skinner v. East India Company* (1668), as well as in *Slingsby v. Hale* (1669).[59] Both of these cases resemble *Shirley v. Fagg* in that defendants were members of the Commons.

In the event, Slingsby withdrew his appeal, so the contest between the houses did not reach the boiling point. But it did mean that the Lords entered the 1675 fracas having recently studied the question of their jurisdiction, with Marvell's acquaintance Denzil, Baron Holles having prepared a 1669 report for the peers' committee on privileges; even Holles located precedent for the disputed appellate function primarily in the Long Parliament.[60] (That they had performed this work in 1669 explains why Shaftesbury has no truck with those Lords who wish to re-examine the question of jurisdiction in 1675, and wished to move immediately to a hearing of the case.) The reasons for the Lords' serving this appellate role may have been practical as much as they were constitutional or political.[61] Yes, some may have worried that courts of Chancery placed too much power over the disposition of estates in the hands of the Chancellor, and by extension the monarch, and that the Lords should offer some necessary oversight. Equally likely, the increase in cases before Chancery in the late Tudor and early Stuart periods would have created a larger number of aggrieved litigants, and ones who felt as though they had been deprived of an avenue of appeal. As the court expanded its activities, it inevitably reached beyond its jurisdictional bounds with greater frequency: while all points of law ought to have been referred to the common law courts, settling estates, and the handling of petitions of discovery in particular, could raise points of law that Chancery implicitly decided—Shirley's appeal, for example, arises from him issuing a bill of discovery of which Chancery had declared that it had no cognizance.[62]

---

[58] See Peacey (2009) 45–6.

[59] See letter to Mayor Hoare, Marvell (1967) 2: 153: "The whole Contest is too voluminous for Letters: but it resembles that wch you may remember upon account of Skinner and the East India Company, but differing by how much members of Pt are herein concerned."

[60] Marvell reports dining with Holles in November 1677; see his 17 Nov. 1677 letter to Sir Edward Harley, Marvell (1967) 2: 330.

[61] Hart (1983) 63–5 and Hart (1991) 47–50, 240–63.

[62] See Finch (1965) 204. Finch cites the case as illustrating the principle that "equity against a purchaser shall not be": "Sir Thomas Fagg purchased land of the Earl of Thanet in Sussex, which was formerly the land of Shirley. The heir of Shirley exhibits a bill against Sir Thomas Fagg, supposing that the land was entailed, and that Sir Thomas Fagg had by money and great rewards procured a servant of the family of Shirley, with whom the evidences were entrusted, to deliver

(We have seen a parallel jurisdictional issue arise in another prerogative court, that of the Council in the Marches of Wales.) Perhaps because the Lords were serving a function deemed necessary, neither the lower house nor the crown seemed to object to it under James I or Charles I. But by Shaftesbury's lights the upper house had now cemented its claim as supreme court of the realm, and, by extension, made necessary its institutional strength and independence.

Marvell's letters repeatedly refer to the great amount of time that the two Houses spent arguing *Shirley v. Fagg*, to the extent that no other legislation, including the Test Act, could be adequately read or debated. He is palpably frustrated that matters of privilege would come to interfere with passing the legislation that Blackstone would later praise, namely those acts limiting royal prerogative and protecting the liberties of the subject: "The Act against transporting men into prison beyond sea is past the Commons and sent to day to the Lords. That of Habeas Corpus and that of Levying no mony but by P[arliamen]t is under Commitment...The Bill of applying the old Customs only to the use of the Navy and that against Popery are ready to be brought in."[63] Even as the dispute between the two houses consumed a great deal of his time and attention, and paraded tendencies in his parliamentary colleagues that we might expect him to lampoon, Marvell, as we have seen, devotes minimal space to the debate in his prose works of this moment. The closest he comes to endorsing Shaftesbury's view is his passing remark in the *Account* on the Lords' ancient jurisdiction. This endorsement looks even less enthusiastic when we notice that he did not object to a resolution in the Commons declaring that "there lyes no Appeale to the House of Lords from any Courts of Equity," stating in a letter to Mayor Hoare that the "Question passed without contradiction."[64]

---

up the deed of entail *etc.*, and prayed a discovery and relief. Sir Thomas Fagg pleads that he was a purchaser for valuable consideration without notice of any entail at the time of his purchase. Ruled by the advice of the Judges, that he should not answer, nor be compelled in equity to deliver or discover any deed against himself, which way soever he came by it, but let the heir recover it at law by Detinue if he can, for equity will not disarm a purchaser." For details of *Shirley v. Fagg*, see also Hart (1991) 251–2.

[63] Marvell (1967), letter to Mayor Hoare, 2: 149. Eliminated in the ellipsis is mention of a pending act "against Pedlers Hawkers &c.," which emerged from a committee on which Marvell served. See also Marvell (2003) 2: 288, on the "Publick Bills" shelved during the two houses' confrontations over privilege, and von Maltzahn (2005) 162; Seaward (2019) 81–4; *Commons Journals* (1802) 9: 332.

[64] Marvell (1967), letter to Mayor Hoare, 2: 154–55. See 28 May 1675 entry in *Commons Journals* (1802), 346–7: "*Resolved*, &c. That there lies no Appeal to the Judicature of the Lords in

Not surprisingly, Marvell is conspicuously less moved than Shaftesbury is to make sweeping claims for the constitutional necessity of the House of Lords. Shaftesbury presents the Shirley case as an assault on the Peers' constitutional function, which he then presents as an assault on the privileges of property. Marvell tells a different constitutional story. The leitmotif of the *Account* is that a long-sitting House of Commons had been corrupted by the realm's steady slide toward Francophile authoritarianism. Ignoring the Lords' jurisdiction becomes yet one more example of a disregard of rule of law. The English, unlike certain "neighbour Nations" (2: 225), have a special claim to enjoying liberty so long as the law crafted by their representatives in Parliament is upheld. And rightly conceived, Marvell makes clear from the start of the *Account*, that law equally constrains monarch and subject:

> here the Subjects retain their proportion in the Legislature; the very meanest Commoner of England is represented in *Parliament*, and is a party to those Laws by which the Prince is sworn to Govern himself and his people ... we have the same Right (modestly understood) in our Propriety that the Prince hath in his Regality; and in all Cases where the King is concerned, we have our just remedy as against any private person of the neighbourhood, in the Courts of Westminster Hall, or in the High Court of *Parliament*. (2: 225; italics in original)

As in Shaftesbury, *lex* is firmly above *rex* in this exordium. But there seems little room here to grant the Lords exceptional status. Marvell is leaning on the broad representation of subjects to argue that Parliament as a whole must be taken as the supreme lawmaking body in the realm. It is on this basis that he later suggests the superiority of the Commons to the Lords:

> although the House of Peers, besides their supream and sole Judicature, have an equal power in the Legislature with the House of Commons, and as the second Thoughts in the Government have often corrected their errours: yet it is to be confessed, that the Knights, Citizens, and Burgesses there assembled [i.e. in the Commons], are the Representers of the People of England, and are more particularly impowred by them to transact concerning the Religion, Lives, Liberties, and the Propriety of the Nation.
> (2: 299)

Parliament, from Courts of Equity. *Resolved*, &c. That no member of this House do prosecute any Appeal from any Court of Equity, before the House of Lords."

The fatal flaw of the Cavalier Parliament, by Marvell's reckoning, is that one-third of the Commons held "beneficial Offices under his Majesty" (ibid.), making them more inclined to serve the monarch than their constituents and also raising the ambitions of those members who had not yet acquired such offices. In this way the *Account* sustains many of the core concerns of the *Advice to a Painter* poems, with their sense that the corruption and incompetence of the court party was rapidly eroding political and economic life in the realm. To suggest anything other than the constitutional centrality of a fully independent Commons is to infringe on the liberty of the subject, who has a right to laws crafted and administered by a faithful representative.

This is a Commons-centric view of English liberty much more than it is an argument for the balancing of the three estates. But Marvell is keen on downplaying differences with Shaftesbury and Buckingham, who are important allies in the emerging Country party even if ones that had not yet been cultivated as personal connections. The remark on the Lords' "ancient jurisdiction" is consciously a sop to their grievances. Legitimate authority in the *Account* arises from representation of the people, rather than a balancing of estates that would justify the institutional strength of the upper house.

And yet this expansive role for the Commons jars somewhat in the *Account* with the great space devoted to aspects of law over which Parliament had very little oversight: the drafting of treaties and negotiation of foreign alliances. Here the parliamentarian, and, by extension, the subject he serves, is reduced to toothless editorial remarks on the benefits of peace and free trade, on the folly of provoking the Dutch and cozying up to the French. We might recall the *Advice to a Painter* poems, and especially the *Second Advice*, with its strong criticism of the Second Dutch War. In this poem Marvell's anxieties on the power of the sword express themselves as a strong opposition to war that exposes its violent realities, most explicitly in the account of the death of Charles Berkeley, Lord Fitzharding and Earl of Falmouth, at the side of the Duke of York:

> Falmouth was there, I know not what to act:
> Some say 'twas to grow Duke, too, by contact.
> An untaught bullet in its wanton scope
> Quashes him all to pieces and his hope.
> Such as his rise such was his fall, unpraised;
> A chance-shot sooner took than chance him rais'd:
> His shattered head the fearless Duke distains,
> And gave the last-first proof that he had brains.
>
> (181–88)

Fitzharding's brain spatter recalls the anti-militarist spirit of Ovid's *Meta-morphoses*, which could be equally grotesque in its accounts of battle—one might think of Theseus hurling a mixing vat at the head of Eurytus, who "spouting forth gouts of blood along with brains and wine from wound and mouth alike, stumbled backward upon the reeking ground."[65] Even so, there are moments across the *Painter* poems where military heroism is praised with a straight face, so long as it flows from a genuine spirit of national duty. What the poem really despises is that the crown's military powers have become an extension of court politics, making war not only disgusting in itself but also expanding the political and economic harm caused by the ambitions of courtiers hoping for a lucky bit of preferment. The effects of the war are highly destabilizing:

> Thus having fought we know not why, as yet
> We've done we know not what, nor what we get.
> ......
> If to discharge fanatics, this makes more;
> For all fanatic turn when sick or poor.
> ......
> If to make Parliaments all odious: pass.
> If to reserve a standing force: alas.
>
> (317–28)

These lines anticipate the pacifism urged in the closing address to the king: "Let Justice only draw: and battle cease. / Kings are in war but cards: they're gods in peace" (367–8). Sweeping as these closing lines seem, they are tied to a set of very specific harms caused by the sovereign's over-willingness to wage war: the corruption of the city's independence, the reduction of Parliament's role to generating supply, the creation of opportunities for courtiers to engage in empty displays of service, the rise in sectarianism that must accompany rising political disaffection, a further slide toward a standing army. Once the gates of the temple of war are opened, power becomes concentrated in the hands of the sovereign and his inner circle—the king starts to resemble Caesar or Domitian as Tacitus saw them.

To return to the *Account*, we find an important case study in these constitutional tensions in Marvell's handling of Parliament's attempts to recall "his Majestyes Subjects out of the French service," a service that had

---

[65] Ovid (1916) 12.238–40.

been negotiated by the crown (*Account* 2: 288). This becomes a powerful symbol of the constitutional tensions animating much of Marvell's tract, and one to which he returns at several points. Much more than in arguments over supply, we find at stake here a battle over the right to set the terms of the subject's life and death. In crafting a treaty whereby the realm's soldiers serve a foreign power, the male body capable of military service is made property of the monarch. One might see this either as a holdover of medieval feudal service, or, more plausibly, as part of a late Stuart ambition of modernizing on the French model by creating large bureaucratic mechanisms, including a standing army, answering directly to the crown.[66] Even as the French had blessed "intolerable and barbarous Piracyes" against English merchant ships, they "were more diligently then ever supplied with Recruits, and those that would go voluntarily into the French service were incouraged, others that would not, pressed, imprisoned, and carried over by maine force, and constraint" (2: 294). For Marvell this is terribly poor policy. It is also a brazen violation of the subject's most fundamental rights, and a trampling upon Parliament's attempts to defend them. The *Account* gives space to John Harrington's tale of meeting with "two Scotch souldiers in Town returned from Flanders" claiming to have been abducted from home "to be carried over into the French service" and "had been detained in the Publick prisons till an opportunity to transport them" (2:307). As with his willingness to trade in anti-Catholic conspiracy theories surrounding the Fire of London, Marvell is willing here to recount an incendiary rumor that will alarm readers into action against the king's authoritarianism.[67]

Rather than having sovereignty embodied in the monarch, the protection of whom is the primary fact and symbol of sustaining the constitution, it is a violation of constitutional principles to demand that the subject be forced by the monarch to serve a foreign power. But even as Marvell invokes a symbolic language of popular sovereignty, it has the air of rhetorical ornament in an essentially pragmatic and juristic approach to political order. Indeed departure from reason of state appears in the *Account* as an absurd defense of the destructive allegiance to the French:

> one of these our Statesmen being pressed, solved all Arguments to the contrary with an oraculous French question

---

[66] I have in mind Steven Pincus' argument on late Stuart "modernization"; see Pincus (2011) ch. 5.

[67] On the Fire of London, see Marvell, *Account* 2: 236.

Faut il que tout se fasse par Politique, rien par Amitie?
Must all things be done by Maxims or Reasons of State; nothing for
Affection?
Therefore that such an absurdity as the ordering of Affairs abroad,
according to the Interest of our Nation might be avoided, the English,
Scotch and Irish Regiments, that were already in the French Service, were
not only to be kept in their full Complement, but new numbers of Souldiers
daily transported thither   (2: 278–9; italics in original)

Marvell similarly faults Lord Keeper Finch for "too grossly prevaricat[ing]
against two very good *State Maximes*," namely that of Sallust against disturbing
the peace and that of Tacitus against doing little things with great agitation (2:
282–3). Shaftesbury deemed certain constitutional matters to be above the
grimy calculations of reason of state. In this passage, Marvell presents
the determination of "interest" central to reason of state as hewing closely to
the determination of public interest that ought to guide public affairs.

Even Marvell's approach to ecclesiology in the *Historical Essay* on religion
is strongly inflected by the reason of state tradition. The core impulse of the
tract, especially in context of the battles of its moment, is to expose the
bishops' threat to civil, rather than religious, order. The essay's peroration is
a catalog of emperors who had embraced toleration not on religious
grounds, but for "Reason of State, and Measure of Government" (2: 163).
This differs from attempting to enforce bishops' religious innovations,
which makes princes "look upon their Subjects as their Enemies, and to
imagine a reason of State different from the Interest of their People; and
therefore weaken themselves by seeking unnecessary and grievous supports
to their Authority" (2: 170). We cannot miss Marvell's invocation twice here
of *raison d'état* and its central imperative of calculating political interest. The
bishops offer flawed reason of state in seeking to convince princes that stiff
religious uniformity will extirpate opposition; in fact toleration is the
sounder reason of state in that it eschews assertions of force and aligns
with the interest of the people as a whole. Time and again in the *Essay*, this
logic of judicious rule is dispositive. Its central claims are thus in harmony
with Marvell and the Cabal's support of Charles II's 1672 Declaration of
Indulgence for Catholics and nonconformists, which they saw as chastening
the bishops and their parliamentary allies.[68]

---

[68] On the 1672 Declaration of Indulgence, see Dzelzainis (1999) 301–2.

Marvell's political commentary in the moment of the *Account* will remind us of several passages of Tacitus that have come up in our discussion of Milton. As in *The Annals*, representative government is corrupted not just by the monarch or emperor's overreach, but by the tendency of the people's representatives to see "a cheerful acceptance of slavery [as] the smoothest road to wealth and office." Such visible "greed of the officials" breeds mistrust.[69] In the *Annals* promotion of unitary sovereignty is the chosen language of such officials. Marvell saw the bishops and the court party in Parliament in precisely the same way. More than Milton, however, he would be drawn to a figure like Manius Lepidus, who managed to advance liberty without earning the hostility of Tiberius:

> [Lepidus] was, for his period, a man of principle and intelligence: for the number of motions to which he gave a more equitable turn, in opposition to the cringing brutality of others, is very considerable. Nor yet did he lack discretion, since with Tiberius he stood uniformly high in influence and favour: a circumstance which compels me to doubt whether, like all things else, the sympathies and antipathies of princes are governed in their incidence by fate and the star of our nativity, or whether our purposes count and we are free, between the extremes of bluff contumacy and repellent servility, to walk a straight road, clear of intrigues and perils.[70]

For Marvell this would read as a manual for a life of public service under Charles II, where one works assiduously in the committee room on pressing public matters, discreetly avoiding "bluff contumacy" without repairing to "repellent servility." And yet he must have felt that there was an element of chance separating standing and falling, between being punished for his ties to the Protectorate and sitting in the Cavalier Parliament, between being vociferous in his support of Shaftesbury and joining him in the Tower. It is precisely the aim of arbitrary government, Tacitus and Marvell recognize, to nurture this sense of precariousness.

Guicciardini observes in the *Ricordi* that "Cornelius Tacitus teaches those who live under tyrants how to live and act prudently; just as he teaches tyrants ways to secure their tyranny."[71] Through his intermittent, though consistent, references to reason of state, Marvell signals an affiliation with this strain of Renaissance thought, much of it centered on Tacitus. If

---

[69] Tacitus (1931), *Annals*, 1.2.   [70] Tacitus (1931), *Annals*, 4.20.
[71] Guicciardini (1970), 45 [Series C, 18].

Shaftesbury separates core constitutional principles from *raison d'état*, Marvell sees a more expansive role for pragmatic political analysis, a means of sifting thought and action that might expand liberties of the subject within the prevailing power politics of the realm.

Sovereign Violence in the Pluralist State

It is the argument of this book that modern political thinkers both assert a position on sovereignty and consciously reject the two major alternatives, so that the three formations become ineluctably linked: unitary sovereignty, divided sovereignty, and overarching principles constraining sovereignty. For Marvell we see a core acceptance of the principle of unitary sovereignty, though with his nose firmly held. He recognizes that in his context political order is determined by a single individual able to wield the threat of force. That recognition drives a core attitude toward politics wavering between skepticism and disgust. In Marvell we see that a "black" unitary sovereignty can be placed in the service of a politics with certain progressive elements: the sovereign's monopoly on violence exists, in ways both destructive and necessary, but political life seeks to limit arbitrary expressions of this violence through rule of law measures protecting the subject. Marvell anticipates the values of modern liberals in these respects.

We have also seen how he gently distinguishes himself from Shaftesbury's Polybian argument for the constitutional independence of the lords. That Marvell might be skeptical of the natural-law view of principles above sovereignty is suggested by one of his first assignments in Thurloe's office: correspondence pertaining to a long-running squabble with the Swedes over the capture of merchant ships during the First Anglo-Dutch War (1652–54). The letters coming across Marvell's desk beginning December 1657, as Nigel Smith notes, make mention of Justinian and Ulpian in making the Swedish case.[72] But these are very minor authorities in the correspondence as a whole, and the Swedes base their claim primarily on the treaty of alliance signed by the two nations in Upsall and confirmed in 1656 at Westminster.[73] They cite Roman authorities as lending further

---

[72] See Smith (2010) 139. For mentions of Justinian and Ulpian, see Thurloe (1742) 6: 736, 737 and 7: 814, 815.

[73] The Swedish ambassadors argue that the English are legally bound to the seventh article of the Westminster agreement, whereby the two nations appoint commissioners to decide upon "the satisfaction for losses sustained by the detaining of... ships" during the war against the

support to their claims, but England's treaty obligations clearly carry greater weight. For their part, the English commissioners point to the "law of nations" as "something common and known on both sides," knowing full well that they could spin their wheels in its vagaries until the treaty's six-month time limit on negotiations had passed and the dispute could be referred higher up the line—a bureaucrat's dream outcome.[74]

Such negotiations are hardly a high-minded engagement of the Roman heritage of *jus commune*. If that tradition can seem the domain of brahminic jurists floating above the hurly-burly of quotidian legal transactions, here it seems far from disinterested and enlightened. The Swedes are engaging in high-pressure diplomacy, knowing that England is reluctant to lose a key Protestant ally after failed attempts at further unification with the Dutch. And the English commissioners are striving mightily to do nothing at all. As an introduction to public service, Marvell would be confirmed in his skepticism, and certainly would not be inspired to see sovereign states as capable of idealism, even when those states are united under confessional causes. The ruthless pursuit of interest, as the reason of state authors had it, would look very much like the determining force of political affairs.

But Marvell also works significantly within the Hull Corporation. Through the example of Lord Saye and the Providence Island Company, we explored in chapter 1 how the corporation as such is increasingly a rival to sovereign power in the period. For Marvell the municipal corporation, of the kind that quadruples in number between 1540 and 1640, is this and more: a true "little republic," to return to Blackstone's phrase, with a republic's capacity to nurture civic virtue. As Phil Withington describes it, Marvell, like Shakespeare, Ben Jonson, John Lilburne, and Milton, was the product of an early modern grammar school system, making his education "a direct product of civic paternalism." Unlike these other beneficiaries, for Marvell the experience left him with a strongly "urban and corporate" sense

Dutch. See "Treaty between Charles Gustavus King of Sweden, and Oliver Cromwell Protector of England...Done at London, Anno 1656," in Chalmers (1890) 1: 38. While the English felt that they had discharged their responsibilities with the return of the ships, the Swedish embassy pressed the claim that the spirit of their provisions argues for full restitution of "expenses, costs, and damages" on behalf of subjects who had been "worn out with charges and vexatious suits." The losses claimed amounted, by English reckoning, to "110,000 pounds sterling." See Thurloe (1742) 6: 679, 737. On Sweden and Denmark in Marvell's later diplomacy, that of Carlisle's Baltic embassy of 1664, see von Maltzahn (2018).

[74] Thurloe (1742) 6: 685.

of citizenship.[75] His politics acquire a Janus-faced quality, at once disdain-fully observing the machinations of the court party and looking more kindly upon the Hull grandees he faithfully serves. Of course that service, too, may be subjected to interest analysis: currying the favor of the Hull Corporation was an effective means for Marvell to maintain his parliamentary seat.

Such dynamics between local, corporate government and sovereign power bring to mind Schmitt's 1930 essay "Ethic of State and Pluralistic State."[76] Here he directly confronts the question of pluralism with reference especially to the thought of Harold Laski, who had argued that the modern state should not monopolize sovereignty. Precisely because it had become the "one compulsory institution," Laski argues, the modern state runs the risk of violating the core Aristotelian principle that citizenship is "the capacity to rule not less than to be ruled in turn."[77] A monistic theory of the state cannot truly value citizens' active participation in rule. Quite the opposite. And so, theoretically and practically, a revivified federalism is necessary, Laski claims, but not one founded in territoriality—capitalism had successfully severed authority and land—but a federalism of social functions. This leads quite naturally to an argument celebrating the trade union as the modern form recovering the "factor of consent" and making the "individual feel significant."[78] Writing in 1919, Laski sees the growing union movement as a "movement for the conquest of self-government" that finds "its main impulse in the attempt to disperse sovereign power."[79]

Schmitt naturally disagrees. As he sees it, Laski's aim is to "negate not only the state as the supreme comprehensive unity but also, first and foremost, its ethical demand to create a different and higher kind of obliga-tion than any of the other associations in which men live. The state then becomes a social group or association which at most stands next to, but

---

[75] Withington (2011) 108. See also Withington (2010) 166, and, on Marvell's association with the corporation of London Trinity House, von Maltzahn (2013). Though I find With-ington's reading of Marvell's Hull association compelling, we differ on Marvell's political sympathies at the national level: his Marvell tends to view the nation under the late Stuart settlement more positively than mine does, and as a site of Ciceronian prudence and civility; my Marvell is more skeptical of politics at the national level and tends to see it as a corrupt forum of power politics suited to the Tacitist prudence of the reason of state writers.

[76] Originally 'Staatsethik und pluralistischer Staat' in Kant-Studien 35 (Berlin: Pan-Verlag Kurt Metzner, 1930), 28–42. Here I use David Dyzenhaus' translation in Mouffe (1999); see also that available in Jacobson and Schlink (2000).

[77] Laski (1921) 235, 241; see Aristotle (1932), Politics, 3.1.4–5 [1275a]. For further articula-tion of his pluralism, see Laski (2014) 69–109.

[78] Laski (1921) 242.   [79] Ibid., 243.

never above, the other associations."[80] Schmitt attacks this position on two fronts. First, that Laski's pluralism is a mere stalking horse for the cause of international socialism. Laski's true aim is to weaken the state, especially in its ability to make ethical demands of its subjects, so that he might make room for other sources of ethical demand: "humanity" or, more specifically, the aspirations of the "Second or Third International."[81] Laski is thus participating in interest-group politics under cover of pluralism. Here, and in a way consistent with Schmitt's abiding hostility toward communism, he argues that "it is a dangerous deception when one single group pursues its special interests in the name of the whole." When "a supreme and universal concept like humanity is used politically so as to identify a single people or a particular social organization with it, then the potential arises for a most awful expansion and a murderous imperialism."[82] (Some have found in such moments a worry over the growing activity of groups on both ends of the political spectrum, but in the context of the essay as a whole it is clear that the statement is directed at the Left.) That Laski would limit state power for the sake of preserving individual liberty is similarly disingenuous, a further attempt to create space allowing the Left to expand its influence. And in a curious twist, Schmitt accuses Laski of an elitist politics. If it was Laski's argument that individual freedoms in a pluralist order allow citizens to engage in forum shopping to advance their political interests, Schmitt retorts that this imagines a "nimble and agile individual who can succeed in the feat of maintaining his freedom between social groups, as one might hop from ice-floe to ice-floe." This does not describe "the mass of ordinary citizens."[83] The conservative Schmitt charges the socialist Laski with advancing a bourgeois politics.

The second major objection that Schmitt mounts is that Laski's political philosophy is out of step with the modern state and inconsistent with Laski's own philosophical sympathies. By limiting the state and seeking to advance international socialism, Laski was imposing on a twentieth-century context a version of the medieval Roman Catholic Church—in his own way Schmitt had already mourned the loss of that possibility in *Roman Catholicism and Political Form* (1923). There is, then, an "intellectual historical alliance between the Roman Catholic Church and unionist federalism which one

---

[80]   Schmitt (1999) 196. Schmitt includes many of his remarks on Laski's pluralism in *Concept of the Political*; see Schmitt (2007) 37–45. On Schmitt's engagements of Laksi, see Schwab (1970) 55–60.

[81]   Ibid., 200–1.   [82]   Ibid., 205.   [83]   Ibid., 200.

finds today in Laski," and in particular in the "quest to relativize the state against the church" which now works "in the interest of a union or syndic-alist socialism."[84] In this translation of theological views to secular political ones, Laski belongs "to that intellectual and historical array of phenomena which [Schmitt has] called 'political theology.'"[85] And because the "monism and universalism of the Roman Catholic Church" lurks beneath Laski's pluralism, he is inconsistent in applying the philosophical pragmatism to which he claims to adhere. As with the argument on individual liberty, Schmitt again outflanks Laski by claiming for his own views a fuller expres-sion of the insights of "William James's pluralistic philosophical picture of the world."[86] In a world without natural foundations of authority, without a set of norms that all can accept, there must be an entity capable of ordering political community. Any factual analysis would conclude that the entity with the strongest claim to this status is the state. Only the state, then, has the vital function of sustaining the normal situation on which depend other associations operating within a pluralist order—a similar claim cannot be made by corporations, or trade unions, or religious organizations. A sustainable pluralism thus depends on the overriding authority of the state, which must exercise its prerogative of deciding on the state of excep-tion in order to maintain the normal situation. Even as this is an argument for the necessity of the threat of force, that necessity does not preclude the importance of consensus in sustaining a dynamic political unity. Schmitt suggestively rejects the view that force and consensus ought to be seen as a dichotomy, with only the latter producing an ethically valid unity. In the case of consensus within the state, they are often mutually constitutive: "every consensus, even a 'free' one, is somehow motivated and brought into existence. Power produces consensus and often, to be sure, a rational and ethically justified consensus."[87] An individual within a pluralistic society will thus have a plurality of associations and a plurality of ethical bonds, but there must be one association that holds the greatest intensity, and that is political unity, which "always designates the most intensive degree of a unity, from which, consequently, the most intensive distinction—the group-ing of friend and enemy—is determined." This remains a thoroughly anti-foundationalist view in that any group that can raise unity to this intensity

---

[84]   Ibid., 200, 197.   [85]   Ibid., 197.
[86]   Ibid. Laski himself had noted that his own moment's "movement for the revival of what we broadly term natural law...derive[s] its main strength from organized trade-unionism"; see Laski (1921) 246.
[87]   Schmitt (1999) 202.

can then make a claim to commanding political unity and thus to commanding the state:

> Because the political has no substance of its own, the point of the political
> can be reached from any terrain, and any social group, church, union,
> combine, nation, becomes political, and thereby of the state, as it
> approaches the point of highest intensity...All human life, even the
> highest spiritual spheres, has in its historical realization at least the poten-
> tial to become a state, which waxes strong and powerful from such contents
> and substances, as did the mythical eagle of Zeus, which nourished itself
> from Prometheus' entrails.[88]

In this telling, there is no single substantive source of political unity that
applies in all places and all times, but rather that unity is achieved by the
entity that "decides, and has the potential to prevent all other opposing
groups from dissociating into a state of extreme enmity—that is, into civil
war."[89] Schmitt's allusion to Prometheus is intriguing, though one wonders
if he is in full command of its implications. The state, eagle-like, feeds on
eternals—religion or nation—which are the source of its strength. But is
Schmitt not, then, presenting the state as the emissary of the gods, and does
this eternalization of the state not align him more closely with Hegel than he
would wish? And is Prometheus' gift of fire not associated with technology?
This would appear to make the state's strength derive from the realm of
technology, the very impulse that Schmitt would later see as a source of
failure in the political mythology of Hobbes.

Here we come to one of Schmitt's readings of early modernity, a reading
important to our discussion of Marvell. Absolutist versions of sovereign
authority, Schmitt argues, were a practical necessity in the sixteenth through
eighteenth centuries, an expression of the state's aspiration to "prevail
against the pluralistic chaos of churches and estates between the sixteenth
and eighteenth centuries.... Even the absolute prince of the seventeenth
and eighteenth centuries was forced to respect divine and natural law—that
is, to speak sociologically, church and family—and to take into account the
manifold aspects of traditional institutions and established rights."[90] For
Marvell the rights-bearing individual is much more important as a limit on
sovereign power than is the "family." He is certainly attuned to the need

---

[88] Ibid., 203.   [89] Ibid.   [90] Ibid., 201.

to curb the wielder of sovereign power, if also aware, like Schmitt, that force enables a consensus that can be accepted on rational and ethical grounds. There is, and perhaps ought to be, an individual maintaining a normal situation with the threat of force. But that imposition can produce a consensus then reinforcing political unity on slightly altered grounds. And in that ongoing process, certain rights and liberties might be secured, so that the normal situation secured by the power of the sword is also one allowing for individual liberty and civic participation. The sovereign's exercise of force against the enemies of this settlement signals that its intensity rises to the level of the political, but this does not prevent the individual member of this political unity from participating in other forms of association.

This Schmittean approach to the pluralist state ties together several of the threads that we have pursued in this chapter. We have noted that Guicciardini saw the political machinations of the Medici, ruthless as they were, as creating a climate in the Florentine republic where civic virtue might be cultivated. For all of its terror, power rightly directed can create conditions for an enlightened political consensus. This is a major lesson of the *Horatian Ode* and *First Anniversary*. In parsing such manifestations of sovereign power one often discerns *raison d'état* in Marvell's thought, whether attacking the deleterious effects of court culture on politics or promoting the political advantages of religious toleration. This signals a practical-minded approach to a pluralist concrete situation, one where Marvell's greatest concern is that an upstart faction—of courtiers, of bishops, of foreigners— will co-opt sovereign power, placing it in the hands of an interest group. For all that we sense his disgust with the scenes of violence he paints, there is also a strong affinity for what Schmitt would call an intensity rising to the level of the political, one creating a unity that can direct state power against enemies. Imperfect as it is, such a unity creates space for a public spirit expressing itself in individual liberty and civic-minded associations.

Epilogue

Uzzah and the Protection–Obedience Axiom

> I have lived through destiny pulling on the reins,
> Victories and defeats, revolutions and restorations,
> Inflations and deflations, bombardments,
> Defamations, regime changes and burst pipes,
> Hunger and cold, camp and solitary confinement.
> Through all of this I have passed,
> And all has passed through me.
>   —Carl Schmitt, "Song of the 60-Year-Old"[1]

Written in the wake of the Second World War, and his questioning at Nuremberg, Schmitt's "Song of the 60-Year-Old" vacillates between passivity and activity. The passage above describes a violent sweep of history in which he is inescapably caught—"revolutions and restorations," "bombardments," and "regime changes." And yet in the final line Schmitt seems to claim his status as a figure through whom his age will be read: we are invited to view his interventions as snapshots of the storms in which he has been tossed. So read the poem nestles easily, perhaps too easily, aside Schmitt's claim before his Nuremberg interrogator, Robert Kempner, that his work simply "diagnosed" conditions of the international legal order, and thus could not be considered as seeking to achieve a "new international legal order in accordance with Hitlerian ideas," specifically the Nazi doctrine of *Lebensraum*.[2]

In Schmitt's telling, he was, during the war years, simply a person sitting "quietly at a desk." "Who else did not leave his desk?" asks Kempner. "Thomas Hobbes," replies Schmitt.[3] Indeed, Schmitt's sexagenarian song is not dissimilar to that of the nonagenarian Hobbes. In 1679, the year of his

---

[1] "Gesang des Sechzigjärigen" appears in Schmitt (2017), *Ex Captivitate Salus*, p. 73–4; an alternate translation, prepared by G.L. Ulmen, is available in Piccone and Ulmen (1987) 130.
[2] Bendersky (1987) 98.   [3] Ibid., 103.

Sovereignty: Seventeenth-Century England and the Making of the Modern Political Imaginary.
Feisal G. Mohamed, Oxford University Press (2020). © Feisal G. Mohamed.
DOI: 10.1093/oso/9780198852131.001.0001

death, appeared Hobbes' Latin elegy, *Vita authore seipso*, which also offers an image of perpetual isolation, of a man blown hither and yon by his unruly age.[4] Hobbes describes returning home in 1651 to an English Commonwealth suspicious of his loyalty:

> In Patriam redeo tutelae non bene certus,
>   Sed nullo potui tutior esse loco,
> Frigus erat, nix alta, senex ego, ventus acerbus,
>   Magnus, equus sternax & salebrosa via.

> Then home I came, not sure of safety there,
> Though I cou'd not be safer any where.
> Th'Wind, Frost, Snow sharp, with Age grown gray,
> A plunging Beast, and most unpleasant way.[5]

Hobbes had also seen revolution and restoration, and he would in after times be seen as a thinker through whom the tumults of the seventeenth century were distilled into political theory. Hobbes, too, styled his work disinterested, claiming to have invented a "Civil Philosophy" in line with natural philosophy's turn away from Aristotle.[6] We should not take either this claim or Schmitt's at face value. In moments of crisis both men strive mightily not only to describe but to alter their political environments. This is evident in Schmitt's arguments for the exercise of emergency powers as the Weimar Republic was teetering on the brink of collapse, and Hobbes' efforts to encourage his fellow royalists to take the Oath of Engagement to the nascent English Commonwealth. That Schmitt chooses at Nuremberg to compare himself to Hobbes is not entirely surprising, given his long-running interest in, and admiration for, the philosopher of Malmesbury. We shall presently suggest that the comparison is more fitting than Schmitt knows, for the two had come to learn the hard way that political obedience is not always compensated by the sovereign's protection. Both men experienced significant moments of betrayal that complicate the views with which they are often associated.

---

[4] As John Hale observes of the poem, it has a "busy traffic of comings and goings, arrivals and departures, presences and absences"; see Hale (2008) 99.
[5] Hobbes (1679) 9; translation is Blackburn's, Hobbes (1680) 11.
[6] Hobbes (1969), *Elements of Law*, ix.

We tend to think of political betrayal as working from the bottom up, in the form of treason. In his recent, full-length exploration of betrayal, Avishai Margalit deals with treason at length, as a "gross violation of one's allegiance to one's sovereign," as "the ultimate sin, something more criminal than murder."[7] But betrayal can also work from the top down. Schmitt's revised view of Hobbes in his later work has been seen as arising in part from the experience of being rejected by the Nazi regime that he publicly endorsed. Despite his service to the National Socialists, Schmitt found himself under suspicion and attack shortly after his embrace of the party in 1933. For this reason the fuller skepticism of his 1938 book on *Leviathan* may be animated in part by resentment that, as he saw it, Hobbes failed to take into account the possibility of a sovereign's arbitrary attack upon a loyal subject. Though he devotes very little space to this form of betrayal, Margalit describes the "conceptually perplexing" case of legally beheading Charles I for the crime of treason as dramatically changing "the notion of treason": "Treason was conceived not as betraying the *king* but as betraying the *people* with whom the ruler was supposed to have thick relationships."[8] That places us, of course, in the moment of *Leviathan*, which resolves this conceptual perplexity with conquest theory: it is not the power of law that is placed above Charles, but a new power of the sword. Because the king is no longer capable of offering protection, subjects are absolved of their obligation of obedience, if also compelled to recognize the new sovereign power offering the benefits of peace. Thus *Leviathan* accounts for England's change of regime while Hobbes' central "protection-obedience axiom," as Schmitt calls it in *The Concept of the Political*, remains intact.[9]

It was clear to Schmitt by 1938 that a subject strenuously defending an existing political settlement might be excluded from the protection of a sovereign who still retained the power of the sword. In the model of political authority that Schmitt and Hobbes espouse, such a subject would have no grounds on which to object to a lack of protection and was reduced to a state of exile, whether remaining in the territory of the sovereign or not. This perceived absence in Hobbes' thought is at play in Schmitt's later reading. I say *perceived* absence because Hobbes did in fact recognize this possibility. Or, to put it more precisely, the Hobbes of *Behemoth* subtly injects this awareness into his typical anti-clericalism and so alerts us to buried aspects of his earlier analysis of England's political troubles in *Leviathan*. Signaling

---

[7] Margalit (2017) 157. 　　[8] Ibid., 172.
[9] Schmitt (2007), *Concept of the Political*, 52.

this awareness is his evident discomfort with the story of Uzzah, who reaches out to sustain the Ark of the Covenant when it shakes on an oxcart, only to be struck dead by an incensed God. To prepare the way for Hobbes' reading, we will explore the exegeses of several early modern predecessors, especially Richard Hooker, Lancelot Andrewes, and John Donne. Here we will find some justification for Schmitt's view of Hobbes as offering secular and political translation of theological concepts, even as we become aware of other dynamics of political theology. After a look at Hobbes' account of Uzzah in the Restoration context of *Behemoth*, we will return to Schmitt's reading of *Leviathan* in the context of his fallen fortunes with the National Socialists. The two thinkers share a skepticism directed at an overly idealistic approach to political philosophy that refuses to acknowledge the dynamics of power. In a way seldom noted, both also acknowledge in their thought the anti-absolutist fact that a subject can endure the fear of exposure when obedient to a sovereign whose authority is stable. Both of these insights adjust significantly how we read Schmitt's claim to have inherited from Hobbes the position that "*protego ergo obligo* is the *cogito ergo sum* of the state."[10]

* * *

Uzzah's appearance in 2 Samuel is brief but memorable. As the Ark of the Covenant is being transported by oxcart, he notices the oxen stumble on the threshing floor of Nachon and intuitively puts forth his hand to steady the holy of holies: "Uzzah put forth his hand to the ark of God, and took hold of it; for the Oxen shook it" (2 Sam 6.6). There is some ambiguity in the Hebrew, but English versions describing the oxen as shaking the ark, or merely stumbling, take some liberty; the Anchor Bible favors "the oxen had let it slip" as a translation of *semato*, a verb that is never intransitive in the Hebrew Bible, lending greater emphasis to the ark's peril.[11] As a reward for this reflex born of a natural, even pious impulse to protect the vessel of the Law, the central object of Israelite worship and national identity, the Lord

---

[10] Ibid. The principle is equally visible in Bodin: "the prince is bound by force of armes, and of his lawes, to maintaine his subjects in suretie of their persons, their goods, and families: for which the Subjects by a reciprocall obligation owe unto their prince, faith, subjection, obeysance, aid, and succour" (Bodin [1606] 69 [Bk. 1, ch. 7]). Schmitt's Cartesian language may explain in part his choice to locate the protection-obedience axiom in Hobbes, pointing as it does to the idiom of natural philosophy, and thus to a fully modern politics, as opposed to Bodin's patriarchal theory.

[11] 2 Samuel, trans. and ed. P. Kyle McCarter, Jr., vol. 9 of *The Anchor Bible* (New York: Doubleday, 1984), 165 [textual n. ad. 2 Sam 6.6].

strikes him dead. An angry David feels that "Yahweh had made a breach in Uzzah," and so the place of this occurrence is named, ambiguously, *Perez-Uzzah*, or Uzzah's Breach (2 Sam 6.7–8).

In a straightforward reading of the story, the Lord is angered by a violation of the proscription in Numbers 4 against touching the ark. And the episode also adds literary complexity to the David narrative, providing a moment of confusion and trial between the battle victories in 2 Samuel 5 and Nathan's oracle on the Davidic dynasty in 2 Samuel 7.[12] In this light, Uzzah's death is a minor distraction that can be easily explained away. The Levites are charged only with carrying the ark and as Jerome, and Pseudo-Dionysius, and Josephus Flavius all point out, Uzzah isn't even a priest.[13] Richard Hooker shares this emphasis in book 5 of the *Lawes of Ecclesiastical Polity*, his extended defense of the rites of the English church against Thomas Cartwright's charges of popish ceremonialism. Uzzah is enlisted in a small brigade of biblical characters showing the error of encroaching upon the prerogatives of the priesthood, and that God is unlikely to accept the "voluntarie services" of those "who thrust them selves into functions either above theire capacity or besides theire place."[14]

The story holds many more riches than this, and allows especially for meditation on the complexities of duty. Uzzah cannot be described as undutiful: charged with transporting the ark he also acts to protect it. But his dutifulness exceeds just bounds and so becomes a violation of duty. Salvianus expresses the point economically: Uzzah "did not do anything in an impudent fashion or with an undutiful intention, but his very service was undutiful because he exceeded his orders."[15] These, in the Geneva Bible's gloss, are the perils of good intentions.[16] In Uzzah's excess lies a mistrust of God's care for the ark, or of its status as earthly manifestation of divine presence. If the ark can carry the Israelites across the Jordan, the medieval rabbi and commentator Rashi remarks, then it can fend for itself on an oxcart. Uzzah not only forgets the letter of the Law, but also implies through

---

[12] See 2 Sam 5.19–25 and 2 Sam 7.12–13.

[13] See Jerome (1893) Epistle 22.23; Dionysius (1987) Epistle 8; Josephus (1934) 47 [7.4.2].

[14] Hooker (1977–1998) 2: 278. Arguing that separatists are wrong to rebaptize those who received the sacrament as infants, Hooker points to Uzzah as revealing that "it behoveth generally all sortes of men to keepe them selves within the limites of theire owne vocation." In the same citation he points to Nadab and Abihu, the sons of Aaron who took their father's censer and offered "strange fire before the Lord" (Lev 10.1), and Uzziah, the king chided by Azariah and fourscore priests also for burning incense upon the altar (2 Chron 26.16).

[15] Salvianus (1930) Bk. 6, ch. 10.

[16] See *Geneva Bible* (2007) notes at 2 Sam 6.7, and 1 Chron 13.10.

his actions that the Israelites are protectors of the ark, rather than the other way around. In this way he reminds us that a touch of hubris motivates the excessively dutiful. So it is not entirely amiss that in the first prebend sermon, Donne likens the overreacher Uzzah to the overgazer Actaeon, who, in Conti's words, is a warning against "getting too curious about things that are none of our business."[17] Uzzah, Donne tells us, "was over-zealous in an office that appertained not to him, ... and suffered for that."[18] Thus Donne's larger lesson in the sermon resembles Saint Gregory's reading in the *Moralia*: that Uzzah overtrusts his own godliness, in a way Gregory likens to the friends of Job pridefully counselling the holy man in his hour of distress.[19]

In a 1610 sermon for James, Lancelot Andrewes runs David and the ark together in reading this story as admonishing us not to lay hands on a godly king: "No more touch *David* than the holy *Arke*. It is not good touching of holy things ... Uzza so found it."[20] But this oddly seamless association of David and the ark may betray an anxiety on Andrewes' part. The story can certainly be read as critical of David, and in fact the harshest words in Rashi's commentary on 2 Samuel 6 are reserved for the king who commits a child's error in applying the law: Uzzah dies because David orders the ark to be transported on an oxcart, instead of having it borne on the shoulders of Levites as he is supposed to do. Andrewes erases this subtext of monarchical carelessness, and the particular occasion of this sermon makes one wonder about the closeted sentiments he betrays in doing so: he was preaching on the tenth anniversary of the Earl of Gowrie's supposed attempt to assassinate James, who had imported from Scotland a tradition of annually celebrating his miraculous escape. The problem was that nobody really believed that James' life was ever in danger. In a famous, if also likely apocryphal, story that comes down to us from Thomas Plume's life of Hacket, Andrewes begged to be released from his obligation to preach on this day of thanksgiving:

> the most Religious Bishop *Andrews* once fell down upon his knees before *King James*, and besought his *Majesty* to spare his *customary* pains upon that day, that he might not mock *God* unless the thing were true: the *King* ... did assure him in the Faith of a Christian, and upon the *Word* of a King, their Treasonable attempt against him was too true.[21]

---

[17] Conti (2006) 564.   [18] Donne (1971), *Prebend Sermons*, 87.
[19] Gregory (1844) 258–59 [Book 5, par. 23–4].   [20] Lancelot Andrewes (2005) 189.
[21] Plume (1675) viii.

By running together David and the ark in his reference to Uzzah, Andrewes glides past the biblical king's infelicitous decision-making in a way that also glides past his own feeling of compromising his role as minister to satisfy worldly powers, of being torn between two masters, God and king.

This quality sublimated in Andrewes' sermon is churned to the surface by Hobbes, not surprisingly. Also not surprising is the atheist inflection of his reading: for Hobbes, God seems rather more blameworthy than does Uzzah. The very brief story from 2 Samuel 6 appears twice in his writings, which give extremely little space to obscure stories from the Hebrew Bible. The first appearance is in chapter 33 of *Leviathan*, where Hobbes is arguing that the books of Samuel were written much later than the reign of David: "when *David* (displeased, that the Lord had slain *Uzzah*, for putting out his hand to sustain the Ark,) called the place *Perez-Uzzah*, the Writer saith, it is called so *to this day*." Comparison to the 1668 Latin edition of *Leviathan* highlights the editorializing packed into this brief mention: "ubi David propter Mortem Vzzae contristatus est, dicit Scriptor, *Vocatum est nomen loci illus Percussio Vzzae usque in diem hanc*."[22] Rather than being saddened by the death of Uzzah, as he is in the Latin edition, David is displeased that the Lord had slain Uzzah in the English edition; and while the Latin offers no reason for Uzzah's death, the English edition justifies David's displeasure with its sympathetic remark on Uzzah putting out his hand to *sustain* the ark.

The editorializing is an aside to the point that Hobbes is making on dating the Samuel books, which may be one reason why he eliminates it in the later Latin text. But he has already given away that the story does not rest easily with him, as is reinforced by the second appearance of Uzzah in his writings, which occurs in *Behemoth* as Hobbes criticizes monarchs who accept the pope's jurisdiction over matters spiritual and thus corrupt sovereign authority. The manuscript version declares that "most bishops" pretend to hold the same jurisdiction in their "several Dioceses," making the problem span the Roman and English churches, but deletes the remark—somewhat gratuitously, for the remainder of the first dialogue makes his assessment of the English bishops clear enough.[23] A separate spiritual jurisdiction granted to the pope or bishops quickly metastasizes and then enlists civil authorities to enforce its decisions. Though not specifically mentioned by Hobbes, the

---

[22] For facing-page English and Latin texts, see Hobbes (2014b), *Leviathan*, 594–5; italics in original.
[23] Hobbes (2014a), *Behemoth*, 113.

Restoration debate on *adiaphora* is a case in point: revanchist bishops eager to impose religious conformity clamor that refusal to participate in the ceremonies of the national church is a violation of civil law, pressing the sovereign to impose civil punishments and thus corrupting the principle of royal supremacy.[24]

Under such conditions, Hobbes argues, the loyal subject is like Uzzah: "He were in an ill case then, that adventured to write or speake in defence of the Civill Power, that must be punisht by him whose Rights he defended, like Uzza that was slaine, because he would needs unbidden put forth his hand to keep the Arke from falling."[25] Striking here, of course, is the blithe criticism of God, who in Hobbes' simile is like a corrupt, self-interested bishop urging the king to punish a loyal subject: Uzzah's impulses are rightly ordered toward the preservation of the ark, here a stand-in for civil order. For that he ought to receive the sovereign's protection. At the time when Hobbes is writing *Behemoth*, likely the late 1660s, the point is personal. Aubrey tells us in his life of Hobbes that shortly after the Restoration "some of the bishops made a motion to have the good old gentleman burnt for a heretic. Which he hearing, feared that his papers might be searched by their order, and told me he had burnt part of them."[26] In 1666–67, the bishops' parliamentary allies took aim at *Leviathan*, which was specifically mentioned in discussion of the bill against "Atheism and Profanity," and Hobbes was summoned to appear before the Lords.[27] The objections to God's treatment of Uzzah visible in *Leviathan* become stronger in *Behemoth* as the story takes on an autobiographical resonance for Hobbes.

Also striking are the limits on absolutism apparent in this reference. In its most familiar arguments, Hobbes' political theory denies subjects a position from which they may legitimately challenge sovereign authority once they consent to form a commonwealth. The exception, visible in the "Review and Conclusion" to *Leviathan* evidently written after the execution of Charles I, is when a monarch is unable to wield the power of the sword in a way that offers protection to the subject. The moment in *Behemoth* we have been examining suggests that such a failure of protection, and consequent release from obligation, may not only occur when a regime has collapsed after a

---

[24] On this debate in the Restoration church, see Rose (2014) 46–7.
[25] Hobbes (2014a), *Behemoth*, 114.   [26] Aubrey (1975) 160.
[27] See Tuck (1993) 339. This was not Hobbes' first such encounter, of course. For a book-length examination of his feud with Bishop Bramhall, see Jackson (2007).

period of civil war. Certain relationships with the church, be it Roman Catholic or English, can corrupt the sovereign's ability to protect the subject.

This is a typically anti-clerical position for Hobbes, who is stridently Erastian throughout his writings. "Experience teaches thus much," Hobbes famously declares in a 1641 letter to the third Earl of Devonshire, "that the dispute for precedence betwene the *spirituall* and *civill power*, has of late more then any other thing in the world, bene the cause of *civill warres*, in all *places of Christendome*."[28] But it is less familiar to the extent that it makes us wonder how deeply it cuts into his absolutist theory. Just as there can be no excess in the sovereign's exercise of power, so too there can be no excess in defending the rights of civil power. In Leo Strauss' suggestive analysis, the moral foundation of Hobbes' political theory rests upon providing individuals this avenue for celebrating and defending civil authority: the acquisition and vanity given free rein in the state of nature is transformed in the commonwealth into the promotion of one's interests through the promotion of civil power. The contract struck at the moment of the polity's founding creates not only the artificial person of the sovereign, but also the artificial person of the citizen, who brackets an insatiable acquisitiveness in favor of the contractually determined obligation of preserving the commonwealth.[29]

We can sense a development in the examples we have traced here, from Hooker's deployment of this story to defend clerical privilege, to Andrewes' nervously exuberant defense of royal holiness, to Hobbes' self-identification with the loyal servant struck down for his efforts. Uzzah can be deployed in straightforward fashion in an early modern political culture of moderation, the kind for which Hooker provides eloquent apology—of knowing and respecting the just bounds on individual activity imposed by station, by church, by monarchy. For Hobbes the story raises different concerns altogether. If the sovereign behaves as God does toward Uzzah, then the subject's defenses of the commonwealth no longer coincide with the primary impulse of self-preservation. And Hobbes' analysis implies that it is common for this to happen: actual sovereigns will rarely measure up to the theoretical categories set forth in *Leviathan*, and tend to allow powerful interests to interfere in the protection-obedience bargain struck with their subjects, whether they have sacrificed some authority to the church, or to foreign powers, or to a class of oligarchs. With this brief reference to Uzzah we gain a glimpse into the friction in Hobbes' thought between absolutist

---

[28] Hobbes (2007) 120–1; italics in original.   [29] See Strauss ([1936] 1963) esp. 8–18.

theory and *raison d'état* analysis of the actual workings of a given political settlement. Hobbes recognizes that sovereignty in its historical appearances is fraught and divided—or widely perceived to be fraught and divided, which in practical terms can amount to the same thing. His utopian impulse is largely directed toward imagining political order without such divisions, thereby preventing such conflagrations as the Thirty Years' War or the English civil wars. Apart from such obvious conditions of civil calamity, however, the subject must determine if his relationship with the sovereign offers the protection that it should. Hobbes' rendering of the Uzzah story shows us that even when ostensibly living in a stable commonwealth, one can be in a condition of exposure. A loyal subject must be chary of being a naive one, of failing accurately to reckon the shifting and multifaceted dynamics of sovereign power. Hobbes' Uzzah shows how the modern subject experiences politics in a way that makes energetic devotion to civil authority seem like a profoundly unwise, even self-defeating, course of action. And yet, for Hobbes, it is also our only legitimate course of action.

It is an important aspect of Hobbes' thought that is overlooked by Schmitt. Indeed, this oversight leads Schmitt to be disappointed when his own obedience to an ascendant sovereign is not repaid with protection. Schmitt's 1938 book on *Leviathan* accuses Hobbes of not providing an effective "sociology of a concept," as he had credited him with doing in *Political Theology,* but instead of advancing concepts that "contradicted England's concrete political reality."[30] Hobbes attempts to form a myth that will reunite the separation of secular and religious authority that Christianity inherits from Judaism, but instead mythologizes the state as machine in a way exploited by liberal Jewish thinkers—this book belongs to the period of Schmitt's most hysterical anti-Semitism.[31] The specific point those thinkers can exploit is Hobbes' handling of the miraculous. In *Leviathan*, the sovereign can determine what the subject publicly professes as belief:

> If, by means of certain spoken words an individual asserted that bread had been transformed into something entirely different, namely, the human body, then, says Hobbes, nobody would have a sensible reason to believe it;

---

[30] Schmitt (2008b), *The Leviathan,* 85.
[31] On the anti-Semitism of Schmitt's *Leviathan in the State Theory of Thomas Hobbes,* including its implicit blaming of Jews for Nazism, see McCormick (2016) esp. 270 and 283–4. McCormick's excellent chapter explores much of the same terrain as this epilogue, though of course with differences in emphasis.

but if the power of a state decrees this to be so, then it is a miracle, and everyone has to obey this command to profess the belief because it was proclaimed by the sovereign state.

In this power to decide the miraculous, "sovereign power has achieved its zenith," but the subject retains the capacity to join, or not join, private belief to this public confession of faith.[32] In articulating that capacity Hobbes creates an opportunity for the "liberal Jew" Spinoza to exploit the distinction between public ritual and private confession, ceding that the state has power over the former while emphasizing the importance of the latter in his political philosophy, so that "the leviathan's vitality was sapped from within and life began to drain out of him."[33] Spinoza thus launches a process that continues in eighteenth- and nineteenth-century Continental thought and culminates in legal positivism, whereby "all the mythical forces embodied in the image of leviathan now strike back at the state that Hobbes had symbolized."[34] In his odd reading of the leviathan image, Schmitt describes it as caught between a biblical association with Satan, as is familiar from the Book of Job, and various natural mythologies where the leviathan, like the dragon, can be a source of protection. Hobbes strives for the latter, but the mythical charge of the former proves to be too strong, so that "all his clear intellectual constructions and arguments were overcome in the vortex created by the symbol he conjured up."[35]

Schmitt's book on *Leviathan*, it is important to note, is published after an embarrassing and precipitous fall from the favor of the National Socialists. He famously joins the party in May 1933 and played a part in having his Jewish senior colleague Hans Kelsen removed from the law faculty at Cologne, even though Schmitt had sought and obtained Kelsen's support for his own hire earlier the same year. Despite best efforts publicly to signal support of Hitler's rise, most visible in his 1934 essay "Der Führer schützt das Recht" ("The Führer protects the law") and in his 1935 celebration of the Nuremberg Laws as "the Constitution of Freedom," Schmitt had seen his ideological support of the Third Reich questioned in several quarters. As early as 1934 he came under the scrutiny of the SD, the branch of the SS seeking to preserve ideological purity, thanks in no small measure to the efforts of his rival jurist Reinhard Höhn, himself rapidly rising in SS ranks. It did not help that the émigré Waldemar Gurian was publishing articles in Switzerland under the pseudonym Paul Müller that pointed out several of

---

[32] Ibid., 55.   [33] Ibid., 57.   [34] Ibid., 62.   [35] Ibid., 81.

Schmitt's pre-war associations with Jews—associations that included Gurian himself. After attacks on him were published in December 1936 issues of the SS newspaper *Das Schwarze Korps*, it became clear to Schmitt that he had fallen out of favor with the Nazis and he resigned his party positions, saved from further disgrace only by the intervention of his friend Hermann Goering, who demanded that the SS newspaper cease its attacks on him.[36]

We might bear that experience in mind as we approach Schmitt's 1938 book on *Leviathan*. Schmitt's account of the "failure" of the myth of the leviathan registers some personal disappointment in Hobbes, whom he identifies as the chief theorist of "the protection-obedience axiom."[37] The *Leviathan* book arrives in the wake of Schmitt's most outlandish attempts to signal his embrace of the Third Reich, including his organization of a 1936 conference on eliminating Jewish influence from German jurisprudence. His keynote address there described such influence as embodying poisonous "anarchist nihilism" and "positivist normativism," ostensible polarities that in fact resemble one another when each is taken to an extreme.[38] Just as Hobbes' version of Uzzah is autobiographical in describing an obedience not repaid with protection, so too is Schmitt's 1938 version of Hobbes. The closing statements of the book read very much like an account of the way in which Schmitt hoped posterity might read him:

> His concepts informed the law state of the nineteenth century, but his image of the leviathan remained a myth of horror, and his most vivid characterizations deteriorated into slogans. Today we grasp the undiminished force of his polemics, understand the intrinsic honesty of his thinking, and admire the imperturbable spirit who fearlessly thought through man's existential anguish.... To us he is thus the true teacher of a great political experience; lonely as every pioneer... and yet in the immortal community of the great scholars of the ages, "a sole retriever of an ancient prudence." (86)

Schmitt's prose very rarely reaches for this emotive register, and we sense a strong personal stake in celebrating a philosopher who has just been associated with a failed idea. If this is a remark on his own legacy, it is prescient

---

[36] Biographical information in this paragraph derived from Balakrishnan (2000) 201–7, Dyzenhaus (2003) 4, and Schwab's introduction to Schmitt (2008b), *Leviathan in the State Theory*, ix–xiii.

[37] Schmitt (2007), *The Concept of the Political*, 52.

[38] Qtd. in Balakrishnan (2000) 206.

in some respects. Some of Schmitt's most potent ideas have deteriorated into slogans: "sovereign is he who decides on the state of exception," "all significant concepts of the modern theory of the state are secularized theological concepts," "the specific political distinction to which political actions and motives can be reduced is that between friend and enemy."[39] More substantive engagements of his work have made effective use of the force and insight of his polemics against the liberal state. But we certainly have not reached the point where Schmitt is celebrated with the warmth he displays here, and likely never will do.

The greatest commonality between Hobbes and Schmitt, then, is the way in which each seeks to anchor political theory in a given political situation, which is defined neither by concepts nor by material conditions but by a complex tangle of the two. This is certainly obvious in Schmitt's writings, which everywhere tell us that an effective legal theory must take stock of the concrete situation in which the law is to be applied. It is the role of the sovereign to sustain the "situation" in which the law can operate: "There exists no norm that is applicable to chaos. For a legal order to make sense, a normal situation must exist, and he is sovereign who definitely decides whether this normal situation actually exists ... The sovereign produces and guarantees the situation in its totality. He has the monopoly over this last decision."[40] Those who would place legal norms above this power of the sovereign, a charge Schmitt levels against neo-Kantian legal theorists, will contribute to the dissolution of constitutional order as political factions use the space liberal parliamentarianism provides to advance their own agendas.

This casts *Leviathan* in a new light, not as a *nuova scienza* of the state but as an effort to inject political ideas into a tumultuous political situation and to alter its shape in a way tending to stability. That is most clear in the "Review and Conclusion," which we have long recognized as an intervention in the debate on the Engagement Oath.[41] Here we see a commonality between Hobbes and Schmitt not only in rooting political theory in a given situation, but also in striving, through their writings, to alter the complexion of that situation. Like Schmitt's polemical works in the late

---

[39] These arise from Schmitt (2005), *Political Theology* (1, 36) and Schmitt (2007), *The Concept of the Political* (26). I have departed from the Schwab translation in the first of them; commentators on Schmitt's thought generally prefer "decides on the state of exception" to "decides on the exception."

[40] Schmitt (2005), *Political Theology*, 13.

[41] See the classic essay on Hobbes' conquest theory and the Engagement Controversy, Skinner (1974). Skinner's account of Hobbes' engagements of *de facto* theory is refined by Hoekstra (2004) esp. 52–7. See also Skinner (1998).

Weimar years, urging time and again that the presidential powers of Article 48 be exercised, *Leviathan* aspires to change the political situation in which it appears by prompting its readership to embrace a core commitment to order, whatever its source.

And yet one detects in both Schmitt and Hobbes a creeping awareness that legal theory and political philosophy seeking to incline readers toward order don't stand a chance in fractious modern societies. There is an unbridgeable distance between the concrete situation they diagnose and the universal acceptance of sovereign power that they imagine. And we have seen that jaded tendency elsewhere in this book, especially in Milton's and Marvell's apparent acceptance that political order is sustained by force as much or more than it is by consensus. We see in these thinkers why sovereignty has always had something of an embarrassed place in modern political philosophy: because focusing our attention on sovereignty casts a harsh glare on the power directing the state, which is indifferent to the good; which is, in the final analysis, an arbitrary power pretending to have great authority; and which in its fearfulness and fragility lashes out at perceived threats at home and abroad.

As with so many modern political theorists, both Hobbes and Schmitt carry with them a rosy picture of lost medieval unity. For Hobbes it is the subject's keen awareness of obligation to the sovereign, more pronounced in feudal order than in a modern age of proliferating voluntary associations, as signaled by rapidly expanding numbers of contracts and corporations. For Schmitt it is the *complexio oppositorum*, the capacity of the medieval Roman Catholic Church to retain a sense of deep unity governing the oppositions of Western Christendom. Each seeks in some fashion to create an absolutist theory of sovereignty that will regain this lost stability. Each also knows the futility of such a project. It is the nature of modern political order to deposit great *potestas* in a sovereign who cannot command great *auctoritas*. Power finds various occluding languages and apparatuses, cultural and legal, but we are naive or disingenuous when we deny its status as organizing principle of the modern state. Once political ideas no longer rest on a set of universally accepted claims, then, for Hobbes and Schmitt, we are ethically obliged to obey the power capable of preserving a normal situation. With this shared impulse to make a virtue of acquiescence to power, they alert us to the core bargain of a politics attaching itself to the state, and to the nihilism lurking under modern political settlements. The ultimate message of these apostles of modern political thought is that we should, Uzzah-like, live enslaved or die trying.

Bibliography

Manuscript Sources

An Act for the Registring and Preserving the Discents of Heires and Orphans. British Library, London. Add MS 32093. f.395.

Bridgewater and Ellesmere Manuscripts. Huntington Library, San Marino. mss EL.

Collections on the Subject of Judicature in Parliament, compiled by John Anstis. [1718–1745.] British Library, London. Stowe MS 1042.

Governor and Company of Adventurers of Old Providence Island: Book of Entries. 1630–1641. National Archives, Kew. MS CO 124/1.

Governor and Company of Adventurers of Old Providence Island: Journal. 1630–1650. National Archives, Kew. MS CO 124/2.

Heath and Verney Papers. 1602–1659. Vol. 1. British Library, London. Egerton MS 2978.

Heath and Verney Papers. 1660–1699. Vol. 2. British Library, London. Egerton MS 2979.

Hobbes, Thomas. 1640. *Elements of Law, naturall and politique.* Chatsworth House, Derbyshire. HS A/2/B.

Jessop, William. Letters as Secretary of Providence Island Company. British Library, London. Add MS 63854 B. Typewritten decipherment of Add MS 10615 prepared by Kenneth L Perrin.

Letter Book 9: 1688–1697. India Office Records and Private Papers. British Library, London. IOR/E/3/92.

The Princes highnes [Charles, Prince of Wales] annual Revenew certen in lands and other thinges. 18 January 1621. British Library, London. Add MS 33469. f.30.

Register of the Council of Wales and the Marches, c. 1586–1634. British Library, London. Egerton MS 2882.

Vane, Sir Henry the younger and Margaret Vane. 1677. [Sermons, Expositions on Job and "A letter of Sr H: Vs: to Mr H: C:y"]. National Art Library, Victoria and Albert Museum, London. Forster MS 606 (48.D.41).

Whitelocke, Bulstrode. *Historie of the Parlement of England. And of Some Resemblances to the Jewish and Other Councells.* British Library, London. Stowe MS 333. Holograph portion of Add MS 31984.

Printed Works

Achinstein, Sharon. 2003. *Literature and Dissent in Milton's England.* Cambridge: Cambridge UP.

An Acte for Certain Ordinaunces in the Kinges Majesties Domynion and Principalitie of Wales. 34 & 35 Hen.VIII c.26.

Adamson, J.S.A. 1987. *"The Vindiciae Veritatis* and the Political Creed of Viscount Saye and Seale." *Historical Research* 60: 45–63.

Agamben, Giorgio. 1998. *Homo Sacer: Sovereign Power and Bare Life.* Trans. Daniel Heller-Roazen. Meridian: Crossing Aesthetics. Palo Alto: Stanford UP.

Agamben, Giorgio. 2005. *State of Exception.* Trans. Kevin Attell. Chicago: U of Chicago P.

Agamben, Giorgio. 2015. *Stasis: Civil War as a Political Paradigm.* Trans. Nicholas Heron. Meridian: Crossing Aesthetics. Palo Alto: Stanford UP.

Andrewes, Lancelot. 2005. "A Sermon Preached before his Majesty, August 5, 1610." *Selected Sermons and Lectures.* Ed. Peter McCullough. Oxford: Oxford UP.

Aravamudan, Srivinas. 2009. "Hobbes and America." In *The Postcolonial Enlightenment: Eighteenth-Century Colonialisms and Postcolonial Theory.* Eds. Daniel Carey and Lynn Festa. Oxford: Oxford UP. 37–70.

Arbesmann, Rudolph, OSA, Sister Emily Joseph Daly, CSJ, and Edwin A. Quain, SJ, trans. 2008. *Tertullian, Apologetical Works and Minucius Felix, "Octavius."* Washington, DC: Catholic U of America P.

Archer, Ian W. 2002. *The Pursuit of Stability: Social Relations in Elizabethan London.* Cambridge Studies in Early Modern British History. Cambridge: Cambridge UP.

Arendt, Hannah. 1998. *The Human Condition.* 2nd ed. Intr. Margaret Canovan. Chicago: U of Chicago P.

Arendt, Hannah. 2005. *The Promise of Politics.* Ed. Jerome Kohn. New York: Schoken Books.

Arendt, Hannah and Karl Jaspers. 1992. *Correspondence 1926–1969.* Eds. Lotte Kohler and Hans Saner. Trans. Robert and Rita Kimber. New York: Harcourt Brace and Company.

Aristotle. 1932. *Politics.* Trans. H. Rakham. Loeb Classical Library 264. Cambridge, MA: Harvard UP.

Ariosto, Ludovico. 1975. *Orlando Furioso.* Trans. Barbara Reynolds. Harmondsworth: Penguin.

Aubrey, John. 1975. *Brief Lives.* Ed. Richard Barber. London: The Folio Society.

Augustine of Hippo. 1972. *The City of God [De civitate Dei].* Trans. Henry Bettenson. London: Penguin.

Aylmer, G.E. 1963. *The Struggle for the Constitution: England in the Seventeenth Century.* London: Blandford.

Badiou, Alain. 2013. *The Incident at Antioch: A Tragedy in Three Acts.* Intr. Kenneth Reinhard. Trans. Susan Spitzer. New York: Columbia UP.

Badiou, Alain. 2016. "Twenty-Four Notes on the Uses of the Word 'People.'" In Badiou et al. (2016) 21–31.

Badiou, Alain, Pierre Bourdieu, Judith Butler, Georges Didi-Huberman, Sadri Khiari, and Jacques Rancière. 2016. *What is a People?* Intr. Bruno Bosteels. Concl. Kevin Olson. Trans. Jody Gladding. New York: Columbia UP.

Balakrishnan, Gopal. 2000. *The Enemy: An Intellectual Portrait of Carl Schmitt.* London: Verso.

Barclaii, Joannis. 1612. *Pietas, sive publicae pro regibus.* Paris: P. Metayer.

Barclay, John. 1628. *Argenis.* Trans. Roger Le Grys. London; STC 1393.

Barclay, John. 2004. *Argenis*. Eds. and trans. Mark Riley and Dorothy Pritchard Huber. Neo-Latin Texts and Translations. Tempe, AZ: Arizona Center for Medieval and Renaissance Studies.

Baron, William. 1700. *Regicides, No Saints nor Martyrs Freely Expostulated with the Publishers of Ludlow's Third Volume*. London; Wing B898.

Bartelson, Jens. 1995. *A Genealogy of Sovereignty*. Cambridge Studies in International Relations. Cambridge: Cambridge UP.

Behnegar, Nasser. 2014. "Carl Schmitt and Strauss's Return to Premodern Philosophy." In *Reorientation: Leo Strauss in the 1930s*. Eds. Martin D. Yaffe and Richard S. Ruderman. New York: Palgrave Macmillan. 115–29.

Bell, H.E. (1953) 2011. *An Introduction to the History of the Court of Wards and Liveries*. Cambridge: Cambridge UP.

Bendersky, Joseph W., trans. 1987. "Carl Schmitt at Nuremburg." Piccone and Ulmen (1987) 91–106.

Benhabib, Seyla. 2012. "Carl Schmitt's Critique of Kant: Sovereignty and International Law." *Political Theory* 40: 688–713.

Benlowe, Edward. 1652. *Theophila, or Loves Sacrifice*. London; Wing B1879.

Benton, Lauren. 2010. *A Search for Sovereignty: Law and Geography in European Empires, 1400–1900*. Cambridge: Cambridge UP.

Benton, Lauren and Richard J. Ross, eds. 2013. *Legal Pluralism and Empires, 1500–1850*. New York: New York University P.

Bierksteker, Thomas J. and Cynthia Weber, eds. 1996. *State Sovereignty as Social Construct*. Cambridge Studies in International Relations. Cambridge: Cambridge UP.

Blackstone, Sir William. 1791. *Commentaries on the Laws of England: Book the Fourth*. 11th ed. London.

Bobbio, Norberto. 1993. *Thomas Hobbes and the Natural Law Tradition*. Trans. Daniela Gobetti. Chicago: U of Chicago P.

Bodin, Jean. 1606. *The Six Bookes of the Common-Weale*. Trans. Richard Knolles. London; STC 3193.

Bodin, Jean. 1992. *On Sovereignty: Four Chapters from* The Six Books of the Commonwealth. Ed. Julian H. Franklin. Cambridge: Cambridge UP.

Bolton, Edmund. 2017. *Averrunci, or the Skowrers*. Eds. Patricia J. Osmond and Robert W. Ulery, Jr. Medieval and Renaissance Texts and Studies 508. Renaissance English Text Society 38. Tempe: Arizona Center for Medieval and Renaissance Studies.

Botero, Giovanni. 1601. *The Worlde, or an Historicall Description of the Most Famous Kingdomes and Common-weales* [*Le relazione universali*]. Trans. Robert Johnson. London; STC 3399.

Botero, Giovanni. 1956. *The Reason of State*. Trans. P.J. and D.P. Waley. London: Routledge and Kegan Paul.

Botero, Giovanni. 1990. *Della ragion di stato*. Rpt. of 1598 Venice edn. Bologna: A. Forni.

Botero, Giovanni. 2017. *The Reason of State*. Trans. and ed. Robert Bireley. Cambridge Texts in the History of Political Thought. Cambridge: Cambridge UP.

Bourke, Richard and Quentin Skinner, eds. 2016. *Popular Sovereignty in Historical Perspective*. Cambridge: Cambridge UP.

Bowen, Lloyd. 2007a. *The Politics of Principality: Wales, c. 1603–1642*. Cardiff: U of Wales P.

Bowen, Lloyd. 2007b. "Prerogative Government: The Council in the Marches and the Long Parliament." *The English Historical Review* 122: 1258–86.

Boyle, Roger Earl of Orrery. 1651. *Parthenissa*. [n.p]; Wing O488.

Boyle, Roger Earl of Orrery. 1655. *Parthenissa, A Romance in Four Parts*. London; Wing O491A.

Boyle, Roger Earl of Orrery. 1676. *Parthenissa, That Most Fam'd Romance the Six Volumes Compleat*. London; Wing O490.

Brathwaite, Richard. 1659. *Panthalia: Or the Royal Romance*. London; Wing B4273.

Brett, Annabel. 2007. *Changes of State: Nature and the Limits of the City in Early Modern Natural Law*. Princeton: Princeton UP.

Brett, Annabel. 2019. "The Post-Machiavellian Poetry of 'An Horatian Ode upon Cromwell's Return from Ireland.'" In Dzelzainis and Holberton (2019) 425–42.

Britton, Dennis Austin. 2014. *Becoming Christian: Race, Reformation, and Early Modern English Romance*. New York: Fordham UP.

Brown, Wendy. 2010. *Walled States, Waning Sovereignty*. New York: Zone Books.

Burke, Peter. 1991. "Tacitism, Skepticism, and Reason of State." In *The Cambridge History of Political Thought 1450–1700*. Eds. J.H. Burns and Mark Goldie. *The Cambridge History of Political Thought, 1450–1700*. Cambridge: Cambridge UP. 479–98.

Bush, Douglas. 1952. *English Literature in the Earlier Seventeenth Century, 1600–1660*. Oxford: Clarendon.

Calamy, Edmund, et al. 1663. *A Compleat Collection of Farewel Sermons*. London; Wing C5638.

Caldwell, Peter C. 1997. *Popular Sovereignty and the Crisis of German Constitutional Law: The Theory and Practice of Weimar Constitutionalism*. Durham and London: Duke UP.

Campana, Joseph, ed. 2018. Special issue, "After Sovereignty." *SEL: Studies in English Literature, 1500–1900* 58 (2018): 1–217.

Campbell, Gordon and Thomas N. Corns. 2008. *John Milton: Life, Work, and Thought*. Oxford: Oxford UP.

Carleton, Dudley. 1609. Letter to John Chamberlain of 27 April. *Calendar of State Papers Domestic*. Available at british-history.ac.uk.

Cartari, Vincenzo. 2012. *Images of the Gods of the Ancients: The First Italian Mythography*. Trans. and ed. John Mulryan. Tempe: Arizona Center for Medieval and Renaissance Studies.

Celikates, Robin, and Yolande Jansen. 2012. "Reclaiming Democracy: An Interview with Wendy Brown on Occupy, Sovereignty, and Secularism." *Krisis*, issue 3: 70.

Cicero. 1927. *Pro Caecina* [*In Defence of A Caecina*]. In *Orations*. Trans. H. Grose Hodge. Loeb Classical Library 198. Cambridge, MA: Harvard UP.

Chalmers, George ed. 1890. "Treaty between Charles Gustavus King of Sweden, and Oliver Cromwell Protector of England…Done at London, Anno 1656." In *A Collection of Treaties Between Great Britain and Other Powers*. London: John Stockdale.

Chernaik, Warren. 1999. "'Every Conqueror Creates a Muse': Conquest and Constitutions in Marvell and Waller." In Chernaik and Dzelzainis (1999) 195–216.

Chernaik, Warren and Martin Dzelzainis, eds. 1999. *Marvell and Liberty*. London: Macmillan.

Clark, Peter. 2000. *British Clubs and Societies, 1580–1800: The Origins of an Associational World*. Oxford Studies in Social History. Oxford: Oxford UP.

Cocks, Joan. 2014. *Sovereignty and other Political Delusions*. London: Bloomsbury.

Coke, Sir Edward. 1697a. *Reports*. Part 3. London; Wing C4968.

Coke, Sir Edward. 1697b. *Reports*. Part 5. London; Wing C4911.

Coke, Sir Edward. 1697c. *Reports*. Part 6. London; Wing C4956.

Coke, Sir Edward. 1697d. *Reports*. Part 8. London; Wing C4937.

[*Commons Journals.*] 1802. *Journal of the House of Commons*. London: His Majesty's Stationery Office. Available at british-history.ac.uk.

A Conference desired by the Lords and Had by a Committee of Both Houses, Concerning the Rights and Privileges of the Subjects. London, 1642; Wing E1284C.

Conti, Natale. 2006. *Mythologiae*. 2 vols. Trans. and eds. John Mulryan and Steven Brown. Tempe: Arizona Center for Medieval and Renaissance Studies.

[Cooper, Anthony Ashley Lord Shaftesbury.] 1679? *Notes Taken in Short-hand of a Speech in the House of Lords on the Debates of Appointing a Day for Hearing Dr. Shirley's Cause, October. 20. 1675*. [London?]; Wing S2897A.

Cooper, Anthony Ashley Lord Shaftesbury and George Villiers, Duke of Buckingham. 1675. *Two Speeches*. Amsterdam; Wing S2907.

Cormack Bradin. (2007) 2013. *A Power to Do Justice: Jurisdiction, English Literature, and the Rise of Common Law, 1509–1625*. Chicago: U of Chicago P.

Cowley, Abraham. 1656. *Poems*. London; Wing C6683.

Cromartie, Alan. 2006. *The Constitutionalist Revolution: An Essay on the History of England, 1450–1642*. Cambridge: Cambridge UP.

Cross, Arthur Lyon. 1917. "The English Law Courts at the Close of the Revolution of 1688." *Michigan Law Review* 15: 529–608.

Crowe, Michael Bertram. 1974. "St. Thomas and Ulpian's Natural Law." In *St. Thomas Aquinas 1274–1974: Commemorative Studies*. Vol. 1. Foreword Étienne Gilson. Toronto: Pontifical Institute of Mediaeval Studies, 1974. 261–82.

Cuttica, Cesare. "Anti-repulican Cries under Cromwell: The Vehement Attacks of Robert Filmer against Republican Practice and Republican Theory in the Early 1650s." In Wiemann and Mahlberg (2014) 35–52.

Davenant, Sir William. 1650. *A Discourse upon Gondibert . . . with an Answer to it, by Mr. Hobbs*. Paris; Wing D322.

Davenant, Sir William. 1651. *Gondibert an Heroick Poem*. London; Wing D326.

Davis, J.C. 2014. "The Prose Romance of the 1650s as a Context for *Oceana*." In Wiemann and Mahlberg (2014) 65–83.

Debates of the House of Commons, from 1667 to 1694. 1763. Vol. 3. Ed. Anchitell Grey. London: D. Henry and R. Cave.

Deleuze, Gilles and Felix Guattari. 1987. *A Thousand Plateaus: Capitalism and Schizophrenia*. Trans. Brian Massumi. London: Continuum.

Dictionary of Welsh Biography Down to 1940, Under the Auspices of the Honourable Society of Cymmrodorion. 1959. Eds. Sir John Edward Lloyd and R.T. Jenkins. Cardiff: William Lewis.

Didi-Huberman, Georges. 2016. "To Render Sensible." In Badiou et al. (2016) 65–86.

Dionysius the Areopagite, Pseudo-. 1987. *Complete Works.* Trans. Colm Luibheid and Paul Rorem. Classics of Western Spirituality. Mahwah, NJ: Paulist Press.

Donne, John. 1966. *Poems.* Vol. 1. Ed. Herbert J.C. Grierson. Oxford: Clarendon.

Donne, John. 1971. *Prebend Sermons.* Ed. Janel M. Mueller. Cambridge, MA: Harvard UP.

Dobranski, Stephen. 2009. *A Variorum Commentary on the Poems of John Milton, Volume 3: "Samson Agonistes."* Intr. Archie Burnett. Ed. P.J. Klemp. Pittsburgh: Duquesne UP.

Dryden, John, Thomas Sprat, and Edmund Waller. 1659. *Three Poems Upon the Death of his Late Highnesse Oliver Lord Protector of England, Scotland, and Ireland.* London; Wing W526.

Dyzenhaus, David. 2003. *Legality and Legitimacy: Carl Schmitt, Hans Kelsen and Hermann Heller in Weimar.* Oxford: Oxford UP.

Dzelzainis, Martin. 1999. "Marvell and the Earl of Castlemaine." In Chernaik and Dzelzainis (1999) 290–312.

Dzelzainis, Martin. 2009. "The Politics of *Paradise Lost.*" In *The Oxford Handbook of Milton.* Eds. Nicholas McDowell and Nigel Smith. Oxford: Oxford UP. 547–69.

Dzelzainis, Martin and Edward Holberton, eds. 2019. *The Oxford Handbook of Andrew Marvell.* Oxford: Oxford UP.

Epictetus. 1928. *The Encheiridion.* In *Discourses, Books 3–4. Fragments. The Encheiridion.* Trans. W.A. Oldfather. Loeb Classical Library 218. Cambridge, MA: Harvard UP.

Elegie on the Untimely Death of the Incomparably Valiant and Noble, Francis, Lord Villiers, Brother to the Duke of Buckingham. 1648. London; Wing E443.

Evrigenis, Ioannis D. 2014. *Images of Anarchy: The Rhetoric and Science in Hobbes's State of Nature.* Cambridge: Cambridge UP.

Felix, Minucius. 2008. "Octavius." In Arbesmann et al. (2008).

Felltham, Owen. "Authori" ["To the Author"]. In Barclay (2004) 78–9.

[Fiennes, Nathaniel and William, Lord Saye and Sele.] 1654. *Vindicae veritatis.* [London;] Wing F884.

Fiennes, William Lord Saye and Sele. 1895. "A Letter from Lord Saye and Sele to Lord Wharton, 29 December 1657." Ed. C.H. Firth. *The English Historical Review* 10: 106–7.

Filmer, Sir Robert. 1652. *Observations Concerning the Originall of Government upon Mr. Hobbs Leviathan, Mr. Milton against Salmasius, H. Grotius De jure belli, Mr. Huntons Treatise of Monarchy.* London, 1652; Wing F918.

Finch, Heneage Lord Nottingham. 1965. *Manual of Chancery Practice and Prolegomena of Chancery and Equity.* Ed. David Eryl Corbet Yale. Cambridge: Cambridge UP.

Fleming, David. 1966. "John Barclay: Neo-Latinist at the Jacobean Court." *Renaissance News* 19: 228–36.

Foisneau, Luc. 2004. "*Leviathan's* Theory of Justice." In Sorell and Foisneau (2004) 105–22.

Foucault, Michel. 1997. *"Society Must be Defended": Lectures at the Collège de France 1975–76*. Trans. David Macey. Eds. Mauro Bertani and Alessandro Fontana. New York: Picador.

Fourty Four Queries to the Life of Queen Dick. 1659. [London]; Wing F1622.

Fox, Charles James. 1888. *A History of the Early Part of the Reign of James II*. New York: Cassell and Company.

French, JM. 1939. *Milton in Chancery: New Chapters in the Lives of the Poet and his Father*. New York: Modern Language Association of America.

Frye, Northrop. 2000. *Anatomy of Criticism: Four Essays*. Foreword by Harold Bloom. Princeton: Princeton UP.

[G.B.] 1662. *The Way to be Rich, According to the Practice of the Great Audley*. London; Wing B71.

Gajda, Alexandra. 2009. "Tacitus and Political Thought in Early Modern Europe, c. 1530–c. 1640." In Woodman (2009) 253–68.

Galli, Carlo. 2000. "Carl Schmitt's Antiliberalism: Its Theoretical and Historical Sources and its Philosophical and Political Meaning." *Cardozo Law Review* 5–6: 1597–617.

Galli, Carlo. 2010. *Political Spaces and Global War*. Ed. Adam Sitze. Trans. Elisabeth Fay. Minneapolis: U of Minnesota P.

Galli, Carlo. 2012. "*Hamlet*: Representation and the Concrete." Trans. Adam Sitze and Amanda Minervini. In Hammill and Lupton (2012) 60–83.

Galli, Carlo. 2015. *Janus's Gaze: Essays on Carl Schmitt*. Ed. Adam Sitze. Trans. Amanda Minervini. Durham, NC: Duke UP.

Gardiner, Samuel Rawson, ed. 1906. *Constitutional Documents of the Puritan Revolution, 1625–1660*. Oxford: Clarendon.

Geneva Bible: A Facsimile of the 1560 Edition. 2007. Ed. Lloyd E. Berry. Peabody, MA: Hendrickson.

Goldie, Mark. 2019. "Marvell and his Adversaries, 1672-1678." In Dzelzainis and Holberton (2019) 703–24.

Gomberville, Le Roy sieur de. 1647. *The History of Polexander in Five Books*. Trans. William Browne. London; Wing G1025.

Gordon, M.D. 1910. "The Collection of Ship Money in the Reign of Charles I." *Transactions of the Royal Historical Society*, 3rd ser., 4: 141–62.

Greaves, Richard. 1990. *Enemies Under his Feet: Radicals and Nonconformists in Britain, 1664–1677*. Stanford, CA: Stanford UP.

Gregory the Great, Saint. 1844. *Morals on the Book of Job*. Vol. 1. Library of the Fathers of the Holy Catholic Church. Oxford: John Henry Parker.

Grimm, Dieter. 2015. *Sovereignty: The Origin and Future of a Legal Concept*. Trans. Belinda Cooper. Columbia Studies in Political Thought. New York: Columbia UP.

Grotius, Hugo. 2005. *The Rights of War and Peace*. 3 vols. Ed. Richard Tuck. *Natural Law and Enlightenment Classics*. Gen. ed. Knud Haakonssen. Indianapolis: Liberty Fund.

Guibbory, Achsah. 2010. *Christian Identity, Jews, and Israel in Seventeenth-Century England*. Oxford: Oxford UP.

Guicciardini, Francesco. 1970. *Maxims and Reflections of a Renaissance Statesman [Ricordi]*. Trans. Mario Domandi. Intr. Nicolai Rubinstein. Gloucester, MA: Peter Smith.

Gündoğdu, Ayten. 2015. *Rightlessness in an Age of Rights: Hannah Arendt and the Contemporary Struggles of Migrants*. Oxford: Oxford UP.

Hackenbracht, Ryan. 2019. *National Reckonings: The Last Judgment and Literature in Milton's England*. Ithaca, NY: Cornell UP.

Hale, John K. 2008. "Thomas Hobbes' Poem of Exile: The Verse *Vita* and Ovid's *Tristia* 4.10." *Scholia: Studies in Classical Antiquity* 17: 92–105.

Hale, Sir Matthew. 1796. *The Jurisdiction of the Lords' House, or Parliament*. London; ESTC T110601.

Hammill, Graham. 2012. *The Mosaic Constitution: Political Theology and Imagination from Machiavelli to Milton*. Chicago: U of Chicago P.

Hammill, Graham and Julia Reinhard Lupton, eds. 2012. *Political Theology and Early Modernity*. Chicago: U of Chicago P.

Hammond, Paul. 2014. *Milton and the People*. Oxford: Oxford UP.

Hampton, Timothy. 2009. *Fictions of Embassy: Literature and Diplomacy in Early Modern Europe*. Ithaca, NY: Cornell UP.

Harington, Sir John. 1618. *Most Elegant and Witty Epigrams*. London; STC 12776.

Harrington, James. 1977. *The Political Works of James Harrington*. 2 vols. Ed. J.G. A. Pocock. Cambridge: Cambridge UP.

Hart, James S. 1983. "The House of Lords and the Appellate Jurisdiction in Equity 1640-1643." *Parliamentary History* 2: 49–70.

Hart, James S. 1991. *Justice upon Petition: The House of Lords and the Reformation of Justice 1621–1675*. London: Harper Collins Academic.

Hawkes, David. 2004. "The Concept of a 'Hireling' in Milton's Theology." *Milton Studies* 43: 64–85.

Helmholz, Richard H. and Vito Piergiovanni. 2009. *Relations Between the ius commune and English Law*. Soveria Mannelli: Rubbettino Editore.

[Herbert, Sir Percy.] 1653. *Cloria and Narcissus, A Delightfull and New Romance*. London; Wing C4725.

[Herbert, Sir Percy.] 1661. *The Princess Cloria, or The Royal Romance in Five Parts*. London; Wing P3492.

Herodotus. 1921. *The Persian Wars. Volume 2: Books 3–4*. Trans. A.D. Godley. Loeb Classical Library 118. Cambridge, MA: Harvard UP.

Herrick, Robert. 1968. *Complete Poetry*. Ed. J. Max Patrick. New York: W.W. Norton.

Hesiod. 2007. *Theogony. Works and Days. Testimonia*. Ed. and tans. Glenn W. Most. Loeb Classical Library 57. Cambridge, MA: Harvard UP.

Hindle, Steve. 2004. *On the Parish? The Micro-Politics of Poor Relief in Rural England c. 1550–1750*. Oxford Studies in Social History. Oxford: Clarendon.

Hirst, Derek and Steven N. Zwicker, eds. 2011. *The Cambridge Companion to Andrew Marvell*. Cambridge: Cambridge UP.

Hirst, Derek and Steven N. Zwicker. 2012. *Andrew Marvell: Orphan of the Hurricane*. Oxford: Oxford UP.

Hobbes, Thomas. 1650. *De corpore politico. Or, The Elements of Law*. London; Wing H2219.

Hobbes, Thomas. 1679. *Vita authore seipso*. London; Wing H2267.

Hobbes, Thomas. 1680. *The Life of Mr. Thomas Hobbes of Malmesbury Written by Himself in a Latine Poem and now Translated into English*. [Trans. Richard Blackburn.] London; Wing H2251.

Hobbes, Thomas. 1839. *The Elements of Philosophy*. In *The English Works of Thomas Hobbes*. Vol. 1. London: John Bohn.

Hobbes, Thomas. 1969. *Elements of Law*. Ed. Ferdinand Tönnies. New York: Barnes and Noble.

Hobbes, Thomas. 1991. *Man and Citizen* (De Homine *and* De Cive). Ed. Bernard Gert. Indianapolis: Hackett.

Hobbes, Thomas. 2005. *A Dialogue Between a Philosopher and a Student, of the Common Laws of England*. Ed. Alan Cromartie. *Writings on Common Law and Hereditary Right*. Vol. 11 of The Clarendon Edition of the Works of Thomas Hobbes. Oxford: Clarendon P.

Hobbes, Thomas. 2007. *The Correspondence of Thomas Hobbes*. Ed. Noel Malcolm. Vols. 6–7 of The Clarendon Edition of the Works of Thomas Hobbes. Oxford: Clarendon P.

Hobbes, Thomas. 2014a. *Behemoth*. Pbk. Ed. Paul Seaward. Vol. 10 of the Clarendon Edition of the Works of Thomas Hobbes. Oxford: Clarendon P.

Hobbes, Thomas. 2014b. *Leviathan*. Pbk. Ed. Noel Malcolm. Vols. 2–3 of The Clarendon Edition of the Works of Thomas Hobbes. Oxford: Clarendon P.

Hoekstra, Kinch. 2004. "The *de facto* Turn in Hobbes's Political Philosophy." In Sorell and Foisneau (2004) 33–57.

Holberton, Edward. 2008. *Poetry and the Cromwellian Protectorate*. Oxford: Oxford UP.

Hooker, Richard. 1977–1998. *The Folger Library Edition of the Works of Richard Hooker*. 7 vols. Gen. ed. W. Speed Hill. Cambridge, MA: Harvard/Belknap and Binghamton, NY: MRTS.

Hooker, William. 2009. *Carl Schmitt's International Thought: Order and Orientation*. Cambridge: Cambridge UP.

Höpfl, Harro. 2004. *Jesuit Political Thought: The Society of Jesus and the State, c. 1540–1630*. Ideas in Context 70. Cambridge: Cambridge UP.

Horace. 1988. *Odes and Epodes*. Trans. C.E. Bennett. Loeb Classical Library 33. Cambridge, MA: Harvard UP.

Horace. 2005. *Satires*. Trans. H. Rushton Fairclough. Loeb Classical Library 194. Cambridge, MA: Harvard UP.

Hosmer, James K. 1889. *The Life of Young Sir Henry Vane*. Boston: Houghton, Mifflin and Company.

Hughes, Ann. 2019. "Marvell and the Interregnum." In Dzelzainis and Holberton (2019) 61–78.

Hughes, Merritt Y, ed. 1957. *Milton: Complete Poems and Major Prose*. New York: Odyssey P.

Jackson, Nicholas D. 2007. *Hobbes, Bramhall and the Politics of Liberty and Necessity: A Quarrel of the Civil Wars and Interregnum*. Cambridge: Cambridge UP.

Jacobson, Arthur J. and Bernard Schlink, eds. 2000. *Weimar: A Jurisprudence of Crisis*. Trans. Belinda Cooper. Berkeley and Los Angeles: U of California P.

Jerome, Saint. 1893. "To Eustochium." In *Epistles. Nicene and Post-Nicene Fathers, Second Series*. Vol 6. Trans. W.H. Fremantle, G. Lewis, and W.G. Martley. New York: Christian Literature Publishing. Available at newadvent.org.

Johnson, Robert C., Maija Jansson Cole, Mary Frear Keeler and William B. Bidwell, eds. 1977. *Commons Debates 1628*. Vol. 2: 17 March–19 April 1628. New Haven: Yale UP.

Jones, Edward. 2013. *Young Milton: The Emerging Author 1620–1642*. Oxford: Oxford UP.

Jonson, Ben. 1640. *Execration against Vulcan*. London; STC 14771.

Jonson, Ben. 1947. *The Poems; The Prose Works*. Eds. C.H. Herford, Percy Simpson, and Evelyn Simpson. Vol. 8 of *The Works of Ben Jonson*. Oxford: Oxford UP.

Joseph, Timothy A. 2012. *Tacitus the Epic Successor: Virgil, Lucan, and the Narrative of Civil War in the "Histories."* Mnemosyne Supplements 345. Leiden: Brill.

Josephus. 1934. *Jewish Antiquities, Volume III: Books 7–8*. Trans. Ralph Marcus. Loeb Classical Library 281. Cambridge, MA: Harvard University Press.

Jurkevics, Anna. 2017. "Hannah Arendt Reads Carl Schmitt's *The* Nomos *of the* Earth: A Dialogue on Law and Geopolitics from the Margins." *European Journal of Political Theory* 16: 345–66.

Juvenal. 2004. *Satires*. In *Juvenal and Persius*. Ed. and trans. Susanna Morton Braund. Loeb Classical Library 91. Cambridge, MA: Harvard UP.

Kahn, Paul W. 2011. *Political Theology: Four New Chapters on the Concept of Sovereignty*. New York: Columbia UP.

Kahn, Victoria. 2002. "Reinventing Romance, or The Surprising Effects of Sympathy." *Renaissance Quarterly* 55: 625–61.

Kahn, Victoria. 2004. *Wayward Contracts: The Crisis of Political Obligation in England, 1640–1674*. Princeton, NJ: Princeton UP.

Kahn, Victoria. 2014. *The Future of Illusion: Political Theology and Early Modern Texts*. Chicago: U of Chicago P.

Kalmo, Hent and Quentin Skinner, eds. 2010. *Sovereignty in Fragments: The Past, Present and Future of a Contested Concept*. Cambridge: Cambridge UP.

Kapust, Daniel J. 2011. *Republicanism, Rhetoric, and Roman Political Thought: Sallust, Livy, and Tacitus*. Cambridge: Cambridge UP.

Karstadt, Elliott. 2016. "The Place of Interest in Hobbes's Civil Science." *Hobbes Studies* 29: 105–28.

Kelliher, W.H. 2008. "Marvell, Andrew (1621–1678)." *Oxford Dictionary of National Biography*. Oxford: Oxford UP.

Kelsen, Hans. 1992. *Introduction to the Problems of Legal Theory*. Trans. Bonnie Litschewski Paulson and Stanley L. Paulson. Oxford: Clarendon P.

Kennedy, Ellen. 2004. *Constitutional Failure: Carl Schmitt in Weimar*. Durham and London: Duke UP.

Kiséry, András. 2016. *Hamlet's Moment: Drama and Political Knowledge in Early Modern England*. Oxford: Oxford UP.

Kneidel, Gregory. 2015a. "Coscus, Queen Elizabeth, and Law in John Donne's 'Satyre II.'" *Renaissance Quarterly* 61 (2008): 92–121.

Kneidel, Gregory. 2015b. *John Donne and Early Modern Legal Culture: The End of Equity in the Satyres*. Medieval and Renaissance Literary Studies. Pittsburgh: Duquesne UP.

Koskenniemi, Martti. 2004. "International Law as Political Theology: How to Read *Nomos der Erde*?" *Constellations* 11: 492–511.

Kupperman, Karen Ordahl. 1993. *Providence Island, 1630–1641: The Other Puritan Colony*. Cambridge: Cambridge UP.

Laroche, Emmanuel. 1949. *Histoire de la racins nem- en grec ancient (nemo, nemesis, nomos, nomizo)*. Paris: Librarie C. Klincksieck.

Laski, Harold. 1921. *The Foundations of Sovereignty: And Other Essays*. New York: Harcourt, Brace, and Company.

Laski, Harold. 1997. *The Rise of European Liberalism*. 1936. Intr. John L. Stanley. New Brunswick, NJ: Transaction.

Laski, Harold. 2014. *Authority in the Modern State*. 1919. Rpt. edn. Clark, NJ: Lawbook Exchange.

Lee, Daniel. 2016. *Popular Sovereignty in Early Modern Constitutional Thought*. Oxford Constitutional Theory. Oxford: Oxford UP.

Legg, Stephen, ed. 2011. *Spatiality, Sovereignty, and Carl Schmitt: Geographies of the Nomos*. Abingdon: Routledge.

Lewalski, Barbara K. 1966. *Milton's Brief Epic: The Genre, Meaning, and Art of "Paradise Regained."* Providence: Brown UP.

Lewalski, Barbara K. 1998. "How Radical was the Young Milton?" In *Milton and Heresy*. Eds. Stephen Dobranski and John P. Rumrich. Cambridge: Cambridge UP. 49–72.

Ley, James, Earl of Marlborough. 1659. *Reports of Divers Resolutions in Law Arising upon Cases in the Court of Wards*. London; Wing M688.

Lindahl, Hans. 2006. "Give and Take: Arendt and the *Nomos* of Political Community." *Philosophy and Social Criticism* 32: 881–901.

Lipsius, Justus. 1590. *Politicorum, sive, Civilis doctrinae libri sex*. London; STC 15700.7.

Lipsius, Justus. 1594. *Sixe Bookes of Politickes or Civill Doctrine*. Trans. William Jones. London; STC 15701.

Lloyd, S.A. 2001. "Hobbes's Self-Effacing Natural-Law Theory." *Pacific Philosophical Quarterly* 82: 286–87.

Lloyd, S.A. 2009. *Morality in the Philosophy of Thomas Hobbes: Cases in the Law of Nature*. Cambridge: Cambridge UP.

Lowe, Lisa. 2015. *The Intimacies of Four Continents*. Durham and London: Duke UP.

Loxley, James. 2019. "Andrew Marvell and Cavalier Poetics." In Dzelzainis and Holberton (2019) 599–613.

Lupton, Julia Reinhard. 2005. *Citizen-Saints: Shakespeare and Political Theology*. Chicago: U of Chicago P.

Machiavelli. 1971. *The Prince*. Trans. George Bull. 1961. London: Penguin.

Mackenzie, Sir George. 1660. *Aretina; Or, The Serious Romance*. Edinburgh; Wing M151.

Macpherson, C.B. (1963) 2011. *The Political Theory of Possessive Individualism: Hobbes to Locke*. Oxford: Oxford UP.

Maitland, Frederic William. 1911. "The Crown as Corporation." *The Collected Papers of Frederic William Maitland*. Ed. H.A.L. Fisher. Cambridge: Cambridge UP.

Major, Philip. 2014. "'O how I love thee Solitudes': Thomas Fairfax and the Poetics of Retirement." In *England's Fortress: New Perspectives on Thomas, Third Lord Fairfax*. Ed. Andrew Hopper and Major. London: Routledge.

Malcolm, Noel, ed. (2007) 2010. *Reason of State, Propaganda, and the Thirty Years' War: An Unknown Translation by Thomas Hobbes*. Pbk. Oxford: Clarendon P.

Malvezzi, Virgilio. 1642. *Discourses upon Cornelius Tacitus*. Trans. Sir Richard Baker. London; Wing M359.

Marcus, Leah S. 1983. "The Milieu of Milton's *Comus*: Judicial Reform at Ludlow and the Problem of Sexual Assault." *Criticism* 25: 293–327.

Margalit, Avishai. 2017. *On Betrayal*. Cambridge, MA: Harvard UP.

Martel, James R. 2012. *Divine Violence: Walter Benjamin and the Eschatology of Sovereignty*. New York: Routledge.

Marvell, Andrew. 1967. *Poems and Letters*. 2 vols. Rev. ed. Eds. H. M. Margoliouth, Pierre Legouis, and E. E. Duncan-Jones. Oxford: Oxford UP.

Marvell, Andrew. 2007. *Poems*. Rev. ed. Ed. Nigel Smith. Harlow: Pearson.

Marvell, Andrew. 2003. *Prose Works*. 2 vols. Eds. Annabel Patterson, et al. New Haven: Yale UP.

Mayers, Ruth E. 2015. "Vane, Sir Henry the younger (1613-1662)." *Oxford Dictionary of National Biography*. Online edn. Oxford: Oxford UP.

McCormick, John P. 1994. "Fear, Technology, and the State: Carl Schmitt, Leo Strauss, and the Revival of Hobbes in Weimar and National Socialist Germany." *Political Theory* 22: 619–52.

McCormick, John P. 1999. *Carl Schmitt's Critique of Liberalism: Against Politics as Technology*. Cambridge: Cambridge UP.

McCormick, John P. 2016. "Teaching in Vain: Carl Schmitt, Thomas Hobbes, and the Theory of the Sovereign State." In Meierhenrich and Simons (2016) 269–90.

McDowell, Nicholas. 2008. *Poetry and Allegiance in the English Civil Wars: Marvell and the Cause of Wit*. Oxford: Oxford UP.

McDowell, Nicholas. 2011. "How Laudian Was the Young Milton?" *Milton Studies* 52: 3–22.

McPherson, B.H. 1998. "Revisiting the Manor of East Greenwich." *The American Journal of Legal History* 42: 35–56.

Meier, Heinrich. 1995. *Carl Schmitt and Leo Strauss: The Hidden Dialogue*. Trans. J. Harvey Lomax. Chicago: U of Chicago P.

Meierhenrich, Jens and Oliver Simons, eds. 2016. *The Oxford Handbook of Carl Schmitt*. Oxford: Oxford UP.

Mercurius Poeticus. Discovering the Treasons of a Thing Call'd Parliament. 1648. London; Thomason E.442[4].

Miller, Jeffrey Alan. 2013. "Milton and the Conformable Puritanism of Richard Stock and Thomas Young." In Jones (2013) 72–103.

Miller, Ted H. 2011. *Mortal Gods: Science, Politics, and the Humanist Ambitions of Thomas Hobbes*. University Park: Penn State UP.

Milsom, S.F.C. 1969. *Historical Foundations of the Common Law*. London: Butterworths.

Milton, John. 1931–38. *The Works of John Milton*. 18 vols. in 21. Eds. Frank Allen Patterson et al. New York: Columbia UP.

Milton, John. 1953–82. *Complete Prose Works*. 8 vols. in 10. Eds. Don M. Wolfe et al. New Haven: Yale UP.

Milton, John. 2007. *Paradise Lost*. Ed. Barbara K. Lewalski. Malden, MA: Wiley-Blackwell.

Milton, John. 2008–. *The Complete Works of John Milton*. Vols. 2, 3, 6, and 8. Gen. eds. Gordon Campbell and Thomas N. Corns. Oxford: Oxford UP.

Milton, John. 2009. *Complete Shorter Poems*. Ed. Stella P. Revard. Malden, MA: Wiley-Blackwell.

Mohamed, Feisal G. 2008. *In the Anteroom of Divinity: The Reformation of the Angels from Colet to Milton*. Toronto: U of Toronto P.

Mohamed, Feisal G. 2011. *Milton and the Post-Secular Present: Ethics, Politics, Terrorism*. Palo Alto: Stanford UP.

Mohamed, Feisal G. 2015a. "Milton's Enmity toward Islam and the *Intellectus agens*." Special issue, "Reading Milton through Islam." Eds. David Currell and François-Xavier Gleyzon. *English Studies* 96: 65–81.

Mohamed, Feisal G. 2015b. Review of Victoria Kahn, *The Future of Illusion*. *Milton Quarterly* 49: 143–8.

Mohamed, Feisal G. and Patrick Fadely, eds. 2017. *Milton's Modernities: Poetry, Philosophy, and History from the Seventeenth Century to the Present*. Rethinking the Early Modern. Evanston: Northwestern UP.

Moore, John. 1653. *The Crying Sin of England, of Not Caring for the Poor*. London; Wing M2558.

Moore, John. 1656. *A Scripture-Word against Inclosure*. London; Wing M2559.

Mouffe, Chantal, ed. 1999. *The Challenge of Carl Schmitt*. Phronesis. London: Verso.

Mouffe, Chantal. 2005. "Schmitt's Vision of a Multipolar World Order." *South Atlantic Quarterly* 104: 245–51.

Moyn, Samuel. 2016. "Concepts of the Political in Twentieth-Century European Thought." In Meierhenrich and Simons (2016) 291–311.

Nedham, Marchamont. 1650. *The Case of the Common-Wealth of England*. London; Wing N377.

Nelson, Eric. 2011. *The Hebrew Republic: Jewish Sources and the Transformation of European Political Thought*. Cambridge, MA: Harvard UP.

Norbrook, David. 1999. *Writing the English Republic*. Cambridge: Cambridge UP.

Nyquist, Mary. 2013. *Arbitrary Rule: Slavery, Tyranny, and the Power of Life and Death*. Chicago: U of Chicago P.

Oakley, S.P. 2009. "*Res olim dissociabiles*: Emperors, Senators, and Liberty." In Woodman (2009) 184–94.

Odysseos, Louiza and Fabio Petito. 2007. *The International Political Thought of Carl Schmitt: Terror, Liberal War, and the Crisis of Global Order.* Abingdon: Routledge.

Osborn, Dorothy. 1888. *Letters from Dorothy Osborn to William Temple 1652–54.* 3rd ed. Ed. Edward Abbott Parry. London: Griffith, Farran, Okeden & Welsh.

Ovid. 1916. *Metamorphoses.* 2 vols. Trans. Frank Justus Miller. Loeb Classical Library 42 and 43. Cambridge, MA: Harvard UP.

Ovid. 1931. *Fasti.* Trans. James G. Frazer. Revised by G.P. Goold. Loeb Classical Library 253. Cambridge, MA: Harvard UP.

Ovid. 2015. *Fastorum Libri Sex: The "Fasti" of Ovid.* Ed. and trans. James George Frazer. Cambridge Library Collection. Volume 3: Commentary on Books 3 and 4. Cambridge: Cambridge UP.

Pagden, Anthony. 1982. *The Fall of Natural Man: The American Indian and the Origins of Comparative Ethnology.* Cambridge: Cambridge UP.

Parker, William Riley. 2003. *Milton: A Biography.* 2nd ed. Ed. Gordon Campbell. Rpt. Oxford: Clarendon P.

The Parliamentary or Constitutional History of England. 1763. Vol. 23. London. Available at books.google.com.

Parnham, David. 1997. *Sir Henry Vane, Theologian: A Study in Seventeenth-Century Religious and Political Discourse.* Madison, NJ: Fairleigh Dickinson UP.

Patterson, Annabel. 1984. *Censorship and Interpretation: The Conditions of Writing and Reading in Early Modern England.* Madison: U of Wisconsin P.

Patterson, Annabel. 1997. *Early Modern Liberalism.* Cambridge: Cambridge UP.

Patterson, Annabel. 2000. *Marvell: The Writer in Public Life.* Harlow: Longman.

Peacey, Jason. 2009. "The House of Lords and the 'Other House,' 1640–60." In *A Short History of Parliament.* Ed. Clyve Jones. Rochester, NY: Boydell.

Pearl, Valerie. 1968. "The 'Royal Independents' in the English Civil War." *Transactions of the Royal Historical Society,* 5th ser., 18: 69–96.

Perry, Curtis. 2006. *Literature and Favoritism in Early Modern England.* Cambridge: Cambridge UP.

Phillips, Edward. 1675. *Theatrum Poetarum, or a Compleat Collection of the Poets.* London; Wing P2075.

Piccone, Paul and G.L. Ulmen, eds. 1987. Special issue, "Carl Schmitt: Enemy or Foe?" *Telos* 72.

Pincus, Steven. 2011. *1688: The First Modern Revolution.* New Haven: Yale UP.

Pindar. 1997. *Nemean Odes, Isthmian Odes, Fragments.* Ed. and Trans. William H. Race. Loeb Classical Library 485. Cambridge, MA: Harvard UP.

Plato. 1925. *Statesman, Philebus, Ion.* Trans. Harold North Fowler and W.R. M. Lamb. Loeb Classical Library 164. Cambridge, MA: Harvard UP.

Plume, Thomas. 1675. "An Account of the Life and Death of the Author." In *A Century of Sermons upon several remarkable subjects preached by the Right Reverend Father in God, John Hacket.* London; Wing H169.

Plutarch. 1917. "Life of Pompey." *Lives.* Vol. 5. Trans. Bernadotte Perrin. Loeb Classical Library 87. Cambridge, MA: Harvard UP.

Plutarch. 1975. *The Roman Questions [Quaestiones Romanae].* Trans. H.J. Rose. Ancient Religion and Mythology. New York: Arno Press.

Pocock, J.G.A. 1975. *The Machiavellian Moment: Florentine Political Thought and the Atlantic Republican Tradition.* Princeton: Princeton UP.

Prokhovnik, Raia. 2007. *Sovereignties: Contemporary Theory and Practice.* Houndmills: Palgrave Macmillan.

Pufendorf, Samuel. 2003. *The Whole Duty of Man, According to the Law of Nature.* Eds. Ian Hunter and David Saunders. Natural Law and Enlightenment Classics. Gen. ed. Knud Haakonsen. Indianapolis: Liberty Fund.

Purkiss, Diane. 2006. *The English Civil War: A People's History.* London: HarperCollins.

Quarles, Francis. 1624. *Job Militant.* London; STC 20550.

Quarles, Francis. 1631. *The Historie of Samson.* London; STC 20549.

Quarles, Francis. 1641. *Enchyridion.* London; Wing Q86.

Quarles, Francis. 1642. *A Feast for Wormes.* London; Wing Q71A.

Quarles, Francis. 1643. *The Loyall Convert.* Oxford; Wing Q104.

Quarles, Francis. 1647. *Argalus and Parthenia.* London; Wing Q39.

Rahe, Paul A. 2008. *Against Throne and Altar: Machiavelli and Political Theory under the English Republic.* Cambridge: Cambridge UP.

Raleigh, Sir Walter. 1658. *The Cabinet-Council Containing the Cheif [sic] Arts of Empire and Mysteries of State.* London; Wing R156.

Raymond, Joad. 2011. "A Cromwellian Centre?" In Hirst and Zwicker (2011) 140–57.

A Remonstrance of the State of the Kingdome of England [The Grand Remonstrance]. 1641. London; Wing E2221D.

Revard, Stella. 2010. "Charles, Christ, and the Icon of Kingship." *Visionary Milton: Essays on Prophecy and Violence.* Eds. Peter E. Medine, John T. Shawcross, and David V. Urban. Pittsburgh: Duquense UP. 215–40.

Rose, Jacqueline. 2014. "The Debate over Authority: Adiaphora, the Civil Magistrate, and the Settlement of Religion." In *"Settling the Peace of the Church": 1662 Revisited.* Ed. N.H. Keeble. Oxford: Oxford UP. 29–56.

Rowe, Violet. 1970. *Sir Henry Vane, the Younger: A Study in Political and Administrative History.* London: Athlone P.

Sailor, Dylan. 2008. *Writing and Empire in Tacitus.* Cambridge: Cambridge UP.

Salvianus. 1930. *On the Government of God [De Prov.].* New York: Columbia UP.

Salzman, Paul. 1985. *English Prose Fiction, 1558–1700.* Oxford: Clarendon P.

Salzman, Paul. 2001. "Royalist Epic and Romance." *The Cambridge Companion to Writing of the English Revolution.* Ed. N.H. Keeble. Cambridge: Cambridge UP. 215–30.

Sauer, Elizabeth. 2014. *Milton, Toleration, and Nationhood.* Cambridge: Cambridge UP.

Scheuerman, William E. 1999. *Carl Schmitt: The End of Law.* Lanham: Rowan & Littlefield.

Scheuerman, William E. 2006. "Carl Schmitt and the Road to Abu Ghraib." *Constellations* 13: 108–24.

Schmitt, Carl. 1996. *Roman Catholicism and Political Form.* Trans. G.L. Ulmen. Global Perspectives in History and Politics. Westport, CT: Greenwood.

Schmitt, Carl. 1999. "Ethic of State and Pluralistic State." Trans. David Dyzenhaus. In Mouffe (1999) 195–208.

Schmitt, Carl. 2000. "State Ethics and the Pluralist State." In Jacobson and Schlink (2000) 300–12.

Schmitt, Carl. 2005. *Political Theology: Four Chapters on the Concept of Sovereignty.* Ed. and trans. George Schwab. Chicago: U of Chicago P.

Schmitt, Carl. 2006. *The* Nomos *of the Earth in the International Law of the* Jus Publicum Europaeum. Candor, NY: Telos P.

Schmitt, Carl. 2007. *Concept of the Political.* Ed. and trans. George Schwab. Expanded reprint. Chicago: U of Chicago P.

Schmitt, Carl. 2008a. *Constitutional Theory.* Trans. Jeffery Seitzer. Duke: Duke UP.

Schmitt, Carl. 2008b. *The Leviathan in the State Theory of Thomas Hobbes.* Trans. George Schwab and Erna Hilfstein. Chicago: U of Chicago P.

Schmitt, Carl. 2014. *Dictatorship.* Trans. Michael Hoelzl and Graham Ward. London: Verso.

Schmitt, Carl. 2017. *Ex Captivitate Salus: Experiences, 1945–47.* Ed. Andreas Kalyvas and Federico Finchelstein. Cambridge: Polity P.

Schwab, George. 1970. *The Challenge of the Exception: An Introduction to the Political Ideas of Carl Schmitt between 1921 and 1936.* Berlin: Duncker and Humblot.

Scott, Jonathan. 2004. *Commonwealth Principles: Republican Writing of the English Revolution.* Cambridge: Cambridge UP.

Scott, Jonathan. 2011. "James Harrington's Prescription for Healing and Settling." In *The Experience of Revolution in Stuart Britain and Ireland: Essays for John Morrill.* Eds. Michael J. Braddick and David L. Smith. Cambridge: Cambridge UP. 190–209.

Scudéry, Madeleine de. 1652. *Ibrahim, or, The Illustrious Bassa an Excellent New Romance.* Trans. Henry Cogan. London; Wing S2160.

Scudéry, Madeleine de. 1655. *Clelia, An Excellent New Romance Dedicated to Mademoiselle de Longueville.* Trans. John Davies and George Havers. London; Wing S2151–S2154.

Seaward, Paul. 2019. "Marvell and Parliament." In Dzelzainis and Holberton (2019) 79–95.

Selden, John. 1726. "Notes upon Fortescue." *Opera omnia.* Vol. 3. Ed. David Wilkins. London; ESTC T153464.

Shakespeare, William. 2008. *Macbeth.* In *The Norton Shakespeare.* 2nd ed. Vol. 2. Eds. Stephen Greenblatt et al. New York: W.W. Norton.

Shirley, James. 1646. *Poems.* London; Wing S3481/S3480/S3488.

Sitze, Adam. 2012. "The Tragicity of the Political: A Note on Carlo Galli's Reading of Carl Schmitt's *Hamlet or Hecuba.*" In Hammill and Lupton (2012) 48–59.

Skinner, Quentin. 1974. "Conquest and Consent: Thomas Hobbes and the Engagement Controversy." In *The Interregnum: The Quest for Settlement 1646–1660.* Ed. G. E. Aylmer. London: Macmillan. 79–98.

Skinner, Quentin. 1993. "'Scientia civilis' in Classical Rhetoric and in the Early Hobbes." In *Political Discourse in Early Modern Britain*. Eds. Nicholas Phillipson and Quentin Skinner. Ideas in Context. Cambridge: Cambridge UP. 67-93.

Skinner, Quentin. 1998. *Liberty before Liberalism*. Cambridge: Cambridge UP.

Slomp, Gabriella. 1990. "Hobbes, Thucydides, and the Three Greatest Things." *History of Political Thought* 11: 565-86.

Smith, Nigel. 1994. *Literature & Revolution in England, 1640-1660*. New Haven: Yale UP.

Smith, Nigel. 2010. *Andrew Marvell: The Chameleon*. New Haven: Yale UP.

Sorell, Tom and Luc Foisneau, eds. 2004. *Leviathan after 350 Years*. Oxford: Oxford UP.

Stanivukovic, Goran. 2016. *Knights in Arms: Prose Romance, Masculinity, and Eastern Mediterranean Trade in Early Modern England, 1565-1655*. Toronto: U of Toronto P.

Stern, Philip J. 2013. "'Bundles of Hyphens': Corporations as Legal Communities in the Early modern British Empire." Benton and Ross (2013) 21-47.

Strauss, Leo. 1953. *Natural Right and History*. Chicago: U of Chicago P, 1965.

Strauss, Leo. (1936) 1963. *The Political Philosophy of Hobbes: Its Basis and Genesis*. Trans. Elsa M. Sinclair. Chicago: U of Chicago P.

Strauss, Leo. 2011. *Hobbes's Critique of Religion and Other Writings*. Trans. and ed. Gabriel Bartlett and Svetozar Minkov. Chicago: U of Chicago P.

Streater, John. 1659. *The Continuation of this Session of Parliament, Justified; and the Action of the Army touching that Affair Defended*. London; Wing S5945.

Stuart, King Charles I. 1643. *A Proclamation Touching the New Seale of the Court of Wards and Liveries*. Oxford; Wing C2715.

Stubbe, Henry. 1659a. *An Essay in Defence of the Good Old Cause... and Vindication of the Honourable Sir Henry Vane from the False Aspersions of Mr. Baxter*. London: Wing S6045.

Stubbe, Henry. 1659b. *Letter to an Officer of the Army*. London; Wing S6054.

Stubbe, Henry. 1659c. *A Light Shining out of Darkness*. London; Wing S6056.

Stubbe, Henry. 1659d. *Malice Rebuked, or A Character of Mr. Richard Baxters Abilities. And a Vindication oe [sic] the Honourable Sr. Henry Vane*. London; Wing S6060.

Syme, Ronald. 1958. *Tacitus*. 2 vols. Oxford: Oxford UP.

Tacitus, 1925-31. *Histories*. Trans. John Jackson. Loeb Classical Library 111 and 249. Cambridge, MA: Harvard UP.

Tacitus. 1931-37. *The Annals*. Trans. John Jackson. Loeb Classical Library 249, 312, and 322. Cambridge, MA: Harvard UP.

Tacitus, 1970. *Agricola, Germania, Dialogus*. Rev. edn. Trans. M. Hutton et al. Loeb Classical Library 35. Cambridge, MA: Harvard UP.

Talaska, Richard, ed. 2013. *The Hardwick Library and Hobbes's Early Intellectual Development*. Charlottesville: Philosophy Documentation Center.

Taylor, Charles. 2004. *Modern Social Imaginaries*. Durham, NC: Duke UP.

Tertullian. 2008. *Apology*. In *Tertullian, Apologetical Works and Minucius Felix, "Octavius."* Trans. Rudolph Arbesmann, OSA, Sister Emily Joseph Daly, CSJ, and Edwin A. Quain, SJ. Washington, DC: Catholic U of America P.

Theophania: Or, Severall Modern Histories Represented by Way of Romance and Politickly Discours'd Upon. 1999. Ed. Renée Pigeon. Publications of the Barnabe Rich Society 10. Ottawa: Dovehouse Editions.

Thucydides. 1919. *History of the Peloponnesian War*. Vol. 1. Trans. C.F. Smith. Loeb Classical Library 108. Cambridge, MA: Harvard UP.

Thurloe, John. 1742. *A Collection of the State Papers of John Thurloe*. Ed. Thomas Birch. London: Fletcher Giles.

Tierney, Brian. 1997. *The Idea of Natural Rights: Studies on Natural Rights, Natural Law, and Church Law 1150–1625*. Emory University Studies in Law and Religion. Grand Rapids: Eerdman.

Toffanin, Giuseppe. 1921. *Machiavelli e il Tacitismo*. Padua: Draghi.

Toomer, G.J. 2009. *John Selden: A Life in Scholarship*. 2 vols. Oxford-Warburg Studies. Oxford: Oxford UP.

Trubowitz, Rachel. 2012. *Nation and Nurture in Seventeenth-Century English Literature*. Oxford: Oxford UP.

Tuck, Richard. 1993. *Philosophy and Government, 1572–1651*. Ideas in Context. Cambridge: Cambridge UP.

Tuck, Richard. 1998. *Natural Rights Theories: Their Origin and Development*. 1979. Rpt. Cambridge: Cambridge UP.

Tuck, Richard. 2006. "Hobbes and Democracy." In *Rethinking the Foundations of Modern Political Thought*. Eds. Annabel Brett and James Tully with Holly Hamilton-Bleakly. Cambridge: Cambridge UP. 171–90.

Tuck, Richard. 2015. *The Sleeping Sovereign: The Invention of Modern Democracy*. Cambridge: Cambridge UP.

Turner, Henry S. 2016. *The Corporate Commonwealth: Pluralism and Political Fictions in England, 1516–1651*. Chicago: U of Chicago P.

van Gelderen, Martin and Quentin Skinner, eds. 2002. *Republicanism: A Shared European Heritage*. Vols. 1–2. Cambridge: Cambridge UP.

[Vane, Sir Henry the younger.] 1652. *Zeal Examined*. London; Wing Z8.

Vane, Sir Henry the Younger. 1655. *The Retired Mans Meditations*. London; Wing V75.

Vane, Sir Henry the younger. 1656. *A Healing Question*. London; Wing V68. Reissue London, 1660; Wing V70.

Vane, Sir Henry the younger. 1660. *A Needful Corrective or Ballance in Popular Government Expressed in a Letter to James Harrington*. London; Wing V72.

Virgil. 1916. *Eclogues, Georgics, Aeneid Books 1–6*. Trans. H. Rushton Fairclough. Loeb Classical Library 63. Cambridge, MA: Harvard UP.

Viroli, Maurizio. 1992. *From Politics to Reason of State: The Acquisition and Transformation of the Language of Politics, 1250–1600*. Ideas in Context. Cambridge: Cambridge UP.

von Maltzahn, Nicholas. 2005. *An Andrew Marvell Chronology*. London: Palgrave Macmillan.

von Maltzahn, Nicholas. 2008a. "Liberalism or Apocalypse? John Milton and Andrew Marvell." *English Now: Selected Papers from the 20th IAUPE Conference in Lund 2007*. Ed. Marianne Thormählen. Lund Studies in English 112. Lund: Lund University.

von Maltzahn, Nicholas. 2008b. "Making Use of the Jews: Milton and Philo-Semitism." *Milton and the Jews*. Ed. Douglas A. Brooks. Cambridge: Cambridge UP. 57–82.

von Maltzahn, Nicholas. 2013. "Andrew Marvell, the Lord Maynard, and the Balla-stage Office." *The Seventeenth Century* 28: 311–21.

von Maltzahn, Nicholas. 2018. "Andrew Marvell's Paper Work: The Earl of Carlisle's Baltic Embassy (1664)." *Marvell Studies* 3: 1–30.

von Maltzahn, Nicholas. 2019. "Marvell and Patronage." In Dzelzainis and Holberton (2019) 43–60.

Walker, William. 2014. *Antiformalist, Unrevolutionary, Illiberal Milton: Political Prose, 1644–1660*. Farnham, UK: Ashgate.

Wall, Illan rua. 2012. *Human Rights and Constitutional Power: Without Model or Warranty*. Abingdon: Routledge.

Ward, Ian. 2003. "The End of Sovereignty and the New Humanism." *Stanford Law Review* 55: 2091–112.

Westcott, Allan F. ed. 1911. *New Poems of James I of England, From a Hitherto Unpublished Manuscript (Add. 24195) in the British Museum*. New York: Columbia UP.

W[hite], J[ohn]. 1660. *The Parallel between David, Christ, and K. Charls, in their Humiliation and Exaltation Delivered in a Sermon Preached at Wadshurst in Sussex*. London; Wing W1785B.

White, Stephen D. 1979. *Sir Edward Coke and the Grievances of the Commonwealth 1621–1628*. Chapel Hill: U of North Carolina P.

Whitelocke, Bulstrode. 1682. *Memorials of the English Affairs: Or, an Historical Account of What Passed from the Beginning of the Reign of King Charles I., to King Charles II. His Happy Restauration*. London; Wing W1986.

Wiemann, Dirk and Gaby Mahlberg, eds. 2014. *Perspectives on English Revolutionary Republicanism*. Farnham: Ashgate.

Williams, Penry. 1958. *The Council in the Marches of Wales under Elizabeth I*. Cardiff: U of Wales P.

Williams, Penry. 1961. "The Attack on the Council in the Marches, 1603–1642." *Transactions of the Honourable Society of Cymmrodorion* Session 1961, Part 1: 1–22.

Willman, Robert. 1983. "Blackstone and the 'Theoretical Perfection' of English Law in the Reign of Charles II." *The Historical Journal* 26: 39–70.

Wilcher, Robert. 2004. "Moseley, Humphrey (b. in or before 1603, d. 1661)." *Oxford Dictionary of National Biography*. Online edn. Oxford: Oxford UP.

Withington, Phil. 2010. *Society in Early Modern England: The Vernacular Origins of Some Powerful Ideas*. Cambridge: Polity.

Withington, Phil. 2011. "Andrew Marvell's Citizenship." In Hirst and Zwicker (2011) 102–21.

Worden, Blair. 2007. *Literature and Politics in Cromwellian England: John Milton, Andrew Marvell, and Marchamont Nedham*. Oxford: Oxford UP.

Woodman, A.J., ed. 2009. *The Cambridge Companion to Tacitus*. Cambridge: Cambridge UP.

Woods, Susanne. 2013. *Milton and the Politics of Freedom*. Pittsburgh: Duquesne UP.

Woolrych, Austin. 1957. "The Good Old Cause and the Fall of the Protectorate." *Cambridge Historical Journal* 13: 133–61.

Zagorin, Perez. 2009. *Hobbes and the Law of Nature*. Princeton: Princeton UP.

Zaller, Robert. 2007. *The Discourse of Legitimacy in Early Modern England*. Stanford: Stanford UP.

Index

For the benefit of digital users, indexed terms that span two pages (e.g., 52–53) may, on occasion, appear on only one of those pages.